THE AUTUMN LEAVES

THE AUTUMN LEAVES

Roger Blount

Book Guild Publishing
Sussex, England

First published in Great Britain in 2006 by
Book Guild Publishing
25 High Street
Lewes, East Sussex
BN7 2LU

Typesetting in Baskerville by
Keyboard Services, Luton, Bedfordshire

Printed in Great Britain by
Antony Rowe Ltd, Chippenham, Wiltshire

A catalogue record for this book is available from
The British Library

ISBN 1 84624 018 2

When the summer tires of her finery,
Autumn sighs in and paints the leaves red and
    gold,
But with winter's horses panting the morning
    mists
The leaves slip through her fingers
To wither and die one by one.

RPB

1

The small town of Wannabee is situated west of the Appalachian range and sits in a shallow valley sided by low foothills to the east and west. A narrow, mostly passive river, the Machohatis, winds its way roughly north to south through the middle of the town, dividing the real estate and the population. Most times of the year, the river almost saunters its way through the valley and only during the brief Spring thaw does it muster enough energy to flush away the discarded waste of careless humans. It is at this time also, that some of the children gather on an old wooden bridge to throw stones at the passing bottles and cans and anything else offering itself as a floating target.

The river was named after an Indian tribe who had set up their encampment in the valley a couple of centuries before and the Indians lived in a sort of quiet harmony with nature until the earliest settlers intruded. The Machohatis tribe, as they were called, had travelled in from the north to get away from a hostile band of Indians who had appeared in their area one day. There hadn't been actual open warfare between them, just a few skirmishes and horses stolen, but it was enough for the elders to get together and decide they would move on. They settled in the valley by the river and erected their tepees, and the morning mists were joined by the spiralling smoke from their camp fires. Small parties went out each morning to hunt and by late afternoon, while the women cut the meat into strips and cooked them over the hot embers, the hides were hung out to dry. They found a peaceful existence by the river; they never travelled much out of their valley, they were happy where they were and tended to be somewhat introspective. From time to time, small hunting bands from other tribes had passed through and they were given hospitality, as was the custom, but the Machohatis were always happy when they moved on.

With the arrival of the first white settlers, the arrangement had at first been quite amicable. They lived apart and traded some, and the settlers' white canvas tents looked temporary, but as the number of white people increased, they began to surreptitiously push the Indians further south when they built more permanent log cabins – these took up more space than tents. The Machohatis waited patiently for the white man to move on but as the number of settlers steadily increased and their wooden cabins looked a little too permanent, the elders of the tribe held a council to discuss the situation. They *talked* around the subject for many hours, chewing words like meat, *talking* at length about the white man clearing trees for cabins and killing animals more for their furs than for food, but they all avoided the only two options available to them: drive the white man away or leave themselves. The tribe had never held a hostile demeanour and after the meeting of the elders, they spoke with each adult member, allowing them time to discuss it in family groups. Then, one night, after they had a consensus, they just up and packed everything and moved further south to find another valley. The white man barely noticed their going and simply built more cabins. The setting was ideal – fertile soil for growing crops, pastures for grazing, plenty of trees to build things, a lot of game for food and furs and a river supplying all the water they needed.

A while after the Machohatis had left, a small wooden

bridge was built to span the river and the cabins moved like a creeping carpet over the eastern bank. The wooden bridge still crosses the river today and although revered as the original crossing point, just about every part of it has been replaced through time. As the town grew and the car dictated faster access, two stone bridges and one ugly iron-framed bridge, painted black, had been added in consecutive decades – the townspeople celebrated each opening with the cutting of ribbons and bands playing the American anthem and the people stood tall and respectful. The first stone bridge was built in the 1940s at the end of the Second World War and the mayor at that time, dabbing his head with a white handkerchief under the hot sun, made an over-long speech. He received grateful applause from the wilting townspeople more for the fact that he had eventually finished. At the end of the 1950s and in the mid-1960s, two further bridges were built, north and south of the first, and in similar fashion they were opened with ceremony, bands playing and the incumbent mayors making over-long speeches. Today, the wooden bridge permits only pedestrians to travel across, and there aren't too many of those except for the children throwing things during the thaw.

The origin of the name Wannabee is shrouded in the mists of the past but most like to accept the suggestion that it was the name of a Machohatis Indian god who was all powerful and protected the valley. The truth of the matter is less romantic. After the Indians had left and the number of settlers grew, the people gathered to debate a name for the town. Most wanted it called after the towns or cities where they had been born or grew up in, which was generally on the eastern coast or some place in Europe. After several hours of claim and counter-claim, one of the more elderly citizens, in frustration, shouted to the gathering, 'I don't care what you call it, I just wanna be

3

here.' The townspeople liked the sound of that and so Wannabee was adopted; it was as simple as that.

On the western side live, as they liked to think, descendants of the original settlers and their houses are large and fashioned to reflect their status and wealth; they are mostly lawyers and doctors and bankers and landowners and businessmen and, of course, the town's officious administrators. A mile or so from the river bank, the land undulates steadily towards the foothills and offers secluded plateaus where the wealthier ones built their grand homes with scenic views of the valley but without being overlooked by neighbours; if there was a chance of that, they grew trees in avenues around them like living walls to secure their privacy.

For a few miles or so either side of the river, the central area is flat and on the western side they built, with careful design, the town centre. The focal point was a large, rectangular green-grassed area; originally, as was the fashion in the late 1800s, it was fenced with ornate iron railings and tall gates and contained trees and flower beds and several small fountains, and wooden benches where the citizens could relax and admire the sedateness of things. But in the latter years, the fencing and gates were removed to create 'open space', as the town leaders liked to put it, and in the centre they erected a square-sided, stone tower, about thirty feet high and with a clock face on each side. Most citizens thought it blended well and that the clocks were useful, but one of the women's groups protested that it was too much like a phallic symbol. It created a small storm for a while but the town leaders handled it diplomatically; they ignored the ladies and it quietly went away. Down one side of the square, in grand style, they built the mayor's office, flanked by the council offices and the courts and banks and people of the legal profession. The other three sides were lined with small shops and

4

restaurants and cafes with tables on the sidewalk, all carefully regulated so that they looked pretty much the same and provided an ambience of equanimity. Away from that area, the blocks of buildings were built in a precise grid system, which from the air looked like a chequered carpet. Here flourished the estate agents, the car sales, the hotels, small clothes stores and the general stores which offer everything from clothing to garden tools, food to haberdashery. But these too were regulated by council by-laws; no building was to exceed two storeys, the message given was: 'build out, not up'. To an out-of-towner visiting for the first time, his first and lasting impression was that he had stepped back into the 50s era, not only from the layout and the style of the buildings, but by the way people seemed to amble around the streets with no urgency to get where they were going. Even the cars seemed to ease down as they approached traffic lights, as if inviting them to turn red and give the drivers a moment to reflect.

To the south of the town, they designated an area for a park and imaginatively called it 'The South Park'. It provided grass pastures and avenues of trees interwoven with tan-coloured gravel paths and a plentiful number of wooden benches for strollers to rest and reflect. In the centre they created a small lake where, at its northern end, they built a high stone outcrop with boulders shipped in from the hills. With ingenuity, they piped water to the top, which cascaded gently down to the lake and provided a spectacle of foaming water with a background of soft, watery noise. At first it had looked bare and stark, but as the years progressed, moss spread itself over the rocks and lichens and water plants sprouted from the crevices until they had painted it to look natural. The townsfolk took their picnics there and played softball games and it became popular as a family gathering place. In the soft light of the Summer evenings, youngsters snuck away to find peaceful corners where they could carry on the timeless rituals of courtship, but the older element of the population, conveniently forgetting how they filled their young lives, demanded a park ranger who patrolled the park and moved on any couples who seemed too interested in each other. In a grove of trees near the lake, they erected a small log cabin which sold food – the fast type – and soft drinks, and the profit from this paid for the ranger. The town leaders always had a good eye for making the people pay for any suggestion they had implemented.

The eastern side of the river had started as a spillover area for the latecomers, who tended to be the artisans and workers who were prepared to spend days out of the sunlight in factories constructed on the outer eastern edge of town that were owned by the richer men who live on the west bank. The houses were built cheaply in clapboard style in estates and the properties lined the straight roads like the houses on a Monopoly board. Here also were built office blocks, sports centres, large departmental stores and supermarkets, which were later replaced by hypermarkets; in latter years, a huge complex was built to house a metal and glass shopping mall and a multi-screen cinema. Anything that was modern and large and was out of style with the western bank was built on the eastern side. If one walked the old wooden bridge from west to east, it was like passing through a time portal and jumping fifty years ahead.

During the 1970s, a highway was built to the north, running east to west, which took a lot of heavy traffic out of the town. It was welcomed by most, not just because it diverted the heavy trucks and the occasional traffic jams from the town centre in the Summer, but mainly because it made the town feel self-contained, with the number of strangers driving and walking around now reduced to an acceptable level. This insular feeling wasn't shared by all

6

– especially the traders, who saw a drop in their passing trade – but it was not a big deal, and within a short while everyone adjusted. Generally, everyone was content with the balance and way of life. Nothing much happened to upset the general flow, and even when some of the men were enlisted to fight in a war, they were sent off to Europe or the Pacific or eastern Asia, where they were too far away to affect the run of things. Over the years, the town quietly grew and modernised itself, and even on the western bank, small cinemas, eat-ins and drive-ins sprouted up away from the town centre. But the administrators drew the line at plans for a huge shopping mall on the west bank; after all, they owned too many of the town centre shops to accept this sort of competition, and anyway, the developer was an out-of-towner, a financier from New York, who was not interested in building on the eastern side. Without realising it, they had developed much the same outlook as the original Indians they had displaced.

*

On the far western fringe of the town, suitably tucked away behind specially planted groves of cedar trees, was the exclusive Wannabee Golf and Country Club, open only to those who could afford its annual subscription. This was set high enough to deter most who lived on the eastern side; it saved time with pointless interviews and rejection letters. Besides, an enterprising mayor in the late 1960s had constructed a cheaper version of the golf club on the eastern bank, and he received thanks from his colleagues for a smart move – he smiled gratuitously as he quietly increased his fortune from the yearly proceeds.

At the Wannabee Golf and Country Club, from early Spring to late Autumn, the members of the club sport their strange golfing attire in extraordinarily bright colours as they carve divots in the manicured fairways and hold endless parties in the clubhouse. In the Winter, when the snows come and the course closes, they retreat to their large houses and hold more parties. Their aim in life, from their earliest years, is to amass more money and to become socially acceptable, usually measured by the number of parties they are invited to.

The golf club members are an exclusive community with provincial views, ably led by the club secretary and general manager, Dinsdale Dryden. He administrates the club with a firm hand, but as he likes to think he is one of the members, his policies reflect their views and without realising it, he is their master and servant at the same time. Dinsdale looks like someone out of the thirties era; his hair is black with a hint of grey above the ears and slicked back with enough cream to reflect a crescent moon shine as he walks under the lighting. He is always impeccably dressed in a dark suit, whatever the weather, with a white shirt with a crisp collar and a club tie knotted in a half-windsor. His shoes are polished daily by his devoted wife and have such a shine as to look like patent leather dancing shoes. On one occasion, when one of the ladies at the club had stood too close to him while ardently complaining about something, he had eased his foot between hers, and while looking down in a pose of studious thought, he had tried to look up her dress in the reflection of his toecaps. He had missed what she said, and when she finally paused, he looked up, smiled and said, 'I shall give a lot of thought to that,' and then moved off. His face was quite handsome – though perhaps his eyes were a bit too narrow like slits – and he wore a pencil-thin moustache that turned upwards with his lips when he smiled. Dinsdale smiled often; most club members were of the class he had always aspired to and so he was happy in his position as their patron, but at that moment, as he gazed out of the window at the eighteenth fairway, he was not smiling. He was watching the slow progress of four men who, despite using motorised golf carts, were holding up a ladies' two-ball behind them. They were the bane of his life; four men around their sixties who, to him anyway, went out of their way to upset the orderly practices Dinsdale employed for the smooth-running of the club. They were not bad in the usual sense of the word, he had to admit, but they were mischievous and took great delight in upsetting the well balanced order of things. There were times when he secretly liked them for the way they challenged the over-pretentiousness of some of the members, especially some of the haughtier ladies, who saw the fortunes of their husbands as a reason for preferential treatment; he hated the way they tended to talk down to him. But aside from that, these four men generated more complaints from the members about their antics than everything else they found to complain about put together. Of the four men, he disliked Harry Menkowitch the most. He was not quite sure why, but if Dinsdale had had a conscience then he would have recognised that Harry would have been it – but Dinsdale didn't have a conscience, and that was perhaps why he disliked him the most.

2

On the eighteenth fairway, Harry eased himself carefully out of his golf cart and studied his ball for a moment. It lay just off the first cut and was nestled down in the semi-rough, barely visible. He looked up at the green ahead and guessed the distance; it was easily within his reach but between him and the flagstick was the worst sand bunker on the course, which had a high, steep face that, when you stood in its cavernous bowl, looked like a brown tidal wave about to break over you. The safe shot, he knew, was to play just short up the centre and leave a chip shot onto the green. On the other hand, he mused, he could try to aim out right and bend it back round the bunker, but his game favoured a fade rather than a draw so he dismissed that option. After so much thinking, Harry felt like he needed a cigar. His three playing partners were all on the fairway and ahead of him so they had the easier shots to the green. He sighed and looked back down the fairway at the two young ladies whom they had been holding up for three holes or more. They were standing on the tee with their hands on their hips watching him; he could tell from their stance that they were angry at the hold-up.

'We'll let the ladies through,' Harry said, reaching into his cart for his cigars.

The nearest friend to him, Sol, gasped his surprise and looked back at the ladies and then to Harry. Sol's face had assumed its normal shade of purple when he was upset by something, which was often.

'What? But this is the last hole. What's the point?' he argued as he stepped agitatedly towards Harry with a seven-iron in his hand. Sol always spoke quickly as if he were afraid he would run out of words before he finished.

But Harry ignored him and waved the ladies through before Sol could protest more. He lit his cigar and watched the smoke waft away with the light breeze. The other two men were not so surprised; they knew what Harry was up to and they walked over to his side of the fairway with amused faces. They always played for a small wager, five dollars each to the winner of the most holes, and Sol, who rarely won, was on a roll; he had won the last three holes and if he took this one, he would scoop the pool. Harry was just breaking his tempo by making him wait and they were happy with that.

'Might as well let them through,' Al said amiably as he came up to them. 'It may stop them reporting us to Dinsdale again.'

'But this is the last hole for Chrissake,' Sol continued to complain, but the others ignored him.

The two ladies hit decent shots from their forward tee and their balls both landed in the middle of the fairway just passed the men's. Harry leaned against his cart and puffed steadily on his cigar while the ladies came towards them.

'This'll add another half hour to our game,' Sol argued on while cleaning some grass from the face of his club with a tee peg.

'So what's the hurry?' Al asked. 'You got somewhere to go?'

Sol didn't answer and his attention turned to the two pretty ladies as they came alongside with their electric golf trolleys. They both had very attractive figures and one was

11

as dark haired as the other was blonde. All four men quietly admired their long tanned legs and tight shorts.

'Thank you,' the blonde one said, not attempting to hide the disdain from her voice.

'Our pleasure,' Harry acknowledged with a wave of his hand and the pleasantest smile he could muster. 'It's always nice to watch you young ladies hit a ball so well.'

The nearest one, the blonde, studied him for a moment. 'You've been holding us up long enough to notice,' she said at last and turned her attention to her ball. She swung easy and her ball flew high and straight and landed on the green.

'That's a lovely swing, you have there,' Harry admired. She again looked at him but considered against another response. The brunette had decided to ignore them and she also hit her ball onto the green and both moved away.

'Who is that?' asked Rick, the fourth member of their group, when they had moved out of earshot. 'She has a lovely ass. Did you see it move in those tight shorts?'

Harry tossed his cigar away into the longer grass and patted him on the shoulder. 'The blonde one is Louise and the brunette is Helen. And you've just ruined your next shot, Rick.'

Rick's face broke into a grin, making him look boyish, despite his years. 'I expect I have,' he agreed. 'How is it you know the names of all the ladies in the club?'

Harry's face broke into a rubbery smile and he touched the side of his nose. 'Not all of them, just the pretty ones.'

Sol looked up keenly from cleaning his club. 'So you fancy yourself as a ladies' man,' he addressed to Harry, with a voice that held a trace of contempt and an expression that resembled a goldfish about to eat an ant egg.

Harry looked down at the short figure and kept his smile going. 'Haven't you heard about my exploits with Ellor Byrne?'

12

'With Ellor…' his voice trailed off. 'That fat carcass that sags all over a seat when she sits down? I don't believe it.'

'You haven't heard about the Ellor Technique?' Al joined the conversation.

Sol looked at him with his eyebrows knitted tightly like a dark bush above his eyes. 'Ellor Technique?' he queried. He didn't like to be the one not knowing something so he looked to Rick. 'Do you know what it is?'

'Sure,' said Rick casually. 'I thought everyone did.'

Sol looked from one to the other and then back along the line of smiling faces. He knew he was often the butt of their jokes, but equally, he didn't like not knowing. Flecks of spit formed at the corners of his mouth and his eyes widened with impatience. 'Okay. So what is it?'

They looked at each other before Rick volunteered the information. 'You smack her on the belly and surf in on the waves.'

Sol's face began to erupt into a laugh but stopped abruptly as he sensed they were playing him along. 'You sonofabitch,' he exclaimed. He cleared his throat with a short cough and then smiled. 'I knew you were jesting. Hey, that's funny. That's a good one.' His voice trailed off and he resumed cleaning his club so that he could look away from them.

Rick relented and patted the small figure on the shoulder. 'Of course you did.'

When the ladies had finally left the green ahead, Harry selected a club from his bag on the back of the golf cart and walked over to his ball. He fiddled with his grip and practised the shot by swinging his club several times in a way one did to show your partners that it was a difficult shot. When he eventually struck, the ball came out flat and hooked into the large bunker. He sighed to himself while he rearranged the grass with his clubhead.

13

'You have to think positive,' Sol said, not attempting to hide his mirth.

'I did,' Harry said quietly to himself as he returned his club to his bag. 'I positively knew it was going in that bunker.' It was after a shot like that that he felt his age.

'Golf is a game of instincts,' Sol said as he walked over towards his ball.

As Harry had predicted, Rick mishit his ball and it went right and short of the green but in no trouble. Al was next and stubbed the ground behind the ball; although it flew straight, it ended about twenty yards short. Sol went to his ball and practised several swings before he settled. He believed he had a full, relaxed swing, but in truth it was about three quarter and he always fell back to his right side with a sort of heaving motion. His ball flew high and straight for a moment and he licked his lips with anticipation, but as it slowed, the sidespin his swing generated took control and the ball suddenly sliced away to the right of the green in some thick grass.

'Sonofabitch,' he muttered. 'Did you see that? There must be a wind up by the green.'

They were all aware that the light breeze was gently wafting from behind them and the flag hung loose on the green, but they knew Sol well enough not to bother to argue. Al and Harry got in their cart and Harry steered it up the track to the side of the green with Rick and Sol close behind in their golf cart.

'I pity Rick,' Al commented drily. 'I bet he's getting Sol's usual excuses for a bad shot.'

Harry gently braked the vehicle near the green and looked sideways at his friend. 'That's why you and I always share the same cart,' he grinned.

Al stubbed his shot again and his ball ended on the green, but twenty feet short of the hole. He walked forward slowly, scooped up his divot with his club and replaced it and patted it down flat – it was his turn to sigh to himself. Rick thinned his ball and it bounced through the green to end at the back fringe, even further away. Sol went over and searched for his ball. When he found it, he was stood knee-deep in the long grass; he practised with exaggerated swings and muttered loudly and incoherently, again to convey the difficulty to the others. When he finally swung, he scuffed it but it still somehow managed to find its way through the grass and roll out onto the green to finish only six feet from the pin. He exclaimed, 'Hah,' loudly to show his satisfaction that he had executed the shot expertly. Harry had watched from his side of the green and he turned and shook his head as he took his sand wedge and stepped down the bank into the yawning bunker from where he couldn't see the flag. The ball was far enough back from the face to give him room to lift the ball and was sitting nicely on a flat area of sand; he had been in there many times over the years and not once failed to flight it onto the green, and this time was no different. With a relaxed swing, the club took sand and ball precisely and the ball elevated quickly over the rim. As he reached for the rake he heard Sol's voice cry out.

'You lucky sonofabitch.'

Harry raked the sand with a smile on his face. He guessed his ball had stopped pretty close to the hole. As he put the rake to one side, Sol's face appeared over the top.

'You lucky sonofabitch,' he repeated. 'It went in the hole.'

Harry straightened up and looked up at Sol's face, which betrayed a hint of purple anger.

'Pure skill,' he laughed quietly.

'Skill?' Sol spluttered as Harry used the wedge as a walking stick to help him clamber up round the side of the bunker to the green. 'Five bucks says you couldn't do that again.'

'That's Harry's hole,' Al interrupted. 'I make it that Harry wins.' He began to take five dollars from his back pocket.

Sol looked from Al to Harry and back. 'Not so. I get a shot on this hole. I still have a putt for a half.'

Rick and Al groaned but Harry walked passed them and took out the flagstick. 'It's only six feet, should be easy enough.' He stood to one side, rested the flag over his shoulder and waited until Sol was lining up his putter behind the ball. 'But that left to right borrow makes it tricky,' he added in a quiet voice.

Sol stepped back and tutted. 'Do you mind not speaking as I'm about to putt?'

'I'm sorry,' Harry apologised. 'I was only trying to be helpful.' He paused until Sol lined himself up again. 'I wasn't sure if you'd noticed the slight slope.'

Sol stood back again. 'Of course I have,' he said, waving one hand in an agitated fashion. 'How long have I been playing this course?'

'I was forgetting,' Harry said, again in an apologetic manner. He looked sideways at the other two and saw there was laughter in their faces.

Sol addressed the ball for a third time and then sent it straight as a die, left of the hole. It did not deviate an inch and he stood for a moment in disbelief. 'There was no left to right borrow.' His voice took on a sort of whine. 'You talked me out of that.'

Harry replaced the flagstick as Al and Rick handed him five dollars each. 'I thought I saw a slight slope,' Harry smiled benignly. 'But then you probably know the course better than me. You should have trusted your instincts.' Sol looked up sharply at Harry; he knew he was throwing the word back at him.

Sol made no attempt to take out his money. 'Five dollars says you couldn't do that shot again from the bunker.'

16

The three of them walked away from him. 'A shot like that is worth more than five dollars,' Harry remarked over his shoulder.

'Okay.' Sol had not moved. 'Make it twenty-five.'

They stopped as one and looked back at the forlorn figure. 'Make it fifty,' Harry said in a steady sort of voice, 'and you have a bet.'

'Fifty!' Sol exclaimed, but then his brain calculated the odds on making a shot like that again. 'Okay, you're on.' He stepped smartly passed them. 'I'll make sure you put it in the same place.'

Harry put his hand in his pocket, took out a spare ball and palmed it to Al. 'Just go and make sure the flag is centred in the hole,' he requested.

Al nodded and walked back to the hole while Harry and Rick followed Sol down to the bunker. Harry passed his ball to Sol. 'Here. You place it.'

Sol took the ball, checked its make and number and placed it carefully in the sand. 'It was about there,' he said, looking back at Harry who nodded his agreement.

By the time Harry had taken his sand wedge from his bag, Al had joined them by the bunker face; he avoided looking at any of them and quietly wiped his nose with a white handkerchief.

Harry stepped onto the sand and moved his feet around until they were firmly planted and he was balanced perfectly. He poised the club over the ball but then stopped and looked back at Sol. 'Do you want to make it a hundred?'

'No,' Sol said with impatience. 'We agreed fifty. Get on with the shot.'

Harry returned his attention to his ball and then, with a fuller swing than before, hit down harder onto the ball. It rose quickly and high and disappeared over the rim. Had they been able to see it, the ball flew high and long

17

and nestled out of sight in the long grass over the other side of the green.

Sol leapt into the air in a futile attempt to see the flight of the ball and exclaimed, 'Hah! That's too much.'

Harry casually raked the sand. 'I think it's about right,' he called out as Sol scrambled up to the green. The other three followed him to the top where he had stopped. There was no sign of the ball.

'There!' Sol said excitedly, 'I said it was too hard.'

'It could be in the hole,' Al suggested.

'Never,' Sol said, and they watched as he went over to the flagstick with quick, short steps. He looked down expecting to see nothing, but he remained half bent over, and they could see his lips muttering something. The others strolled over to him and he straightened up as they neared.

'I don't believe it,' and he bent quickly and retrieved the ball from the hole. He looked from them to the ball in repeated movements and then suddenly cupped his fingers round the offending ball. 'What were you playing?' he asked.

'My normal ball,' Harry said in a relaxed manner. 'A Titleist. A number two or three. I'm not sure.'

'Which?' Sol was becoming more agitated and uncurled his fingers enough to check the number on the ball.

'I can't remember,' Harry admitted, 'but there should be my initials, H and M, marked on one side. You know, for Harry Menkowitch,' he said, pronouncing the 'w' as a 'v'.

Sol rolled the ball in his palm and saw the initials. 'Well, I'll be...'

He looked over to the far side of the green. 'I was sure you hit it too hard.'

'Must have been the spin,' Al remarked, trying hard to keep the smile from his lips. 'Coming out of sand it probably spun back into the hole.'

'That's fifty dollars,' Harry said casually. As Sol took his wallet from his back pocket and grudgingly leafed out two twenties and a ten, Harry added, 'and five for the game.'

Sol shook his head and added the five. 'I still can't believe it.'

*

Dinsdale had watched them on the green from the lounge window and saw everything that had happened. He shook his head sadly. 'They're like children,' he thought. At least, he admitted to himself, they had played the trick on Sol whom he disliked almost as much as Harry – he wasn't a jester like the others, he was just mean. Members were not supposed to play for money on the course but Dinsdale checked and saw there was no one else near the windows and so decided he would say nothing to them. From the look on the faces of the two ladies as they had come off the green a while before, he knew they would be bending his ear with another complaint about the men's slow play. He strolled down the passageway to his office; he preferred to take complaints in his own domain. It was then he met Travers Delaque, the club captain, who was coming the other way – Travers was tall and willowy and a very decent fellow, socially that is, but as captain he was hopeless. The problem with Travers was he didn't like making decisions, or rather, he couldn't bring himself to make a decision. This derived from him listening to all sides of an argument and then agreeing with them all, unable to discern which was right or appropriate. He floated like a leaf on a stream, happy to let the currents and eddies of life carry him along, fearing only a confrontation with one of the more vociferous members who would insist he make a decision. Dinsdale never understood why he had been nominated in the first place or why Travers had accepted it, but it suited his own purpose to have a weak captain and when Travers' name was put forward, Dinsdale quietly canvassed for him behind the scenes.

'Ah, Travers,' Dinsdale hailed him heartily, 'just the man.'

Travers returned the welcome with a weak smile; he knew Dinsdale only spoke to him when there was a problem. He tried to edge pass as he muttered something about being late but Dinsdale, accustomed to this manoeuvre, moved sideways and blocked his path. 'There's a small matter I wanted to mention, Travers.'

Travers halted. He was a clear head and shoulders taller than Dinsdale but somehow he felt diminutive, overshadowed by the beaming and effusive general manager. He instinctively looked at his watch; he wasn't late for anything but he felt this action may prompt Dinsdale to keep whatever it was to the minimum. He sighed inwardly when Dinsdale reached up and placed his hand on his shoulder, rooting him to the spot and daring him to move away.

'I saw Harry Menkowitch and his usual playing partners exchanging money on the eighteenth green.' Dinsdale paused to make sure Travers was listening and he tilted his head to make eye contact.

'You think they were playing for money?' Travers asked.

'That is what it looked like.'

'But you're not sure. I mean, you haven't asked them.'

It was Dinsdale's turn to sigh inwardly. 'When three men give money to a fourth on the eighteenth green it usually means they have played for money.'

'Is that against the club rules?' Travers queried. 'I haven't read that anywhere.'

'It's not a written law but it is frowned upon.' Dinsdale released hold of Travers' shoulder and patted it three times. 'Just have a word with them, will you?' He smiled and moved on, happy that he had passed the problem to someone else. He admitted it was something he wouldn't have bothered with himself, but as Travers was to hand, a word from him would let them know they were being watched.

*

When they had showered and changed, the four men went up to the lounge area, sat at their usual table and ordered drinks. Throughout their shower, Sol had complained about being talked out of his putt and then about Harry's sand shot and only stopped when Rick flicked his towel across his bare behind, which made him yelp.

'You know,' Sol started again, pointing his finger accusingly, 'I know you guys have stitched me up somehow. I know you have.'

'I'll have to keep my eye on Wall Street this week,' Al said seriously. He waited until the other three looked at him with attention. His face began to break into an easy smile. 'I expect Sol could cause a crash when he cashes in a lot of his stock to pay for the fifty dollars he lost today.'

'Is that supposed to be funny? So what do you know about stocks?' Sol said with a hint of bitterness in his voice.

'I dabble,' Al said quietly.

'I dabble,' Sol mimicked. 'You'll never make money by dabbling. It's a science.'

Harry knew they were in for a long diatribe about the Exchange and cut him off. 'How many hours do you spend a day on the Internet and on the phone with your broker, Sol?'

Sol hunched shoulders while he thought about it. 'Two. Maybe three hours a day. Why?'

'That's about fifteen hours a week, assuming you don't

trade at weekends.' Harry drew aimless, small circles on the table with his finger. 'Take in the cost of your calls, your computer and the Internet plus your own time, and of course your broker's charges, you'd have to make a lot to show a profit.'

Sol looked at him with suspicion. 'I make enough.' Then he felt they were having fun with him again so he said in a hushed voice, looking first to ensure they weren't being overheard, 'I make a lot of bucks and I mean a lot. You guys have no idea what's out there.'

He waited for some response but there was none.

'Fifteen hours,' Harry mused. 'If you spent fifteen hours a week practising your golf, you wouldn't have lost fifty-five dollars today.'

Sol noticed the grins from the other two. 'Okay. So I don't win much. But I'll show you guys. Before the snow comes you'll see a different Sol out there on the course. It'll be me taking the dollars from you three.'

The waiter, a young, fresh-faced youth wearing a white jacket and dark trousers and carrying a tray with their drinks, interrupted Sol's assurances and placed the four drinks on the table.

'He'll pay,' Sol indicated towards Harry. 'Mister Moneybags over there. He hit a couple of streaky shots today,' he offered as way of an explanation. The lad smiled without understanding and handed Harry a chit for the drinks which Harry signed.

When he had left, Rick leaned forward in the manner of a conspirator. 'Have you heard they are going to franchise out the catering and the bar?'

'Who did you hear that from?' Al enquired. 'That usually means higher prices and less service.'

'It's the thing to do these days,' Sol said with a knowing look. 'All the big corporations are doing it. They call it outsourcing.'

22

'Whatever they call it,' Al argued, 'it'll still increase the price of everything.'

'No,' Sol countered. 'It's the way to keep costs down. You identify your essential services and outsource all non-essential ones. Hire it all out and take in the money without doing anything.'

'Are you saying the bar and catering are non-essential?' Rick queried.

'And the service level will go down and the prices go up.' Al wouldn't let it go. 'They will have to make more profit to pay the club for the franchise.'

Harry wasn't so concerned with the semantics of the argument. 'Where did you hear this from, Rick?'

Rick seemed reluctant to reveal his source. 'Just talk in the locker room.'

Harry gently whirled his glass round so that the ice clinked against the sides before he sipped his Jack Daniels. He sucked on his lips and savoured the taste. 'Maybe I'll go and ask Dinsdale. It's a while since I had a chat with him.'

Al smiled. 'And he enjoys that so much.'

Harry stood up. 'I won't be long,' and he sauntered across the lounge. On his way to the passage leading to Dinsdale's office, he had to pass a table where several ladies were seated. As he approached, he could see from their glances that he had been part of their conversation. He paused by their table and his rubbery face broadened into a lopsided grin. 'Did you have a good game this morning?' he asked, amicably.

The brunette he had called Helen looked at her watch deliberately. 'It's afternoon now. It would only be morning had we not been held up so much.'

Harry ignored her sarcasm and looked at Louise. 'You'll have to show me sometime, how you swing so easy.'

'Will it make you play more quickly?' she responded.

Harry shrugged. 'I guess.' He winked at her in an inoffensive way. 'At least the other guys will admire it.'

Louise couldn't help a smile. 'But you have to have the figure to go with it.'

'Ah well,' he shrugged again. 'Then I guess there's no hope for me.'

Harry moved on and they waited until he had disappeared down the passageway, out of earshot.

'How could you talk to him like that?' one queried to Louise.

'He's not so bad. Kind of cute in a way,' Louise said, with a smile. 'I hope when I'm his age I can still enjoy a round of golf.'

'And hold everyone up,' the same woman retorted.

A large lady at the end of the table grunted; her name was Ellor Byrne and she was the Lady Captain. She was large, as Sol had described, in every area; she was at the age when her breasts had begun to sag in unison with her expanding waistline, and when she wore shorts, her large rear end was a sight to avert every eye in another direction. When she smiled, which was not often, her whole face came in to play, and when she spoke her tone reflected her status as Lady Captain. She was over-officious, over-bearing, and as Harry had once remarked, over the hill. She was very proud of the fact that her husband was high up in one of the banks; she reminded people of this often enough, but had she known that he had been carrying on with his secretary for nigh on fifteen years, she may have changed her views.

She waited until the ladies had settled before speaking. 'We really must do something about that man.'

'And the other three,' a mouse of a woman, sat at one corner of the table, interjected.

Ellor did not like the interruption and glared at the offender, who suitably wilted in her chair and looked down at her hands as if inspecting a piece of cheese. 'And the other three,' she repeated. 'It's no good complaining to Dinsdale. He doesn't do anything.'

'I think I have an idea,' Louise said quietly. The others looked to her with interest.

'An idea for what?' Ellor Byrne queried with an abrupt tone.

'Oh, a way to bring him down.' Louise angled her eyes to the ceiling and curled her lips in a secretive manner.

Ellor did not like someone else to have the ideas. 'We want all four, not just Harry Menkowitch,' she insisted.

'Bring Harry down and you topple all of them,' Louise said, and waited as the ladies leaned closer. 'It'll be like the domino effect.' And she slowly spread her fingers down onto the table one at a time like an unfolding fan, to illustrate her point.

'Go on,' said Ellor, conceding she was interested.

*

Dinsdale's office was situated at the end of the thickly carpeted passageway and Harry paused at the door. To one side of the door there was a small box with a red glass front and this was illuminated to reveal the word 'Engaged', which meant Dinsdale did not want to be disturbed. Harry ignored the sign and tried the door, but it was locked. He walked back to the next door and pushed down the handle; the door opened and Harry stepped into a small office used by Dinsdale's secretary, Felicia. She was not there so Harry went over to the door connecting to Dinsdale's office and he paused a moment while he tried to make out the sounds coming from Dinsdale's room. It was a sort of a steady panting that reminded him of the old steam locomotives and he eased the door open just enough to see in. A smile began to spread over his rubbery

25

lips. Felicia was lying across Dinsdale's desk with her skirt around her waist and her legs held high and Dinsdale was standing between them with his trousers and boxer shorts round his ankles. The lasting impression Harry would always carry with him was Dinsdale's white, half-moon cheeks pumping away while Felicia, with her arms spread wide across the desk, made the impression of the steam train as she gasped with each thrust. Harry gently moved the door further open and quietly stepped forward.

*

Dinsdale was the first to become aware that someone was standing close. His head snapped up and his mouth fell open and he paused in mid-thrust, his face purple with exertion. 'Harry! What the hell are you doing here?'

'Somehow, I don't have to ask you that question,' Harry smiled. He moved closer so that he was looking down at Felicia's face. She had quickly lowered her legs and pushed her skirt down to cover herself, and her eyes were pressed tightly shut as her mind repeated over and over, 'God, this is not happening. God, this is not happening.'

'The sign said engaged,' was all Dinsdale could think of to say.

'And so you are,' Harry said, the smile remaining on his lips. 'I came in through Felicia's office. I heard a noise in here and thought you were in trouble. I guess I was wrong,' he added sardonically.

'Didn't you lock your door?' Dinsdale asked Felicia with an accusing edge to his voice.

Her eyes didn't open. 'Apparently not,' she said in a caustic voice.

'It was only a small thing,' Harry said in a matter-of-fact way. 'It can wait until later. Unless you'd like to talk about it now...'

Felicia's eyes opened and stared up at Harry's face. 'Will you get the fuck out of here, Harry?'

Dinsdale's mouth fell open again. 'Felicia?'

'And you can get that thing away from me,' she spat, raising her head to look at Dinsdale.

Harry reached forward and patted her shoulder. 'Now, now my dear, let's not be hasty. Let me leave first before you adjust yourselves.' He turned and made towards the door where he paused and looked back at the two distraught figures. 'I'll catch you later,' he said to Dinsdale and winked.

'Harry?' Dinsdale called after him, but Harry had left, closing the door behind him.

*

Harry returned to the others and sat down. They looked at him with keen expectation but he just lifted his glass and swirled it around; the ice had long melted, but when he sipped, he was pleased it was still chilled the way he liked it. As usual, Sol was the impatient one.

'Well?'

Harry reached for his cigar packet but it was empty. He crumpled the packet and placed it in the ashtray. 'He was engaged with some sensitive negotiation,' Harry said, thinking that he must remember to pick up some cigars from the corner shop on the way home. 'He'll call me in to see him soon.' And before Sol could say anything, he added, 'He'll want to see me alone.'

'What?' Sol queried. 'Why just you?'

'We have some other matters to discuss,' Harry said without further explanation.

Al sensed something from his friend's expression and stood up. 'Well, I've got to be going.' He placed his hand under Sol's arm and gently lifted him to his feet. 'And you've got to ring your broker. Fifty-five dollars, remember?'

Sol pulled his arm away with irritation. 'You'll never let me forget that,' his voice whined.

'I guess not,' Al said, and waved to Harry as he walked away. 'See you at eight tonight.'

'What's at eight?' Sol queried.

'Nothing to concern you,' Rick said as he got up and gently pushed Sol in the direction of the door. 'See you Wednesday, Harry.'

'Same time,' Harry answered and watched them depart.

*

Harry sipped his drink and looked out the window to the eighteenth green where four men were putting out. He smiled as he remembered his trick on Sol and considered if he should repay him the fifty dollars; he didn't think long about it and promptly forgot it. As he looked back, he noticed Travers coming towards him. Harry watched him keenly; like Dinsdale, Harry wondered how Travers had made captain but it didn't bother him. The lanky figure halted in front of him and Harry noted his eyes betrayed a little nervousness.

'How are you, Travers?' Harry tried to sound light to put the other at ease.

'Can I sit down?' Travers asked.

Harry looked at the three empty chairs and then nodded. 'You look like a man with a mission.' Travers sat on the edge of the seat and looked uncomfortable. Harry thought of offering to buy him a drink but he wasn't that keen on his company. 'Let me guess, the ladies have complained about our slow play.'

Travers shook his head. 'No, it's something else.' He paused and his lips moved without sound as if shaping the right words in his mouth. 'You were seen paying money out on the final green.'

28

Harry ran a finger along the line of his mouth. 'Betting, you mean.'

Travers nodded. 'Not that I think it's a serious offence when it's only for a few dollars, but Dinsdale asked me to mention it.'

'Well, well, Dinsdale,' Harry murmured. 'It was not what you would call a heavy bet. Five bucks each, that's all. It adds a little interest to the game.'

For some reason, Travers seemed relieved. 'Well, perhaps...' Travers paused a moment, '...perhaps you could settle your bets in the locker room.'

'I guess we could,' Harry said laconically. 'It would take away the excitement though.' When Travers looked at him with some confusion, Harry added, 'It's our tradition that when you win the fifteen bucks, you do a lap of honour round the green.'

'You do?'

'No, we don't. Don't worry about it, Travers, we'll keep it discreet.'

Travers seemed happy that it had all been resolved; at least he thought it may have been, so he stood up and just said, 'Good,' repeating it several times as he moved away.

*

A short while later Dinsdale bustled across the lounge and sat opposite Harry at his table. Harry noticed that his clothes were as impeccable and smooth as usual, but the same couldn't be said about his face, which had a high colour, and his eyes seemed even narrower.

'Would you like a drink, Harry?'

'There's no need,' said Harry, but Dinsdale had already clicked his fingers to the boy behind the bar. 'In that case, I'll have a cigar as well,' Harry added.

29

Dinsdale looked at him and then to the bar. 'And a cigar,' he ordered. 'Now look, Harry...'

But Harry held up his hand. 'Dinsdale, there's no need for an excuse or explanation.'

'There's not?'

Harry finished his drink as the young boy placed another drink and a cigar in front of him. 'No there isn't,' he said as the boy moved away with the empty glass. 'What you do in your office with your secretary is your business.'

Dinsdale studied him in disbelief. 'Do you mean you are not going to say anything?'

Harry shrugged. 'Why should I? What is to be gained except a lot of talk, which would upset things.'

'I'm very grateful,' Dinsdale began to relax.

'You do a great job running this place,' Harry said genuinely as he took the wrapper off the cigar; he noted it was very expensive and rolled it through his fingers. A grin eased across his lips. 'Besides, I don't blame you. I wouldn't mind a crack at Felicia myself. She's quite a beauty.'

'You would?'

'But I wouldn't,' Harry corrected Dinsdale's thoughts. 'But what I can't understand is why you did it in your office. There are plenty of cheap motels you could use.'

Dinsdale face tightened. 'That would be sordid.'

'I suppose it would,' Harry said, looking to the ceiling and wondering what the difference was between having sex in an office and a cheap motel room.

Dinsdale became flustered again by his silence. 'You have to understand. Mrs Dryden and I ... well, we don't...' His voice trailed off. He always referred to her as Mrs Dryden, and not many knew her first name; it was Dinsdale's way of keeping her detached from the club which she rarely visited.

Harry put a lit match against his cigar and puffed a cloud of blue smoke towards the ceiling. Satisfied it was burning evenly, he flipped the match into an ashtray where the flame died and a thin wisp of smoke signalled its passing. He looked across at Dinsdale. 'Let's consider the matter closed and forgotten.'

Dinsdale recovered his composure a little. 'That's very good of you, Harry.'

Harry puffed more smoke for a moment and then looked across at Dinsdale. 'What's this I hear about franchising out the catering and the bar?' he said quietly.

Dinsdale stiffened. 'Just talk. A rumour. There's nothing to it.'

'I hope so,' Harry said, looking at him directly in the eyes. 'I'd hate to think this club would lower its standards for a quick profit. The members would end up paying more in the end.'

'I said, it's just rumour,' Dinsdale repeated. 'It won't happen.'

'That's good to hear,' Harry said and stood up. 'Well, it's been good to talk with you, Dinsdale. We must do it more often.' Dinsdale didn't reply; he knew Harry didn't mean it. As Harry began to move away, he stopped and came back. 'Oh, by the way, Travers has had a word with me about...' he looked around like a conspirator not wanting to be overheard and spoke in a hushed tone, '...the betting.'

Dinsdale tried to smile. 'Oh right. He said he would.'

'I told him we wouldn't exchange money in future. We'll write out cheques.'

Harry smiled to disarm Dinsdale's suspicious mind but it had the reverse effect. When Harry had left, Dinsdale noted he had not touched his drink. He looked around and, making sure nobody was watching, quickly lifted the glass to his lips and swallowed the drink with one gulp, feeling the liquid warm its way down his throat. When he stood up, he pulled his shirt cuffs down to reveal an inch

31

of white linen, set back his shoulders and strode out of the lounge.

*

Back in his office, Dinsdale virtually collapsed into his expansive, leather chair and ran his hands along the padded arms. He was getting careless and that bothered him more than anything. He had not meant it to happen at that moment; he and Felicia were usually more discreet and waited for the evenings when the clubhouse was empty. But Felicia had stood too near to him and her breast had brushed against his arm as they looked at a document she had brought in. He could tell from a coquettish look in her eyes that she had noticed as well, and then it all happened it a rush.

He looked at the closed door to her office and judged she was better left alone. She had been in a mean mood when Harry had left and as she had adjusted her dress, he had held up her panties, meaning to be helpful. But she had snatched them away and sobbed as she rushed into her office, slamming the door behind her.

*

And then there was the franchise business. He wasn't happy with that and where the hell had Harry got to hear about it? The president and owner of the club, Jay Don Winchester, known by all as JDW, had only mentioned it to him a few days before, so how had it got out so quickly? When JDW confided to him about it, Dinsdale had rejected the idea quite firmly and the president had raised his eyebrows with surprise; Dinsdale was usually a 'club man' and went along with most things, but Dinsdale knew what would happen – the members wouldn't like it and all the complaints would be directed at him. And he also knew that it would drag on like a festering sore. Every rise in prices – which would happen – and every incident of bad service – which would also happen – would bring the members hammering on his door. Life would become unbearable.

Dinsdale guessed that JDW had probably set the rumour in motion himself. That was his style – ease it in quietly from the back door and let them chew it over until they got used to the idea. Dinsdale made up his mind – he would oppose it and somehow find a way to prevent it from happening. He rested his head back and began to search for a solution.

3

Sol was the first to leave the club; he always was for some reason, as if it were important to be in front. He drove down the drive to the club gates too fast and had to brake hard before easing his big Buick out into the traffic, ignoring the horn of a fast-approaching truck; his mind was too full of negative thoughts to notice. Solomon Riley was of part Jewish and part Irish descent; how his mother, fleeing from a troubled Europe in the 1930s, had met, was impregnated by and finally married his father in Dublin, was a story in itself, but the mixture of their blood was the cause for his fiery, short temper and obsession with money. Rick had once offered an apt description of him when he had lost his patience with Sol's manic behaviour – he called him neurotic. In fact, Rick had surprised the others with an unusual vehemence: 'That guy's obsession with cents makes no sense. He's fucking neurotic!'

Sol's head was mostly bald with a hint of black, curly hair tracing round the back of his head to his ears which he nurtured daily with a hair-growth hormone shampoo that had little effect except to irritate his skin. His face was wide which placed his eyes too far apart like black buttons either side of his flat, stubbed nose. He was short and tubby with a waistline that eased over his waistband, and although he sat on an extra cushion in his car, he had to tilt his head slightly upwards as he drove so that he could peer over the steering wheel. His wife, Catherine, had died many years before. It had been a good marriage to start with – in an opposites attract kind of way – and initially they savoured a close harmony, but living together soon took the shine off and somewhere in her distant ancestry there must have been Irish blood too because from being a quiet, adulating wife, his neurosis steadily cut through her until it awoke a dormant fire inside; he suddenly found she could match his temper. Sol never realised that he was to blame for unleashing the beast which scorned his obsession and berated his ears about his neglect for his children, leaving her to bring them up while he immersed himself in his money-making schemes. She had lived a good, clean life, caring and bringing up the children on the small allowance he gave her, but Fate's fickle finger had sought her out one day and she had died a slow, painful death from cancer. Through that time, Sol had become a changed man, investing all his time and energy to care for her, and when she went, he felt a mixture of sadness, relief and exhaustion. After that, he lived alone in his over-large house, except for the once a month visit from his three sons, whom he barely tolerated, and their wives, who irritated him by talking incessantly and all at once. He also hated their children, of which there were many; they were too active and too noisy and one of them would always be crying about something that another had done. Their visits had started as a routine when his wife had died; somehow his sons felt it was their duty to see their father even though they had never truly got on with him. Throughout their young lives, he had been forever preoccupied with work and making money and he had always felt that they were only waiting for the time when his fortune would pass on to them. If they had been able to talk openly with him and he had had the patience to listen, they would perhaps have found some meeting ground and the irritating, regular visits would have ended.

In fact, most things in life irritated him, especially being beaten at golf, which was most times. What he didn't realise was that the solitude he thought he wanted after his wife died made him a watcher – he watched the world from the outside like a lonely child at the window of a toy shop, peering in with fascination but not daring to venture in and be part of it. As a consequence, in the evenings he sat, a small man in a large house, reclining in his chamois-covered, electronic, automatic, executive-style armchair watching cable and sipping beer. But from time to time, his gaze would drift around the room and absently take in the dark mahogany furniture – ornate occasional tables which he never used and glass-fronted cupboards with hidden lighting that subtly illuminated expensive silverware and crystal. There were two large sofas that he never sat in, positioned either side of a large stone hearth which was never warmed by a log fire. Finally, his gaze would return over the soft, light-brown Wilton carpet which eased itself across the room like a sandy beach across the desert island he lived on, and his attention would slowly return to the television. He would then sigh for no reason.

As Sol drove down the highway, his mind seethed with his failure at golf, except he didn't quite see it as a failure. He felt that just about everything conspired against him: a sudden gust of wind that angled his ball into the rough grass; an unlucky bounce which diverted it into a bunker; or the lip of a hole which bent his ball away when he was sure it was about to drop. Whatever power there was who watched over him, he felt its malignant finger pointing down at him. Perhaps it was his wife getting her own back.

The fifty dollars irked him as well; he was sure the others had done something but he couldn't quite work out what. He decided to invest another fifty bucks with the club's professional and get his swing sorted out. 'I just want one round,' he said aloud to himself, 'to show those sonsofbitches and rub their noses in it.' A motorist passing him by in the outside lane had glanced across and seen his mouth working and assumed he was singing along with his radio. Sol felt eyes on him, looked sideways and raised his hand with one finger lifted. 'So what's with you?' he shouted. The driver simply put his foot down and sped forward, shaking his head and wondering who the crazy guy was.

When he got home, Sol decided he would have a quick lunch and then phone his broker to get the latest status on his shares. He felt a little better from the thought.

*

Rick got into his BMW; it was one of life's luxuries that he permitted himself. He felt relaxed as the big engine quietly purred as he drove at an easy pace down the club's drive to the gates. His real name was Ricardo, but he had hated it from an early age when he found it difficult to pronounce. He had also taken beatings at school for being Spanish, which he wasn't. The solution had been simple – he changed his name to Rick and thereafter became popular. Ironically, he married a pretty Spanish girl called Anna, who had the darkest ebony eyes. They had one son whom he named Ricardo and he had waited for the day he wised up enough to change it to Rick. He loved his wife, who became even more beautiful with the years, and they had found a fulfilling harmony which transgressed any of the problems that life seemed to throw up with too much regularity. Although financially comfortable – his parents had left him a fair-sized fortune when they passed on – he had never kept a job for long; he always found he was at the front of the queue when lay-offs were made and at the back of it when promotions were given out. When he retired early in his mid-fifties, he made a point of never queuing for anything.

As he drove home he thought about his current problem – his son Ricardo. He had dropped out of college without discussing it with his parents and had lived at home doing nothing; that is until Rick had bought him a small apartment in the hope that independence would stir him to make something of himself. But Ricardo had simply moved into the apartment, lived alone and carried on doing nothing. That was until recently, when Ricardo came round to see his parents one evening to announce that a friend had moved in with him and they were in love. Under normal circumstances Rick would have been over the moon, but the fact that the friend was a boy whom Ricardo had been to college with kind of took the edge off his joy.

Rick's wife, Anna, seemed to take it in her stride. Women tried to understand these things, but Rick could not see past a red neon sign flashing in front of his eyes which said, 'Your Son Is Gay'. Ricardo had awkwardly tried to explain the way he felt, but as he didn't understand quite what had happened to himself, he failed to penetrate through his father's stigmatic views. He finally gave up when he saw the vacant, uncomprehending stare in his father's eyes. He left with an uttered, 'Sorry'. A few days later, Anna had visited Ricardo at his apartment and tried to explain – and in some way excuse – Rick's disposition. It would take time, she told him, but she was sure he would come round eventually. In his own way, his father was trying to come to terms with himself; he knew he couldn't change things, but the wall was too high to climb, there was no doorway and his only hope was to find a way round it.

*

Al was next to leave the club and he drove out slowly in his ageing Mercury; he could have treated himself to a newer model but he was comfortable with its feel and, like a pair of worn-in slippers, he was loathe to break in a new one. He was tall, tanned and athletic-looking, with a slim build and could have been taken for less than his sixty-two years; except for his face, which was grooved by time and was softened only by his ever-humourous grey eyes. He was an easy-going sort of guy who let most things slip over his head without a glance upwards to see what it was; even when he found out his wife, Phillippa, was having an affair he had felt sorry for the guy. This bemused Harry, whom he told one time in confidence. You had to live with her to understand, he had tried to explain; she was ten years younger than he was and had come from a poor family on the eastern side of the river and the transition to a large house and his wealth had brought on a dramatic change soon after their marriage. He had allowed, even encouraged, her to spend and buy things she didn't really want. Initially he had been fascinated by her excitement, which was like a child in a toy shop, but after restocking her wardrobe, she then turned to the house and had it totally redecorated and refurnished; everything had to be the best and soon he found he wasn't allowed to touch the best in case he broke it or simply didn't put it back in its precise place. The house and every possession became her obsession and her temple. Her only concession to him was his own room, a study, which he deliberately kept in a state of permanent untidiness. She had only ever entered it once, turned without speaking and never entered it again. It became his haven and he spent most of his leisure time there relaxing with whatever he wanted to do or watching cable. They had no children; he decided he didn't want to take the risk.

When they had first met, Al was taken by her open sort of beauty: her fair skin, her long, honey-blonde hair, her blue eyes, her wide mouth and her even teeth, which she showed often with a ready smile. But the years were not kind to her and she put on weight easily. As a result, her face became puffed and lost its smile. One day she became aware that men were not looking at her in the same way they had when she was younger and trimmer and so she went on a strict regime of diet and exercise. She became slimmer – perhaps too thin, Al thought – and she had her hair cut shorter in a bob. She selected more formal clothes, usually a jacket and skirt, giving her that 'businesswoman' look and wore higher heels to show off her shapely legs. She noticed that men were beginning to notice again.

A few years ago, Al came home unexpectedly one day and found her in bed with an interior designer she had hired to 'go over' the kitchen. He had stood in the doorway to the bedroom and watched them, curled in each other's arms, breathing quietly in sleep. The one thing that stuck in his mind was their clothes strewn about the room; it was unlike her to be so untidy. He had left without disturbing them and driven down to a local diner he frequented. It was called the 'Ever After Diner', and from the outside it looked like most other diners, with plenty of glass and steel and plastic. Inside, though, it offered blue and white checked tablecloths and wooden moveable chairs, and it was always exceptionally clean. The food was wholesome and the coffee fresh and the diner also had a waitress called Aritha; she was middle-aged and sort of attractive, with a smile for Al that said, 'I like you'. Al talked with her a lot and he confided in her things he told no other; not even Harry. It almost became an affair between them, but it was an affair without touching and never left the confines of the diner. Had he asked her to go to a cheap motel and make love, she would have readily agreed but he never asked and somehow she knew he probably never would. On that particular day when he had caught Phillippa in bed with the kitchen designer, Aritha could tell from his face as he sipped his coffee that something was troubling him and eventually he told her. As she eased a cloth round a clean plate and put it on a stack on a back shelf, she came over and leaned towards him over the counter. 'So what are you going to do?' she asked.

Al had sighed and his shoulders sagged in an almost defeatist way. 'Nothing, I guess.'

She had covered his hand with hers, their first real touch. 'You can't just let her get away with it.'

'Why not?' he asked with a sort of hopelessness. 'We haven't done that sort of thing in a long while and I expect the poor bastard will pay for it eventually. She has expensive tastes.'

She squeezed his hand gently. 'If there's anything I can do.'

'Another coffee,' he said without realising what she really meant.

Now, as he drove into town, he thought about the diner and decided he needed a coffee; Phillippa was probably out at one of her lady's clubs or having her hair done or shopping for expensive clothes or something. Perhaps she was screwing with someone else; whatever, he convinced himself it didn't bother him and he wanted to talk with Aritha.

*

When Harry left Dinsdale Dryden, he wandered into the Professional's shop to look over any new clubs on offer. He frequently did this after a game just to pass a little time, but he never bought anything and the Professional knew it. Harry selected a club from a rack and swung it gently in his hands; he then replaced it with a shake of his head that indicated he knew what he was doing. The Pro watched him and in turn shook his head. Eventually, after handling several more clubs, Harry approached the shop counter where the Pro had buried his head in a golf magazine.

'I've heard a lot about these graphite-shafted clubs,' he began. 'Would they improve my game?'

The Pro lifted his face and looked tired from similar questions asked every day. 'They would make a round of golf easier.'

Harry rubbed his hand over his loose chin. 'How so?'

'Your bag would be lighter.' The Pro's voice was monotone. 'Make it easier to carry.'

Harry looked upwards and sighed – he knew the Pro was making fun of him. 'Trouble is, I always use a cart. Don't have to carry.'

'So what do you want to improve in your game?' the Pro queried.

Harry thought for a moment. 'I want to drive three hundred and fifty yards, hit a wedge in from one-fifty and make the ball spin back to the hole.'

The Pro just looked at him without responding.

Harry smiled at the Pro's straight face. 'I guess you are right,' he said, and left the shop.

He drove his Ford out onto the road and headed for town. Harry drove the car the same as he walked; he ambled, and traffic stacked up behind him until there was a gap in the outside lane to slip into. Some drivers shook a fist at him as they sped past but he didn't see them; Harry watched the road ahead and smiled as he thought of Sol and Dinsdale and Felicia.

When he got home, his wife Rosemary was putting on her coat. She offered her cheek for a quick kiss and then picked up her bag. 'Did you have a good game or is that a silly question from the look on your face?'

'I had a good final hole. I'll tell you about it later. Are you going out?' he asked the obvious.

'Yes, Harry,' she quipped. 'Otherwise I would be taking my coat off.'

Harry grinned and went over to the fridge and took out a beer. 'So if you are going out, where are you going?'

She hesitated and seemed reluctant to tell him. 'I'm going to the supermarket,' she admitted at last.

'Damn,' he uttered as he flipped the top off the bottle of Budweiser. 'I meant to call into the local shop on the way back. If you wait until I finish this beer I'll come with you.'

'No you won't,' she said deliberately, which made him look up from rummaging for something to eat from the fridge.

'Why not?'

'Because whenever you come shopping with me, you fill up the basket with a lot of things we don't need.'

'I need some cigars and a bottle of Jack Daniels,' he said, giving a reason to go with her.

'I know you do and that's another reason why you're not coming with me.' Her face had become set and he knew her well enough not to argue. 'You know what the doctor said and it is time for your next check-up. I've booked you in for tomorrow at ten.'

'I don't need to see that quack.' He tapped his chest and drew in his waistline. 'I'm just fine.' He sipped his beer and spilt some down his shirt front.

Rosemary saw this and laughed in the way that always fascinated him; it sounded like water tripping over stones. He smiled with her. 'I guess you had better book me in to see the paediatrician, as well.'

'That's the wrong type of doctor,' she laughed again, but then she paused. 'No. I guess it may be the right one. You're just like a big kid.' She kissed him on the lips and then went to the door.

'Are you sure you don't want me to come?'

'I'm sure.'

'Don't forget the cigars and JD,' he called after her.

'I can't hear you,' her words trailed off as she closed the door.

Harry stood for a moment looking down the empty hall to the front door and waited for her car to depart. He had had a new door fitted a year ago with a large multi-coloured glass pane that he had designed himself, and as the sun progressed west through the afternoon, its rays painted a dapple collage of colours across the floor, which crept up the hall like a wavelet slowly creaming over a sandy shore.

Harry took his beer out to the back porch, where he sat in a canvas chair at a wooden slatted table. The sun was beginning to dip and the back porch was in shade, but a light, warm breeze made it comfortable and he began to think of his father who had died several years ago.

His father had moved to Wannabee sixty years earlier from New York and had rented a small shop with a two-room apartment over it on the eastern side of the river. Harry was very young and only had vague memories of those hard times as his father tried to establish a business. He was a watchmaker and jeweller by trade and was astute enough to realise that life would be better on the western side of the river.

He came up from the shop very late one night and told his wife about his dream. She listened to him intently, knowing that she should not interrupt, and when he had finished she patted his arm affectionately.

'That sounds very nice, Harry, but where will we get the money?'

Harry Senior had also given that some thought. He worked well into the early hours writing out his plans, and the next morning, without opening his shop, he went down to see the local bank manager. He listened to Harry's plans and read through his proposal. Despite it being written in pencil, the manager was sympathetic; he knew all too well that the western side of the river was the place to be and had long yearned for a position in the bank's branch on that side. Harry's plan was quite simple: a watch and jewellery shop in an upmarket part of town, selling personally made watches and jewellery to the wealthy who thought more of uniqueness than price, and who would pay marked up prices believing they must be the best because they were expensive. Harry had assured him also that his goods were of the highest quality and that evening the bank manager stopped off at his shop to look over his stock. He didn't know a great deal about them but he could see that everything was expertly made.

'And you make all these yourself?' the manager queried.

'Just about everything.' Harry indicated over to one side to some glass cabinets. 'I have some cheaper stock I buy in but then this area of town isn't exactly rolling in money. I have to cater for most of them.'

'But the ones you make are all unique? You don't make copies.'

'Never. They're all my own design.'

The manager fingered a small bracelet and thought what a fine gift it would make for his wife. 'And what would you charge for this item?'

'Fifteen dollars.'

'And to me?'

'Fifteen dollars.'

The manager put down the bracelet. In a strange way, Harry's refusal to reduce the price, or even make a gift of it, made him realise that Harry was also a good businessman.

'Come and see me in the morning, Mister Menkowitch, and we'll sort out a loan.'

Within a month, they had moved to the western side of the river into a larger shop not far from the town centre

45

with a four-roomed apartment above it. Paying back the loan and getting established was difficult but within a year, Menkowitch's Watch and Jewellery shop was renowned for its high quality, high standards and high prices. The most frequent question Harry Senior was asked did not refer to the price of an article.

'It is unique, isn't it?'

'There is no other on this earth like it,' he would smile in response. 'You may find one on the moon, and if you do, I'll give you your money back.'

Although Harry Senior did not try to persuade his son to enter the trade, the young boy had a natural talent for it and did not bother with college; he went into the back room and began his apprenticeship, earning a princely two dollars a day. When he met Rosemary and began to talk of marriage, his father took him outside the shop early one morning and pointed to the sign over the shop front. Harry looked in amazement and then hugged his father. The sign read: Menkowitch and Son. As a wedding present, he had been made a partner.

They worked well together; their ideas for design were sometimes diverse but always complementary, and business was thriving. Harry admired his father greatly and respected his business acumen as well as his skills. There was one time, when young Harry had been married a year and lived in a small house away from the town centre, that he suggested opening a second store, but his father had shook his head slowly.

'There is no need. It would serve no purpose.' To Harry's questioning look, he added, 'We make enough money, wouldn't you agree? Do you want for anything?'

Young Harry shook his head. 'No, I guess not. But I'm not against earning more.'

'There is something about the jewellery business in a small town like this that you must understand and always remember.' He paused to check his son was listening. 'When you sell the best, only sell it in one place. Make the customer come to you.'

Harry had understood what his father meant and nodded and remembered. As his father grew older, his eyesight began to fade and his hands became arthritic. Finally he conceded and handed the business over to his son. But the years had taken their toll and within six months he had died; the doctor had said that his body was simply worn out. Harry remembered that lesson as well, and as soon as one of his sons had learnt the business, Harry retired and took up golf.

He came out of his thoughts when he heard a noise in the house. At first he thought it was Rosemary returning but then a small express train burst through the back weather door, full of noise and action.

'Well, well.' Harry smiled and held out his hands. 'And how is my favourite grandson.'

The young boy ran to him and fell into his arms. 'I'm your only grandson.'

'Ah. But that makes you even more special.' Harry kissed him on top of his thick, curly hair and leaned back to look at him. 'Where did you get that eye?' he queried, noticing the young boy sported a shiny, black bruise around his right eye. 'Has your father been beating you?'

'No,' the boy said with some indignation. 'I got it at school.'

'You've been fighting?' Harry asked with some concern.

'Yep,' came the short reply.

Harry noted the boy had the same laconic way of speaking his father had; why use five words when one would do? 'Tell me what happened.'

The young boy stepped back, his face full of mixed emotions; he felt proud of what he had done but he was unsure his grandfather would see it that way. 'A boy called

Rizzo was bullying a friend of mine so I wupped him.' He punched his fist through the air to demonstrate how he did it.

'Was this friend a girl?'

'Yep. Sophie Pearson. She's in my class. Does it matter?'

'No. It's just when it's a girl it makes it more worthwhile.' He touched the boy's cheek just below the eye and the boy leaned away quickly, not wanting the pain if his grandfather touched the bruise. 'And he gave you this.'

'Yep. But you should have seen what I did to him. I kicked his ass.'

Harry sat back with mock horror. 'Where did you get that expression, young man?'

'From you, Gramps.'

'Me? When have I ever said that?'

'Every time you watch the ball game on TV.'

At that moment the weather door opened and Harry's son, Dave, stepped out onto the porch. 'You should know, Harry, that children hear everything, see everything and remember everything.'

Harry laughed as he stood up and touched his son on the arm. 'I was forgetting,' he said easily and motioned his son to the canvas chair next to him. 'There's a beer in the fridge if you want one.'

The young express train gathered up steam and crashed through the weather door again. 'I'll get it,' he shouted as he disappeared.

'You've got him trained well,' Harry smiled. 'You never brought me a beer like that.'

'You didn't drink beer when I was his age.'

'True. I was just thinking back to those days with my father. Funny thing, there were some hard times but they were good times.' Harry relaxed back into his chair with his hands idly lying in his lap. 'How is the business going?'

Dave looked out to the garden where the sun, now

arching downwards to the western foothills, was stretching shadows across the lawn. 'Same as always. It runs itself.' He looked back at his father. 'People just want to keep spending, Harry.'

When Harry had made Dave a partner all those years ago, he made him promise never to call him 'Pops' in front of the staff or the customers and Dave had thought about it for a while. Then, in a casual sort of way, he started calling him by his first name. It took a while to get used to, but Harry felt it was a moment of special bonding and although he noticed it every time his son called him Harry, he felt comfortable and proud.

The weather door banged open and his grandson appeared holding an opened bottle of Bud that he handed carefully to his father. Dave held up the bottle and looked at the level of the beer.

'Did you take a sip, James?'

The young boy was as honest as his father. Harry remembered the times he had questioned Dave when he was the same age, over some mishap or something missing or broken, and he could never quite manage a lie. His face would contort with effort but then he would blurt out the truth.

'Just a little one,' young James admitted. He screwed his hands in front of him, waiting for his father to scold him.

'Did you like it?' Harry questioned.

'Pretty good. But it made me burp.'

They both laughed. 'You have to sip it gently,' Harry said and lifted his own bottle. 'Let it run over your tongue. Like this.' Harry tilted the bottle and sipped and then smacked his lips in an exaggerated fashion. 'That way you get the full flavour and it doesn't make you burp.'

Young James laughed also and Dave noted how his father had quietly intervened and prevented a reproach, but he didn't mind. He reached to the floor beside him, lifted a

49

brown paper bag and handed it to his father. 'I guessed you might be wanting these.'

Harry opened the top of the bag and peered in. He looked at James with big eyes. 'A present. It's not my birthday is it?'

James was eager to know what was in the bag and his voice was excited. He pummelled his hands on his grandfather's knees. 'Take it out, Gramps. What is it?'

Harry took out a bottle of Jack Daniels and a packet of five cigars and placed them on the table. James was disappointed.

'Have you got a present for me?' James asked.

Dave was about to say something but Harry interceded again. 'If you look in the freezer, I expect you'll find some chocolate chip ice cream Grandma bought.'

'How much can I have?'

'How much do you want?'

'This much,' and James motioned his hands round in a shape of a large bowl.

'Try a small amount first,' Harry advised. 'You may not like it.'

'Oh yeah? I always like chocolate chip ice cream.'

'And so do I,' Harry said, 'so don't take all of it.' He grinned to ease his grandson's tense face. 'Off you go.'

'Bring the bowl out here so I can check,' Dave ordered as the door swung shut with a bang.

The door opened slightly and his young face reappeared. 'I want to watch TV.'

Dave shrugged. 'Okay, but not too much ice cream.' He looked to his father. 'Was I like that, Harry? Always asking for things?'

Harry reached for the cigars, took one out and expertly stripped off the cellophane wrapping. 'Always.' He lit the cigar and blew smoke. 'But we didn't have chocolate chip ice cream then. I seem to remember it was always vanilla.'

'We didn't have a TV either.'

Harry puffed easily for a moment. 'Did you feel deprived in those days?'

Dave shrugged the way his father often did. 'Nope. I had all I wanted. What we didn't have I guess we didn't miss.'

'True.' Harry nodded and puffed on his cigar. 'Have you heard from Rob at all?' he asked, referring to his other son.

'No.'

Dave always felt uneasy talking about his brother; he had caused a lot of hurt. When Rob had left college with good results, he wasted his time for a while and then just upped and went with little reason given and without saying where he was going. They had heard little from him except when he needed money, which Harry always sent him. But it had hurt his mother more; she had borne it quietly, but he saw the pain in her eyes whenever Rob was mentioned. He rarely remembered birthdays and Dave noticed their quiet disappointment each time a birthday was missed; but then they would be over-excited when on the odd occasion he did remember.

They heard a noise in the house and James's excited voice; Rosemary had returned. She stepped out onto the porch and her eyes alighted on the cigars and Jack Daniels on the table. Dave looked suitably guilty.

'From your look I guess you bought those,' she nodded towards the bottle and cigars. 'Are you trying to kill your father?' she admonished.

Dave got up and gave his mother a bear hug. 'I bought you some flowers,' he offered to temper her reproof.

'I saw them,' she said, relenting some. She stepped back while still holding his arms and looked at him with a critical eye the way that mothers often do. 'Thank you, they're lovely.' But then she added, 'But you don't have to buy him those.'

51

Dave shrugged in his familiar way and looked at his father and winked. 'I reckon he's past saving. Let him go quietly.'

'Quietly?' Rosemary queried with a laugh. 'Have you ever known your father do anything quietly? He'll go out kicking and screaming. I reckon the only reason he's lived this long is because the Lord is worried about the turmoil he'll cause in Heaven.'

'Now, Rosemary,' Harry chided, pronouncing her name with four syllables – Rose-a-ma-ree – in a way that irritated her. 'If He has a bottle of JD and a few cigars up there, He knows I won't be any bother.'

'You have them down here and you cause enough,' she replied quickly, not letting him slip so easily off her hook. She let go of her son's arms. 'You're filling out. Is Pam feeding you too much or are you not getting enough exercise?'

'A bit of both, I guess,' Dave responded with a smile.

'Where is she?' Rosemary asked.

'She's at an interview. I picked James up from school so she could go. That's why I left the shop early.'

'A job?' Rosemary's lower jaw dropped a few degrees. 'Whatever for?'

'Boredom,' he replied. 'She's a qualified dentist,' he offered as an explanation, but when his mother's expression didn't change, he added, 'With James at school, she gets bored at home with so little to do. It's only for a few days a week.'

'But you don't need the money,' Rosemary still argued, not understanding.

'It's not the money,' Harry interjected. 'She's got a lot between her ears that needs exercise.'

Rosemary turned her attention to her husband. 'Is that supposed to mean something?'

Harry lifted his bottle but it was empty. 'Another beer, Dave?'

'Now I understand what that means,' Rosemary said with a little annoyance. 'It means you want to change the subject.' But then she relaxed and smiled at her son. 'I'll get the beer. You talk to your father.'

When she returned with the two uncapped bottles, she put them on the table and interrupted their conversation. 'Don't forget we're going out tonight.'

Harry's face screwed up with thought. 'I'm seeing Al at Sam's bar.'

'No you're not. We've been invited round to the Sinclairs'. I knew you'd forget. You can give Al a call and tell him you can't make it.'

Harry's gaze got somewhere lost in the distance. 'I'll just have a couple with him and...'

'And that will become four. The Sinclairs are our new neighbours and I don't want you to make a bad impression by breathing alcohol all over them.'

Harry's gaze came out of the distance and he noticed the stubborn look on Rosemary's face; it was a look which said, 'do as you're told', but without the need for words. But Harry was in a stubborn mood himself. He liked his quiet evenings with Al, besides which he had met Mike Sinclair over the garden fence the day the Sinclairs had moved in and he had taken an instant dislike when he had introduced himself with an over-firm handshake and then tried to sell him an insurance policy.

'I'll just have a couple with Al. We've got something to talk over. I promise I won't be long.'

Dave had watched the clash of wills and was laying odds with himself who would win but he was surprised when Rosemary conceded, 'All right. But if you are late...' She left the rest unsaid.

*

Al sat at the counter in the small diner in the town centre. He sipped his coffee patiently, waiting for Aritha to finish serving someone and return to him.

'Do you want to eat?' she asked, wiping the counter in front of him with a cloth. It was an unnecessary action, since the chrome surface was already gleaming, but it was her way of getting to talk with him. 'I can do you some scrambled eggs with bacon.'

Al shook his head and she was left disappointed; it meant he would finish his coffee and return to his wife. Somewhere inside she felt the same ache she always did when he sat in front of her. She admired his tanned face and grey eyes and his lean, healthy body, which she fantasised about most times when she thought of him when laying in her bed at night. Her husband, in her own description, was nothing more than an overweight slob and she knew Al's wife was a mean woman – Al's description. It just wasn't right in her mind that two people, so suited, would be forever separated by some vows uttered so long ago, vows that at the time had some meaning but from which time and circumstances had rubbed away the shine.

'I've got some nice pancakes. You know, the way you like them with maple syrup.' She tried to tempt him but he knew her game and shook his head again.

'I have things to do,' he lied, hating himself for it. He wanted to stay and he wasn't quite sure why he wouldn't. Perhaps he knew the risk if he stayed too long listening to her honeyed voice. 'I'll stop by tomorrow.'

'It's my day off,' she reminded him; she never worked Tuesdays. 'I was thinking of going to the park and taking a picnic. Do you fancy coming with me?'

Al stepped back from his stool. 'I'd like to, Aritha, but I promised Phillippa I would fix a few things around the house.'

Aritha knew this was a poor excuse – she avoided the word 'lie' but knew from experience there was no point in chasing him. Phillippa never let him touch anything round the house; even for the smallest jobs she got someone in as she wouldn't trust Al to tamper with her palatial home.

He flipped a few coins on the counter. 'I'll probably stop by Wednesday after golf.'

'Be sure you do.' She gave him a special look that said everything and then busied herself clearing his cup and picking up the coins before wiping the counter again.

When Al returned home, Phillippa was descending the stairs. The way she moved reminded him of some Hollywood movie actress entering a ball down a wide avenue of marble steps, expecting all heads to turn towards her. He noted she was wearing a pale blue suit with a white blouse and a dark blue ribbon at her throat, and he regrettably wondered why they were so far apart; was it too far to ever bridge the gap again? Her bobbed hair was freshly brushed and her high cheekbones shaped her face around her mouth in a sensuous way; at that moment, he wanted to kiss her. But then he remembered bitterly the time he had found her in bed with the kitchen designer who was half her years.

'Are you going out?' he asked.

'You make it sound as though you want me to.' Her voice was flat and whatever desire he had to kiss her disappeared.

'No. This house is yours,' he said rather pointedly. 'It's just the way you're dressed.'

'As a matter of fact, I am,' she said, stepping past him and offering no explanation. 'I suppose you are going to lock yourself away in your study so it doesn't matter what I am going to do.'

'I could take you out for lunch,' he offered, not knowing why he said it.

She stopped and looked back at him, searching his face

for sarcasm but not seeing any. 'I'm going to my aerobics class and then on for tea with Melinda. I don't know what time I'll be back.'

'I'm out with Harry tonight.'

'Oh yes. It's Monday.' Her statement carried fact and no emotion. She did not like Al's friends, especially Harry. He had a way of looking at her as if he could see inside her head and he knew her; it made her feel uncomfortable. He also had a habit of patting her bottom when he kissed her in a greeting but she guessed he only did it because he knew it annoyed her; Al probably told him about their relationship or lack of it.

'Besides,' she added, 'I suppose you have been to that diner and had lunch. The one in the town square.'

Al examined his wife closely. 'You know I go to the diner?'

'I've seen you in there a few times.'

'A few times and you've never said anything?' he queried.

'So? You've never mentioned you go in there.'

He hated the way his wife always had an answer which turned the guilt back to him, but he accepted that this time she was right. Why hadn't he ever told her? But he knew why; it was Aritha, but his wife didn't know about her or she would have said something derisory. 'I just go there for a coffee after golf sometimes.'

Phillippa went to the wall mirror by the door and checked herself over. Satisfied, she picked up her sports bag containing her aerobics clothes and went to the door and opened it. 'And the large blonde female,' she said, allowing a knowing smile to form on her mouth, before she slipped out.

Al crossed the room to his study and quietly closed the door behind him. He sat in his well-worn favourite chair and waited until he heard her car start up and move out of the drive. He was seething with anger over many things.

Aritha was not large. He accepted she was not slim, but she was tall and carried her weight well. And she was not just a female; Phillippa had called her that because she knew it would annoy him. Aritha was a friend and confidante, someone he felt easy with and could talk to about pretty much everything. He was also angry that Phillippa had stored away the information to use at a time when she knew it would hurt him. He reached for the phone and dialled a number. A man's voice answered and he asked for Aritha. A moment later he heard her voice.

'It's me,' he said without giving his name. 'What time are you going for that picnic tomorrow?'

'About twelve-thirty.' He could hear the brightness in her voice. 'I'll be at the lake near the waterfall. I'll pack extra food.'

'I'll see you then,' and he rang off without saying any more.

*

Rick arrived home and his wife, Anna, came out from the direction of the kitchen and enveloped her husband in her arms. He kissed her lips in a lingering fashion, not wanting it to end. 'So did you win?' she asked, after finally pulling her head away from him.

He kissed her many times around the mouth and across her cheek and spoke words between the pattering kisses. 'Nope, Harry did. I guess I was too distracted to concentrate on my game.'

'Oh?' Her dark eyebrows raised in perfectly matching arches that widened her eyes with the question. 'What was the distraction?'

He slipped his arms round her and pulled her close again. 'You. I kept thinking about kissing you when I got home.'

57

'So I am your excuse for playing badly.'

'Of course you are. I've got to blame someone.' At that moment he lifted his head and sniffed the air. 'What's that you're cooking?'

'A surprise.'

'Will it take long?'

She looked at him suspiciously. 'A while. Why?'

'How long is a while?'

Her eyes narrowed. 'A couple of hours. It has to simmer. Why? Are you hungry?'

'Yes,' he said and suddenly scooped her up in his arms. She was small and light and he carried her easily up the stairs to the bedroom while she squealed with delight. 'I'm hungry for you.' He growled like a bear as he laid her down on the bed, but then he suddenly stopped and she saw his face was contorted with pain.

'What is the matter?' she asked with growing concern when he didn't move and remained bent over her.

His head dropped and she heard him start to snigger. 'My damn back! I think I've pulled something.'

She relaxed a little and couldn't prevent a girlish chuckle slipping from her lips. 'You're not as young as you think. Perhaps you're not up to it any more.'

He rolled over her and lay on the bed next to her. 'Is that all the sympathy I get?'

She tried to suppress her mirth and she leaned over him and stroked his forehead. 'Is it really that bad?'

'No,' he lied. 'I just need a minute.'

She began to unbutton his shirt. 'You always complain about your back but you won't go to the doctors.'

'It's nothing. Just a twinge now and then.'

'Like a woman getting a headache?' She pattered kisses down his exposed chest.

'What's that supposed to mean?' he asked, experiencing a feeling which numbed the ache in his back.

She raised her head for a brief look at him, smiled and then slipped his belt buckle as she resumed kissing down his body. 'Perhaps I ought to do it for you if you're not up to it.'

He began to say something but then he dropped his head back on the pillow. He wasn't going to argue.

His breathing was soft but Anna noticed that his face twitched occasionally as he slept. Rick always tried to make light of it, but she knew how much their son caused a pain inside him; he had devoted himself to Ricardo as much as he had to her, and his son's recent revelation about living with a gay friend had driven deep. It was tearing out his heart. She tried to ease her arm from under him since it was losing feeling, but the movement stirred him and he looked across at her.

'Is dinner ready?' he asked.

'Is that your first thought?' she laughed softly. 'It'll be a little while longer.'

'Good.' He snuggled in close to her and felt for her breast. Since that night when their son had told them, Rick had become even closer to her, making love more often and more passionately, and she knew he was trying to lose himself in her. But she accepted it and was content that she could help him find some comfort. She stroked his head and then pulled his face into her breast.

4

That evening, Harry entered Sam's Bar and saw Al already seated on a stool at the counter, supping a beer and watching baseball on the TV monitor set on the wall at the far end. It wasn't the best bar in town, just a small oblong-shaped room with a bar in it and Harry couldn't remember when or why he and Al and Rick started to use it as a regular meeting place. Sam, the owner, kept the place clean and served a good chilled beer and it was always quiet, with never more than a handful of men either sitting at the bar or at wooden tables along one wall facing the bar. That said, there was little else to recommend it but Harry and his friends felt comfortable to use it to sit and chew over things. They never invited Sol to join them. He was not the sort to enjoy a quiet conversation that slipped around most subjects and he was sure to talk incessantly about his shares and stocks; he would be about as intrusive as a jukebox would have been, blaring out and flooding the bar with noise.

Harry ambled over and patted his friend on the shoulder as he sat down next to him.

'Hi, Harry. Another beer,' he called to Sam. Harry grabbed a handful of nuts from a bowl and scooped some in his mouth in an untidy fashion, dropping some on the bar. 'You not eaten?' Al asked, watching Harry's mouth working over the nuts.

'You're early,' Harry said, ignoring the intended sarcasm. Sam put a chilled glass of draught beer on the counter in front of Harry.

'So how's you?' Sam asked. 'You're looking good,' he answered his own question.

'Tell my wife that,' Harry said, 'she's booked me in to see the quack tomorrow.'

'So what's the matter?' Sam asked. He spoke a little through his nose that made it sound as though he had a permanent cold, and he began most sentences with 'So'.

'Nothing's the matter.' Harry lifted the beer and took a long drink. 'She thinks I drink and smoke too much.'

'Have you got insurance?' Sam enquired, scooping away the scattered nuts and tossing them into a bin.

'Of course I have,' Harry answered.

'So what's her problem?' He took out a bag of nuts from under the counter and emptied it into the dish. 'Women? Huh. I've never understood them. That's why I've never married one.'

Al laughed as Harry grabbed another handful and spilt more nuts over the counter. 'You'd think that would help you to understand them?'

Sam looked at the scattered nuts. 'Harry, why don't you tip the whole friggin bowl in your mouth. You'd make less of a mess.'

Harry kept a straight face while he held up a nut between his forefinger and thumb. 'If you were married, Sam, you would know all about eating nuts.'

'So what is there to know?'

'Well. If you ate nuts at home you wouldn't spill any because your wife would get angry and make you clean them up.'

'So what's different eating nuts in my bar?'

Harry flipped the nut in the air and expertly caught it

61

in his mouth. 'The difference is, you clear them up.'

Sam shook his head despondently and moved down the bar to another customer.

'So what's with you?' Harry mimicked Sam's voice.

Al smiled. 'That's pretty good Harry. Do it when Sam comes back. I bet he doesn't notice.'

'Five bucks, but it's not a good bet. That sonofabitch don't miss anything.'

Al began to laugh. 'Hey, that's a good impression of Sol. Can you do one of me?'

'No. You're too ordinary.'

'Now that's an impression of my wife except you didn't sound like her.' The humour went out of Al's voice.

'Still giving you a hard time?' Harry said quietly, feeling for his friend's long-time grief.

Al took a long pull at his beer. 'She'll never change now. I missed the chance a long time ago.' But then his face lit up some. 'But I have found the solution.' He drank some more and emptied his glass.

'Are you going to tell me?' Harry asked.

Al thought about it and then began slowly, choosing his words carefully. 'There's this woman in a diner I use. I've been going there a while and we talk a lot. Tomorrow we're going for a picnic in the park.'

Harry waited for more but Al just looked at his empty glass in thought. 'And?'

'And nothing. It'll be just a picnic.'

Harry sounded disappointed. 'Just a picnic.'

'Yes.'

Harry expelled air through his mouth that made his rubbery lips quiver. 'It's a start, I guess.'

Al half turned on his stool and put his hand on Harry's shoulder. 'I'm not sure if I want more. She's nice but she's married too and I don't want to create complications. Do you understand?'

Harry looked steadily into his eyes. 'You still love Phillippa.'

Al sighed. 'I guess I do, even though she's a bitch most of the time. When I got home today she was dressed in one of those suits. You know the ones she wears.' Harry nodded. 'She came walking down the stairs and do you know I got the hots for her.' He held the image of her for a moment and then added, 'But when she opened her mouth it was like pouring cold water over me.'

'What about this woman from the diner? Do you ever feel the hots for her?'

Al shook his head. 'That's the strange thing. I like to talk to her and maybe I would like to get her into bed, but if I did, I think that would be it. It would become a different kind of relationship. I like it the way it is.'

'Then keep it that way,' Harry advised. Al watched him as he took out his handkerchief and spread it out on the bar. He emptied the bowl of nuts into it and folded it and put it away in his pocket.

A moment later, Sam came back and eyed their empty glasses.

'So what's with you?' Harry asked.

'Are you making fun of the way I speak?' Sam asked, spreading his hands wide on the bar and looking from one to the other. Harry held out his hand and Al put a five dollar bill in it. 'So what's this? Are you playing a game or something?'

'Or something,' Harry smiled innocently. 'Two more beers, Sam.' As he refilled their glasses, Harry added, 'And some more nuts.'

Sam put the full glasses in front of them and looked at the empty bowl. 'So what are you two doing? Eating all the friggin nuts?'

They both leaned over and closely inspected the bowl.

'I didn't eat them,' Harry said truthfully.

Al shook his head. 'Me neither.'

'So who was it? The friggin mice?' Sam moved away, muttering as he went, to get another bag from the end of the bar. Harry took out his handkerchief and emptied the nuts back into the bowl. When Sam returned with the bag he stopped and studied the bowl of nuts. 'Okay. So who's the comedian? It has to be you Harry.'

'Guilty as charged. Let me buy you a drink, Sam. Oh, I was forgetting, you don't drink.' He lifted the bowl. 'Here. Have a nut instead.'

Sam stepped back and pointed his finger at them. 'I'll ban you two nutcases from here one day. You bet I won't.'

'You won't?' Al queried, but Sam didn't work that one out and he went down the bar to watch the game on the television while shaking his head again.

They supped their beer and looked over the rim of their glasses at each other; their smiles were in their eyes.

'What happened in Dinsdale's office?' Al asked.

'You know,' Harry said with consideration, 'the trouble with a secret is that it hurts to get it out, but if you tell someone, it's no longer your secret and you pass on the hurt to the one you told.'

Al thought about that and slowly untangled the meaning. 'Does that mean you're not going to tell me what went on?'

'I shouldn't,' Harry said.

'But you will,' Al smiled.

Harry related everything that had happened and Al sat quietly listening and chuckling until he had finished.

'Tell me something,' Al asked at the end. 'Is Felicia a natural blonde?'

'Now that's a secret I cannot divulge,' Harry said. 'But I'll tell you this. She has a fine pair of legs which go right up to her...' and he stopped, his eyes glazing over from the memory.

Al tutted. 'Don't stop at the good bit.'

It was Harry's turn to chuckle. 'There's nothing like imagination to improve on reality.'

Al patted him playfully on the cheek. 'You're such a tease.' But then they became aware that Sam was standing across the bar in front of them.

'So what's the game now? You a pair of friggin queers?'

'Give me a kiss and I'll tell you,' Harry said, leaning forward over the bar.

Sam sneered and moved away again. 'Friggin nutcases,' he muttered under his breath. Although he was frequently the butt of their jokes, Sam admitted to himself that they were his favourite customers. He just liked the way they fitted into the ambience of the bar, but he wouldn't have used the word 'ambience', as it wasn't in his vocabulary.

After one more beer, Harry said he had to go. 'We've been invited round to the new neighbours.'

'What are they like?' Al enquired.

'He's an insurance salesman,' Harry replied with a flat tone.

Al just said 'Oh.'

*

When Harry arrived home, Rosemary made out he was late but he wasn't, and she fussed around insisting that he change into something that didn't smell of Sam's Bar.

'Why?' he protested with some frustration. All the same, he pulled on a clean pair of pants.

'First impressions,' she replied, 'they're important.'

'I've already met him,' Harry eased his feet into a pair of casual shoes, 'and my first impression didn't amount to much.'

'There,' she brushed some invisible thing from his shoulder. 'That should do.'

'Shall I get the car out the garage?'

She ignored his sarcasm. 'Do you think we should take something like a bottle of wine?'

'Flowers would be better. I'm not so keen on wine.'

She tutted. 'We're not taking something for you to drink. Besides, I forgot to get some flowers.'

'You forgot to get my...' he said with an exaggerated tone, but when she looked sharply at him he gave her a lopsided grin. 'I'll fish out a bottle from the cupboard.'

While he looked, Rosemary said with some anguish, 'But flowers would be better and I went to the shop but didn't think of it.'

Harry came back with a bottle of white wine. 'They'll have to chill this for a while so perhaps they'll serve something better. Here, you give it to them.'

She looked at the label and guessed why he'd said that. 'This is a cheap one with the supermarket name on the label.' She brushed passed him and he heard bottles clinking while she searched for something better.

'Will anyone else be there?' Harry enquired, admiring her rear end as she bent to look into the cupboard. 'I hope that weasel from across the road won't be there. He must be eighty if he's a day and he wears his hair round his shoulders like an old fan from Woodstock.'

Rosemary came back with a bottle that had gold foil wrapped round the cork. 'This looks more presentable.'

Harry glanced at the label. 'And so it should. That's grade one champagne. Perhaps I can crack it over his head to launch the new house.' He took the bottle from her and replaced it in the cupboard.

'Why do you make your mind up about people so quickly?' she admonished. 'You only had a brief talk with him while they were moving in.'

'You'll see,' Harry defended himself weakly. 'Have you met his wife?'

'Yes,' Rosemary said quickly and in a way that made Harry look at her with suspicion.

'And would it be that you don't like her?'

Rosemary looked coy. 'She just seemed a little ... well ... tarty.'

'So,' Harry summarised, 'I don't like him and you don't like her. This is sure to be a great evening.'

'What about the wine?' she asked, noting he had nothing in his hands.

'Forget the wine. We'll just take our good selves.'

'But...' she began to argue, but Harry was already heading for the door.

*

Mike Sinclair opened the door. 'Harold and Rosemary,' he greeted them with a wide smile full of teeth. 'Glad you could come. The others have arrived. Come in.' He stood back and waved them forward with his arm.

'By the way, Michael, it's Harry,' Harry said as he moved passed him.

'And I'm Mike. Just plain Mike. And this is Dolores. But not plain Dolores, if you get my drift,' he kept the grin going.

They were ushered through the door and Harry came face to face with the 'not just plain Dolores'. She was slightly taller than Harry – he wasn't used to looking up to women – and had platinum-blonde hair (from a bottle he was sure) sweeping to her shoulders, wide, blue eyes and an over-wide mouth, which she kept permanently open to reveal her gleaming (capped he guessed again) white teeth. She wore a red dress which Harry would later describe to Al as atomic – a lot of fallout – and when she noticed Harry's eyes slowly drifting down and taking in her figure, she giggled in short bursts, ending each one with a squeak. Harry guessed she probably did this when she made love and hoped they kept their bedroom window closed, but he quickly pushed the image from his mind and held out his hand.

'I'm pleased to meet you, Dolores,' he smiled.

'And arhm glad to make your aquaintance,' she responded.

My God, he thought, when she drawled the 'I'm' to sound like 'arhm', she's a southern belle straight from the Belle Star Saloon. Another image hit his mind of a saloon gal in fishnets and high boots and it took more effort than before to dismiss it. 'Would you be from Mississippi?'

'Ma,' she drawled again, 'aren't you so perceptive?'

Harry winced; he was sure nobody outside *Gone with the Wind* spoke like that any more.

She took his arm and led him into the lounge, leaving Rosemary seething behind in the hall. Mike came forward quickly and offered his arm. 'Would you do me the honour ma'am,' he mimicked his wife. She took his arm reluctantly. 'My wife does have some fancy southern ways but that is what I love about her. She has been getting so excited about tonight.'

I bet she has, Rosemary thought, and she hoped there wasn't a band to strike up a rebel song. There wasn't, but in the background she heard a Dolly Parton CD tripping its way through the conversations. The room was quite full and she recognised many of the nearby neighbours drinking or precariously balancing plates of food whilst trying to avoid dropping crumbs and crusts onto the lush pile carpet. They each paused from their conversations and waved or shouted 'Hi' as Harry and Rosemary were guided across the room to a large table laden with plates containing mountains of food.

'I guess you know everyone,' Mike flashed a smile. 'Saves having to do the introductions. Here, help yourselves to eats and over there are the drinks. Don't stand on ceremony, just serve yourselves. Hey, Dolores, we need some more ice.' He guided her away towards the kitchen.

Harry looked at Rosemary and she looked back at him. 'Have I got a smut on my nose?' he asked.

'No, why?'

'He seemed in a hurry to get away.'

Rosemary shrugged and eyed the plates of food. 'I guess they need some ice.'

'Is that what I think it is?'

Rosemary followed his gaze to a large stone fireplace. To one side, leaning against the wall, she saw a huge wagon wheel, painted white with a black rim. 'I wonder where the rest of the wagon is?' she queried.

'It's where they keep the horses that worries me,' he replied.

Harry was going to pass on the food. He had spotted a bottle of Wild Turkey on the drinks table but on his way over he was intercepted by the long-haired weasel who lived opposite. He took hold of Harry's arm and arrested his progress. 'Saw you trimming your hedge the other day, Harry.'

'I thought of doing it at night but you can't cut it even when it's dark.'

'Perhaps you can take a look at mine,' the weasel continued, missing the jibe. 'Can't reach those high spots any more.'

Harry noticed a powdering of dandruff on the older man's shoulders and it made him think of the Winter snows that would be coming. 'It's good to keep the hedges trimmed. It's like hair, needs to be cut to give it strength. By the way, have you ever been to Woodstock?'

'Woodstock?' The weasel released Harry's arm to stroke his beard. 'Don't think so.' But Harry had moved on to the drinks when the arm had released him.

Rosemary looked over the food but had somehow lost her appetite. She put a few items on a plate to be sociable

69

and as she turned away, May Heathburn, her neighbour from the other side, was at her shoulder.

'So what do you think of them?' May asked. 'They've certainly done a lot to the house. Have you seen the bathroom?'

'Hello May. No I haven't. We've only just arrived.'

'I tell you, they have a mural made out of small tiles in the shower and the floor is a mosaic, and there's a sunken bath. It's just like a Roman bathroom I saw in one of those films. *Cleopatra*, I think? The only thing missing is a fountain. You know, one of those cherub things spouting water from its ... well, you know where.'

Rosemary was glad when May paused to take a breath. 'I suppose you've had a guided tour.'

'Oh no,' May touched her lips. 'I snuck around when they were meeting people at the door. I'm not the nosey type, you know that, but their bedroom ... do you know they have a water bed? It's a huge thing. When I touched it, the whole thing went into motion. I'd get seasick. And the kitchen. You must see that. There's...'

'Have you tried one of these?' Rosemary lifted something off her plate which was covered with fried breadcrumbs. May looked at it and shook her head. 'They're fantastic,' Rosemary lied, not having eaten one, and she jammed it against May's lips until her mouth opened and Rosemary forced it in.

May's face took on a strange, inquisitive look while she chewed and tried to analyse what Rosemary had forced into her mouth. As she chewed, she looked to the ceiling for inspiration but it didn't come. 'There's a hint of fish. No, lobster, crab or something like that.' When she looked down again, Rosemary had moved on.

Harry was gently supping his drink when Rosemary sidled up to him. 'Any of that sipping whiskey available,' she whispered from the side of her mouth.

Harry glanced sideways. 'You sure you can take it, little lady.'

'Ain't sure but I need it.'

Harry measured out a shot of Wild Turkey. 'What say you and me saddle up and mosey out back to our place.'

Rosemary winced as Lileth, an elderly spinster from down the road, let out a shriek of laughter, and she downed the shot in one. She clenched her lips tightly together to suppress spluttering it over Harry as the liquid took her throat by surprise. 'Now that is some drink,' she said in a hoarse whisper.

'And you always thought I enjoyed drinking it,' Harry chuckled.

'We'll have to stay a while,' she said, regaining some power of speech. 'It wouldn't look good leaving...' but her words trailed off as Mike and Dolores entered the room.

Mike carried an easel with flip-chart paper and Dolores carried a small box containing marker pens. Conversations round the room died as they watched Mike set up the easel and Dolores stand to one side with a wide smile, and in a pose that was usually assumed by a magician's assistant.

'Now folks,' Mike started, and gave a little chuckle as if he was about to tell a joke. 'You all know ... well, if you don't then you soon will ... I sell insurance. Life insurance, that is.'

'I don't believe this,' Harry muttered under his breath.

'We, that's Dolores and I, asked you all here this evening primarily to meet you all and for you to partake of our hospitality. But I just want a moment of you time. Now, looking round this room, I see that you are, how do you say politely, not of a young persuasion. Though I must say that the ladies in this room contradict that statement.' He paused for the expected laughter but got none.

'Harry. I don't want you to say a word,' Rosemary warned

71

him, sensing his agitation, but Harry was already moving forward.

'Young feller,' Harry interrupted Mike. 'You know, that's really great to hear you sell insurance. I'm in jewellery myself. Retired now, of course. And Bill over there,' he turned and pointed him out, 'he was in tailoring. The best tailor shop in Wannabee. He's retired now as well. That right Bill?' Bill nodded and smiled. 'And Joel over there,' he pointed him out too, 'he sold cars. I've still got one of his I bought ... about ten years ago, Joel?'

Joel laughed. 'Never could talk you into buying a newer model.'

'I can't afford to buy another. The prices he charges, I'm still paying off this one. Joel, take a bow.' Harry leaned towards Mike and spoke in a softer voice but loud enough for everyone to hear. 'He's retired too, but you wouldn't think so to look at his wife.' He winked at Joel's wife, Isabel, who gave him a coy smile and a flap of her hand. 'And Bartholomew over there,' he indicated towards the long-haired weasel, 'he was a hairdresser, but you can tell by looking at him that he's retired too.' This brought hoots of laughter from everyone except Mike and Dolores, who stood rather bewildered by Harry introductions. Everyone had started talking at once and the air was full of laughter.

'That was a great way to break the ice, young feller,' Harry complimented him, but Mike was not grateful for it. 'It's got everyone talking.'

Mike looked frustrated and Dolores looked mean. Eventually he nodded his head. 'Okay Harry, I get it. So this was not the time to sell insurance.'

'It's not for me to comment on what you do in your own home,' Harry said, 'but you're right, this was not the time.'

'I guess I should have left it until later,' Mike shrugged, 'when they'd all had a bit more to drink.'

'By time I meant the occasion,' Harry explained, but Mike wasn't listening. He had turned and was folding up the easel.

'I guess we'll try again later,' he said to his wife.

Harry wandered back to the drinks table where Rosemary was downing another shot.

She held the empty glass at eye level. 'You know, after three, it doesn't taste half bad.'

'Three?' He took the glass from her hand. 'Perhaps you ought to have something to eat.'

'Nope,' she said, snatching the glass back and refilling it. She raised it towards Harry. 'Thanks Harry. You sure know how to bring a party to life.'

'Are you angry with me?'

Rosemary shook her head. 'I compli … I comp … you did swell.'

Harry laughed as she downed the drink. 'Maybe we should leave,' he suggested. 'I don't think we are the most favourite guests and you are getting puddled.' But before they could move, people came over and started to congratulate Harry and slapping his arm.

'You know,' the weasel said, 'I wasn't a barber.'

'I know,' Harry said. 'I hope you don't mind a joke at your expense.'

'Not at all. In fact, I keep meaning to cut my own hair but I can never get round to it,' he exploded with mirth.

Harry looked over their heads and saw Mike and Dolores carrying the easel out of the room. They looked crestfallen, and he would have felt sorry for what he did, but, he reasoned, Mike sells insurance.

The easel didn't make a later appearance and Mike and Dolores, after cooling their anger in the kitchen, decided to make the most of it. Mike lived his life on the premise that days pass but insurance is there forever. He'd tackle them one by one at a later date, except Harry – he was a no-go area. They returned to the room and Dolly Parton was replaced by Tammy Winnette. Dolores tried to teach some of the women how to line dance – they never quite got the hang of it but found it a lot of fun. Rosemary remained with Harry to one side, her lips were numb and she didn't trust her legs.

Later, back at home, Harry made them both a strong coffee and they sat at the kitchen table, laughing through the evening. They agreed they were both right about their new neighbours, but they were harmless. Harry watched Rosemary carefully lift the cup to her lips and try not to spill it.

'You know, in all the years we've been married, I've never seen you drunk before,' he observed with a grin.

Rosemary slowly lowered the cup to the table. Her face assumed an indignant look. 'I'm not drunk.'

He reached across and patted her knee. 'Of course you are not, my dear.' Somehow he managed to keep a straight face. And then he mumbled something which she only half caught.

'What did you say?'

'I said I bet you couldn't stand on one leg and drink your coffee without spilling it.'

Rosemary studied him for a moment before a look of defiance came over her face. She slowly stood up and lifted her cup and then surprised him when she gingerly began to raise one foot. 'Who says I can't?'

At first she looked like succeeding, but as the cup reached her lips, her attention switched from her precarious balance to sipping the coffee, and that was her undoing. Harry leapt to his feet and caught her as she began to career sideways with coffee splattering all over the floor and down his trousers.

He held her in his arms and began to laugh when she smiled up at him and uttered, 'Oops'.

He took the cup away from her and eased her back into her chair. 'I shall remind you of this in the morning and you won't remember a thing about it.'

'Remember about what?' she asked and laughed in a pretty way.

5

The next morning, Harry sat in the doctor's waiting room and leafed through a pile of *Time* magazines, but they were months out of date and he tossed the last one aside. The receptionist was a large, beefy woman with wild, red hair, sagging breasts and small eyes. She looked up.

'They're all old ones,' he said to excuse the untidy pile he had created.

'They're what people bring in,' she explained in a voice that made Harry question her sexuality.

'I'm glad you don't buy them that old,' he said caustically.

She ignored him and looked down, busying herself with some paperwork. Harry watched her and noticed that she kept her face close to the paper in a short-sighted way. And when she wrote something, her index finger on her other hand preceded the pen across the paper as if pointing out the way her pen should follow. Harry thought of mentioning that she ought to get some glasses but decided against it; he considered she might be a heavyweight wrestler in her spare time and he didn't fancy being put into an arm-lock.

The door to the doctor's room opened and an old man shuffled out, his feet slipping across the bare floor without actually leaving it and making a scuffing noise like a train slowing into a station. He handed the receptionist a slip of paper that she looked at briefly before handing it back.

'Your next appointment is in two weeks.' She spoke

76

loudly and Harry assumed from the volume that the old boy was deaf, at least he hoped he was.

He took back the paper and nodded and then turned by edging his feet round. When he was pointing in the direction of the outer door, the old man set forth in another series of shuffles. Harry guessed he must be at least a hundred years old and wondered if it was worth his while leaving. He waited until the old man had left before commenting, 'Looks like he needs a doctor.'

The receptionist's small eyes glanced up briefly. 'You think he's bad. You should see his father,' and her shoulders shook with quiet mirth.

Harry allowed himself a small laugh; it was good to know that even wrestlers had a sense of humour. 'Shall I go in?' Harry asked.

'No!' came the abrupt reply. Obviously her humour was restricted. She resumed writing using two hands again.

Harry quietly sighed to himself and looked around the room; the walls were painted a lemon yellow and were bare except for some pictures of matchstick animals and people, drawn by young children on ragged paper and taped to the walls. Each one was signed by a scrawling hand with the age of the child written underneath. He wondered who had done the first one and set a trend.

'Are those pictures for sale?' he enquired.

The receptionist didn't bother to look up. 'You can have a crayon and paper if you're bored.' Before he could reply, a buzzer sounded. Harry was about to get up but the receptionist gave him a curt look and then continued writing. Harry had just adjusted himself back in the seat again when she looked up. 'You can go in and see the doctor now,' she said.

Harry stood up with an audible sigh and ambled casually over to the door marked 'Consultancy Room'. 'A grand name for a quack's office,' he said before opening the door.

77

She looked at him with some disdain. 'He's only a quack when he sees you.'

Harry edged the door open. 'I'm glad to hear it. He might find something serious if he knew what he was doing.' She screwed her mouth up in a sort of sneer, and he smiled back as he went in.

Doctor Harmsworth was making up some notes. Harry stood for a moment, waiting for some recognition, but when it didn't come, he sat down and coughed.

'I know you're there, Harry,' the doctor said without looking up. 'Just be patient for a moment.'

'I've been a patient since I got here but everyone is just concerned with paperwork.'

The doctor laid his pen to one side and looked up with a sigh. 'I spend more time writing than I do examining, Harry. You just here for a check-up?'

'Didn't you get Rosemary's message? I'm here for heart surgery,' Harry quipped.

Doctor Harmsworth studied his face for a moment and then let a smile gently slip over his face. 'You will be one day, Harry, you can be sure of that. Tell me, how many cigars are you smoking a day?'

Harry waved his hand casually. 'Three. Maybe four.'

'Hmmm. That means six, maybe seven. And how many glasses of Jack Daniels do you drink a day?'

Harry waved his hand again. 'Two. Maybe three.'

The doctor made the 'hmmm' sound again. 'That means four, maybe five.'

'Do you believe anything I tell you?' Harry asked.

'No. Not a lot.'

'Perhaps Rosemary should come here instead and answer your questions,' Harry said with a trace of rancour.

The doctor laughed in a short way that sounded like a hiccough. 'Maybe she should. I might get the truth. Do you have any chest pains, get out of breath, have any

78

headaches or does it hurt when you pee or have motions?'

Harry studied his face for a moment; the doctor looked tired or bored or perhaps both. 'No, but I keep having these nightly fantasies about your receptionist.'

Doctor Harmsworth chuckled. 'I'll tell her that. It must be the uniform. I can't think there's anything else attractive in that woman.' He stood up, picked up his stethoscope and came round the desk. 'Strip to the waist and sit over there on the bed, please.'

When Harry had sat on the bed, the doctor listened to his chest and asked Harry to breathe steadily.

'I thought JD was good for the arteries,' Harry queried, flinching from each touch of the cold stethoscope.

'The odd one might be, but the amount you consume won't do your liver a whole lot of good.' He moved the stethoscope to his back. 'And don't talk while I'm trying to listen.'

Harry ignored him. 'And I only smoke the occasional cigar to help me to relax.'

The doctor stood back and clipped the stethoscope round his neck. 'Oh, they'll do that all right. One day ... poof ... you'll be relaxed for all eternity.' He took Harry's arm and wrapped a rubber strip around it above the elbow and pumped it up while studying the blood pressure gauge. 'Do you get stressed, Harry?'

'Stressed? Of course I'm not. I'm so laid back I keep falling over backwards.'

'Then why do you need cigars?'

Harry smiled. Neat trick, he thought, but he had the quick response. 'They are the reason I'm so laid back. You see, they work.'

The doctor unwound the rubber strap from Harry's arm, went back behind his desk and sat down while he made some notes. 'You can get dressed,' he said without looking up.

'So what's the verdict?' Harry asked as he slipped his shirt back on and began to button the front. 'Will I live long enough for another check-up in six months?'

The doctor finished writing and leaned back in his chair. 'There are a lot of people your age who smoke and drink too much.'

'So it can't be so bad.'

'But they don't live for much longer,' he continued. 'What do you want, Harry? A few years enjoying life as you want to live it, or twenty more with careful living?'

'Isn't there a third choice?' Harry asked. 'You know, somewhere in between?'

Doctor Harmsworth shook his head slowly. 'Think about it, Harry. And then ask Rosemary for her opinion.'

Harry's face straightened from a smile. 'You know where to hit where it hurts.'

'No pain, no gain,' the doctor said simply. 'What you've got to understand is that life is a bitch. Do you want me to prescribe something that will help your blood pressure and cholesterol?'

Harry knotted his tie and slipped on his jacket. 'Are you asking me?'

'I think you need something but I see no point if you're not going to take them or you wash them down with Jack Daniels.' The doctor shrugged in a way that put the decision back into Harry's court.

'If I start taking pills then Rosemary will really think there's something wrong.' He scratched his chin. 'I could kiss goodbye to my cigars and JD.'

'That's how I figured it.' The doctor leaned back in his chair. 'So what's it to be?'

'I'll take a rain check on that. Give it another six months.'

'That's how I figured it,' the doctor repeated. 'Give my receptionist a kiss as you go out. It'll confuse her for hours.'

'If I do, I'll tell her it's from you.'
'Now that she won't believe.'

*

Al arrived at the park early, but then so did Aritha. The pair of them felt like naughty children stealing a few hours from the watching eyes of their parents. She had selected a spot near the small waterfall and sat in the shade of a leafy birch tree where they could watch the water tumbling over steps of outcrop rocks and finally plunging into the pool with a bubbling sound that was easy on the ear. Al had brought a blanket from his car and spread it out while Aritha unpacked some bags of food and a flask of coffee. When they were settled, he noticed the sunlight was shining through the swaying leaves and was playing moving patterns over her hair like glittering specks of silver dust.

'Is something wrong?' she asked, noticing him looking at her hair, which she then touched with her hand.

'No,' he said, 'nothing at all. It's just the sunlight on it. It looks magical.'

'That's nice,' she smiled. 'Have you any more compliments?'

'I might when I've had some coffee,' he nodded towards the flask. 'Is it from the diner or your own?'

'My own,' she said, and unscrewed the cap. She poured the coffee into a small metal cup and handed it to him black; she knew that's how he liked it. He sipped it and made a suitable noise of approval. 'It's Brazilian with a mix of Colombian. I find they go well together.'

'You'll have to give me the recipe,' he said, feeling relaxed with her.

'Are you hungry?' she asked.

'What have you got?'

She opened two paper bags and took out small, square

81

sandwiches, which she laid out on a plate. 'There's salmon with a drizzle of lemon juice and these are duck pâté. Which do you fancy?'

He just said 'Yes,' with a broad grin.

'All right. Then help yourself.' She sat with her hands in her lap and watched him try one of each. 'Do you approve?'

He nodded while chewing. 'Superb. You're a great cook,' he chuckled.

'I wish I was.' She saw his look of surprise and added, 'I only serve in the diner, I don't do great cooking there. It's all fast stuff.'

'Aren't you eating?' he queried when he saw she hadn't taken a sandwich.

'Later,' she said, resting her body against the tree and making a small sound of contentment. 'What made you change your mind? About coming here.'

'Something my wife said. Well, not exactly what she said,' he corrected, 'just the way she said it.'

'Does she know you are with me?'

Al shook his head. He didn't want to talk about his wife; he had come here to get away from her. He took another sandwich and bit into it as he looked around; there were many other people with the same idea of having a picnic, mostly young women with children. 'A popular place,' he observed.

'I come here a lot,' she said quietly. 'The sound of the water is kind of peaceful and the air is clean.'

At that moment the peace was shattered by the scream of a young boy who had toppled into the water. Al jumped to his feet but then relaxed when he saw the boy's mother grab him with two hands and haul him out. The boy was now crying, more from the shock of the cold dousing, and he shook himself like a dog, with the water spraying over his mother.

'Were you going to play the local hero?' Aritha chuckled.

Al sat down again. 'It was just a reaction to the scream,' he said modestly.

'More coffee?' she asked, noticing his empty cup.

'Thank you.'

As she leaned forward to pour the coffee he caught a glimpse down the front of her dress, which exposed the deep cleavage between her firm breasts. But he felt no excitement, at least not the way he had felt when Phillippa had walked down the stairs. He wondered why, and at the same time silently cursed Phillippa for intruding again into his thoughts. He realised Aritha was looking at him – her face had coloured a little from his staring down her dress. He started to feel hot with embarrassment.

'Is there anything else I can offer you?' she asked with just the hint of a smile. He said nothing and she misread his hesitation as discomfort at being caught out. He looked like a lost child and she felt he needed a helping hand. 'Al. Can we go somewhere else where it is quiet? Somewhere we can be alone.' She regretted the words as she saw a sort of alarm come across his face, but they had been said.

'Aritha,' her name stumbled out of his lips.

'It's all right, Al. I guess you still love your wife. My mistake.'

He saw her downcast eyes and hated himself. 'No. That's not it exactly.' He wanted to tell her how he felt about the friendship they had built up between them, but he knew she would not understand and it would only serve to make matters worse. She had declared her intentions and her feelings and anything short of that would be a slap in the face.

'I guess the picnic wasn't such a good idea,' she said to break the silence between them.

'I'm sorry,' was all he offered. They sat in silence for a while, each feeling they were responsible for the breakdown.

Al was the first to speak. 'You know, I find this situation difficult.'

Aritha wanted to avoid his eyes and was looking at the lake. The mother and her wet child had disappeared and the view was peaceful, with water tumbling over the rocks and frothing the surface below with bubbles that floated and sparkled in the sunlight. She spoke without turning her head. 'It's no different for me.'

He thought he detected a little bitterness in her voice. 'I know,' he said, but then stopped, wondering if she was listening.

At last she looked at him. 'What do you want, Al? A fantasy affair in the diner? Is that all you want?'

'No.' He felt stung by her words that carried some truth and he brought his knees up to rest his arms on them. 'Do you know, when I'm with my wife I often think of you.'

'And when you're with me?' she queried.

'I sometimes think of her but not in the same way. She intrudes.' He flapped his hands against his sides with exasperation at not finding the right words. 'I have a wife and you have a husband.' His voice trailed off when she looked away again.

'Is that what's holding you back? Because I have a husband?' She looked back at him and it was his turn to look away. 'I've told you about him.'

'I know,' he said weakly. 'Phillippa can be mean and hurtful and all of those things, but at the end of it all, she is my wife.'

'And you can't be unfaithful to her.'

'I guess not.'

Aritha felt a hopelessness build up inside. When Al had rung her, she had thought, wrongly, that something had happened and this picnic may be the start of better things. She felt that he was close to taking that small step and perhaps he just needed a little push, a little nudge.

'You know, Al,' she said softly, 'there are times when you sit in the diner that I want to reach across and hold you and kiss you.' She paused to see his reaction and was encouraged by the way he looked at her with appealing eyes. 'I want so much to make love with you. It hurts sometimes.'

'In the diner?' he tried to make a joke.

'I don't care where,' she almost cried. 'I just want to feel you close to me. I want to feel you inside of me.'

There, she thought, it's been said. His eyes visibly widened and his mouth dropped open, but he couldn't speak. He waved a hand with a pathetic motion and he shook his head.

'I never knew you felt that much.'

'Have I shocked you?' she asked, wondering what was going round in his head.

'I guess.'

'Tell me, Al. Have you ever wanted me like that?'

'Yes,' he said.

'But you keep putting obstacles in the way.' She saw him nod and was comforted that she was breaking through. 'Al, I'm not asking you to leave your wife. Hell, I just want a part of you.' She sucked in her breath and thought, 'Well, here goes for nothing'. 'Al, I'm offering myself to you. Don't reject me.'

He reached across and touched her arm and she quickly grasped his hand. 'I'll not reject you. I couldn't hurt you. I don't know if it's Phillippa or your husband or what, but let's not rush into this. I'm sure it will come, but I want to ease into it in a natural way.'

He ran out of ways to say it and he could see from her expression that she didn't understand. He stood up slowly and looked down at her but she refused to look up; she didn't want him to see the tears forming in her eyes.

'I'll call into the diner and see you tomorrow.'

85

She said nothing and he walked quietly away, hating himself. She dabbed a handkerchief at her eyes, and when she finally looked after him, hoping he may have changed his mind and be coming back, he was quite a way off. 'See you tomorrow at the diner,' she repeated, and began putting food back in the bags.

On his drive back across town, Al pulled into the side of the road and switched off the engine. His mind was full of Phillippa and Aritha, two women who offered him different things, and he couldn't make a choice. 'Damn!' he uttered, punching a fist on the steering wheel. What was the matter with him?

6

The next day, like most days that Summer, the sky was clear except for a few puffball clouds which drifted slowly and dragged small, inkstain shadows across the land. Harry was happy, and his relaxed swing hit the ball straight, most times. Al was preoccupied and mishit most shots, and Sol was over-determined as ever, losing three balls on the front nine holes. Rick played with a permanent smile on his face that widened considerably when he collected five dollars from each of them after the last hole. Sol grumbled, but this was more from the money he felt he had wasted on a lesson with the Professional the day before.

Harry was the last to shower and change and the others were already in the lounge as he made his way up the wide staircase from the locker room. As he neared the top, a shapely pair of suntanned legs came into view and he followed them up until his eyes came level with the smiling face of Louise.

'Hello young lady. I wish it was me you were waiting for.' His face creased into several smiles.

'As a matter of fact, I am, Harry.'

'What have I done now? Are you going to scold me or, even better, spank me?'

She slipped her arm through his. 'Behave yourself. I wanted to ask you something.'

'Ask away. The answer's yes, whatever it is.'

'Good,' she said and guided him over to a noticeboard. 'I want to enter this.'

He looked at the notice she pointed to. 'You want to enter the mixed competition?' he said reading it. 'You have my permission.'

He began to move away, but her hand remained gripping his arm and she pulled him back. 'I need a partner.'

'Who had you in mind?' As he asked the question he knew the answer from the cute smile she gave him. 'Me?'

'You. And don't say no.' She pouted her mouth in a provocative way. 'You said your answer would be "yes" to whatever it was.'

'It begs the question, why?' he said. 'There's a hundred men in this club I could name who would give a month's pay for a round with you.'

'Because I want to play with you,' she said, opening her blue eyes wider.

'That doesn't answer my question.'

'I think we will make a good pairing.' She tugged at his arm with encouragement. 'Does that provide an answer?' She saw a hint of suspicion remain in his face and added, 'I want to prove something to the ladies.'

'That I'm not such a cantankerous old mule?'

'Exactly that,' she said, surprising him with her candour. 'We were talking the other day and, to be honest, they didn't have much good to say about you and your friends. I said you weren't as bad as they made out, and I quite liked you, which shocked them a bit.'

'I bet it did.'

She lowered her eyes and he thought he detected a quiver in her bottom lip. 'I said you were just like a mischievous boy and really, you were...' She hesitated and he looked keenly at her, waiting for her to finish the sentence.

'Were what?' he asked gently when she said nothing.

She raised her eyes to his face and smiled in a shy sort of way. 'I said you were sort of cuddly.'

'You said that?' he said with an astonished voice.

She tightened her grip on his arm. 'I only said what I thought. You're not angry, are you? Please don't be.'

'I'm not angry,' he said, feeling the complete opposite. 'I've never been described like that before, that's all.'

'Oh good. Then you want to play with me?'

He avoided the obvious response that may have upset her and said instead, 'It will be my privilege,' and he bowed his head slightly towards her. 'But what about your lady friends?'

Her face darkened slightly and her mouth set firm. 'I'm not worried what they think. They're not talking to me right now.'

'I'm sorry if I've been the cause of a rift between you,' he said genuinely.

She let go of his arm and turned back to the notice as she took a pen out of her purse. 'Tush. Don't worry about them. They're just a bunch of frustrated old hens.' She added their names to the list. 'There, we're in. It's in two weeks. On a Sunday. Is that okay?'

Harry's mind turned immediately to Rosemary; somehow he was going to have to square it with her. 'No problem,' he lied.

Her face was full of smiles again. 'Perhaps we should have a practice round together. How about Thursday next week?'

That's two games he would have to explain to Rosemary. Things were getting worse. 'Sounds great.'

She touched his cheek with her hand. 'Thanks so much, Harry.'

He still felt her hand even when she had withdrawn it. 'I guess I ought to thank you for siding with me.'

'Oh tush.' He was to hear her make that sound a lot

during the next two weeks but it sounded girlish and he liked it.

'I'll see you Thursday next week. I'll get a start time and let you know.'

'Fine,' he said and raised his hand in a wave which she didn't see as she descended the stairs to the locker rooms. 'Well, I'll be,' he muttered to himself as he went into the lounge. Then he saw his three friends sitting at the usual table and wondered how he was going to tell them.

Al was the first to notice him. 'I've got you a drink, Harry. Where have you been?'

Harry sat down and decided to go in feet first and get it over with; he knew they wouldn't let him off lightly.

'I've just been talking to Louise. We've entered in the mixed competition.' He kept his voice level and matter-of-fact.

'You mean the blonde with the nice ass and long legs? I don't believe it,' Sol said excitedly.

'Look on the noticeboard,' Harry said calmly and sipped his drink. 'And please use a bit of decorum when you're referring to my partner.'

Sol hooted. 'A bit of what? Did you hear this guy?' he said to the others.

They looked surprised but refrained from adding to Harry's discomfort. Al said, 'What made you ask her?'

'I didn't,' Harry shrugged. 'She asked me.'

'Yeah, right,' Sol snorted. 'So she just came up to you and said, "Hey Harry baby. Will you partner me in the mixed competition?"' He tried to put on a feminine voice but it came out too high and added to his sarcasm.

'That's about it,' Harry said. Outwardly he looked calm but inside he thought, 'Just once more, Sol, and I'll loosen some of your teeth.'

'I have to see this.' Sol got up and crossed the lounge.

'Not another word,' Harry warned the remaining two.

90

Al shrugged. 'I have nothing to say.'

'Me neither,' Rick agreed.

'Then take those silly grins off your faces,' Harry ordered.

They sat obediently and sipped their drinks, careful not to look at each other and risk a fit of the giggles. Sol came back and punched Harry on the shoulder as he sat down.

'Hey! You old stag. You were telling the truth.' Sol's eyes were gleaming with devilry and he pressed his hands together as he gazed up to the ceiling. 'It looks quite impressive. Van Brockenhurst and Menkowitch.' He drew his hands apart expansively to describe an imaginary banner strung across the lounge. 'Has an international flavour about it.'

Al and Rick had to smile at that, even though Harry looked uncomfortable. Sol dropped his hands and his face turned serious, but his eyes still betrayed his merriment.

'I do suppose you have the permission of your wife,' Sol said with a hushed voice.

'Why would it be a problem?' Harry hedged, but he knew Sol had smelled the scent of his blood.

'Exactly.' Sol hunched his shoulders with innocent agreement. 'There won't be any problem. Why should there be a problem? I mean to say, what problem is there playing with the sexiest, most beautiful and vivacious girl in the club?' Each time he emphasised the word 'problem', and slowly leaned forward. 'But you haven't told her yet, have you?'

'How could I?' Harry's voice was underlined with irritation. 'We've only just arranged it.'

Sol sat back and nodded to the other two who had remained quiet throughout the exchange. 'You wouldn't have any problem telling your wives, would you guys?'

Al thought of Phillippa and guessed what she would say, so he said nothing. Rick, though, was seeing the funnier

91

side to it and despite Harry's discomfort could contain himself no longer.

'No, no, no, no, no,' he said rapidly while shaking his head and avoiding the look he knew Harry was giving him. 'Why. Anna would say, "You go and play with any woman you like".'

'Of course she would,' Sol agreed gleefully. He looked across at Harry. 'And Rosemary will say the same, I'm sure.'

'Perhaps you would like to ring her and tell her yourself,' Harry suggested phlegmatically.

'Oh no,' Sol said deliberately. 'I wouldn't deprive you of that. It'll be far better coming from you.'

Whilst he had been amused, Al thought it had gone on long enough. 'Isn't it time you were ringing your broker?' he asked Sol.

Sol instinctively looked at his watch and then quickly across at Al. 'Ah. I see. You think Harry has had enough.' Then he relented. 'I guess you're right. I must be going anyway.' He stood up and patted Harry's arm. 'Good luck old buddy. Give me a call if you need any support.' He waved to the others and they could hear him chuckling as he crossed the lounge.

'That's made his day,' Al said flatly.

'I guess it has,' Harry agreed. 'Thanks for your support fellers.'

They sat in silence for a minute before Rick asked, 'So what *are* you going to say to Rosemary?'

*

That evening, Harry waited until they were halfway through dinner before he got round to telling Rosemary, although even then he was really forced into it.

'This is really good,' he said, dabbing his mouth with a cloth napkin. 'You've excelled yourself tonight, my dear.'

Rosemary laid down her knife and fork. 'That's the third time you've complimented my cooking. What's up?'

He looked at her with some surprise. 'What's up? Nothing.' He continued eating but Rosemary just watched him. He avoided looking at her but he felt her penetrating glare. 'A funny thing happened at the club today,' he said in a casual way. 'The darnedest thing. One of the ladies asked me to play with her in the mixed competition.'

'What's so strange about that?' Rosemary asked, noting he was still not looking at her.

'Well, the Ladies Section doesn't have a very high opinion of me or my playing partners.' He casually cut into a potato and forked it into his mouth.

'I'm not surprised, the way you four carry on. So why did she ask you?'

Harry finished his food and dabbed his mouth again. 'Couldn't get anyone else, I suppose.'

'Who is she? Someone I know?'

Harry looked to the ceiling as if trying to remember and shook his head. 'I don't think you've met her.'

'What's her name? What does she look like?'

He felt it was getting like an inquisition but he knew his wife well enough not to tell her she was asking too many questions; it would simply make her even more suspicious.

'Her name's Louise van Brockenhurst. Now that's a name, isn't it,' he said weakly to make a joke of it. 'She's a peroxide blonde, overweight, getting on a bit and doesn't play golf very well.' Hidden under the table he had his fingers crossed; at least he was truthful about her name.

'That's probably why she's asked you to play with her,' Rosemary said as she stood and started to clear the plates.

'Thank you, my dear, for that vote of confidence.' He smiled at her as she made her way to the kitchen.

As Rosemary returned, the telephone rang. She put a

plate of mixed cheeses and a cup of coffee down in front of Harry and said, 'I'll get it,' and went out to the hall. He heard her speaking briefly and then she appeared in the doorway. 'It's that ageing, peroxide blonde you mentioned.' She came back and sat at the table with a stern expression on her face.

Harry went to the telephone hoping Louise hadn't heard what Rosemary had said. 'Yes?'

'Hi Harry. It's Louise.' Her voice dripped with honey and he hoped she hadn't spoken to Rosemary in the same way. 'I got us that tee time at eight-thirty. I hope you don't mind starting that early.'

'Not at all,' he said, looking back into the room and seeing Rosemary had not moved a muscle.

'We can have some lunch together afterwards. Talk strategy,' she giggled down the line.

'That sounds like a great idea,' he kept his voice flat. 'I'll see you then.'

He rang off, took a deep breath and returned to the table.

'That was Louise,' he said as he sat down. 'She wanted to know if we could have a practice round. I told you she wasn't very good.'

'She didn't sound overweight,' Rosemary said casually.

Harry stopped cutting into a piece of cheese. 'How can you tell someone's weight down a telephone line?'

'Just by the sound of her voice. She sounded young and vivacious. It was the way she said, "This is Louise. Is Harry there?"' Rosemary made her voice sound kind of dreamy.

Harry looked up from his cheese and saw Rosemary was smiling at him. He grinned, 'Okay, so she's not overweight and she's quite young and she looks like a natural blonde. And I haven't a clue why she asked me to play with her.'

'Perhaps she likes older men,' Rosemary suggested, still smiling from making Harry squirm for a moment.

He speared a piece of cheese with his knife. 'Maybe she does.' He bit some cheese from the end of the knife. 'Perhaps I've still got it.'

'Can you still remember what "*it*" is?' Rosemary poked at him.

Harry looked sideways at her. 'Do you want me to show you?'

'Right now?'

'There's the couch.'

'But the curtains are open.'

Harry chuckled. 'It'll give the neighbours something to talk about for a while.' He got up and went round the table, put a hand under her arm and lifted her to her feet.

'Harry. Don't play games,' she protested with a coyness he had not heard in a while. 'At least pull the curtains.' He led her over to the couch. 'And you'll get indigestion so soon after dinner.'

*

A few days later, Dinsdale Dryden sat in his office and fidgeted with a pencil through his fingers. Jay Don Winchester had phoned to say he would be calling in and Dinsdale knew what he wanted to talk about. To add to his troubles, Felicia was hardly speaking to him and only came into his office when she had to; even then she avoided looking straight at him. He had tried to soothe things over but her eyes had begun to moisten again, so he left it. He was finding it extra difficult concentrating on things and, to make matters worse, he was missing the late-night sessions with Felicia in his office. He had begun stopping off at a bar on his way home but he usually drank alone and it was becoming as boring as it was going home to his wife.

The door to his office opened without a knock and Jay

Don Winchester's huge frame filled the doorway. Dinsdale dropped the pencil and leapt to his feet. He held out his hand as he came round his desk.

'JDW, it's good to see you.'

Dinsdale found his hand engulfed in JDW's meaty paw and tried to keep his face straight despite the bone-crunching grip.

'Hello Dinsdale. I hope I'm not disturbing you from something important. Like counting the profits.' The big man laughed loudly, slapped Dinsdale heartily on the back and then hugged him with his arm round his shoulders until they cracked.

Dinsdale wilted under the assaults and felt he would need an appointment with a chiropractor by the time their meeting was finished. He moved out of range and offered JDW a drink from his cabinet lined with various bottles.

'That's some collection you got there,' JDW observed drily. 'I don't hold with drinking until the sun goes down.'

Dinsdale hurriedly closed the door of the cabinet. 'They're just for a complimentary drink with special guests,' he said hastily, cursing himself for forgetting JDW's drinking habits. 'Perhaps some coffee?'

'Nope. Don't bother with any of the usual courtesies. I've come here to talk business.' JDW slumped down into Dinsdale's chair and swung it round from side to side using his feet. 'Some fancy chair you've got here,' he observed. 'Must have cost a few bucks.'

Dinsdale cursed silently again; he normally shepherded JDW to the conference room but he had arrived early and unannounced and had caught him out. 'I brought it from home,' he offered as a lame excuse. 'It's very comfortable. Helps my back.' He smiled, but his face did not reflect his thoughts; he was thinking other things like: 'Don't break it with your overweight carcass.' Dinsdale sat on a small wooden chair on the other side of his desk and had a view of his office he had not shared before. 'So, what brings you down here?'

JDW did not speak immediately and turned his attention to a large cigar he had taken from a leather case. He puffed on it quietly on a flame from a very expensive-looking lighter until it was burning evenly and creating a large, blue fog above his head. Dinsdale cursed silently again; it would take a week for the smell to dissipate.

JDW waved the cigar about. 'I was passing through on my way to an important meeting and I thought I would drop by and ask what thoughts you had about the franchising.'

Dinsdale did not miss JDW's put-down about going to an important meeting. 'I've given it a lot of thought,' he said tightly, still bristling. 'I've drawn up some figures. Projected costs. Savings. I'll get the file.' He started to rise but JDW waved him down.

'Just tell me about them.'

Dinsdale sat back and thought, 'Right, you fat schmuck', but he said: 'The cost of franchising out the catering and the bar would increase the cost of those services to the members by around ten per cent. I've seen the tenders and there's no way any of them could operate without raising the prices across the full range.'

'But what about the club, for chrissake,' JDW interrupted. 'The whole idea of franchising out is that it costs us nothing and they pay us to do it. We make savings all round.'

'But we'd lose the profits we currently make from providing those services,' Dinsdale argued, beginning to feel heated.

'All right,' JDW conceded, 'I know what you're saying, but what is the bottom line?'

Dinsdale hated that expression; it brushed away all the detail and left only one figure. If it was a profit, JDW

97

would insist on it. 'Overall, the club would make about fifty, maybe sixty thousand a year.'

'And that's not good?' JDW queried.

'It will look good on the balance sheet,' Dinsdale said. 'But it would be the members who would be paying for it.'

JDW nodded as he easily accepted that fact.

'You don't play golf, do you?' Dinsdale queried. He could not imagine that great, fat hulk could even swing a club round the circumference of his belly.

JDW saw the angle he was coming from. 'I own several clubs and they're all operating a franchising system. And they are all showing a good profit on the bar and catering.'

'And have they retained their membership levels?'

The big shoulders heaved a shrug. 'I'm not interested in that.'

'Well, I am,' Dinsdale stated firmly. 'You see, I've made some quiet soundings and I think we could lose members. Maybe a lot.'

'So what?' JDW sucked at his cigar but it had gone out. He felt around in his pockets for his lighter.

'I've made some more calculations and if we lost twenty members then the franchise profit would be wiped out.' Dinsdale then added in a cold voice to emphasise his point, 'If we lose more then we would make an overall loss. Not only would we lose their subscription but there would be less members eating and drinking. And we'd lose a lot of bookings for private functions. That would have a knock-on effect on the prices and as they rise, the members would probably spend less. It would be a downward spiral.'

JDW made a mental note to make enquiries at his other clubs. Dinsdale wasn't as dimwitted as he thought. He heaved himself to his feet without relighting his cigar. 'Okay Dinsdale. I hear what you say. But it's up to you to find a way round it. That's what I pay you for.'

Dinsdale would find a way round it, he was sure, but it

98

would not be what JDW was expecting. 'Leave it with me,' Dinsdale assured him with a fixed smile.

Dinsdale was pleased that JDW left without touching him again and he closed the door as JDW left his office knowing that would annoy him; JDW expected his hirelings to see him out to his chauffeur-driven limousine.

But it still left him with the problem of what to do; he hadn't figured that one out yet. He had come to one conclusion though – there was no way he could win without playing dirty, and he had someone in mind who could help him with that. He went into Felicia's office.

'Can you get me Harry Menkowitch's home number,' he asked, noting she didn't look his way.

Felicia tapped into her keyboard and wrote down a number from the screen onto a piece of paper and handed it to him. 'You really ought to learn how to use one of these things,' she said, referring to the computer on her desk.

Dinsdale ignored her advice. 'And could you book a meal for two, for this evening, at the Crighton Hotel. And book a double room for one night.'

Felicia noted that down and looked at Dinsdale for the first time. 'Is that for you and Mrs Dryden?' Her voice had a sour tone.

'No. It's for me and you.'

Felicia's head snapped up with surprise. Dinsdale saw different emotions pass over her face but then she smiled. 'And what name do I book it under?'

He relaxed with her smile and felt he had finally broken through the blockade. 'Mr and Mrs Dryden, of course.'

'Of course,' she repeated. 'And would that be the best room they have? Like a suite or something?' A mischievous glint in her eyes warned him not to argue.

'Whatever you feel is appropriate.'

'Right,' she said efficiently. 'Consider it done.'

Dinsdale nodded. He was going to add something like 'it's good to be friends again', but he thought he would heal the wounds that evening and so he turned without speaking.

Back at his desk, he rang his wife and asked her to pack him a small overnight bag; he told her JDW was in town and he wanted a long meeting that would go on late into the night. He even told her where he would be staying; he had learnt long ago that if he fed her all the information, she was satisfied and didn't check up.

He rang Harry next.

'Harry. It's Dinsdale.'

'Oh yes? What have I done now?' His voice sounded distant as though he had the phone away from his mouth.

Dinsdale tried to put laughter into his voice. 'I need your advice.'

There was a pause on the line. 'My advice?' Harry queried.

'Just a small matter. I wondered if we could have a drink one evening.' And then he added a bit too hastily, 'Not at the clubhouse.'

When Harry spoke, Dinsdale could sense a wariness from his tone. 'I guess so. When had you in mind?'

'Whenever it suits you.'

Harry had nothing arranged but he was reluctant to see him and he wanted some time to think a few things through. 'Can we make it next week? I'm pretty tied up at the moment.'

'That'll be fine,' Dinsdale agreed. 'How about ... er...' he glanced at his diary, '... Tuesday? I'll meet you in the Tobago Bar. At about seven? Do you know where it is?'

'That's on the eastern side,' Harry said, wondering why Dinsdale would choose a bar over the other side of the river; it sounded too clandestine. 'Okay.' And Harry rang off.

Dinsdale looked at the silent phone in his hand and wondered if involving Harry was the right thing. He sighed – he didn't have much choice.

*

After their game on the Friday morning – with Rick winning again and collecting fifteen dollars – they gathered at their usual table in the lounge and sipped their drinks.

'What's new?' Sol asked. 'Any more young ladies ask you to play with them?' he directed the question to Harry.

'Several,' Harry said casually. He felt more comfortable about playing with Louise, especially now Rosemary was happy with it, and he was determined not to let Sol get him rattled again. 'The word must be out that Harry Menkowitch is the stud of the month.'

'Yeah right,' Sol said, annoyed that Harry had deflected his attempted barb.

'But I had to turn them down,' Harry continued. 'I suggested they ask you but they said they only play for fun.'

Before Sol could respond, Al said, 'Don't look now, stud, but I think your young partner is coming this way.'

Louise came up to their table and smiled all round. She was wearing a green dress which somehow shimmered and showed off her figure. 'I hope you don't mind me interrupting you boys.' They all smiled back at being called 'boys'. 'I just wanted a word with Harry.'

Sol got up and fetched a chair for her. 'Please, rest those pretty legs and join us,' he said, happy to see that he had irked Harry by his invitation.

Louise put her hand on Harry's shoulder and dragged her fingers round his neck as she moved to the chair and sat down next to him. 'Why, how nice of you.'

'Perhaps you would like to get the lady a drink as well,' Harry suggested coolly.

Sol was about to sit down but stood up again. 'Yes. Okay,' he said with less enthusiasm. 'What would you like? Louise, isn't it?'

'Yes. I would like a vodka with orange juice please. No ice but with a twist of orange peel.' As Sol went to the bar she turned to Harry. 'How kind all your friends are.'

'Oh yes,' he said sardonically, 'you can always rely on them.'

'I didn't want to intrude, I know how you like your men's talk, but I expect Harry has told you that I'm not the flavour of the month with the Ladies Section.' She smiled sweetly in turn to Rick and Al.

'No.' Al returned the smile without looking at Harry. 'He hasn't told us anything. He's the bashful type.'

'Tush. Haven't you told them we're playing together?' she said in a playful, scolding tone and she patted Harry's knee.

Harry almost spluttered into his drink and moved his knee away from her hand. When he had recovered, he said, 'I did tell them we were in the mixed competition. He's just joking with you. He's the comedian type.'

'And next Thursday,' Louise added.

'No. I don't think he told us about that,' Al said, raising his eyebrows. 'Did he say anything to you, Rick?'

Rick slowly ran his hand round his jaw. 'No. No, I don't remember him saying that.'

'They're right. You are the bashful type,' Louise gushed. 'You're Al and you're . . .'

'Rick.'

'I'm sorry I didn't introduce you. I didn't think you were staying,' Harry said rather pointedly. 'And this is Sol,' he added as Sol brought her the drink and sat down.

'Why, thank you, Sol.' She lifted the glass almost to her lips. 'Bottoms up.'

'I'll drink to that,' Sol said with so much enthusiasm

that it made Louise laugh. 'So what have you been talking about?' he asked.

'Harry playing a round with Louise,' Rick said, keeping a further smile from his face.

'Is that so?' Sol said in a suggestive way. 'Oh, you mean the mixed competition.'

'Not just that,' Al corrected. 'Thursday as well, was it?' he asked Louise.

'We're just going to have a practice together,' Louise explained innocently. 'We need to get to know each other's game.'

'Of course you do,' Al commented rather too drily for Harry's comfort.

'That's what I came to tell you, Harry,' she said as she turned her big eyes on him. 'The format for the competition is foursomes so we need to decide who drives which hole. I expect you are quite a big hitter.'

'He has that reputation,' Rick added, not resisting a small chuckle.

Harry said nothing; he knew he was in a corner and now was not the time to fight his way out of it.

Louise took another sip from her drink and put the glass down. 'I had better leave you now. Thanks for the drink, Sol.' As she stood up, she touched Harry's shoulder again. 'I hope your wife didn't mind me ringing you last night, Harry. She sounded such a nice woman.'

'She didn't mind at all,' Harry said, pleased when Louise withdrew her hand. 'In fact she was quite excited about the whole idea.'

'Oh, that's good. I'll see you next Thursday.' She looked round the table with just the hint of fluttering eyelashes. 'Bye for now, boys.'

'Bye,' the three of them said in unison. Harry said nothing.

103

They sat in silence until she had moved away out of earshot.

'Nice girl,' Al said at last.

'Very friendly,' Rick added.

'I wish I could play around with her,' Sol fantasised.

'All right,' Harry broke in at last. 'So you've had your fun.'

'Did she really ring Rosemary?' Al queried.

'No, she rang me but Rosemary picked up the telephone,' Harry said, sighing that it was obvious they hadn't finished with him.

'And Rosemary's quite okay with the idea?' Rick asked.

'I told you she was.'

'Nice to have an understanding wife,' Al added. 'I hate to think what Phillippa would have said.'

'I know how it is,' Rick consoled him, feeling they had had enough fun at Harry's expense. 'Anna would have been the same.'

Sol said nothing. He didn't like these times when they talked about their wives. He looked out of the window and thought of Catherine – she was long gone but it only seemed like yesterday that he had watched her die slowly; it was like a bright light being gradually snuffed out. It was strange – when she was alive, they were continually slogging it out over trivial things, but after she was gone, he realised that there had been no venom and somehow it had been a form of affection between them. Life could be a bitch but death was a lot worse.

'Hey Sol.' Rick had noticed him sitting quietly, gazing out of the window. 'You thinking about your stocks?'

Sol nodded. 'Yeah. Taking stock. Something like that.'

With the end of the jesting at Harry's expense, they seemed to have exhausted their conversation and they parted, each to return to their different lives.

7

It was raining hard as Harry eased his car into the Tobago Bar parking lot. When he turned off the engine he heard a distant rumble of thunder; the storm was probably coming in from over the western foothills. A good night, he thought, for this type of meeting. He had parked as close as he could to the front entrance but he still got his head and shoulders wet as he ran through the rain and splashed his shoes in the puddles which reflected the garish neon sign across the front of the bar. It read 'Tobago Bar' in high red letters with green palm trees arched round it at each end. It was a cheap sign and Harry considered it appropriate for a cheap bar. When he entered and shook the rain from his coat, he looked round and was surprised by the number of people in there; most sat at side tables and a few on stools at the bar. There was a group of unsavoury-looking men at the far end clustered around a jukebox and watching two men shooting a game of pool. They each gave him a brief glance as he entered and then resumed their conversations. The air was thick with smoke and a smell of stale beer; Harry wondered why Dinsdale had chosen this place and regretted his choice. The jukebox was playing some music he didn't know, but it was turned down enough not to be obtrusive. He went to the bar and waited for a barman to come his way. One finally noticed him, a guy with a shaven head and wearing a stained sweatshirt, who stood in front of him with a look that questioned why he was there. Harry ordered a bottled beer. At least that would be fresh, he guessed, but he noticed a glass was not offered so he wiped the bottle top on his sleeve in front of the barman to show his disapproval. He leaned back against the bar and looked around again. He couldn't see Dinsdale through the haze, but then he suddenly appeared at Harry's side; he guessed Dinsdale had been sitting in his car waiting and watching for him to arrive and then let him go in first.

'Do you want a beer?' Harry asked, not willing to give him a choice of drink.

'Fine,' Dinsdale nodded. 'There's a table over there. I'll go and grab it.'

Harry thought that the expression of 'grabbing a table' was unusual for Dinsdale and he'd probably said it to suit their surroundings. He ordered another beer from the same barman and said, 'No glass this time', taking the bottle over to the table. Dinsdale said 'thank you' and looked at the bottle but didn't attempt to drink it.

'Have you been in here before?' Harry felt he had to ask the question to satisfy his curiosity.

Dinsdale shook his head emphatically. 'No. I've driven past and seen it. I hope you don't mind. It seemed enough out of the way.'

'So you didn't want anyone to see us together,' Harry said, not attempting to hide his chagrin.

'Please don't take it that way,' Dinsdale said hurriedly. Someone had turned the music up and he had to lean towards Harry to make himself heard. He was about to say something else when a huge man in a plaid shirt and dirty slit jeans stood up from his stool at the bar.

'Shut the fucking music down,' he shouted. 'I can't hear myself fucking think.' The volume was turned down. The guy at the bar was obviously too big to argue with.

106

Dinsdale coughed and lowered his voice. 'I had no idea it was quite like this.'

'Don't worry about it,' Harry said, taking a sip of his beer. 'Just tell me why you wanted to see me.'

Dinsdale paused for a moment as if gathering himself. 'Do you remember you asked me about the franchising?' Harry nodded. 'Well, I wasn't exactly truthful.'

'I knew you weren't,' Harry said.

Dinsdale coughed again. 'Well, nobody was supposed to know about it.'

'I'm not surprised,' Harry admitted.

Dinsdale hoped that Harry wouldn't keep interrupting him. 'It's all JDW's idea.'

'Jay Don Winchester,' Harry interrupted again. 'Now that's a name to wrap around your tongue. No wonder you call him JDW.'

'Quite. The point is, I don't agree with him over it but he's insisting it happen.'

'Before you go on,' Harry said, 'tell me first why you don't agree with him.'

'Frankly I think it will do a lot of harm to the club. You may not believe it, Harry, but I am a club man. I put the smooth running of the club before anything else.'

'I understand that,' Harry admitted, 'but what sort of harm will franchising do?'

Dinsdale looked surprised. 'Well, for a start it will put up the prices. I won't be responsible for the level of service and it will upset the members. I think many could leave. JDW doesn't realise we are a very prestigious club with wealthy members who expect the highest standards.'

'And it will take the catering and the bar out of your control,' Harry said in a cool tone.

'There is that to it as well, I suppose. And that is an important point,' he insisted. 'I pride myself that we provide the highest levels of service at the moment. And not wishing to sound immodest, I think that is due to my handling of things.'

'So why is JDW so insistent? The big dollar?' Harry asked, knowing the answer but asking the question anyway. The more he kept Dinsdale talking, the more he felt he would get from him.

'He thinks so. But I've pointed out that I believe we could end up being losers.' Dinsdale shook his head despondently. 'I've tried to explain but he seems set on it.'

Harry took another sip from the bottle and then leaned back in his chair. 'So how do I come into all this?'

Dinsdale tried to choose his words carefully. 'I want you to help me stop him.'

'You mean you've exhausted all other avenues and now it's time to play dirty.'

Dinsdale saw Harry's smile and relaxed and smiled back. 'You're very astute, Harry. Yes, that's about it.'

'Have you thought of hiring a hit man?' Harry kept a straight face. He meant it as a joke but he wanted to see Dinsdale's reaction – to what lengths would he be prepared to go to bring down JDW? 'I hear they come quite cheap these days. Some do it just for the fun of it.'

Dinsdale audibly gasped at the suggestion but then realised Harry was just playing with him. 'Perhaps something less drastic. I thought it could be something that would make him think again.'

'Like a little blackmail.'

Dinsdale shrugged. 'I don't like that word but yes, something like that. But I can't think what we could use against him. He's a very careful man. Quite upright in his ways.'

'Every man has a weakness,' Harry demurred. 'Tell me, what is his wife like?'

'You'll get nothing from that angle,' Dinsdale said coldly.

'She's a regular church person and a first-class bitch. She's the only person I've seen him afraid of.'

'Then that is his weakness,' Harry said and finished his beer, feeling better.

'Do you have anything in mind?' Dinsdale asked, hoping there was a spark of light.

But Harry poured cold water over his optimism. 'Nothing yet, but leave it with me. I'll give it some thought.'

'I know I already owe you one, Harry, for not saying anything about me and Felicia.' Dinsdale looked down with some embarrassment. 'And I would forgive you for turning me down, but this is for the club rather than me.'

'Oh, I think I may enjoy this,' Harry smiled.

Dinsdale didn't know what could be enjoyable about this type of problem and put it down to Harry's quirky sense of humour.

'There is one point I need to make,' Dinsdale said carefully.

'Oh what is that? Or can I guess?' Harry said with a knowing look. 'You don't want to be seen as part of it.'

In one way, Dinsdale admired Harry for his shrewdness, but at the same time he hated him for it. 'I do have my position to think of.'

'Does that mean I am expendable?' Harry was enjoying seeing Dinsdale squirm a little.

'Not at all,' Dinsdale expressed hastily. 'I'm sure you know how to cover your tracks.'

'And so do you', Harry thought, but said aloud, 'Okay, leave it with me. I'll give it some thought.'

'Good, good,' Dinsdale regained his enthusiasm.

When they stood to leave, Harry noticed that Dinsdale had not touched his beer. He guessed he didn't want to take the risk of catching anything.

*

109

The rain hung around for a few days but by the Thursday morning the skies were clear and Harry stood on the first tee with Louise. He looked down the fairway that appeared washed and fresh with sparkling droplets of water waiting to be dried. The avenue of trees down both sides of the fairway moved only gently in a waving sway in the upper branches to indicate there was a breeze, but it was light enough not to trouble them. Even for that early hour, the warm air had returned and Louise was dressed in her usual tight top and short shorts.

'Are you going to wear those clothes for the competition?' he asked her.

She opened her eyes wide. 'Don't you like them, Harry?'

'Quite the opposite,' he said lightly.

She giggled in a girlish way. 'Just keep your mind on the game.'

He couldn't hide a grin as he put his ball on a wooden tee peg, setting the ball so the name painted on the side faced up at him – he found it helped him concentrate to keep his eye on the ball. 'I'll try.' He waggled his driver a few times to get her legs out of his mind and then swung easily. The ball flew straight and took a favourable kick on the fairway up the middle that gave him more distance than usual.

'It's right what they said about you,' she said as she admired his shot.

'Who said what about me?' he asked, retrieving the wooden peg.

'Your friends did. They said you were a big hitter.'

They climbed into his buggy and Harry smiled to himself as they drove forward to the ladies' tee. Perhaps this wasn't going to be too bad. He noted that Louise did not waggle her club when she addressed the ball; she waggled her bottom instead, and in a very provocative way. He decided that in future he would stand on the other side of her.

She had a full, easy swing and connected perfectly. Her ball rolled just past his.

'My tee is quite a bit in front of yours,' she excused her long drive. 'It must be at least forty yards forward.'

'There are three things you should remember about playing golf,' Harry advised as they made their way up the track in his buggy. 'Never make an excuse for a good shot and never complain about a bad one.'

'What is the third thing?' she asked.

'I'll tell you that later,' he said secretively.

'I know another one,' she said as he pulled up level with his ball. 'Never give your opponent an even break.'

He selected a club and went over to his ball. 'That sounds like fighting talk,' he laughed over his shoulder.

She came and stood next to him. 'You have to think that way to win. I don't like losing.'

He looked up from his ball and studied her face. 'Five bucks says you lose today.'

'What game?'

'Matchplay. Play for holes. No shots given, just the distance on your tees,' he rattled off the rules crisply.

'Sounds fine.' She stepped back and let him prepare for his shot. As he was ready to play, she lifted her jumper a little to reveal bare skin and scratched her midriff. Harry stepped back from his ball.

'Now that's dirty play, young lady,' he grinned at her.

She smiled sweetly. 'Sorry, I didn't think you'd notice. I thought you were concentrating on your shot.' She pulled her jumper back over the top of her shorts.

What she didn't know about Harry was that he could be just as determined. Her attempt to put him off only served to harden his resolve and he hit the ball sweetly. It rose high but then fell away slightly to the right before pitching onto the green, where it rolled up towards the right of the flagstick.

111

'I think there is a little breeze blowing around up there,' he said, almost to himself.

He went happily over to the golf cart and leaned against it while she went forward to play her shot. She spent a lot of time looking at the type of shot she had to play, and when she finally played it, she caught the ball a little open and it kicked right into a bunker by the green. Her lips were smiling as she came over to him but he could see her eyes did not share the humour. Everyone has a weakness, he thought, and now I know yours.

She played a very good bunker shot to within ten feet of the hole and walked around the hole several times before she two-putted down for a five. Harry noted how her ball had curled a little near the hole, so he took a brief look and eased his ball to the side of the hole, tapping it in for a par four. He knew he could have gone for a birdie three but he wasn't taking the chance of running passed the hole and having one of those tricky putts back.

'Well done, Harry,' she complimented him as she replaced the flagstick. 'The first hole to you.'

As they walked back to the cart, she said, 'You don't take long over your putts. You barely looked at it.'

'I play a very instinctive game on the greens,' he said in a casual way. 'Don't like to think about it too much. You can clutter your brain with too many negative things.' He put the cart in gear and drove across to the second tee. 'Try it out. Just take a quick look and let your instincts take over.'

She said nothing and they both played reasonable shots up the fairway and both hit the green with their third shots. She was a little further away and Harry held the flag while she putted. He noticed she barely gave it a look and then hit the ball about four feet passed the hole. She tried to hide her annoyance.

'I guess it doesn't work for me,' she said a little tersely.

'Keep trying it,' he said as he measured the distance with his eye and again laid his ball next to the hole.

She missed with her putt and picked her ball up. 'Two to you.' Her smile was weaker.

'I think we'll make good partners,' he commented as he put his putter in his bag.

'I hope I don't let you down.'

'You'll be all right,' he said as they moved forward. 'Just strengthen your grip a little.'

'What do you mean by that?' she queried. 'Do I hold the club too loose?'

He stopped at the next tee and shook his head. 'No. But you need to bring your right hand over your left more.'

The next hole was a short par three and he hit easy again and put his ball just short of the hole, about ten feet away. Louise took a long time over her ball; she seemed to be having trouble getting her grip right. When she finally swung, she pulled it left into some thick stuff.

'Don't worry,' he consoled her. 'Early days yet. Plenty of holes to go.' She didn't respond.

After six holes, Harry was five up. The next tee area offered a wooden bench under the shade of a tree and he strolled towards it.

'The course is quiet today and there's no one behind us. Do you mind if we take a break and I have a cigar?'

'No. Not at all,' she said quietly. 'I need to think about my game.'

Harry lit his cigar and turned to her beside him. 'That's exactly what you shouldn't do,' he advised. 'Remember I said there was a third rule?'

'Yes,' she said, rather dejectedly.

'Harry's third rule is, never listen to anything your opponent says, be it advice or even just a comment on the breeze or how the green slopes or anything like that.' He

113

noticed she was looking at him keenly. 'Your opponent never says anything for your advantage. Listen and you lose your game.'

'You mean you have been talking me out of it?' He nodded to her. 'Oh, you're so mean, Harry Menkowitch,' she chided him, but not in a spiteful way. She prodded him playfully in the side.

He smiled. 'Remember what you said? "Never give your opponent an even break." Well, your opponent will never give you one either. From now on, go out and play your natural game. You're pretty good.'

'Do you really think so?'

'Yes. You have a good swing.' He tossed his cigar away and as he stood up he added, 'but not good enough to beat me.'

'We'll see about that, Harry,' and she got up with a new-found determination.

By the eighteenth hole they were all square and both on the green in three shots. Harry putted-up close to the hole and Louise conceded the putt. Harry picked his ball up.

'I didn't see that slight borrow to the left,' he said quietly as Louise crouched down behind her ball.

'You'll not talk me out of it again,' she said. 'This is for five dollars.'

'Do you want to make it ten?'

She stood back and eyed him suspiciously. 'You're a dirty player, Harry Menkowitch. No. We'll keep it at five.'

She took her time about lining up and finally stroked the ball towards the hole. At first it held the right line, but at the last moment it veered away to the left. She looked up at Harry's face and he was grinning. 'You did it again,' she pouted at him. 'At least we halved the game.'

'Not yet,' he said and looked down at her ball, barely three inches from the hole.

'Aren't you going to give that to me?'

'No,' he said smiling. 'Never concede the final putt.'

She stepped over to her ball. 'Is that another Harry rule?' she asked, betraying a little petulance.

He waited until she had addressed the ball and then he stooped and picked it up. 'Just joking,' he said. 'Thanks for the game.'

She seemed relieved. 'I enjoyed that, Harry. I think we'll do well in the competition.'

He replaced the flag and then she said, 'That's five dollars you owe me.' She held out her hand.

'I thought we halved the match,' he queried.

'We did. But you said, you bet five dollars you'd beat me.'

Harry thought about it. 'You're right,' he admitted, 'that was the bet.' He took out a five and gave it to her. 'I'll have to watch how I word my bets in future.'

Now it is normal at the end of a mixed game that the man and woman trade kisses on the cheek, but as Harry took off his cap and stooped his head, Louise cupped his face in both hands and delivered a firm kiss on his lips.

Harry stood back and sucked in his breath. 'Well, after that, I guess I had better buy you lunch.'

*

Up in the clubhouse lounge, the Lady Captain, Ellor Byrne, had watched their progress up the last hole. When she saw Louise deliver an over-amorous kiss at the end of their game, she smiled to herself. Everything was going according to plan.

Harry ordered the food and got them a drink and they settled at a table in the window overlooking the course. As he gazed out, the course looked green and lush but he knew that before long, Autumn would begin to paint the leaves; for a while, everything would be colourful until the Winter snows came and golf would be suspended until the thaw. Another year was passing.

'Well, young lady,' he said, turning to face her. 'I must say I enjoyed that game with you, despite you winning.'

'Oh tush,' she said, 'it was only on a technicality. We halved really.'

'That's nice of you to say so,' he smiled at her. 'Have you thought about the competition?'

'Yes,' she said, reaching into her bag and taking out a scorecard. She moved her chair closer to him and he was conscious of her knee touching his. 'I made some notes going round. You seemed better on the holes I've marked with an "H" and on those with an "L", that's me, where I had the advantage off the tees.' She showed him the card and he looked over it.

'Your approach is very scientific,' he said with some admiration. 'I wondered what you were writing on your card.'

'We have to take alternate drives and I think it works out that you drive the odd numbers and me the even ones.' She looked to him for agreement.

He nodded. 'I'm happy with that.'

She was pleased and rested her hand on his arm. 'I think we make a good pair, don't you?'

He patted her hand. 'I think we'll go out there and kill them.'

'I didn't mean just on the course,' she said, with a slight expression of shyness. 'We seem to get on well generally.'

'Like a father and daughter, you mean.'

'Nooo,' she dragged out the word. 'I don't see you as old. You have a lot of life in you, Harry. I bet you've had your moments.'

Harry chuckled. 'When I was your age I used to make them last a few hours.'

She clutched his arm tighter as she laughed from somewhere deep in her throat. 'I bet you haven't forgotten, either.'

'There're some things you never forget,' he said with a broad grin that creased his face into folds.

The food arrived. They had both ordered a light meal of scrambled eggs with salad which they ate with relish, having gained a big appetite from the golf and from the many compliments they had swapped. Life feels good, Harry thought, but something was tugging at his mind. Well, almost good, he admitted.

*

That evening over coffee on the back porch, Harry explained their game, hole by hole, to Rosemary, who sat patiently listening but not always understanding. When he told her about Louise winning on a technicality, Rosemary merely commented, 'She seems a determined young lady.'

Harry sipped his coffee. 'That she does,' he said quietly, deep in thought.

'So what's bothering you?'

'Did I say something was?' he asked, glancing sideways at her and seeing perceptive eyes.

'No. But I can tell something is.'

He ran a finger along his lips. 'I'm not sure. Am I full of life?'

'You were the other night on the couch. Quite frisky I seem to remember.'

He plucked at his lips. 'Do you think I am still attractive?'

'Were you ever?'

Harry tutted at her refusal to be serious. 'She's always touching me. She puts her hand on my arm or my shoulder.'

Rosemary tried to keep a smile from her mouth. 'Some people are like that. They communicate by touch. It adds

117

a little something to their words. Like shaking hands when you greet someone.'

'No, it's not like that with her.'

Rosemary put her hand on his arm. 'Are you thinking that she fancies you?'

Harry looked at her hand on his arm. 'That is what bothers me,' he said, looking up as if suddenly seeing it more clearly. 'She acts as though she does but I know she doesn't.'

Rosemary withdrew her hand. 'You've lost me somewhere.'

Harry leaned across and kissed her. 'Good.'

8

At the weekend, Sol's family gathered for their ritual 'One Sunday a month with Dad'. He had thought of going out for the day and phoning them later to apologise that he had forgotten, but he couldn't think of anywhere to go on his own; he'd have been quite happy playing with his computer or having a beer while watching movies on cable. They arrived, as always, at the same time, and their three cars filled the crescent drive which ran round a half-moon grass island in front of the house. The hoards of kids screamed straight through the main door and the passageways to the rear garden or disappeared up the stairs to the upper rooms without the slightest acknowledgement of their grandfather. He imagined the neighbours had their wall planners marked with a big red cross on the last Sunday of every month and the area was vacated for the day.

What he noticed, and what frustrated him most, was that he never achieved a complete conversation with anyone. He would be talking to his sons and then be interrupted by one of their wives, or one of the kids would come in crying or something would happen to end the conversation in mid-sentence and somehow it was forgotten. The three wives – he always got their names mixed up – would take over the kitchen to cook the lunch, but they were forever poking their heads round the door to say something, usually to correct what their husbands were saying. He was fascinated by their ability to hold one conversation but still hear another one going on in the next room.

And lunch was no better. There were too many of them, and chairs were brought round the table from all parts of the house; everyone sat cramped, too close together and all talking at the same time. Dishes of food were passed round and if you missed one, it was empty by the time it came your way again. There was one time when one of the wives – Gloria he thought her name was but wasn't sure – kept distracting him by pulling his arm as she tried to emphasise something and he kept missing the dishes passing by. He ended up with three potatoes and a sprig of broccolli. She had touched his arm again. 'You really ought to eat more,' she advised him. He seethed but said nothing.

Sol had considered changing the arrangement to having each family on separate Sundays, but he went off that idea when he realised he would have to put up with them for three Sundays a month instead of one. After lunch, he wandered out to the garden for a moment of peace but then one of them had noticed he was missing and they sought him out and joined him. Then his sons proceeded to talk over his head; Sol was very short and for some reason, perhaps Nature was against him as well because his sons all grew to be giants. He would stand among them with his head upturned, looking from one to the other as they spoke.

He hated their way of living as well. They seemed to think that the more you owed on your credit card, the better your standard of living. He listened to them bragging about buying this and that – a new car, the latest hi-fi system or whatever – and he suddenly felt a surge of anger.

'You are a bunch of boneheads,' he said too loudly. The garden suddenly went quiet – even the birds sitting in a tree ducked their heads. All eyes turned down to Sol. He lowered his voice. 'How can you live happily, owing so much money? Don't you ever think of saving some or investing in shares. Dollars make dollars if put in the right place. Don't you ever think of the security of having some money put away?'

'Like for a rainy day,' one of his sons guffawed, and the others laughed with him. At that moment, Sol wanted to lash out and hit his son in the balls – his head was too high and out of reach. He stepped over in front of him and looked up.

'Listen, you schmuck.' He reached up and tapped his finger hard on his son's chest. 'All the while you pay for things with your credit card, you think you're getting a good deal but you'll be paying interest on the amount you don't pay off. And the rates are high. So what you think is a good deal costs you more in the long run.'

His sons looked at him in silence. He wheeled round slowly to look at each of them in turn. 'It's a false economy you live in. You think you're being clever and smart and have something better than the next guy. But look around you,' he waved his arm round to take in his house and garden. 'Have you got anything like this?' He stepped over to a small pond with a fountain sprinkling melodic water. 'How did I get this?' He turned and waved his arms to indicate the spread of his enormous house. 'And that. I didn't inherit anything. I didn't win on the lottery. And,' he emphasised the conjunctive, 'I didn't work my balls off for it.' He paused to see their reaction but they were standing, just staring at him. 'Whatever money I saved, I made it work for me. Work for me,' he repeated. 'That's what you guys should be doing.' They still said nothing, and as he looked round at them one at a time, each looked away from his stare. 'Are you understanding what I am saying?'

121

'Hey Pops,' one of them said at last, 'aren't you taking it all a bit too seriously?'

'Too seriously?' Sol homed in on him and he stepped forward. 'What have you got besides your fancy stereo and a car you can't afford to buy gas for? You live in a two-bedroomed tenement with no garden and three kids sharing one room and a guy next door who keeps you awake at night playing music. And you,' he turned to the next son in line. 'You have an extra job at night humping frozen beef just to pay off the interest on your debts. And you,' he turned to the next in line, 'you live in a hutch and breed like a rabbit. What do you feed on? Carrots?' They laughed nervously, but he cut them off with a dark glare. 'Wise up fellers. I didn't bring you up to keep some fat schmo working in a bank living on champagne and caviar while you struggle to make ends meet just to pay off his interest.'

He stopped when he saw their horrified faces and a sense of guilt began to swell up in his throat. 'Look guys. Life can be a bitch and when you least expect it, she can deliver you a swift kick in the guts. It can take a long time to recover if you've got nothing behind you.' He paused to see if they understood. 'Of course,' he said, forcing a smile on his face, 'there's always Papa to come to. I want you to know you can.' Their faces showed relief and then he laughed. 'I may not be in but you can try.' Their expressions dropped once more, so he laughed again. 'Just kidding.' He held out his arms. 'Hey. How about a family hug?'

They came forward as one and crowded round him, slapping each other's backs and all talking at the same time. From somewhere beneath them, Sol's voice cried out, 'Okay. Enough of that. I'm suffocating down here.'

Sol stood alone with his hands on his hips, watching his sons and their wives begin to file back into the house, and he wondered if that had been a sensible thing to say. At least he gained some satisfaction when he overheard one wife saying to her husband as she tugged at his arm, 'He's right, you know.'

At last the time came when the wives cleared everything away, the dishes were washed and put back in the cupboards, the chairs were replaced round the house and the kids were collected and counted. Sol stood on the drive with a smile and a wave as the three cars drove away. He imagined that his neighbours would be checking their watches and soon their cars would be arriving in convoy as they returned home.

All he wanted at that moment was a cold beer and to watch a movie on the TV as he relaxed in his easy chair. He went into the kitchen, opened the fridge and cursed. They'd drunk all his beer.

*

At the Wannabee Golf and Country Club, the men, with their wives, girlfriends or mistressess, gathered for the Summer Mixed Golf Competition. The car park was filled with expensive cars and the clubhouse was bedecked with bunting; the air was filled with their chatter and laughter. They wore a variety of caps and straw hats to keep the high sun from their eyes or from burning balding heads, and sported clothes of every colour, shape and size. Golf carts bumped and wheezed along the tracks siding the fairways, carrying overloaded bags and overweight golfers. It was a collage of colour and movement and noise, and anyone who considered themselves someone was there, either playing or making sure they were being seen at the clubhouse. Even the mayor, who was invited to make the presentations later, arrived early to partake of the free drinks and free lunch, wandering around pretending he knew everybody; after all, it wasn't that long before the next mayoral election was due. Dinsdale kept close to his side and whispered the names of members in the mayor's ear when he spoke to them; many were amazed he knew their names even though they had not met before. It was a good time for all.

Harry and Louise were in the last group to tee off and they were paired with a young couple who took their game too seriously. The young man was trim with clean-cut lines and white, even teeth, but his partner was something nearing plain. Harry winked at Louise. 'They may have lower handicaps but that means they get less shots than we do. Just play your natural game and follow my lead.' She smiled, but her eyes reflected her nervousness.

Harry introduced themselves to their playing partners. 'I'm Harry and this is Louise.'

'Jim and Babs,' Jim said, and he shook hands with an over-strong grip. 'Who's taking the odd holes?'

'I am,' Harry informed him.

'Me too,' Jim said. 'Man against man then.'

'Looks like it,' Harry smiled easily. 'You have the lower handicap so why don't you start.'

Jim and Harry mounted the wooden steps to the tee area and Jim swung his club several times to loosen up.

'We're the holders,' Jim informed him proudly between swings. 'We've won this competition for the past two years.'

Harry ignored this information; he didn't like the way Jim was talking down to him with a 'superior than thou' look in his eyes. 'Is Babs your wife?' Harry asked as Jim began a series of exercises.

'Yes.' He stopped exercising and looked passed Harry's shoulder to Louise.

Harry glanced back at Louise and then shrugged to Jim. 'Oh, she's not my wife. She's my mistress.'

Jim just said, 'Oh,' not concealing his surprise.

'I find that at my age I need someone to keep me young. Watch her swing and you'll know what I mean.' He winked and Jim nodded knowingly.

Jim looked at Louise again and she smiled sweetly back. For some reason, he didn't connect too well and pulled his ball just off the fairway where it settled down in the second cut. Harry smiled as he put his club behind the ball and he swung easy, hitting shorter but straight up the middle.

As they drove up the cart track, Louise asked, 'What did you say to him?'

Harry smiled. 'Just being friendly.'

'Oh yes,' she said in a knowing way.

As Jim and Babs toiled behind them carrying their heavy bags as low handicappers seemed to do, Babs asked a similar question. 'What were you talking about and why did you keep looking at her?'

'She's his mistress. Can you believe that?'

Louise went over to her ball while Harry stayed in the cart; he wanted her to play her own game. He noticed Jim had positioned himself behind her to gain full advantage of her swing. Somehow, Louise sensed this and gave her bottom an extra wiggle. She hit the ball clean and made the front of the green.

Babs walked on and stopped to look down at her buried ball with disgust. Jim came up to her and she gave him a withering look. 'Thanks,' she said coldly. 'If you thought more about your shot and less about her wiggling ass, you wouldn't have put it here.'

Jim tried to make light of it. 'Just play it up and I'll put it near the hole.'

She tried to hit it too hard and caught it thin, not managing to find the fairway. Jim sighed with disappointment and his wife glared at him. He walked forward and found the ball was again low in the grass. He tried for

125

the green but hit too heavy and the ball hit a bunker to the left of the green. It was Babs's turn to sigh.

As Harry drove the cart, Louise grinned. 'Whatever you said has put him off.'

Harry glanced at her. 'And I suppose that extra wiggle you gave was for her benefit.'

'I have a sixth sense that tells me when a man is watching my bottom.'

He stopped the cart by the green and they waited for the pair to slowly come up. 'Don't sympathise,' he said quietly.

When the hole was finished, Harry marked the scorecard. 'I made that a six for you and four for us.'

Jim broke the pencil as he wrote down their score on his card.

Louise had the honour to start the second hole and she went through her usual routine of moving just about every part of her body before she settled. Before she hit, she lifted her jumper slightly and scratched her bare midriff; Harry quietly smiled to himself. She drove sweetly down the middle, and then went over to stand by Jim while Babs prepared herself. Jim made some comment to Louise about how nice her swing was and Louise gave him an extra-sweet smile. Babs heard him and looked up. Her drive hooked left and Babs swore as Jim cursed quietly to himself.

'Do you want to play a provisional ball?' Harry asked. 'That's in the trees.'

Neither replied as they walked off.

When they had completed the ninth hole, they went over to a small wooden hut with a straw roof to receive a complimentary drink. For some reason, Jim and Babs were having a bad day; they talked little during the preceding holes and only used short sentences like 'You're swinging too fast' and 'God, we'll never find that one' and 'Will you keep your eyes off her ass.' By the time they got their drinks, they were not talking at all.

Louise went over to Harry, slipped her arm round his waist and pressed herself against him. 'How's it feel to have a young mistress?' she smiled at him.

'How do you know about that?'

'Babs asked me when we were looking for their ball in the trees.'

'What did you say?' Harry asked with a little surprise.

'I said it was good with an older man.' She squeezed his waist. 'I said they took their time about it.'

Harry slipped his arm round her and patted her behind. 'No wonder they're not playing so good.'

'You're a wily old fox, Harry Menkowitch. Remind me never to play against you again.' She leaned her face closer and kissed his cheek.

'Now you be careful,' he warned. 'You'll be putting me off.'

Babs and Jim stood a short way off and watched them in silence.

By the end of the game, Harry and Louise had put together a very low score and Jim and Babs were left wondering how they could have hit so many bad shots. Louise gave Jim the briefest of kisses on his cheek and Harry did likewise with Babs. While Louise then put her arms round Harry's neck and gave him a full kiss on the mouth, Jim shook hands with his wife.

After they had showered and changed, they met in the dining room and passed a quiet meal together. Jim and Babs said little and Louise began to feel sorry for them. Harry just sat with a big smile and commented, 'That was some game you played, my dear. It's nice to know we can get it together on the course as well.' Jim spluttered in his drink and Louise kicked Harry under the table.

After the meal, the competitors made their way to the

127

lounge area for a drink and a chat with friends they met as they made their way round the room. For some reason, Jim and Babs had disappeared. Finally, Dinsdale mounted a low stage at one end and was joined by the Mayor. He made an over-long speech about how well everyone – or most, he tried to joke – had played, how good the course was and how nice it was to see so many members and guests present. When they thought, or hoped, he had finished, he then went on to say how good it was of the Mayor to give up his important time to present the prizes. The Mayor smiled and held it while the local newspaper cameraman took his picture with Dinsdale. He also made a speech, but having heard Dinsdale, he thankfully kept it short.

'And now for the results, which I'm sure you're all eager to hear,' Dinsdale announced with a broad smile. 'I'll give them in reverse order.' He presented prizes for the fourth, third and second places and each couple made their way to the front to receive their prizes from the Mayor, who seemed more concerned with smiling for each photograph. Dinsdale waited for the room to settle before continuing, trying to build up their expectation.

'In first place, and winners of the cup, with a very low score, ... Harry Menkowitch and Louise van Brockenhurst.' The room erupted with applause and some whistling from the back of the room. Harry let Louise go in front of him; she was surprised they had won but Harry had sneaked a look at the scoresheet earlier and as he stepped onto the stage, he smiled in a casual way. The Mayor was too eager to give Louise a congratulatory kiss and almost forgot to smile for the camera. Louise took the cup and then turned to Harry, giving him a long kiss on the lips; there were many hoots from the audience. Harry tried to look embarrassed but failed.

'Well done, Harry,' Dinsdale clapped him on the back. He leaned close to his ear. 'Just make a little speech.'

Harry knew this was the custom and he stepped in front of the microphone. He didn't mind making speeches, but it was then that he saw Rosemary standing over to one side. His eyes locked with hers, but then she smiled and gave him a little wave. He coughed and couldn't remember what to say, mumbling something about how nice it was and what an honour it was to receive the cup and how he owed it all to his playing partner. Those that knew him wondered what was wrong – he usually had too many words to say. Harry was glad when it was over and they gave him generous applause.

As Harry made his way through the crowd, he came across Travers who was smartly dressed in his Captain's jacket. 'Well done, Harry,' he congratulated him and patted him on the shoulder.

'Well, thank you, Travers. Did you have a bet on me to win?' Harry asked him.

'A bet?' Travers' eyebrows rose and then he smiled. 'Oh, I see, a bet.' He shook his head like a chiding schoolmaster. 'Yes, very good.'

Harry passed on and made his way over to Rosemary, not quite knowing what she was going to say. She smiled and took his hand in hers. 'I thought I would surprise you,' she said.

'Oh you have,' he admitted.

'And you won, how nice. You didn't expect to but then I guess you'll put it down to your partner. She looks very ... athletic.' Harry eyed her suspiciously but she squeezed his hand in that special way she did and he relaxed. 'And this must be Louise,' Rosemary said, looking over his shoulder.

Harry turned his head and saw Louise was standing close behind him, holding the cup. She came forward, put her hand on Rosemary's shoulder and gave her a light kiss on the cheek. 'And you must be Rosemary. I recognise your voice.'

'And I recognise you from Harry's description.' She gave Harry just the hint of a look. 'How wonderful to have won.'

'You know,' Louise leaned closer to her in a conspiratorial way, 'Harry's a better player than he makes out.'

'Oh, he keeps himself quite fit,' Rosemary smiled, and then added, 'for his age.'

'I don't see him as old,' Louise confided. 'I think he's cuddly,' and she patted him playfully in the stomach.

'He can be that as well,' Rosemary kept her smile going.

'And he's a wily old fox too,' Louise added.

'So I've heard.'

Harry was getting more uncomfortable and coughed. 'If you ladies want to talk about me, perhaps you would like me to go somewhere else.'

'We're only teasing,' Louise giggled. 'Oh, the Lady Captain is waving at me. I'd better go and see what she wants.' She kissed Rosemary lightly on the cheek again. 'It was nice meeting you.' As she moved away she said, 'I'll see you later, Harry.'

They watched her move through the crowd of people around them and Harry finally looked back at Rosemary. 'Well, say something.'

'She's...' and Rosemary paused, '...she's very enthusiastic.'

'That's one way of putting it.'

'And she obviously likes the older man,' she said with a glint in her eyes.

'Rosemary?'

'And you are right,' she added. 'She's up to something.'

'I'm glad you agree with me,' he began to relax. 'It's working out what it is.'

'I expect you'll have fun finding out.'

He looked at her expecting a smile, but she kept a straight face. 'There are times when I feel like putting you across my knee.'

130

'Wait until we get home, dear.' She allowed just enough of a pause before adding, 'If you still have the energy, that is.'

He was about to reply when Rick and Anna came over. 'Hi stud,' Rick said with a wink to Rosemary. 'I said you two would play well together. They make a fine couple, don't they Rosemary.'

Anna did not see the wink and felt she had to help Rosemary. 'So why didn't any of the ladies ask you to play with them?' She poked Rick in the side.

'I hear Ellor Byrne was looking for a partner,' Harry put in quickly.

'And who's Ellor Byrne?' Anna asked just as quickly. Harry looked around and, when he spotted her, pointed her way. Anna gave out a shriek of laughter. 'Now that I would like to have seen.'

Rick gave a concessionary smile. 'And what if Louise had asked me to play with her?'

'I would have hidden your clubs.' As soon as the words had slipped out, Anna realised that was not the thing to say in front of Rosemary and added hastily, 'but then Harry is a perfect gentleman.'

Rosemary felt the humour was getting out of hand. 'Actually, my dear, I knew it was Louise I could trust.'

'You did?' Anna said with some surprise.

'Of course. Harry may have the will but not the way.'

This made Anna laugh again and Harry and Rick exchanged glances. 'I think that's a cue for us to get a drink and drown our sorrows,' Harry said with an exaggerated sigh.

'I think you may be right, old timer,' Rick said with a cracked voice as he put a hand on Harry's shoulder. They moved away with shuffling feet like two old men.

'You know,' Rosemary smiled to Anna, 'those two could be mistaken for brothers.'

131

'They're good for each other,' Anna agreed.

'Come on,' said Rosemary, 'let's have a drink with them. We have to cheer them up.'

'Make them feel like men again,' Anna laughed.

'Absolutely,' Rosemary said, taking her arm and leading her towards the bar. 'Besides, I just noticed Louise has joined them.'

9

A little while later, when they had got home, Rosemary told Harry she'd had a phone call from her sister in Seattle who'd broken her leg and an arm in an accident. She was going to stay with her for a week. She was having difficulty getting around and, as she lived alone, Rosemary felt she ought to go and help. Harry raised no objections but didn't offer to go with her; he wasn't so keen on her spinster sister.

'What will you do with yourself?' Rosemary asked.

'Get a few jobs done round the house,' he said. 'The garden needs tidying. I can find plenty of things to do. Besides, I expect Dave will call round.'

'As long as you don't just put your feet up and watch that thing,' she nodded towards the TV.

'Do you want me to draw up a checklist so you can tick it off when you come back?'

'Don't be silly, dear.' She bustled around, packing a case and tidying odd things unnecessarily, then checking the fridge and freezer to make sure he had enough food for the week. She made a meal planner for him to vary his diet every day, even though she knew he would ignore it. Harry booked her on a flight and the next morning drove her out to the airport on the south-eastern fringe of the town.

He could see she was nervous of the flight and gave her an extra-long hug at the exit gate. 'Now don't worry about me. And give my love to your sister. If she remembers who I am. And don't stay longer than a week,' he pleaded.

He saw in her eyes an unusual tenseness even though her mouth was smiling. 'Don't forget the meal list I made out for you,' she reminded him.

'Of course not.'

'And get Dave to help you with that tree stump you said you'd dig out. I don't want you straining your back. You're not as young as you think you are. Despite Louise,' she added.

'I'll give Dave a call.'

'And the garbage man calls on Wednesdays. Make sure you've put all the trash in the bin.'

'Are you going to catch this plane or wait for the next one?' he asked her with a broadening grin.

She flapped her hands with some anxiety. 'Is it time?'

'The captain's over there looking at his watch.'

She half turned but only saw the check-in girl at the gate. 'Oh, you're just trying to get rid of me.'

'The sooner you go, the sooner you come back.' He kissed her cheek. 'I'll miss you.'

'I hope so.' She gave him a final kiss on the cheek and then went over to the departure gate. He watched as the girl checked her in and he gave Rosemary a last smile before she disappeared.

He went out onto the balcony and watched the small plane climb into the sky and head west. He wondered if she was looking out of the window and could see him. Perhaps she was waving down to him so he waved up to the plane, just in case. He missed her already.

*

On the Monday, he played golf, as usual, but something was missing from his game. Unfortunately, it wasn't missing from Sol's, and he had a rare win, letting everybody know about it. Harry stayed longer in the shower, soaping himself several times; he hoped it would wash away his melancholia. By the time he had dressed, the others had gone up, and as he was about to enter the lounge, a voice behind him said, 'Hello partner.'

He stopped and turned just as Louise came up to him and kissed him on the cheek. 'How's my champ today?' She leaned away from him. 'Hey? Why the sad eyes?'

'Just out of sorts,' he shrugged. 'And Rosemary's off for a week at her sister's.'

Louise slipped her arm through his. 'Then how about taking me out for dinner one night? Say tomorrow.'

'I don't know,' he sounded reluctant.

'That's not like Harry,' she questioned, and then pouted her lips. 'And it's not nice to turn down a lady.' She looked at him with big eyes, which slowly brightened as her lips broke into a grin. 'Come on. You look as though you need cheering up.'

'All right,' he finally conceded.

'Good. I'll pick you up at your place around seven.'

He hesitated at that. 'Perhaps I ought to pick you up,' he said, thinking of the prying eyes round neighbouring curtains.

'No,' she said firmly. 'It's your night out so I'll drive.'

He conceded again and nodded.

'Good.' She pecked his cheek again and set off down the stairs.

This was one thing he wasn't going to mention to the others, he thought. Especially as Sol was in his crowing mood.

As it turned out, their evening together was very good. She had chosen an out-of-the-way place, guessing that he didn't want to meet anyone who knew him. The food was plain but very good, and she kept the conversation bubbling

135

along with humorous tales of her childhood. She spun a story about her wacky father who was an inventor in his spare time, and told Harry about all the weird 'home help' machines he made and how they always ended in disaster; sometimes they flooded the kitchen or ran beserk around the room damaging furniture or once even catching fire.

'You sound like you had a good childhood,' Harry said as they sipped their coffee after the meal.

'Too good in some ways,' she said, her eyes still remembering them. 'My mother died when I was very young and I have only vague memories of her, but my father made up for it. I am an only child and he devoted himself to me. I loved my father. There was so much good in him. He could be so funny at times and I never remember him losing his temper. You know, that's quite something to say about someone.' She paused in thought and then reached across and touched Harry's hand. 'You're like him in some ways.'

'I'll take that as a compliment,' he said, and put his other hand on top of hers. He had not seen this side of her, and he was touched by her apparent loneliness. 'From the way you talk of him, I assume he's gone,' he said quietly.

She nodded, her eyes holding a sadness. 'A while ago now but I still miss him. You know, in a funny way, I think that's why I've never met anyone I can settle down with. I'm always comparing them with my father.' She raised her eyes slowly and then they suddenly brightened, quickly banishing away the sadness. 'Hey! I'm getting morbid and I'm supposed to be cheering you up. Tell me something about Harry.'

'Me? What you see is what you get.'

'No,' she contradicted him. 'I think there is another Harry deeper down.'

'Well, if you find him you can tell me what he's like.'

'He's...' she paused for a moment, '...he's a caring man

136

who loves his wife but he never tells her. He is mischievous and can't take anything seriously. How am I doing?'

'I do tell my wife I love her.'

'Not enough, I bet,' she contradicted him, 'but I could see she adores you. Now tell me about the other Harry. The one in the jewellery business. Your business has quite a reputation.'

'Well, it's not mine anymore. I own part of it but my son, Dave, runs it.'

'You're a sleeping partner,' she mused. 'That sounds a nice position to be in.'

There was something in the way she said it that made him glance up, but when he looked at her she smiled back sweetly.

'It was a deliberate move,' he went on to explain. 'My father started the business and although he made me a partner, he just went on too long. I gauged when the time was right to retire and let Dave take over.'

'So now you play golf. And you have your friends. Sounds idyllic.'

'It is. And the icing on the cake is Rosemary.'

'I guess you are missing her while she's away,' Louise said tenderly.

'That I am,' he conceded.

When she drove him home, she drove up his drive near to the house and switched off the engine. 'Are you going to invite me in?'

'I wasn't,' he admitted.

'Just for a coffee? I don't want our evening to end yet.'

'Okay. Just for a coffee,' he repeated.

When they got inside he put her coat in the cloakroom. 'I'll get the coffee,' he said as he entered the lounge. 'Black and one sugar?'

As he moved towards the door she said 'Harry?' in a way that made him stop and turn. She moved towards him until she was standing close. She averted her eyes from him. 'Harry. I don't know how to say this.'

'Are you in some sort of trouble?' his face showed concern.

'No. Not trouble exactly.'

'Then what is it?'

She moved closer and gently slipped her arms round his neck. 'Will you make love to me tonight?'

Harry remained motionless with his hands hanging loosely by his sides and said nothing for a moment. 'Don't you think that talking about your father has, well, you know.'

But she cut his words off with a deep kiss. When she leaned her face away, her eyes were wide and appealing. 'Please. Just tonight.'

Harry nodded slowly. 'If that's what you really want.'

'Yes. I'm not an infatuated young girl. I know I want you. Have for a while, I suppose.' Her mouth widened into a smile. 'Where is your bedroom?'

Harry gestured over to a set of double doors.

She giggled slightly. 'Your bedroom is downstairs and has double doors?'

He obviously hadn't thought about it by the way he shrugged. 'It was the dining area but we wanted a bigger bedroom.'

'Will you do something for me? Go in there, take all your clothes off and lay on the bed?' she asked coyly.

'And what are you going to do?' he enquired.

'I'll get myself ready in here.' She smiled uneasily. 'I'm a bit shy, I guess.'

'Okay. But don't be too long.' He turned and opened one of the doors, slipped through and closed it behind him.

Louise waited for a moment and then stepped carefully to the front door and eased it gently open. She held her finger to her lips as four ladies from the golf club filed quietly passed her. She indicated for them to line up across the double doors and they raised their cameras at the ready.

Louise checked they were set and then called out, 'Are you ready, Harry?'

'Just about,' she heard him call from the other room. 'Come on in, baby.'

She took hold of both handles and swept the doors open.

Harry looked up and blinked as the cameras clicked and flashes flickered like a broadside from an old sailing warship. The flashes slowly stopped and their cameras were lowered in unison with their jaws.

Louise stepped forward. 'What are you doing?'

Harry blinked the lights out of his eyes. 'Just having a game of poker with the boys. You know Al and Rick and Sol,' he said, waving his hand round the table. They all waved and said 'Hello' in unison.

Her facial expression passed quickly through several emotions. 'Harry Menkowitch!'

Harry dropped his cards on the table and slowly got up. 'I hope you got some good pictures, ladies. I had a good hand there.'

They stood, cameras in their hands, with their mouths open.

'You would make quite a picture yourselves right now,' he smiled along the line.

Their mouths shut in unison and they hurriedly put their cameras away as if to hide their embarrassment. Louise stood still, rooted to the spot; only a muscle twitching in her cheek gave away her inner frustration.

'If you ladies wouldn't mind leaving, we'd like to get on with our game. Unless you'd like to join us,' he added. Harry advanced towards them and they turned and almost fled to the front door. Louise alone stood her ground.

Harry put his arm round her shoulder and led her back into the lounge, closing the doors behind him.

'How did you know?' she asked, her short breaths betraying her anger. 'Who told you?'

Harry shrugged and smiled at the same time. 'You did, I guess.'

'Me? How?'

'Well, let's put it like this. I'm at an age now that if a girl asks me to take her home from a party it's because she feels safe with me.' He saw that she didn't fully understand and he explained quietly. 'I'm too old for a beautiful girl like you to want someone like me.'

'I guess you must hate me,' she said quietly.

Harry let a small laugh slip from his mouth. 'No way.' He reached up and put his hands on her shoulders. 'I'm the trickster, remember. And you have to accept them when the jokes are on you.'

She slipped her arms round his waist and buried her head against his chest. 'Oh Harry. I'm a fool. We've had such a good time together.'

'Yes we have,' he admitted. 'I've enjoyed every minute of it.' He tucked his finger under her chin and tilted her head up so he could see her face; she had small tears running down her cheeks. 'You're too beautiful to stain that face with tears.' He kissed her on her forehead.

'You are just like my father. Never losing his temper. Forgiving everything.'

'I'm not quite a saint like that,' he argued mildly.

She kissed his cheek and lay her head on his shoulder and whispered in his ear: 'You know, there was a moment in the restaurant when I was going to ring the ladies and call it off.'

'Oh? And what stopped you?' he asked without admonishment.

She sniffed her tears away. 'Because if I did, I knew I

would try to get you to make love to me anyway. And that wouldn't have been right, I guess.'

He stroked her hair. 'I'm glad you didn't try.'

She tilted her head back again to look at him. 'Does that mean you wanted to make love to me?'

'It means I'm glad you didn't try.'

She stepped away from him and blew her nose gently in her handkerchief. 'I suppose you won't want to talk to me again,' she said with downcast eyes.

'I'm afraid I'm going to have to.'

She looked up with a question on her lips.

'Well,' he smiled, 'we've got to defend our title next year in the Mixed Competition.'

She rushed to him, knocking him slightly backwards, and hugged him. 'Thanks Harry.'

When Louise had departed, Harry went into the other room. His three friends looked at him and waited for him to say something. He looked round at their expectant faces.

'Well?' he asked, 'Whose turn is it to deal?'

*

Rosemary was returning on the Sunday afternoon flight, and on his drive out to the airport, Harry wondered if he should tell her about the little game. If he did, he knew she would smile and not mind, but she would also tuck it away in some corner as she always did and bring it up at a moment when she was reprimanding him for something. If he didn't tell her, she may find out and then there would be no smile and she would question why. He decided to take the risk; it was one thing to mention the game, but it was quite another to explain to Rosemary why he took Louise out for dinner in the first place.

'How is your sister?' he asked, as he manoeuvred round a slow, overloaded truck and into the fast lane.

141

'She's okay. I could've stayed a month but I guess she'll cope. She has good neighbours.'

'How did she have the accident?' Harry asked as he turned onto the freeway back into town. 'Did she fall off a bar stool?'

'Now that's unkind,' Rosemary chided him. 'You know she doesn't drink. She was doing voluntary work in an old people's rest home and one of the old men upset a large tureen of soup. In an effort to jump out of the way, she tripped.'

'What was wrong with the soup?' he asked, almost to himself.

Rosemary said nothing but tutted to show her disapproval. They sat in silence for a while before Rosemary asked, 'Did you get many jobs done?'

'All I had planned,' he said with a self-gratifying grin; he'd known she would ask him that before they'd got home. 'Dave came over and we dug out the tree stump. I've made that space into a bed for asters and dahlias. Should look nice. Oh, and the boys came round one evening for a game of cards.' He thought he had better tell her that much about the evening in case one of them let slip they had been there.

She smiled at the way he referred to them as 'the boys'. 'Poker I suppose. Did you win?'

'Oh, it was a very successful evening.'

'And have you aired the house to get rid of all the cigar smoke and whiskey fumes?'

'I opened every door and every window.' He reached across and patted her knee. 'The air's so clean, it's like standing outside.'

She made a noise in her throat to show she doubted his claim.

When they arrived home, Rosemary unpacked in a way that took her round the house, checking that everything

142

was neat and tidy as she had left it. Harry went out to the back porch and sipped a Jack Daniels while she busied herself, knowing what she was doing and wanting no part of it. She eventually joined him and sat with a sigh in the other canvas chair.

'Autumn is coming,' she observed, feeling the slightly cooler air. 'Have you said anything to Dave about Christmas?'

'Christmas? That's still a way away,' he said, glancing sideways at her with mild surprise.

'It'll suddenly come up on us. We went to him last year.' She ran her hand up her arm as a cool breeze crept up. 'I thought maybe they would want to come to us. It'll save Pam having to cook and all.'

'I'll ask him. He did say last year that they may go away, skiing or something.' Harry finished his JD with a flourish and smacked his lips. He had to give Rosemary a reason for the question he knew would be coming.

'Have you been drinking and smoking much?' she asked on cue.

'Why do you ask when you know I won't tell you the truth?' He reached across and put his hand on her arm and gave it a gentle squeeze. 'I've missed you.'

'Because you had no one to cook for you or to clean up after you,' she smiled to take the edge off her remark.

'What else could it be?' he said as he leaned across and kissed her. His lips lingered on her cheek and then she pushed him away.

'Harry Menkowitch! I've been back five minutes and already you're getting randy.'

'I only kissed you!'

'And I've known you long enough to know that kiss.'

Harry released her and leaned back in his chair. 'You'd complain if I didn't kiss you that way.'

'Of course.'

143

'I can't win.'

'Have you ever with me?' She patted his knee but quickly got up and went in the house before he could make more of it.

10

After their Monday game, Harry went in to see Dinsdale. He went in through Felicia's office; she looked at him with cautious eyes, expecting him to say something sarcastic, but he just waved in a friendly sort of way and asked if he could see Dinsdale. Over dinner, when she had spent the night in an hotel with Dinsdale, he had assured her that Harry had taken their episode across his desk in his usual casual way and promised he would say nothing. She got encouragement from Harry's smile that didn't carry even a glint of humour.

'Go right in,' she said lightly. 'He's expecting you.'

Dinsdale looked up with a smile of expectation as Harry entered and waved him to a chair. 'I'm hoping you have some good news for me, Harry.'

'Well, I have an idea,' Harry said easily, 'but I don't know if you'll think it is good.'

'Tell me what it is and let me decide.' Dinsdale clasped his hands together on the desk to show Harry he had his full attention.

'Are you sure you want me to tell you?' Harry queried. 'I mean, perhaps it is better if I keep you out of it.'

Dinsdale thought about his proposal. He was a careful man by nature and, although he had approached Harry for assistance in the first place, being a part-conspirator was not a role he relished. 'Is your idea, sort of ... drastic?'

'Tell me something more about Jay Don Winchester,' Harry avoided answering Dinsdale's question. 'Does he drink much?'

Dinsdale paused again, trying to work out the reason for the question, but nothing came to him. 'Not while the sun's up. He's always saying that. But I've been to a few of his business conventions. He gets all his management together once a year. He owns quite a few companies – five golf clubs, several communication firms and then...'

Harry was slowly becoming impatient with Dinsdale's long diatribe that did not tell him anything. 'So what happens at these annual conventions?'

Dinsdale leaned back in his chair. 'He pays for it all – drinks, food and the entertainment.'

'What sort of entertainment?' Harry interceded again.

'Usually some singer. Sometimes a comedian.'

'And that's it?'

'Oh, he always makes a speech. It's usually over-long and tells us how we can work harder. Things like that.'

Harry was disappointed. 'So they're quiet, sort of formal affairs.'

'No.' Dinsdale sensed Harry's disappointment and wondered why. 'They get a bit rowdier late in the evening. You know what it's like when the wine begins to flow.'

'I suppose JDW leaves before all that occurs.' Harry assumed it was like a jewellers' convention he had attended once. Everyone behaved with utmost decorum until the members at the top table left and then all hell let loose. He didn't bother to go again.

'Oh no,' Dinsdale corrected him. 'He always gets as drunk as a skunk.'

The expression surprised and pleased Harry at the same time. 'Good.'

Dinsdale studied Harry for a moment, his narrow eyes

becoming mere slits in his face. 'Why do you say that? Perhaps you had better explain your idea to me.'

As Harry went through it, he watched Dinsdale's face pass from initial doubt to a shade of concern, but by the time he had finished, his face had blossomed into a broad smile.

But then as he thought more about it, his face clouded. 'Do you think it will work?' he queried. 'I mean, if something went wrong.'

'If it doesn't come off then he will be none the wiser,' Harry tried to reassure him. 'I'll make sure you are not involved. Unless it's successful, of course; then it's up to you what you do.'

Dinsdale licked his lips. The risk was small and if it worked, the franchising was dead. What really appealed to him was that JDW would keep clear of the club in future. Besides, Harry was right when he said he wouldn't be implicated, and if the shit hit the fan, Harry and his little band would be thrown out of the club. He was in a win-win situation.

'All right,' Dinsdale said at last. 'Go ahead. But I don't want to know any more about it. You don't have to give me update reports.'

Harry nodded. He knew exactly where Dinsdale was coming from but he always held a small ace in reserve. 'I won't say another thing,' he assured him. 'Just leave it all to me. Oh, there is one small matter.'

Dinsdale raised his eyebrows, which left his narrow eyes seeking refuge with his straight nose. 'What's that?'

'I shall need a few bucks for expenses. You know, the cake and things.'

'The cake?' Dinsdale queried and then he remembered. He slipped his wallet out from his jacket. 'How much do you want?'

'A couple of hundred should cover it.' Harry inwardly

smiled; he knew Dinsdale wouldn't take the risk of using club money that would connect him to the plan.

Harry left and went out of Dinsdale's door, but went straight round to see Felicia. He leaned with both hands on her desk, which made her nervous, so he stood back and spoke in a quiet voice with a disarming smile. 'I'm getting up a surprise for the Christmas dance. I wondered if we could talk somewhere private. I need your help but I don't want Dinsdale to know about it.'

Felicia relaxed. Harry confessing he needed her help was very flattering and she assumed, from the secrecy, that it was a surprise for Dinsdale. 'Of course,' she matched his quiet voice while glancing quickly at the closed door to Dinsdale's office. 'He's going to the bank in half an hour; I'll meet you in the lounge.'

Harry leaned forward and patted her shoulder in a similar way he had when she was stretched across Dinsdale's desk, but she didn't tie the two events together. He winked in a conspiratorial way and left.

*

When Al had left the club, he went straight home. He had toyed with the idea of going to the diner but he was unsure of his feelings and it was too soon after the failure of the picnic in the park. He didn't like being in this confused state but he felt any attempt at a reconciliation with Aritha might give her the wrong impression, and he would merely be stepping back into a mire where he didn't trust his own feelings.

Phillippa was penning a letter at her small wooden writing desk when he walked into the lounge. She barely looked up. 'Good game?'

'Not really.' He stopped and watched her, wondering if she wanted an explanation but he guessed not. He began to ascend the stairs when she called after him.

'Don't forget to put your clothes in the laundry bag. They'll be calling in an hour.'

He didn't bother to answer and went to their bedroom. Everything in there was 'his and hers': separate beds, separate wardrobes, even separate laundry baskets. The only thing shared was the ensuite bath and shower room but even this had separate towels hanging at a discreet distance apart, hers a light pink and his a deep blue colour. Although he had showered at the club, he felt he needed another – the torment of his mind had somehow made him perspire on the drive back and he wanted to change into his shorts before seeking the haven of his study. He stripped off and let his clothes fall to the floor before he noticed Phillippa had put a plastic laundry bag on his basket; she had suggested they get a maid or cleaning woman who would do the washing and pressing and he had argued that he felt it was an unnecessary expense. In the end, he had conceded to using a laundry service who washed, ironed and folded the clothes neatly and delivered them back in plastic covers.

While he showered, he sang quietly to himself, trying to sound like Frank Sinatra – he chose *The Lady is a Tramp*, which suited his mood. When he'd towelled himself dry, he slung the towel over his shoulder and went back to the bedroom. Phillippa was changing her clothes and he caught her as she slipped her panties up her legs. He stopped close to her and watched her, admiring the curve of her bottom, her flat stomach and how her breasts had remained so firm and upright. She noticed him watching and said, 'Put that towel in the bag as well.'

She reached for a bra and covered herself as she fastened it, aware that he hadn't moved. 'What's the matter?' But then she noticed his swelling manhood and her bottom lip almost turned down. 'The laundry man will be here in a minute,' she said by way of an excuse.

Al moved a little closer and slipped a hand round her

149

waist and then let it slide over her bottom. 'So what? He can watch if he wants.'

She didn't move away but her eyes hardened. 'Don't be disgusting.'

'I want to be disgusting. It's a long time since we were disgusting together.' He drew the finger of his other hand up between the top of her legs and rubbed gently.

He saw a glimmer in her face as the idea appealed to her, but it lasted for barely a few seconds. She moved away, turning her back to him and slipped on a skirt. 'I have to go out. I'm late as it is.'

He didn't bother to ask what she was late for. He sighed and let the towel drop to the floor. He went to a chest of drawers and took out a pair of boxer shorts; when he slipped them on, he noticed how quickly his ardour had died down. By the time he had pulled on his shorts and a tee shirt, Phillippa was fully dressed and had picked up his towel and put it into the laundry bag. The doorbell chimed and she glanced at him with a look which said, 'I told you so'. She said nothing as she stuffed the rest of his clothes into the plastic bag and left the room, carrying the two 'his and hers' bags.

He heard her talking amiably to the laundry man and imagined her smiling; he was probably young. Al waited until he heard her leave and her car drive away. Then he changed his clothes again. He was going to the diner for lunch.

*

Harry quietly supped another JD and smoked a cigar in the club lounge while he waited for Felicia. She eventually came and sat opposite, her face bright with expectation. 'He's gone to the bank. Now Harry, tell me what you are cooking up.'

He noticed she used his first name, which was very rare, and he guessed she had assumed the wrong thing about his surprise. He would have to explain it carefully and in such a way that she would feel she had to agree for Dinsdale's sake.

'You know, Felicia,' he began, 'a lot of people think Dinsdale and I don't exactly hit it off. But we do,' he added quickly as he saw her mouth forming a word. 'I think he runs this club effectively and efficiently. In fact, I have the highest regard for him.'

'I'm glad to hear that,' she said, wondering if Harry meant what he was saying.

'Dinsdale and I went out for a drink the other night. He's under a lot of pressure right now and he felt he had to confide in me.' He saw a surprised look cross her face. 'I know. You're astonished, but Dinsdale and me, we're like that,' and he crossed two fingers and held them up. 'We don't go round hugging each other, I know. He has his position to think of, and I don't have...' he gave her a knowing wink, '...the best of reputations with some of the members.'

'You do,' she paused to choose the right words, 'play your little games sometimes. But I know it's just for fun.' She admitted to herself that she had not been aware of this close relationship, but now she understood why Harry had said nothing about her little indiscretion in Dinsdale's office. He really was a good friend.

'You probably know about Dinsdale's problem with JDW and the franchising,' Harry said, hoping she did; he didn't want to go through all that. She nodded. Dinsdale had confided in her, especially during their night in the hotel; while other men smoked cigarettes, he talked a lot after having sex and she knew how much it troubled him and how determined he was to ensure it didn't happen. That Harry knew about it confirmed he and Dinsdale were close.

151

'Well,' he continued, feeling he had her firmly on his side, 'when he asked for my help, he also made me promise not to mention it to anyone else. He doesn't even know I'm speaking to you about it.' He saw her look of apprehension at that and quickly added, 'But I've explained my idea to him and he's given me the okay.'

She looked a little confused. 'What is it you plan?'

He told her. As the plan unfolded, her eyes widened in fascination, but when he told her what part he wanted her to play, a brief look of horror contorted her face. 'I couldn't do that.'

Harry looked suitably disappointed. 'I'm sorry,' he said with an apologetic tone. 'I was sure you would want to help Dinsdale. I'll have to find someone else. I guess he will appreciate whoever it is. I'm sorry I asked.'

Inwardly, Felicia was a confusion of mixed emotions. On the one hand she wanted to help Dinsdale – she was sure it would finally cement his feelings for her, if only in gratitude – but what Harry was suggesting was ... well ... bordering on the outrageous. Harry said nothing and averted his eyes by looking down into his lap while he guessed her thoughts were pinballing around in her head.

'Who else could you get?' she asked finally.

Harry shrugged. 'I shouldn't say really but I guess Louise may help Dinsdale out. I think they're good friends.'

Felicia was unaware of any relationship between them. For sure, she had noted Dinsdale watching her out on the course from the window, but half the men in the club did that from time to time; she had that sort of figure that attracted their stares.

'No,' she said slowly. 'I'll do it.'

'I'm glad to hear that,' Harry said with an inner relief. 'I know Dinsdale will appreciate it.'

Her smile was faint and her eyes didn't share it. 'I hope he will.'

'But you mustn't say anything,' he requested. 'Not even to Dinsdale.' She immediately looked suspiciously at him. 'This has to be done with the utmost secrecy,' he said hurriedly. 'A secret shared is no longer a secret. Dinsdale insisted I just got on with it. I'm not even going to discuss it further with him. He has to think of his position.'

'Does he know you were going to ask me?' she queried, the suspicion receding but not entirely gone.

'When he asked who I would get to help out, I told him to leave everything to me and not ask questions. I simply said it would be someone who I knew thought a lot of him. He gave me a sort of knowing look and was happy with that.' Harry expected her to say something but she merely nodded. 'Good,' he concluded, standing up. 'I'll let you know when I've sorted a few things out.'

She also stood up. 'I won't say a word,' and she left for her office.

Later, when Dinsdale returned, he noticed Felicia had a special smile for him. He didn't ask why, but assumed she was still remembering their clandestine night together.

11

As the Summer tired and wilted under its own heat, the trees began to reflect the change. The chestnuts became heavy with prickly conkers, which they dropped gratefully to the ground with muted thumps like sporadic rain, and the sycamores released their seeds in spirals like helicopters, spinning away in the breeze. The oaks gave up their acorns and the beeches came under attack from the squirrels, eager to store their nuts for the coming Winter. As Autumn came in and the air cooled, the trees took their cue and began to assume multiple shades of reds and tints of yellows and gold before tiring of the display and discarding their leaves carelessly over the streets of the town and the fairways and greens of the golf course. Along both sides of the drive up to the clubhouse, robinias had been planted in tight avenues and their Summer pastel green turned to bright yellow like ripening wheat. The golfers noticed the beauty as it happened, but then cursed the debris as they had to clear a path on the greens to the flagstick so they could putt their golf balls. The early morning mists became a regular feature and they ghosted through the trees, letting their moisture reveal secretive spider webs like gossamer strung among the gorse and bushes. But again, the golfers complained that the mist made it difficult to judge distances and was responsible for losing balls from errant shots which had disappeared off into the haze. Most of all, they complained because they knew it heralded the coming of Winter and the snows that would close the course.

Before going out to play, Harry looked at the noticeboard in the locker room. 'It says here,' he addressed to the other three, 'the course will close Thursday as it's expected to snow at the weekend.'

Al stopped behind him and read the notice. 'They always need a few days to prepare the course before it snows. They do that every year.'

'I know that,' Harry said, turning to face him. 'But it won't snow until next week.'

Sol joined them. 'The Weather Bureau says this weekend. I heard it this morning.'

'And when have they been right?' Harry queried.

'Fifty bucks says they are,' Sol offered. Somehow he had to get that money back; it wasn't that he needed it, but he was still annoyed that he had lost a dubious bet.

Harry didn't take him up. 'I'll have a word with Dinsdale.'

'A lot of good that will do,' Sol quipped. 'I can see him announcing, "Harry says it won't snow until next week so I'm deferring the closure a few days." Hah!'

But Harry, Al and Rick were already going out of the door. Sol looked at the closed door and felt his anger rising. Today, he promised himself, I'm going to beat you guys off the park.

Now to play a decent game of golf, you have to be relaxed. Harry was relaxed, but then he was most times; Al was relaxed – his relationship with Aritha was back to normal, if not better than before the picnic way back in the Summer; and Rick was relaxed – he had celebrated his wedding anniversary the night before by taking Anna and Ricardo out for a meal and Ricardo had not asked to bring along his flatmate. It had made it feel like a family evening again. But Sol's earlier promise to himself did not help him to relax; in fact, from the moment his first tee

155

shot had hit a tree and rebounded back about fifty yards to nestle down in some thick stuff, his thoughts were only of evil things – his muscles responded accordingly to the negative impulses flashing from his brain through his network of nerve fibres. He pulled and heaved and thrashed, and he lost three balls in as many holes. By the halfway point, he had not won a hole and Rick was three clear of the others. Sol collected his thoughts on the tenth tee; he had nine holes to turn it round and as this was the last game before the Winter closure, he was determined to show them he could come back. He knew they thought he was dead. He told himself he wasn't hitting through the ball and took a lesser club than usual, drawing it back in a fuller arc until he could see the clubhead over his left shoulder and hitting through it fast. He powered his whole body into the shot and promptly carved it into the only water on the course.

'Calm down,' Al advised quietly as Sol stood, gritting his teeth and watching the ripples broaden out from the point the ball had entered the water. 'You need the Winter break. You're getting too worked up.'

'It's only a game, for Chrissake,' Harry said, mimicking one of Sol's favourite sayings and noting the purple tinge colouring his face. 'Think of that lovely scotch and water you'll be having soon in the clubhouse.'

'Hey!' Rick playfully poked him in the stomach with the butt end of his club. 'Think of those lovely long nights when we get together for cards. Oh sorry. You lose then as well.' Rick walked away chuckling to himself.

At that moment, Sol wanted to break his club in half, but not over his knee.

By the eighteenth green, Sol's only consolation was that Al had clawed his way back and was poised to take the hole and win the game from Rick. Al was barely ten feet from the hole and Rick was at least forty feet, having thinned his last shot almost through the green. Harry wasn't in it and had picked up his ball as had Sol. Rick asked for the flagstick to be taken out and struck his ball with hardly a glance at the run of the green. His ball sped too fast it seemed, but within the last few yards it applied unseen brakes, enough so that when it hit the side of the hole, it ran round almost a full circle and then dropped.

'You sonofabitch!' Sol shouted as Rick punched the air. 'You lucky sonofabitch. That ball should have been twenty feet past, at least.' He looked suspiciously at the green, wondering what had slowed the ball so much.

Rick retrieved his ball. 'It must have been the backspin I always get from my putter,' Rick joked with some relief – as soon as he had struck the ball, he knew it was too hard and expected it to shoot at least ten feet past.

Al waited for the noise to abate and took his time over looking for a possible break around the hole. He didn't mind who won and was relaxed at the thought that he needed one for the win and two for a half. He thought he had given the ball just enough to reach the hole, or close to it, and although he only missed the hole by an inch, as it passed it was fed by some unseen slope and carried five feet on.

'What are you doing?' Sol spun round with an upturned face and raised his hands to the heavens with despair. Al looked at him in surprise; he wasn't aware how much Sol wanted Rick to lose. Sol went over and bent down behind Al's ball. 'There's shade left to right,' he said, moving his head from side to side. The other three looked at each other and shrugged. Sol stood up and looked at Al. 'Did you hear me?'

Al walked over to his ball. 'Yeah, I expect Dinsdale could hear you from his office.' He looked at the putt and guessed correctly that it was straight at the hole. He hit it and it kept its line, except that it stopped an inch short.

157

'Sonofabitch!' Sol almost howled. 'It only needed hitting,' ignoring the fact that the ball had run straight.

Al picked up the flag and replaced it before picking up his ball. 'You win some, you lose some,' he said in a matter-of-fact way and handed Rick five dollars. Harry did the same and they then looked at Sol. He was standing by the flag and seemed to be thinking it over, but he finally reached into his back pocket and peeled off a note. He slowly put the other notes back and then stood, looking down at the five-dollar note.

Rick began to say something, but as his mouth opened, Sol began to buckle and he slumped forward onto the green, first to his knees and then followed by his body like a slow-motion replay; his head made a soft thud as it hit the ground last of all. It was one of those moments when a second becomes timeless, and they stood looking at the inert, small figure before they came to life as one. They bumped shoulders as they bent over him and Harry knelt and turned Sol's head to one side – he didn't like the blue tinge in his cheeks. Al rolled him over onto his side and felt for a pulse.

'Al?' Rick queried, but Al shook his head.

'I've got a mobile in my bag,' Al said, already moving away. 'I'll ring for an ambulance.'

Harry felt for a pulse at Sol's neck but didn't find one. He knew he was dead.

'What can we do?' Rick asked, suddenly feeling helpless.

'Give him mouth-to-mouth,' Harry suggested.

'Yeah. That's good,' Rick said and looked to Harry, waiting for him to begin.

Harry shook his head. 'I've just had a cigar. It wouldn't do him any good.'

Rick twisted his mouth and looked down at Sol. 'He looks so peaceful. All the meanness has gone out of his face.' He slowly lowered his head closer to him and applying

158

one hand around the sides of Sol's mouth to open it. Rick began to breath into him. There was no response. He tried for a short while longer, but eventually sat back on his feet with a forlorn look.

'He's still got hold of the five dollars,' Harry nodded towards Sol's right hand.

Rick reached forward and eased the bill out of his fingers.

'You can't take money from a dead man,' Harry said, mildly surprised by his action.

'It's mine, I suppose,' Rick said without thought, but then realised what he was doing and folded the note and tucked it into Sol's pocket. 'You sonofabitch,' he said quietly and stroked Sol's balding head.

Al came back and informed them he had rung for an ambulance and had told Dinsdale, who was on his way from the clubhouse. He felt for a pulse again but shook his head. 'Have you tried mouth-to-mouth?'

'Yeah,' Rick drawled slowly. 'Nothing. I can't believe the life went out of him so quickly.'

They stood up as Dinsdale bustled over; it was the first time they had seen him break into a sweat. He stopped to look down at the motionless figure. 'Is he...?'

Al nodded. 'I've called an ambulance.'

Dinsdale looked perplexed. 'Should we move him off the green to one side?'

Harry glanced back down the fairway. 'There's no one coming. We're not holding anyone up,' he said with just a hint of sarcasm.

'I didn't mean it like that,' Dinsdale said, but his embarrassment was saved as they heard the wail of a siren coming from the freeway. A moment later an ambulance came down from the direction of the clubhouse, across the grass. 'I'd better stop him before he drives onto the green,' Dinsdale uttered, and he ran forward and waved the vehicle to stop by the edge.

'I'm glad Dinsdale's got his priorities right,' Al said pointedly.

*

The snows came that weekend. Had Harry taken the bet, and had Sol lived, he would have finally won his fifty dollars back, but that was perhaps how his life had been. The snow started late in the evening, light and powdery at first, and was swept by the light wind into pockets under bushes and into lines along the kerbs. It fell heavier during the night and the folks of Wannabee woke on the Sunday morning to a white blanket. Snow has some strange effects: it mutes the sound of traffic and reflects into rooms and brightens them with a cold, white light; and the streets seem to widen with no boundaries from the sidewalks and everything seems virgin and clean, for a while anyway. The earliest risers gazed from windows or stood on their porches and admired Nature's handiwork. The trees were tinselled like Christmas cards around the thin, outer edges, and nearer the trunks along the thicker, steel-hard branches, white stripes of snow had been carefully painted by the wind; a sparkling whiteness covered the ground with undulating curves like a rumpled blanket with no rough edges. Those that had to travel cursed that the snows had come early, while children looked out from bedroom windows and thought of the fun to be had and that Christmas couldn't be too far away. People got up early to clear their drives with long-handled shovels and the kids built snowmen and had snow fights. But by midday, the ploughs and the gritters had moved the snow into orange-stained ruts. In no time, the soft blanket was churned and piled into untidy heaps and Nature sighed with a cold breath as she watched her night's work undone.

The coming of the snow made Dinsdale happy. The

160

course was closed, which meant there were no members around to complain about trivial things and he could get on with preparing the year-end accounts in peace. It also meant he and Felicia were often the only ones in the clubhouse and when she reclined backwards over his desk, it added something special to their relationship.

*

Later that week, Sol's funeral was held at the small, white clapboard church on a hill close by where he had lived. The weather had turned mean with a wind that cut through even the thickest clothing and carried flurries of snow that stung exposed faces. The headstones in the graveyard stuck out singularly like stark stubs of decaying teeth and the trees were black and angular; they showered ice as the wind swayed their bared branches. Sol's family – all three sons, their wives and their quarrelsome children – huddled closely together against the wind round the open grave while the priest tried to hurry through the service before the snow completely matted his beard. Harry stood with Rosemary, Al, Phillippa, Rick and Anna at the back of the circle. They could not see anything and from somewhere in the group they could hear the priest's soft words, which were dragged away by the wind and barely audible to them at the back. All three men were thinking pretty much the same. Sol had been mean and complained a lot, but they would miss him. The three sons were each thinking their father hadn't been too fond of them and they wondered why. But now there would be no more Sunday visits to find out.

As the families moved away at the end of the service, Harry overheard Rick saying, 'And I always thought he was Jewish.' Harry smiled at that because he had thought so too. They waited until the families had driven off in their cars; the sons had invited them back to Sol's place but they had each declined – they knew Sol's sons and disliked them as much as he had, and they suspected there would be some discussions over dividing the spoils which they didn't want to hear.

They hung around, somehow not wanting to leave even though their bodies were now feeling the warmth drain out of them. The three men left their wives and edged closer to the graveside, seeing for the first time the coffin lying stark and alone, with the snow beginning to lay a thin cover over it like an angelic mantle.

'It's funny,' Rick was the first to speak. 'This is how it ends. You spend your life filling it with things and it is all taken away so quickly and easily.'

'Better that way,' Al said sombrely, 'than the way his wife died. I want to go that quickly.'

'But not too soon,' Harry commented. The other two looked at him and he shrugged. 'Sol will be up there waiting for us. I'm in no hurry.'

'He'll be wanting to win his fifty dollars back,' Rick chuckled.

Al and Harry smiled at that as they remembered Harry's bunker shot over the eighteenth green; it had been Summer then, which seemed a long while ago.

'Well, Sol,' Al said down to the coffin, 'we're down to a three-ball now. I guess we won't be holding people up so much, but it'll seem a little lopsided without you.'

'Amen to that,' Rick said quietly.

They stood a moment longer, finding it difficult to make their final farewell and turn away.

Al said, 'I expected Dinsdale to come.'

'I didn't. Not for Sol,' countered Rick.

'Everyone back to my place for some warm refreshments?' Harry offered at last.

'Sounds like a good idea,' Rick agreed. 'Jeez, I'm so cold.'

162

Al looked back to the three women and noticed how attractive Phillippa looked in a black fur hat that hugged her face and the snow hung about it like crystals. Her long, black coat had trimmings of fur around the collar and cuffs and reached down to her boots. It was fashioned to her body and the snow had powdered her shoulders like icing sugar sprinkled over a cake. She was smiling at something Anna had said and he wondered if she would smile and dress like that at his funeral.

Back at Harry's place, he filled glasses with JD for the men while Rosemary was in the kitchen with Phillippa and Anna, making some tea and warming some bread. They toasted to Sol with a simple raising of their glasses and then swallowed their drinks in one gulp – each gasped as the strong liquid purged their throats and then permeated through the extremities of their bodies.

'Now that is better,' Rick said and licked his lips to capture any drops from around his mouth. 'Why, thank you,' he said as Harry refilled their glasses.

'Do you want tea?' Anna asked, peering round the door, but when she saw their glasses she slipped back without waiting for an answer.

Harry shepherded them down to the far end of the room where a large picture window overlooked the rear garden; the snow out there was untouched and thick from accumulated falls.

'I expect they've covered him over by now,' Rick surmised quietly, thinking of Sol, as he watched the snow begin to fall more heavily, with large flakes that swirled in the wind and disappeared when they touched the settled snow covering the ground. 'The last traces of the little feller gone.'

Harry and Al both looked at him. Harry said, 'It's strange how someone can be an irritation, but now he's gone, you miss him because there is no longer anywhere to scratch.'

Rick touched Harry's shoulder lightly. 'That's very true and nicely put.'

The ladies came in bearing a tray with tea things and plates of hot bread with melted cheese. Rosemary looked at the three figures silhouetted against the brightness of the window and just stopped in time from saying, 'You look as if you've been to a funeral'. Instead she said, 'Get some of this food down you.'

They turned and went over to the table. Whether it was the soporific effect of the Jack Daniels or their thoughts of Sol, none of them felt like eating. Rosemary saw their hesitation and didn't press them.

'Well,' she said, turning to Anna and Phillippa, 'would you like some tea?'

Phillippa was looking at Al with some disdain as Harry refilled their glasses again. 'You will be alright to drive?' she phrased it as an accusing question.

Al barely glanced at her and raised his glass, finishing his drink in one swallow. 'Nope. You can have that privilege.'

Phillippa twisted her lips in a way that wrinkled her nose. 'I don't want to drive that heap of yours, especially in these conditions.' She turned to Rosemary and Anna. 'Can you believe a man with his money still drives that old thing.' She never referred to it as a car. 'It's rusted and dented and it smells like something's died in there, I'm sure.'

'I think I did,' Al said quietly, not meaning to speak his thoughts.

Phillippa had a riposte on her lips but Harry cut her off by quickly taking a slice of the bread. 'Well, somebody's got to eat.' He bit into the baked bread. 'That sure is good.'

Rick and Al followed his cue and started eating.

'Have you been to see Dave about Christmas?' Rosemary asked, changing the subject. She turned to Anna, 'I want a Christmas at home. You know, with the family?'

'Does that mean Rob will be coming home?' Phillippa asked, feeling bitter that Al had got away with his remark and, wanting to lash out at somebody, she knew Rob was Rosemary's weak point.

Rosemary felt stung. What was it about this woman that made her feel so uncomfortable when she was around? 'I'm not sure. We're hoping so,' she kept her voice level.

Harry could see Rosemary's troubled eyes and reached out with his words to comfort her. 'It'll be a full house anyway. That young tiger of Dave's will see to that.' He glanced at Al, hoping he would understand what he was doing and Al smiled back – he knew he wasn't aiming the barb at him.

'Ours will be a quiet one, as usual,' Al said. 'I was thinking of booking somewhere to eat out.'

Phillippa's face coloured. 'You haven't said anything to me.'

'I was going to save it as a surprise,' Al said, 'but you may have been thinking of arranging something else, so I thought I'd better mention it.' He could see Phillippa was simmering just beneath the surface. 'Just think of the cooking it will save you.' He tried to sound light.

'Will Ricardo be coming to you at Christmas?' Harry neatly steered the conversation away but as soon as he asked the question he regretted it. He and Al knew about Ricardo's 'coming out' – Rick had brought himself to talk about it one time – but they avoided mentioning it.

'I hope so,' Rick said amicably and he smiled to Anna. 'He's sharing his apartment with some young man. I'm hoping they will both come.'

Anna's face lit up with surprise and pleasure.

*

When the two pairs got to their homes, their reception

165

was very different. Anna waited until Rick had closed the door and then hugged him. 'Thank you. I know it's not easy for you.'

Rick held her as close as he could without hurting her. 'I guess I've got to get up with the times,' he whispered in her ear. 'If he's happy then I suppose that is the important thing.'

She pulled her face away, wanting to see his eyes. 'When did you decide?'

'Oh, I've just kept thinking about it,' Rick admitted. He stepped away from her. 'I guess it was Sol's funeral.' He stopped while he searched for the right words to express his feelings. 'It was the way he died. So quick. So final.' He shrugged his shoulders. 'It just made me rethink about the value of being together while we're alive. I'll give Ricardo a call. Invite him out for a beer. We'll talk about it then.'

Anna moved forward and kissed him in a way that said thank you for Ricardo and for being my husband.

*

After a journey made up mostly with expletives uttered by Phillippa as she battled with the old Mercury through the rutted roads, she finally slithered it to a halt at an awkward angle across the drive by braking too hard. She cut the engine and, with a final, 'Fuck this heap', got out in one movement and went to the house. Al sat for a moment and then sighed. He slid over to the driver's seat, started the engine and straightened the car in the drive. It was unnecessary to do it then but he was in no hurry to follow her into the house. Inside, he expected the silent treatment; she was probably already at her dressing table, brushing her bobbed hair furiously. But when he entered, Phillippa was standing a few yards inside the hall, waiting for him.

166

'You bastard,' she seethed. 'You did that deliberately to embarrass me.'

His arms hung limply by his sides as the words whipped over him with a storm force. He couldn't deny it and to give a reason would only provoke a long argument that he wasn't in the mood for. He walked passed her and headed for his study; somewhere in one of his cupboards he had a bottle of scotch, and he wanted that more than a fight.

Phillippa stood in disbelief as he passed, but then spun round and gripped his arm. 'Don't walk away from me!'

Al stopped and looked down at her hand in a way that made her let go. He looked up at her face and she saw steel in his eyes she had not seen before. 'Do you want a divorce?' he asked with a steady voice.

'What?' It was like the moment of dying when your whole life is supposed to flash before you. Phillippa saw her style of living and all the material things she had stacking up in front of her and then begin to sway. 'Of course not,' she said more quietly.

'Then shut the fuck up,' he said and went to his study. He closed the door quietly behind him, not giving her the satisfaction of knowing if he was upset or angry.

She stood motionless in a state of shock as she watched him walk away from her. She knew she had driven him to the edge this time and if she pushed him too far, it could so easily rebound on her; he could make her world come tumbling down. He had allowed her to build it and fashion it to her choice, but she suddenly realised for the first time that throughout their marriage, he had kept the gold out of her reach and she reflected on the old saying: 'He who held the gold could call the piper's tune'. When Al had closed the door, the anger began to return and she stomped up to the bedroom to begin brushing her hair furiously.

In his study, Al fished out a glass and the bottle of scotch and poured himself a liberal measure. He held it up in

167

front of his face: 'To you, Sol.' He sipped until he felt the liquid warming his insides. He sat in his chair and turned sideways to look out of the window – the snow was falling thicker and he didn't like the idea of being holed up in the house with Phillippa for a few days. He comforted himself with thoughts of what it would be like to be snowed in with Aritha and it drew him to a conclusion: he would have to get this sorted out, and soon.

12

A week before the Christmas festivities had begun, the golf club held its Christmas dinner and dance. The parking area and roads had been cleared and gritted, and small lights strung between the flagposts in front of the main entrance swayed precariously in the cold wind. More lights had been wired across the roof and round the gables to reflect the shape of the clubhouse and they stood out in the black night like illuminated pine Christmas trees. The members with their wives, husbands, live-in partners or 'just' friends, arrived in their expensive cars or hired, chauffeur-driven limousines or taxi cabs, and talked noisily as they entered the main hall. The men were dressed smartly in evening suits with black bow ties and the ladies were in their new dresses that they had spent hours selecting, with assurances that nobody else had bought similar. The younger ladies, with figures they were proud to show off, wore cocktail-type dresses that hugged their bodies and were low slung to reveal mesmerising cleavages. The older ladies wore more flouncy dresses that hid the unwanted curves and plump waistlines and displayed sparkling necklaces to attract the eye away from the sagging or scrawny necks. The men first made for the bar, gathering in groups of high and low handicaps, the way golfers sometimes do. The ladies' first port of call was the powder room, where they traded cheek kisses without touching with their lips and did little else except check that the hours of preparation were still intact. They talked all together and all at once, admiring this dress and that jewellery. When someone left, they said what they really thought about them.

A few days before, Rosemary had gone down with a heavy cold. Her nose was red with wiping and she lay in bed with balls of used tissues around her, looking like the untidy snow heaped outside. Under normal circumstances, Harry would have stayed with her, but that night was when his plan would be put into action. He had not told her about it – she would have strongly disapproved – so he made the excuse that he had promised Dinsdale he would make and serve the punch; that was the only bit of truth he told her. Rosemary was in no state to question him. Her mind was as muzzy as her nose and all she wanted was to sleep in a hope that in the morning her cold may have cleared, or at least relented somewhat.

Al had not mentioned it to Phillippa; they were still passing through a period of avoidance and silence. Even Christmas Day had not been discussed and he was beginning to wonder if it would pass like any other day. He dressed and drove off without a word, leaving her writing another letter; he'd never asked who the recipients were.

Rick and Anna arrived late. Anna was already dressed, as Rick, slow as usual, came out of the shower. When she twirled around to show off her new party dress, she squealed as she saw his ardour rising. She backed away, trying to ward him off with a wagging finger and a scolding voice that didn't sound too convincing. 'Now don't you even think of it. I don't want this dress creased.' But then she couldn't suppress her giggling as he pushed her over onto the bed.

Dinsdale busied himself by standing at the main door and greeting all the arrivals but he was becoming increasingly agitated and constantly looked at his watch.

170

Dinner was due to start soon and JDW, the guest of honour, hadn't arrived yet. He saw Harry and went over to him. 'Are you sure we should be doing this?' he queried for the hundredth time, the anxiety oozing out of every word.

'We are not doing anything,' Harry assured him, emphasising the 'we'. Dinsdale was momentarily confused and then nodded when he understood.

'Of course not,' he said with a short laugh. He touched his nose and then laughed again as he moved away. He had to remember not to talk with Harry again that evening.

Dinsdale went back to the front entrance and sighed twice with relief as he saw a stretch limo draw up outside. The first sigh was on seeing JDW get out and the second was for the fact his wife was not with him. When he had rung JDW and invited him, he had at first baulked at the idea, but when Dinsdale said he was to be the guest of honour – and that if he couldn't make it then he would invite the Mayor – JDW had quickly agreed, feeling elevated by the mention of the substitute. Dinsdale had casually mentioned that he could bring his wife, if he really felt he should, but JDW had jumped in and said his wife would be unable to attend. He had said it in a voice that betrayed relief even down a phone line.

Dinsdale opened the door to go out to greet him but he felt the cold wind whip past him, so he decided to hold the door from the inside and let the big man come to him. He held out his hand and prepared himself as the paw wrapped itself around it, but the grip was surprisingly light and brief. JDW was in too much of a hurry to get out of the cold and pour a few warming drinks inside him. He spoke as he walked passed. 'Seems like a lot of folks are here tonight.'

Dinsdale let the door swing shut and hurried after him. As instructed by Harry, a waiter stood by the door to the

171

main hall with a tray holding a single, large glass of Southern Comfort. JDW gulped some down. 'That's a friendly way of starting the evening,' he smiled back at Dinsdale and then set off into the mêlée of guests. Dinsdale didn't follow him; he looked back at the waiter and nodded. The waiter went to a side table, put another large glass of Southern Comfort on it and followed Dinsdale into the crowd. It was easy to locate the big man, who was pumping hands and slapping shoulders; he knew no one but he made them feel like he did. Dinsdale noticed his glass was almost empty and motioned the waiter forward. In a professional manner, the waiter took JDW's glass as he was shaking hands – it was a deft, practised movement, and JDW was hardly aware a full glass had been slipped into his hand.

The Wannabee Golf Club prided itself on providing sumptuous functions and this one was no exception. The dinner was extremely well organised, with superb food finely presented; no expense had been spared. After all, the members were paying enough for it. An army of waiters and waitresses moved efficiently up and down the columns of tables and served the food and wine in a way that did not interrupt conversations and the many jokes the men had been putting aside especially for this evening; everybody had to have a humorous story. On the top table, Dinsdale fussed until JDW told him to relax; everything was just fine, he assured him. The same waiter hung around the back of the table and gave JDW his personal attention, refilling his glass whenever he turned the other way to talk with someone down the table.

When everyone was fed and watered like horses, it came time for the speeches. Dinsdale spoke first, and after a brief welcome to all with the usual thanks to the people who had made it happen, he passed over to JDW. Before JDW stood, Dinsdale leaned over and asked him not to

172

mention the franchising and he nodded. 'Not the time or the place,' he agreed. His speech was very good, delivered in his slow Texan style, and his jokes were original and topical; he had paid a speechwriter a lot of bucks to prepare this one for him. When he sat down, he received generous applause – his jokes would be repeated for many weeks after in offices and bars.

A five-piece band played music in the main lounge and the people slowly drifted away from the tables in the restaurant area. The tunes had been carefully selected: to start with there were slower waltzes and shuffles to encourage people to dance, and a solo singer sang some Sinatra ballads – nobody wanted to shake their dinner around. But as the evening progressed, the tempo was upped in stages until the solo singer, casting his jacket aside, had them jiving around the floor to renditions of the faster numbers from the likes of Elvis, Eddie Cochrane and Bobby Darin.

Harry had taken his place by a side table, serving a mildly alcoholic, tropical fruit-flavoured punch which he had prepared himself. It was particularly popular with the ladies, and he was kept busy, ladling the punch into small rounded glasses with handles. Hidden behind the large punch bowl, he had a smaller bowl of straight Southern Comfort, and when the waiter looking after JDW brought back an empty glass, Harry half filled it with the punch, topping it up from the smaller bowl. The routine was going fine until Ellor Byrne, the ladies' captain, stopped at the table and looked at him suspiciously.

'What's in the punch?' she asked abruptly.

'Just a Harry Special of tropical fruits and a touch of crême de menthe for colouring.' Harry smiled as disarmingly as he could through gritted teeth.

She thought about it. 'I'll try one.' It was a demand rather than a request. As Harry took a glass and began to ladle the punch, she noticed the smaller bowl. 'And what's in there?'

Harry was about to say 'You don't want that', but he stopped himself and looked at her in a secretive way. 'That's the real expensive version. You know, real fruit, not canned juice.'

'Then I'll have that.' Again it was a demand.

Harry couldn't take the smile from his lips. 'Right you are.' He topped her glass up from the smaller bowl and handed it to her. 'I'd rather you didn't mention it to anyone. It's for the special guests like JDW.'

'But I am the Lady Captain,' she said, trying to glare down his smile. She sipped and sucked on her lips and sipped again. 'I must admit it does taste very good,' she conceded, and emptied the glass. 'Here, fill it up again.'

Harry did so and then tapped his nose. 'Not a word now.' She turned away without reply.

Louise came over to his table. Harry stepped back and held his arms wide with exaggerated admiration. 'My, you look beautiful tonight young lady. Who's the lucky fellow?'

She wrinkled her nose. 'No one that matters.'

'I can't believe that. Do you want some punch?'

'No,' she shook her head. 'I want a dance with someone who won't step all over my feet.'

'Who had you in mind?'

She laughed. 'Now don't play coy with me, Harry Menkowitch. And I know your wife isn't here.'

'I'd like to but I really can't.' He looked around to see that no one was in earshot. 'I'm doing this as a favour for Dinsdale,' he said in a hushed voice.

'For Dinsdale?' Her eyes squinted with suspicion. 'What are you up to?'

He shrugged. 'Me? Nothing.'

She came forward and leaned over the table. 'I don't

care what it is. When you've finished you dance with me. Okay?'

'Even if it's the last waltz. And it could well be.'

She gave him another funny look and drifted away.

By late evening, all the punch had been consumed and the smaller bowl had been emptied, not only by JDW but Ellor Byrne, who had returned several times. With each glass, Harry altered the mix in favour of the Southern Comfort. The last time she came back, she didn't say anything and just held out her glass – she couldn't trust her lips to move as she wanted them. Harry moved across the room looking for JDW. He wasn't difficult to find, he just followed the noise. He was gyrating in a strange fashion in the middle of a cleared space, with the other dancers wary of his flying, high-heeled cowboy boots. Harry stood and watched with amazement as Ellor Byrne was being swirled round in the grip of JDW's huge paw and her dress was flaring out to expose dimpled, fat knees. Harry averted his eyes and saw Dinsdale looking at him with concern. He nodded sideways with his head and Dinsdale moved away. Feeling that Armageddon wasn't too far away, he sought the sanctuary of his office and waited, still unsure and wondering if he was doing the right thing. Harry looked to the doors at the far end and nodded to Al and Rick who reciprocated the nod and went into the adjoining room.

Anna had noticed and came over to him. 'What are you three getting up to?' she asked.

Harry shook his head in an innocent fashion. 'Nothing at all my dear, just a little surprise for our guest.'

She looked across at JDW still heaving his heavy body around in an attempt to keep up with the music, but somehow he had lost the rhythm. 'Ah hah. What sort of surprise? Rick hasn't said anything to me.'

'No, it's a secret.' He wished Anna would move away.

Rick had signalled from the doors that they were ready. 'If you stand over there, you'll get a better view,' he suggested.

Anna finally moved away, but not before she gave him a last suspicious look.

Harry sucked in his breath; what were the words of that Elvis song that the solo singer had sung earlier? 'It's now or never.' He moved over to the band and said something to the leader, who deftly brought the current tune to an end. Everyone stopped, wondering what had happened as Harry moved to the centre.

'Folks,' he said into a hand microphone, noting that JDW and Ellor Byrne were still on the floor. 'For our guest of honour tonight, JDW, who I'm sure you've all noticed by now...' Cue ripples of laughter. '...we have prepared a little surprise, so if you could make some space out here.' The dancers began to withdraw and Ellor Byrne staggered to one side, not quite sure who or where she was. JDW stood tall, but a slight swaying betrayed the amount of Southern Comfort swilling around inside him. Harry fetched a chair and made him sit down. 'Now JDW, just for you!' The far doors swung open and Al and Rick appeared behind a large cake sat on a board with rollers. It was round, about five feet across and four feet high and made out of pink-painted cardboard, but with real icing trimmings. They wheeled it forward until it was in front of JDW. He was breathing heavily from his exertions and his bootlace tie was askew; he squinted his eyes to focus. He started to stand but Harry, poised at his shoulder, eased him back onto the chair. Harry nodded to the band leader and the band started playing *The Stars and Stripes*. As the first notes struck up, the lid of the cake flew off and Felicia, dressed in a skimpy red, white and blue sequin costume and fishnet tights, stood up with her hands raised to the ceiling holding two American flags. Some of the ladies 'oohed' with hands to their mouths, and the men smiled as their eyes travelled down Felicia's shapely body to the fishnet tights. Few noticed the sparkling tiara on her head. She smiled in a nervous sort of way and then, gathering her courage, opened a door in the front of the cake. She stepped out and danced across to JDW, jumping into his lap with her arms about his neck. After delivering him a kiss, she shouted, 'Happy Christmas, JDW!' Even Harry was surprised when JDW tilted his head back, yelled 'Yeehaaa' and threw his arms around her. The room was lit with flashes as Al and Rick clicked away with their cameras; JDW, through the haze of whiskey and Felicia's perfume, thought it was just part of the festivities.

Harry had withdrawn quietly to one side, not wishing to be captured on film. He was just congratulating himself on a successful operation when Ellor Byrne, with a shrieking 'whoop', half ran and half fell across the floor and dumped herself on JDW's other knee. The seismic shock trembled through his giant frame and his face was painted with confusion as Ellor lifted her skirt to reveal an ample thigh. The ladies gasped and the men looked away, suddenly feeling sick, but from a point right in front of them, Al and Rick dutifully carried on snapping.

The party ended quickly after that, with the members having plenty to talk about on their way home. Felicia freed herself from JDW's clutches and ran off, while JDW stood, almost reeling on his feet, wondering what the hell had been happening and where was the angel with the fishnets. As he stood, Ellor rolled off his knee to the floor and tried vainly to lever her body from the ground. In the end, she lay back and watched the room revolve around her.

'Where's Dinsdale?' JDW growled, not knowing why he wanted him.

'He had to leave early,' Harry said at his side. 'Your

limousine is outside to take you to your hotel. I think the party's over.' Harry nodded to a couple of the staff and they guided him to the door, careful to remain out of reach. 'I hope you enjoyed it,' Harry called after him, but JDW was still in a mist of too much alcohol to hear him.

From his office, Dinsdale had heard the noise and when the band struck up *The Stars and Stripes* he clasped his hands to his head – it was too late now. His head snapped up when he heard JDW's 'Yeehaaa' and the ensuing commotion – he feared the worse and buried his head again. Negative thoughts flashed through his mind and he began to wonder what other job he could find at his age; perhaps he would have to leave town. It suddenly went quiet and he slowly lifted his head. He wanted to see what was happening but was afraid to venture out in case JDW was looking for him. He waited a suitable time and then heard the band playing a waltz. He rose slowly and peered out of his door – the passageway was clear and he walked slowly down towards the main hall.

When the hall had pretty much cleared, Louise appeared at Harry's side. 'So nothing's going to happen, huh? What do you call that?'

Harry looked sideways at her with an innocent expression and then down at the prostrate Ellor Byrne. 'Oh, just some folks enjoying themselves.'

'Have you forgotten something?'

Harry caught the glint in her eyes. He went over to the band who were beginning to pack away their instruments. He spoke quietly to the band leader and slipped him some money. Harry went back to Louise. 'A promise is a promise,' he said as the band began to play a waltz. 'May I have this last dance?' he asked, bowing from the waist.

Louise curtsied and they then began to dance together in a wide circle so that they skirted the prone figure of Ellor Byrne. Al came across with Rick and Anna and they all began to waltz; Al held his arms around an imaginary figure – he wasn't sure if it was Phillippa or Aritha.

As Dinsdale entered the hall, he came up abruptly as he saw the strange sight of five people dancing and something lying in the middle of the floor. He made his way over and stood with hands on hips until Harry noticed him.

'So what's going on?' Dinsdale asked. His voice was loud and the band stopped playing.

Harry nodded over to the band leader and, for a second time, they began to pack away their instruments. 'The last waltz,' Harry explained. 'It's customary.'

Dinsdale was about to say something else but he was distracted by a soft, snoring sound from the floor. He gazed down at the sleeping Ellor Byrne. 'What's she doing there?' Dinsdale enquired.

Harry shrugged. 'Punch drunk by the look of her.'

Dinsdale avoided the obvious question; he didn't want to know the answer. Instead he asked, 'Where's her husband?'

'In Boston on bank business,' Louise offered.

'And probably with his secretary,' Rick added, but received a dig in the ribs from his wife.

Dinsdale looked at him briefly and then across to the members of staff who were clearing away the debris of the evening. 'Will one of you call for a cab for Mrs Byrne?' He looked back. 'We can't leave her lying here.'

'She looks peaceful enough,' Harry said with a smile. 'I don't fancy waking her.'

'Or trying to lift her,' Al added.

Dinsdale ignored the banter. 'Harry, can we have a few words?' He walked away to a safe distance and when Harry came up to him, he asked in a strained voice, 'So what happened?'

Harry patted his shoulder in a reassuring way that made

179

Dinsdale feel uncomfortable. 'Everything went perfect. In fact, it was better than I anticipated. Wait until you see the photographs.'

Dinsdale felt relieved and suspicious at the same time. 'You have them?'

'No. Of course not,' Harry said. 'I know a place that will be open tomorrow. It'll process them in a few hours. I'll bring them in Monday morning.'

Dinsdale relaxed a little. 'Do you think it will work?'

'It's now up to you,' Harry said, emphasising the 'you'.

When they rejoined the others, Ellor Byrne had been woken and helped to her feet. She looked around with misted eyes trying hard to focus, as if she were in a strange place and shouldn't be there. At that moment, two waiters came over and looped her arms over their shoulders and, staggering under her weight, half walked, half dragged her across the floor towards the main entrance for a cab.

'Well, I'm for home,' Harry said. 'It's been a long night.'

'Any chance of a lift?' Louise asked with a smile and big eyes.

'Where's your friend?' Harry queried.

Louise wrinkled her nose. 'Long gone,' was all she said.

'Does anyone else want a lift?' Harry offered, but they all shook their heads.

As they walked out to his car, the wind whipped into them and another light fall of snow had begun.

'You seemed afraid to take me home alone,' Louise said as she slid into the car and quickly closed the door, shivering against the sudden cold.

'Just being courteous,' Harry said as he started the engine.

'It didn't sound like it to me.' Louise sounded as if she were pouting in the darkness of the car as Harry steered out onto the main highway. 'You can come in for a coffee and tell me what little game you have been playing tonight.'

'I'm afraid I can't,' Harry said. 'Rosemary is down with a heavy cold. I didn't want to leave her this evening so I ought to get back to her.'

'Is that the truth?' Louise questioned.

'The whole and nothing but.' Harry patted her knee. 'Anyway, it's better that you don't know for the time being. I'll explain it all to you later.'

When he got home, Harry looked in on Rosemary who was fast asleep. Her breathing was light but rasped through her lips, and it made him think of Ellor Byrne; he smiled as he went to the spare bedroom. That was some successful night, he grinned to himself with satisfaction.

Al returned to a darkened house and slipped quietly up to his bedroom. He could just hear Phillippa breathing and so he undressed in the dark. He slipped into his bed and had just relaxed his head in the softness of his pillow when Phillippa spoke out of the darkness. 'I didn't know the diner stayed open 'till this late.'

Al sighed. 'I haven't been to the diner,' he said without offering an explanation. A loving wife would have asked where else he had been, but as she wasn't, she turned over and went to sleep. Al wished she had asked him.

*

On the Monday, Harry allowed himself the luxury of another hour in bed to get over a Sunday filled with questions from Rosemary, which he answered truthfully, if not a little scantily. When he finally rose and dressed, he went to his son's shop. He wanted to see if Dave and his family were coming for Christmas Day, and to check the progress of a necklace Harry had specially designed for Rosemary that Dave was making. The shop had maintained the same appearance it had since Harry's father had first opened it. The counter bounded three sides and was constructed of dark oak panels with glass tops; with the thick pile, blue carpet, it gave the aura of 'expensive'. The walls were lined with glass showcases, dimly lit from concealed lights that spotlighted the jewellery with pencil-thin beams which made the encrusted sapphires, diamonds and emeralds sparkle with fire. When he entered, the familiar faces of the two staff looked up and chorused 'Hi Harry'. They had worked for him for years and he never stood on the ceremony of them calling him anything else except 'Harry'.

'Decided you prefer work and are coming back?' a tall, bald-headed man asked, as he always did when Harry paid a visit.

Harry grinned as usual. 'And put up with you again?' was his usual reply.

The other server was a woman in her sixties who, as far as Harry could remember, always wore a black dress with a wide white collar and a simple pearl necklace. She came round the counter and offered her cheek for a kiss. 'You just can't stay away from me, Harry.'

'Now that's the truth,' he said, delivering the awaited kiss.

He peered passed her and through a glass partition to the work room, where his son was studying one of his creations through an eyepiece. It had been one of Dave's first suggestions to put in the glass panel so that customers could actually see their orders being made. Harry had baulked at the idea at first because he liked the privacy of the back room, but he eventually saw sense in it and finally conceded. He had to admit it added a personal touch to the business even though he felt like a monkey in a cage; he once put up a 'Please do not feed' sign and it was the one time that Dave had got angry with him. It was about that time that he decided to retire; he realised that Dave had the skill for making jewellery and a better business head for running things. He tapped on the window and when Dave looked up and waved he went in through the door.

'Checking up on me?' Dave asked in an amiable way.

'I'm from the Department of Quality Assurance,' Harry said, looking over his shoulder and letting out an admiring whistle as he saw all the items on shelves ready for collection. 'I've had a complaint that you're making duplicates.'

'Yeah, right,' Dave laughed. 'I wish I had the time to make them.'

Harry stood back. 'Busy time then.'

'You know it always is at this time of year,' Dave sighed. 'I wish people would order earlier. I'm working near sixteen hours a day, seven days a week.'

'They never did and they never will,' Harry said, moving along a bench and looking at several bracelets and necklaces in various stages of completeness. 'Have you finished that little thing for your mother?'

Dave got up, opened a drawer and took out a small box. 'That "thing" was finished over week ago. I gave it priority attention.' He eased the crimson velvet box open and passed it to his father. Harry studied the intricate design he had drawn himself – it was a silver bracelet of entwined roses, and at the end of each stem, the flower bud was shaped by small rubies; at spaces up the stems, small diamonds traced their curves with sparkling leaves.

'Think she'll like it?' Harry asked, turning it in his fingers.

'A Menkowitch original? How can she not?' Dave smiled. 'A team effort, Harry,' and he slipped his arm easily round his father's shoulders. Using his father's first name had the same effect again and Harry felt close to his son.

'Is it still okay for Christmas?'

'Of course,' his son's smile turned into a grin. 'You ask me that every time you see me. And Pam is happy with it,' he said, pre-empting the next question.

'Good,' Harry said, replacing the bracelet in its box. 'I'll write you a cheque. Your mother checks the Visa statements. How much was it?'

Dave tugged at his chin and kept a straight face. 'To you, let's say fifteen hundred dollars. Family discount included, of course.'

Harry looked at him keenly. 'Let's say eight hundred and forget the discount.'

Dave sucked in his breath. 'You drive a hard bargain, Harry Menkowitch. The cost of high-grade silver, diamonds and rubies is on the up but seeing as you did the design, let's say a round thousand.'

Harry wrote out a cheque for a thousand dollars. 'Can I have it wrapped?'

Dave punched him playfully on the shoulder. It was another custom of the firm never to hide beauty in paper. 'With Christmas bears, I suppose.'

'I don't suppose you have time for a late lunch?' Harry asked, ignoring the comment about the bears.

'Nope,' Dave shrugged in a tired way. 'Pam packs me some sandwiches and a flask of coffee and I barely have time for that. I must think about retirement some day.'

'Sure.' Harry couldn't conceal a smirk. 'In about twenty or thirty years when you have that young tiger of yours trained up.'

'Funny. I was thinking about that,' Dave commented quietly. 'You followed Grandad into the business, I followed you, but Rob didn't. Perhaps we ought to think of having more kids to make sure one follows me.'

'I'd have a word with Pam about that,' Harry advised. 'She's just started work again.'

'I know,' Dave said, with a trace of concern in his voice. 'I was wondering about that too.'

*

184

When Harry left he went straight to the golf club. He had the photos and was eager to see Dinsdale's reaction; he was in for a surprise. When he entered Felicia's office he expected a sheepish look from her but her face was wreathed with smiles when she greeted him.

'You were just great at the dance,' he said jovially.

'So everyone keeps saying,' she said, showing extensive white teeth. 'I worried about it all over the weekend, but this morning everyone has said how they enjoyed it, especially the men. But then I suppose they would. But even the ladies said it was a good idea for JDW. But I wasn't so sure some weren't being catty.'

It was only when she paused for breath that Harry got a word in. 'I must admit that you took my breath away.'

'That's just what the men said,' she cut back in again. 'But I'm not sure how they meant it. I had a few offers which I turned down, of course.'

'Did Dinsdale appreciate your effort for him?' Harry asked carefully.

The smile faded and her face showed disappointment. 'That's the funny thing. He hasn't mentioned it. He seems preoccupied. He's hardly been out of his office.'

'Can I go in?'

'Oh sure, he'll be glad to see you,' the smile returned to her lips.

Harry went into Dinsdale's office. He was sitting with his head bowed, looking at a blank pad on his desk, and he spoke without looking up. 'Not now, Felicia.'

Harry closed the door and moved to the front of the desk, placing the photographs in a neat pile where Dinsdale could see them. He focused on them and his head snapped up. 'I'm sorry, Harry, I didn't know it was you.' He glanced at the pile of photos and seemed reluctant to look at them. He brought his hands together and rubbed the palms against each other slowly. 'I have been wondering if this has been such a good idea.'

Harry sat down and ran a finger along his lips. 'Why don't you look at them?'

Dinsdale lowered his hands and took the top one. He studied it for a brief second before his narrow eyes widened considerably. 'That's Felicia!'

'What a good girl she is,' Harry enthused quickly. 'You know, she'd do anything to help you.'

'But that's Felicia!' Dinsdale repeated, his cheeks turning a definite purple. 'What is she doing on JDW's lap? And look at that costume!'

'Beautiful, isn't she. What a gal.'

'But you didn't tell me.'

'You said you didn't want to know.'

'But I wouldn't have let her.'

'But she said she wanted to.'

'She did?'

'She did, and just for you.'

Dinsdale calmed a shade on the Beaufort scale, edging from force ten down to six. He started to leaf through the other photos. 'My God! That's Ellor Byrne. Did she agree too?'

'Ah. Well, not exactly. She just got into the act.'

'And look at JDW's eyes. He's drunk!'

Harry sighed loudly. 'Look Dinsdale, I think you are forgetting why we did this.'

Dinsdale looked at him through slitted eyes. 'We?'

'Well, you,' Harry corrected deliberately.

Dinsdale thought about it, dropping the pictures onto his desk. Then he picked them up and went through them again. 'Yes. Quite.' he said rather slowly. 'I suppose JDW's wife would not be very impressed with these.'

'Precisely.' Harry was glad he was beginning to remember why the pictures had been taken. 'And there's an added bonus.'

186

'There is?'

'Ellor Byrne,' Harry reminded him. 'You know – that constant thorn in your side? Do you remember her on the dancefloor?'

'Yes,' Dinsdale said quietly, and then more loudly, 'Yes!'

Harry sat back with relief. 'I think you can kiss the franchising goodbye. And I wouldn't forget Felicia in all this. None of it would have happened without her help. She was very good.'

Dinsdale glanced back at a picture of Felicia standing with arms outstretched as she rose from the cake, and his mouth began to water. 'I see what you mean.' He coughed to clear his throat. 'I see what you mean. I'll have to thank her.'

'A special Christmas treat,' Harry said casually. 'Like a bonus.'

Dinsdale coughed again. 'Yes, of course. I was thinking along those lines myself.'

'Glad to hear it,' Harry agreed, standing up. 'I'll leave you to do what's necessary.'

Dinsdale didn't reply; he was looking through the photos again. Harry went in to see Felicia. He winked as he passed through her office. 'He's very impressed,' he told her and paused at the door. 'He said something about a bonus.'

When Harry had gone, Felicia checked herself in her compact mirror, touched her hair unnecessarily and then went in to see Dinsdale. 'You want to see me?'

Dinsdale looked up at her and then again at the picture of her in the skimpy costume. 'Oh yes,' he said. He got up and came round his desk. He slipped his hands round her waist and then eased them over her bottom. 'Is your door locked?'

Felicia pulled away from him. 'No. I thought you wanted to talk about a bonus.'

187

'A bonus?'

'Harry said you were going to give me a bonus,' she said with a raised voice.

'Oh yes. I was thinking of a little something. Just to show my gratitude.'

'A little something! Huh!'

'Well, more than a little,' he corrected hastily. 'I ... er ... I don't suppose you've still got that costume?'

Felicia turned on her heels and went back to her office, slamming the door behind her.

Dinsdale suddenly felt deflated. He eased himself back and sat on the front of his desk. 'So Harry,' he thought, 'you've played a double game getting Felicia involved.' His head began to fill with negative thoughts again. One thing was for sure – he was going to find a way to get rid of Harry. But then his thoughts lightened – a little matter of a phone call to JDW.

*

When Harry got home, Rosemary was looking decidedly better – her nose had almost assumed its normal colour and her face was literally beaming. 'I have some news for you,' she said, slipping her arms round him. 'Rob phoned this morning. He's coming home for Christmas.'

She noticed Harry's smile did not crease his face as it normally did. 'Did he mention needing money?'

'Harry!'

Harry shrugged. 'That's usually the reason, isn't it?'

'Harry,' she said again, this time with softness in her voice. 'You think of that boy more than you care to admit.' She touched his shoulder briefly. 'It'll be good to have the whole family together.'

'It will at that,' Harry allowed his smile to broaden. 'Who knows, perhaps he's got himself a job.'

188

13

Rick eased his car by the kerb and noticed his son's car parked in front of him. This wasn't a meeting he was looking forward to, and when he had wavered at the last minute, Anna had pushed him out of the door and insisted he go – and she was usually right. Rick had selected the bar – he didn't want Ricardo choosing some gay place. It was a quiet bar downtown he had visited a few times and he stood before its neon sign, looking up at the sky. There were no stars showing – perhaps another fall of snow was imminent because the wind was certainly colder. He sighed and went in. Ricardo was sat at the far end, near a pool table, and far enough from the bar to ensure some privacy. He stood up and came forward to greet him.

'Hi Pops.'

Rick took his hand and patted his arm. 'Good to see you, son.' He tried to sound amiable.

'Let me get you a drink. A Bud?'

Rick nodded. 'That'll do fine. I want it in a glass.'

When they were seated, there was a short period of silence that almost became embarrassing, but Ricardo conveniently bridged the gap. 'So, what did you want to talk about? Christmas? Have I got a job yet? Or did you want to talk about my flatmate?'

Rick could easily have taken offence, but Ricardo smiled broadly to show he didn't mean any harm. 'All of those,

I suppose.' He still felt uneasy. 'How about Christmas for starters? What are you doing then?'

Ricardo sipped from his bottle. 'Not much, actually. Just another quiet day.'

Rick coughed lightly and moved in his chair. 'Your mother and me, of course, would like you to come round for Christmas Day. It would be nice being together. It is a special day. Once a year and all that.'

He was rambling on, not knowing where to stop, and Ricardo cut in to help him. 'Is that just me?'

'No,' Rick dragged out the word. 'You can bring your friend.'

Ricardo leaned back and studied his father's face. 'Do you want him to come?'

'If I'm to be truthful, no, but your mother feels it is right.'

'And how are you going to handle it?' Ricardo questioned.

Rick seemed lost for a moment. 'Look son. You have to understand, it's not exactly what a father expects his son to do. Parents tend to think of wives and grandchildren and things like that.'

'I guess,' Ricardo said quietly. 'But I can't help it. I don't know why I'm like this. Something just grew differently in me.' He wondered if he was getting through because his father's face remained blank. 'Look Dad, perhaps it would help if you didn't think so graphically. We don't speak in a feminine way and we don't wear women's clothes. Just look upon Joshua as a friend of mine.'

Rick was surprised that his son had spotted his problem; that had been it all along, but every time he thought about them together, the pictures had made him turn his mind away. 'I'll try,' he conceded.

'And I have a job,' Ricardo said, moving away from the subject.

'You do? That's good,' Rick's face brightened.

'Not really. It's only as a packer down at Sturgess's over on the east side, but it earns a few dollars.'

'You're capable of a lot better.' He saw a look of disappointment in his son's face. 'But it's a start. You know, I started as a sweeper in a butcher's shop.'

'You did? You never told me that.'

'Well, it was a part-time job while I was in college. As you said, it brought in a few dollars. I had to be there at six in the morning to sweep the place out and sprinkle fresh sawdust over the floor and do a few other odd jobs. Then I went to college and returned in the evening to help clean down the chopping blocks and bag up all the bones and waste meat which was sold for people's dogs.'

Ricardo pulled a face. 'Sounds gruesome.'

'It was.' Rick thought back to those times. 'But you learnt to switch your mind off.' He laughed and thought, 'I've got to learn to do that again,' but he didn't say it. 'What does your friend do?'

'Joshua,' Ricardo reminded him. 'He's in fashion. Women's clothes. It's full of queers.' Rick spluttered into his beer, which made his son laugh. 'So it is. They have a talent for it.'

'I'll take your word for it. Have you thought about it?' He regretted it as soon as he said the words.

Ricardo's face shaded a little and his smile disappeared. 'I don't see myself like them. They're so overt. Joshua and I are just very good friends.'

Rick realised that Christmas Day was going to be difficult; he had to get the pictures out of his head. 'Do you want another beer?'

'Sure. Do you want to shoot some pool? The table's clear.'

Rick looked round at the table. 'I used to be pretty good when I was your age. There used to be a pool table in the college restroom.'

191

'I'm learning more about you,' Ricardo smiled. 'I'll set the balls up while you get us a beer and then you can tell me more about your misspent youth.'

Rick had a better feeling inside when he went to the bar and ordered their drinks. When he returned, Ricardo had set up the balls and passed his father a cue.

'Is this the bent one?' Rick asked, holding it up and sighting down the cue.

'Of course it is,' his son smiled a reply. 'Just in case you are as good as you say you are.'

'Were,' Rick corrected him. He chalked the end of the cue and lined up behind the cue ball. 'You don't mind if I start?' he asked as he sent the ball into the pack. He stood back with satisfaction as two balls disappeared. He moved round to the side of the table and eyed a ball near the corner pocket. 'You know, this brings back some warm memories.' He pocketed the ball and admired the way the cue ball screwed back to centre table. 'I haven't lost my touch. I used to subsidise my allowance by taking on all-comers at college.'

Ricardo watched his father smoothly work his way through the balls and began to see another man. He wondered where he had been through his younger years. 'Hey Pops,' he called out, 'leave me something to play with.'

Rick stood back while he chalked his cue and looked across at his son. 'Okay,' he said with a grin and then bent over the table. He hit the ball softly to kiss the eight-ball and position the cue ball hard against a cushion, leaving no shot.

Ricardo came to the table. 'Thanks a million.' He miscued his shot and Rick quickly cleared the table.

Rick supped his beer while Ricardo set up the balls again.

'How about a little wager?' Ricardo asked as he stood back.

'You can't afford it,' Rick said.

'Five bucks a game. I can afford that.'

Rick shrugged. 'Okay. But I must warn you – when there's money at stake, I don't play for fun.'

Ricardo moved to the table. 'I'll break.' He hit the ball hard and saw two balls disappear; the rest were scattered to nice positions.

Rick sat at a side table drinking his beer and watching his son finish the fourth game – he had won three in a row. 'Do you know what the penalty is for hustling your father?'

Ricardo went to the bar and ordered two more beers. He came back and put the glasses on the table as he sat down. 'That's fifteen dollars. Do you want to quit while you're down?' His grin showed he meant no offence.

Rick leafed out three notes and passed them across. 'I'm not a quitter but the years have taught me to know when I'm bettered. You played some good pool there.'

Ricardo lifted his glass to his father. 'Thanks for this evening, Dad; we must do it more often.'

'When you're short of a few bucks, you mean?' Rick chuckled.

'No.' Ricardo sounded serious, 'When I'm short of seeing you.'

'I'll drink to that,' Rick said as he raised his glass.

*

On Christmas Eve, Al went to the diner for lunch; he ordered his usual scrambled eggs, bacon and toast with a large black coffee. It was a quiet time, with only one other customer – a guy in denim and a white baseball cap worn back to front – sat at the far end. Aritha was glad he had come in. Their affair by proxy had been improving since the picnic and she held secret hopes that one day

193

Phillippa would overstep the mark and he would turn it into something more real. When she served his lunch, she stood in front of him, watching as he carefully forked the egg into his mouth. 'So, what are you doing tomorrow?'

He rocked his head from side to side. 'I really don't know.'

'You haven't discussed it?' she asked, surprised.

This time he shook his head. 'I don't even know if she's got me a present.'

'Al, that's ludicrous. Are you telling me you two are not talking at all?' Inside her, she felt hope rising.

Al ate some toast and she waited for him to swallow. 'Only when it is necessary. I don't quite know what has happened.'

Aritha paused and thought about her next words; she and Al had always been open with each other. 'Do you think she is having an affair?'

Al shrugged as if it were a small matter. 'Possibly.'

'Don't you mind?' Aritha was again surprised by the matter-of-fact way he said it.

Al didn't answer. He looked as if he had remembered something and reached into his pocket. 'Here, this is for Christmas.' He passed over a small, dark blue, velvet box.

Aritha had wondered if he would buy her something – she had bought him a present and tucked it under the counter just in case he did. She slid it out and across the counter. 'I got you something too,' she smiled. 'Just a small thing.'

'You first,' he smiled.

She opened the box slowly and her eyes widened quickly. 'Oh my, a Menkowitch watch. Oh, Al. That's expensive.'

He shook his head. 'Harry gave me a special price,' he said, trying to scale it down. He guessed from her face that she had only bought him something small. He reached

194

across and took it out of the box, fastening the gold band round her wrist. 'I noticed you never wore a watch.'

She held it up and studied the pearl face with minute numbering, noticing how the light caught the sculptured gold casing. 'Oh, Al, it's so beautiful.' Her face then slanted towards an embarrassed look. 'I haven't got you anything like this.'

'I'm glad you haven't. It wouldn't look good on my wrist,' Al laughed, trying to ease her. He opened the green-coloured paper with decorated trees and stars and 'Happy Christmas' printed at angles. Inside there was a slender box that contained a stainless steel pen with his name engraved along the side that had cost her five bucks extra. 'That is just perfect,' he said, reading his name. 'It's the sort of thing I've never got round to buying myself.'

'I thought I would buy you something,' she explained, 'that wasn't obvious. You know, like a tie.'

He understood and stood up from his stool and leaned across to kiss her. She slipped her hand round his neck so that the intended peck became a full kiss on the lips. The guy in the denim called up from the other end. 'Hey! Does that only come with the scrambled eggs?'

*

At about that same time, Harry was studying the tall Christmas tree he had placed in the corner of the room in a large, green plastic pot and had spent over an hour decorating. He gave it the same attention and designer eye he would have given to a piece of jewellery. Rosemary occasionally looked into the room, smiled and left without a word. It would look as beautiful as it always did – it was his little job for Christmas. He switched on the lights, stood back and, after adjusting a streamer of tinsel, was satisfied. He switched off the lights, called to Rosemary

195

and stood in the centre of the room. She came in and slipped a hand round his waist and squeezed him gently.

'That's lovely, Harry,' and rewarded him with a kiss on the cheek. 'Really lovely.' She sighed as it brought back all the Christmases they had spent in that house.

'Ah, wait a minute.' He slipped away from her hand and switched on the lights.

Her hand went to her mouth – he had positioned the lights carefully so that they caught the silver and gold streamers and glinted off stars hidden in the branches. Suddenly, it had been transformed into sparkling life. 'Watch this,' he said, and took out a fan from behind an armchair. He placed it near the tree and switched it on – its gentle breeze moved the branches and it became a motion of light.

Rosemary began to laugh. 'That's wonderful, but we can't have a fan on in December.'

He slipped his arm round her. 'I know. I just wanted you to see the effect.' He looked down at her face but she was looking past him.

'There's a cab in the drive. It must be Rob,' and she left him to hurry to the door.

Harry watched her and then looked out of the window and then back to the tree. He shrugged to himself. 'Well, it was good while it lasted.' And he went outside after Rosemary.

Rob was taking his case out of the trunk as Rosemary came up at a half run and her embrace took him back a step. 'Hey Mom!' They kissed and then she quickly pulled back.

'When did you grow that beard?'

'Oh, a while ago. Let me look at you,' and he held her at arm's length. He then saw Harry approaching. 'Dad!' He let Rosemary go and shook his father's hand vigorously. 'It's good to see you.'

Before Harry could say anything, the cab driver coughed; Christmas Eve was a busy day for him. Rob heard the prompt and said, 'Can you pay him?' Harry was about to say something again, but Rob laughed and took a wallet from his back pocket. 'Just joking.' Harry noticed a thick wad of notes protruding from the wallet.

After paying off the cab, they went inside and Rob had hardly put down his case when his mother ushered him into the lounge. 'Come see this.'

Rob watched the moving lights. 'Dad's tree. You still do it.' He put his arm round Harry's shoulder. 'Like old times.' Then he noticed the fan. 'A fan in December?'

'Just for effect,' were Harry's first words to his son. He switched it off and put it away. The tree stilled. 'So how long are you staying here?'

'Oh, Harry,' Rosemary flapped her hands. 'He's just in the door and you ask him when he's going. Come into the kitchen, I've got some coffee ready.'

Rob put his hands round his mother's waist and led her out of the room. 'Dark and strong as I like it.'

'As you like it.'

Harry stood for a moment looking at the tree; Rob had called it 'Dad's tree' and his feeling of reservation slipped away – it was good to have him home. He went out to the kitchen and slipped his hands in his pockets as he leaned against the doorway. Rob was seated at the table sipping coffee. He looked a lot older – he guessed the beard did that a bit – and his face was leaner and etched with lines. A hint of grey was flecked in his hair above his ears.

'So how are things going?' Harry asked when Rosemary paused from an endless list of questions to pour more coffee.

Rob's eyes moved to his. 'Pretty good. I got into computer graphics. I've done a lot of work for Disney and Fox and Universal. I have a small set-up with six guys working for

197

me. We're into TV advertising as well. It's going good.' He saw a smile in his father's face. 'You'd be proud of me, Dad.'

'I am,' Harry said simply.

Rob put down his cup and went over to Harry. 'I know I don't write or call. There have been some rough times. Getting it set up and all. At one time I nearly went under but now it's coming together.' He studied his father's face. 'It's been like you and your jewellery. I wanted you to see the finished product.' He ran out of explanation.

'I'd like to see it.'

'That's something I was going to mention.' Rob's smile was weak and unsure; he was waiting for a sign of approval, but Harry's face was set and his eyes were probing, as if checking for the truth. 'I have this big place by the beach. I want you and Mom to come out in the Spring. Stay a while.'

Harry relented. 'We would like to.' He looked to Rosemary, who smiled in agreement. He touched his son's shoulder. 'I'm glad you've found what you wanted.'

Rob moved forward and surprised him by wrapping his arms round him in a hug. 'I know you wanted me in the firm but it wasn't for me.' He leaned his head away. 'But it shows I have inherited your talents. I just use them in a different way.'

'It's good to know there's something of me in you,' Harry smiled.

'More than you realise.'

'Sit down and drink your coffee,' Rosemary ordered, 'before you start me weeping. Now,' she said as Rob settled. 'Tell me all about it from the beginning.'

'Well,' Rob thought for a moment. 'I was born at an early age.'

Rosemary slapped his wrist playfully. 'You know what I mean.'

Rob gave them a potted history and somewhere in it he casually mentioned a girl. They waited for him to finish and then Rosemary asked the question that Harry knew she would.

'So this girl, who is she?'

Rob chuckled; he also guessed she would pick up on his comment about a girl, no matter how brief it had been. 'Her name is Miriam. We met when we were doing a shoot for a soap advert. She had to lather her face and say how creamy it felt. The soap was computer generated and it spoke to her.'

He paused and Rosemary made a clucking sound with her tongue. 'And?'

'And I asked her out and we've been going steady for, oh, about year or so.'

'Why didn't you bring her here for Christmas?' Rosemary asked.

Rob shuffled in his chair a little awkwardly. 'About six months ago she moved in with me.' He looked to his parents, and while he detected a little reservation in his mother's eyes, Harry just smiled. It didn't bother him. 'Her parents aren't too happy with the arrangement. They're a little puritan in their outlook, but she's twenty-five and old enough to make her own decisions.' Rob relaxed when his mother refrained from comment. 'I wanted her to come and she did too, but she decided she ought to stay with her parents.'

'Well, that's nice,' Rosemary said, taking the girl's side. 'It shows she's had a good upbringing.'

Rob exchanged a humorous glance with his father. 'I guess so.'

'Perhaps you'd like to unpack,' Harry suggested. 'Your mother has spent a lot of time preparing your old room.'

'I bet it's just the same as the day I left,' Rob chuckled softly.

'No it's not,' Rosemary said with mild indignation. 'I changed the curtains. They were getting faded.' She wasn't quite sure what Harry and her son found amusing from her comment.

14

Christmas happens in different ways for different people. Some celebrate it as it's meant to be – going to church and then a quiet festivity at home – but most prefer the commercial idea and use it to invade each other's homes. They drink their drinks and eat hot chestnuts or savoury things and give presents which require a smile and words of gratitude, regardless of the usefulness of the gift. It is a time for giving over-size jumpers and garish ties, which are worn for a brief time before being put away and forgotten; for unfathomable puzzles, which are regarded with scepticism and never tried; for gadgets which use up their batteries all too quickly and are not used again; and for books, which will never be read and simply collect dust on a shelf. But it is mostly a time when families reunite and for a brief while at least, they feel a closeness that they hope will carry into the new year; mostly.

*

Dinsdale always made a point of getting up before his wife on Christmas morning and bringing her a cup of tea in bed. It was a moment she cherished as she saw it as suitable recompense for the three hundred and sixty four other times she did it for him. They opened their presents while drinking their tea and each was received with a brief kiss of thanks. When that was done, Dinsdale would recline back, pleased that his wife was happy. Then he would turn his thoughts to Felicia. He wondered briefly what sort of day she would be having with her parents and her brothers and their wives, but these thoughts were quickly replaced by ones of her wearing the skimpy sequinned costume and wishing again that he had remained in the hall to actually see her rising from the cake. They had restored their relationship in exchange for a large Christmas bonus, a point that reminded him that somehow he had to get even with Harry.

Dinsdale's thoughts strayed to JDW and he congratulated himself again for the way he handled the meeting in JDW's sumptuous office in Chicago. Dinsdale had said nothing directly; there had been no need as the photographs spoke volumes. Dinsdale had a selection of them framed and offered them, in an innocent sort of way, as souvenirs of the evening. JDW's aghast expression as he looked through them, and his furtive glances across at him, was enough for Dinsdale to be sure he saw them in a different way. They had talked their way around the pictures without directly addressing their implication until JDW had tired of the game.

'Damn it Dinsdale. Who the hell took these.'

'Just one of the members. Don't you like them?' Dinsdale said with a virtuous sound in his voice.

JDW made a sound in his throat like growl. 'Has anybody else seen these?'

'I don't think so. No, I'm sure. I was thinking of perhaps one or two being displayed...'

JDW cut him off. 'Now, I'm no sort of fool. I see what this is.'

Dinsdale raised his eyebrows in a way that dragged his thin moustache into a smile. 'What is it that you see?'

JDW studied his face carefully, looking for some betrayal, but Dinsdale was also a master at this game and his face remained blank. 'What do you want?'

202

Dinsdale shrugged. 'Want? I don't understand.'

'Alright,' JDW conceded with a heavy sigh. 'Let me put it this way. Is their some sort of favour I can do for you?'

Dinsdale looked to the ceiling for a moment. 'Well, if you are in the Christmas spirit, I would ask that the franchising be dropped.'

'Consider it done. Now I want one from you.'

'Anything,' Dinsdale's smile became a permanent fixture. 'Just name it.'

JDW stood up and stretched himself to his full height; he looked down at Dinsdale the way a vulture would, waiting for the lion to finish feeding on a carcass. 'I don't want to see your greasy face around my office again,' he said, breathing heavier than usual. 'I don't want to hear your slimy voice again. In future, you will contact me by e-mail only. And if I find out that anybody else has seen these pictures then I'll skin you alive and use your pelt to light my cigars with.'

Dinsdale stood also. The time for denial was over, but it was also not the time for admission. 'As you wish,' he said simply, and left JDW's office. Only when he got outside and had closed the door, did he punch the air and silently shout 'Yes!'

*

'Would you like some breakfast now?' Dinsdale's wife's voice invaded his thoughts.

'Now that would be nice. I'll have a shower and be downstairs in ten minutes.' He afforded her a wide smile; after all, he was feeling very happy. In the evening, they had been invited to the Mayor's house for dinner along with a number of top people from the town, and Dinsdale would replace his loss of JDW's friendship by binding a few new ones. Yes, it was a time to be happy.

Ricardo arrived with his friend Joshua just before lunch and Rick was surprised by the latter's firm grip when he shook his hand; even after his talk with Ricardo, he had expected a limp hand. Joshua was older than Rick had expected and stood about six-six, with startling blue eyes, a firm jaw and square shoulders. Rick thought he would be a good catch for any girl, and an admiring Anna thought the same. At first, there had been some unease, at least on Rick's part, but Joshua was relaxed and talked with an easy manner. They drank some beer before lunch and Joshua impressed Rick with his tales about his experiences in the Gulf War aboard a destroyer protecting the carriers. Rick had been in the navy many years before and also served on destroyers; they had found a common bond, and it was only Anna's intervention that lunch was ready and on the table that broke up their conversation. In the afternoon they played canasta and the conversation slipped easily round the table. Rick was on top form with tales about his golfing exploits with Harry, Al and Sol, and he related the story about JDW, which was encouraged by their laughter. He was, though, unaware that the humour stemmed mainly from their relief that he was accepting Ricardo's friend. In the evening, Anna played some tunes on the piano and the three men gathered round it and sang, their arms linked round each other and with Ricardo feeling closer to his father than he had during his whole lifetime.

They left late and exchanged handshakes and Rick, surprising them all, invited Ricardo and Joshua to come round more often. It had been a good day and Rick only spoilt it with a comment he made as he and Anna ascended the stairs for bed. 'Funny, he doesn't seem like a faggot.'

Al woke and glanced over his pillow at the other bed where Phillippa was still asleep and breathing lightly. He eased himself out of bed, slipped on his dressing gown and slippers and padded softly down to the kitchen where he made a pot of coffee. He took the mug out to the conservatory at the back of the house and sat in a cushioned cane chair. The sky was blue and clear and the air looked crisp; it had snowed again in the night and the tracks across the lawn he'd noticed a few days ago, made by some burrowing animal, had been filled in and covered over. He wondered what the day held. He had bought an expensive necklace from Dave Menkowitch's shop, a cluster of emeralds and sapphires which would hang low from Phillippa's neck and match with her favourite dress. The problem was, while he supposed she would have bought him something, he wasn't sure and expected a game of who would admit to buying a present first. He hated the idea that the presents would remain not given at the end of the day because they didn't trust each other.

When he went back upstairs to shower and dress, he noticed that Phillippa had turned in her sleep and her body was part uncovered. He stood for a moment looking at the soft curve of her back through her transparent, white nightdress. Something tugged inside him – perhaps it was regret – and slipping off his robe, he eased himself in behind her. She stirred a little.

'You smell of coffee,' she murmured.

'You smell of nice things,' he said gently.

She half rolled over and looked at him. He could see a look of indecision in her eyes as he moved his hand over her breast. 'Is it Christmas morning already?' she queried.

'Yes.' She had not responded and he felt unsure. 'It doesn't matter what morning it is really.' He moved his hand in a gentle caressing motion. She sighed and he stopped.

'Don't stop, I like that,' she said, surprising him.

Afterwards, while he stood for a long time soaping himself in the shower, he thought of Aritha for the first time. He grudgingly admitted to himself that when things were good with Phillippa, then Aritha slipped to the back of his thoughts.

Al had made a reservation for lunch at an expensive restaurant, not knowing if they would use it. After exchanging their gifts, Phillippa had been lost for words as she put on the necklace. They spent a quiet morning together, talking more than they had in the previous six months. Al's spirits were high as they went out to the car to drive to the restaurant. He had kept it a secret, 'a surprise' he told her every time she asked where they were going, but as they sat in the car and he started the engine she said, 'I hope we're not going to the diner.'

Al sighed; it had been too good to last.

*

In the Menkowitch household, everyone was late rising. The evening before, Rob had told his parents more about his exploits, failures and eventual success, and from what he described, Harry realised that his son had grown up in a hard sort of way. He came to accept that Rob had a restless spirit inside him that would not have been satisfied had he gone into the family business. Harry had not recognised earlier in his son's life – perhaps it was good he had not – that Rob had to make it on his own, without his father's helping hand. He was an individual who needed to make his own stamp on his life. After they had drunk plenty of beer, Harry, without a word or hard look from Rosemary, had got out the Jack Daniels and the two men relaxed on Havana cigars. Even Rosemary had accepted extra glasses of her favourite Californian white wine, which was probably why she felt soporific and had not bothered to complain about their cigars. She was happy the two of them were talking amiably, and Harry's deep-rooted fear that his son would be a perpetual failure had slowly dissolved with each tale Rob had told.

The next morning, Rosemary was the first to rise. She made coffee and woke the two men with steaming mugs, eager like a child for them to go downstairs and open their presents. Harry had rolled over and complained that he wanted another half hour in bed, but Rob had come in and had whipped his bed covers to the floor.

'Come on, Father,' he laughed as Harry made sure his pyjamas were in place as the covers disappeared. 'Mom is getting so excited she'll wet herself if we don't open our presents soon.'

'Christmas Day is for relaxing,' Harry grumbled, eventually accepting the robe he had been offered by his grinning son and following him down to the lounge. 'Damn, I've forgotten my coffee,' Harry cussed mildly.

'No problem,' Rob shouted as he bounded back up the stairs. While he was gone, Harry switched on the tree lights.

Rosemary came in carrying a plate of hot, freshly baked, buttered bread as Rob returned with his father's coffee. 'Now it feels more like Christmas,' she enthused when she saw the tree lit up. 'So where are my presents?' she asked them both.

When Rosemary opened her present from Harry, she suspected it would be jewellery – it usually was – but her mouth fell open when she saw the intricately woven roses topped with rubies. She slipped it onto her wrist. 'It is so beautiful,' she breathed softly. 'You designed this, didn't you?'

Harry nodded modestly. 'But Dave made it.'

Rob leaned over closely and examined it. 'So my younger brother has inherited your skills,' he admired.

Just before lunch, Dave, Pam and an overexcited James arrived and the house was suddenly full of noise. Rosemary showed off her bracelet to Pam, who gasped at its beauty even though Dave had already told her about it. Dave and Rob clasped each other like long-lost friends and both asked the other the same questions at the same time. Harry knelt on the floor as his grandson insisted he show him each of the presents he had received from his parents. Harry had a go with a hand-held computer, but within a few seconds it flashed red and buzzed angrily as Harry was killed off. James snatched it back with impatience and showed his bemused grandfather how killing aliens should really be done.

'Anyone want a beer?' Harry asked when all the presents had been exchanged.

'Sure, I'll have a Bud, Harry,' Dave said without thinking.

'Harry?' Rob queried.

'I was forgetting,' said Dave. 'We always used first names when Dad was in the shop.'

Rob chewed this over, somehow feeling that he had missed out on something. 'I'll have a Bud too, Harry.' It came out rather stilted but Harry went into the kitchen feeling a little younger.

Rosemary served an excellent lunch and everybody ate too much and then drank too much to wash it down. The rest of the day revolved very much around young James; it was after all, the day for children. By late afternoon, though, with a belly full from a cocktail of foods, and a brain overwhelmed with so many presents and too much excitement, he tired, and Dave took him up and laid him down on Rosemary's bed. They sat around and caught up on each other's past, and when Rob let slip about Miriam, Dave teased more information from him and raised the question Harry and Rosemary had avoided – when were they getting married?

Rob raised his hands in mock horror. 'Hey. We've not been living together long. Give us a chance.'

'Well that's halfway house,' Dave said, keeping a straight face. 'You'll soon feel the noose tightening and then, bam, before you know it ... what's that song? The Tender Trap?'

He started to sing the first line but Pam cut him off with a dig in the ribs. 'A noose? When did that become a part of our marriage?'

'I wasn't talking about our marriage,' Dave said hastily. 'My feet have been off the ground since I met you but I'm not dangling by a rope.'

'Now that was quick thinking,' Rob laughed. 'I'll have to remember that one.'

Harry quietly noticed how his sons knitted together again like they had in their youth. The years in between had made no difference and he felt an inner contentment, especially as they were now both calling him Harry.

Late in the evening, when Dave, Pam and a tired young James had left and Rosemary had excused herself to go to bed, Harry and Rob supped another Jack Daniels and smoked a final cigar in the lounge.

Rob eased back in his armchair and sipped his drink. 'It's good to hear Dave is doing so well. But then he's had you to thank for that.'

'No,' Harry contradicted. 'He's his own man. He has the talent and the business has prospered since he took it over.'

'Don't get me wrong, Pops, I didn't mean it that way,' Rob said quickly. 'I owe you a lot too. I know I was a disappointment to start with but you helped out when times were hard, and I'm grateful for that.'

'You were never a disappointment,' Harry corrected him. 'I was just concerned for you. There's a difference.'

'True,' Rob nodded and puffed his cigar. He looked at

his father through the cloud of blue smoke. 'I want to pay you back somehow.'

Harry was surprised. 'I don't need paying. The fact you have got on your feet and created a career for yourself is all I ever wanted.'

They talked for a while longer and then Harry rose and yawned. 'Well, I'm for bed.'

Rob got up, moved towards him and wrapped his arms round Harry in a hug. 'Thanks Dad.'

'Thanks for what?' Harry asked, a little taken aback.

'Just thanks for being you.'

15

The build-up to Christmas is slow. For the kids, the shorter Winter days seem longer as it approaches, and for the adults there is the planning and preparation and the shopping; people dodge each other on the slippery sidewalks and vie with each other to catch the overworked shop assistants' attention. But then the day is suddenly upon you and passes in a wink before everything returns to normal, for a few days at least, before the New Year celebrations. People return to work, a few wearing their presents of over-sized jumpers and garish ties with painted cartoon characters. But even these disappear quickly and Christmas is quietly filed away with all the other memories.

A few days later, Harry met Al and Rick at midday in Sam's Bar to review what had happened in the past year, discuss their aspirations for the new year and generally put the world to right. They sat on stools at the bar and supped their Buds from hourglass-shaped glasses with the Budweiser logo painted on the side; Sam, on the pretext of cleaning the bar, hovered around in front of them like a nervous moth round a light bulb. Finally he settled in front of them.

'So, what's with you?' But he didn't wait for a response. 'Personally I'm glad friggin Christmas is over. It's not good for business.'

'Everywhere else looked pretty busy,' Al commented dryly.

'This isn't everywhere else,' was his lame explanation. 'I don't exactly get office parties in here. It ain't a family bar either.'

'Just a place for friggin nutters like us,' Harry said, without the trace of a smile.

'That's it,' Sam agreed, without thinking, 'and that's how I like it.'

'Except we're not nutters.' Rick nudged the bowl of peanuts forward. 'The bowl's empty.'

Sam looked disdainfully at the empty bowl. 'You know, you guys eat all my profits. So don't your wives feed you?' He went off to get another packet of nuts, muttering something about 'friggin' something or other.

'By the way,' Harry said, 'thanks for your help at the golf club. I think it was a success.'

'You think?' Rick queried.

Harry drew a wet circle on the bar with the bottom of his glass. 'Well, I gave Dinsdale the photographs. He seemed pleased at first until he saw the one with Felicia rising out of the cake.'

'I told you, you should have mentioned it to him,' Al said.

Harry shook his head. 'He wouldn't have agreed to it. Besides, she was my insurance. If things went wrong he'd have tried to land it all on me, but with his secretary involved, he couldn't have denied knowing about it. I think he guessed that and it upset him.'

Rick laughed. 'You're a distrusting, devious old schemer, Harry. That's your problem.'

'Something I learnt early in life,' Harry sighed. 'Always make sure you cover your ass.'

Sam came back and poured peanuts from a small packet, but it didn't fill even half the bowl; he had decided to economise. Then he noticed the large wet ring on the bar round Harry's glass and tutted as he lifted the glass and wiped the bar with a cloth. 'Do you know how much work it is to keep cleaning up after you guys? You give this bar a bad reputation.'

Harry looked round the empty room. 'To whom?'

'You want to provide coasters,' Al suggested.

'Just something extra to clean,' Sam grumbled, wiping the bottom of the glass before replacing it.

'Clean?' Al questioned. 'Get the cardboard ones.'

'They'd get soggy when I'd wash them, stupid,' Sam grunted.

Harry grabbed a handful of nuts, dropping a couple onto the bar that Sam quickly picked up and dropped back into the bowl. 'You throw them away,' Harry said through chewing.

'Throw them away? Yeah right,' Sam said with disbelief. 'And that's more expense. It's easier to wipe the bar with a cloth.' He moved away as three older men ambled in, slapping their hands against their bodies and trying to restart their circulation after the cold outside. Sam wasn't sure if he had come out right from the exchange and was glad to go to the other end of the bar to serve them.

'What will happen about Ellor Byrne?' Rick queried.

'Dinsdale didn't mention what he would do about her,' Harry answered. 'But I wouldn't be surprised if she resigns as Lady Captain. It'll keep her quiet whatever.'

'A lesser man would have had his leg broken...' Al chuckled, '...the way she leapt onto JDW's knee.'

'How did she get into that state in the first place?' Rick wanted to know. 'She's usually sobriety personified.'

'I think she got her bowls mixed up,' Harry smiled, and took some more nuts without offering a further explanation.

'And the franchising won't happen?' Al asked.

'Not if Dinsdale handles it right,' Harry replied. 'He probably won't tell me. He didn't even thank me.' The other two looked at him with surprise. 'Hey Sam! Three more Buds,' Harry called down the bar. He waited until Sam uncapped the bottles and refilled their glasses. 'So, how was your Christmas?' Harry mimicked to Al and Rick. Sam gave him a suspicious look and moved away again.

'Quiet but very pleasant,' Al said.

'Did Phillippa like her necklace?' Harry enquired, scooping another handful of nuts.

'Oh, she loved that.' Al sipped his beer. 'But then any woman would. It was a good day,' he surmised, and then paused before adding, 'I hope it lasts.'

Harry tactfully didn't ask about the watch for Aritha and turned to Rick. 'And how was it with you?'

'Just great. We had a swell time.' His face smiled effusively. 'Do you know, we sang songs round the piano in the evening. It was like the old Christmases we used to have.'

'Did Ricardo bring his friend?' Al asked carefully.

'Yep.' Rick sighed, wondering if he should leave it at that but he was comfortable with his friends. 'You know, I guess I can be a bit of an old bigot at times, but this guy he's living with, well, he was just like any other guy. I swear, if he were straight, he'd have the girls running after him. I know Anna was attracted to him in a motherly sort of way.' He ran out of words and looked appealingly to the other two.

'That's good,' Harry smiled, and touched his friend's arm.

'I'm glad for you,' Al said sincerely. 'We both know how difficult it's been.'

'You know,' Rick continued, seeming that he wanted to get it all off his chest. 'Ricardo and I went for a beer before Christmas. To discuss things and get it all cleared, I guess. And he helped. Do you know what he said to me? He said, "Look Dad, perhaps it would help if you didn't think so graphically. Just look upon Joshua as a friend of mine." It made it a whole lot easier.'

'That's good,' Harry repeated. 'So you'll be seeing a lot more of them?'

'It's funny,' Rick studied his glass of beer and was almost talking to himself. 'In the evening we sang those songs with our arms round each other. Why couldn't it have been like that when he was younger? I must have gone wrong somewhere.'

'Nah,' Harry drawled. 'They don't come with an instruction book. Look at the difference between my Dave and his brother Rob.'

'Was Rob home for Christmas?' Al asked.

'He turned up the day before. He's finally found something and made a success of his life.' Harry's face reflected his happiness. 'Something to do with computer graphics. He's invited Rosemary and me out to California next Spring.'

'Seems the season of goodwill has worked a few miracles for all of us,' Rick laughed.

'I wish it would work one here,' Sam said, breaking into their conversation; they hadn't noticed he'd drifted back to their end of the bar.

'God works in mysterious ways,' Al said.

'He helps those who help themselves,' Rick added.

'*Hallelujah* brothers,' Harry sang out.

'What are you? Three friggin disciples?' Sam growled.

'No. We're your customers. Three more beers,' Rick demanded.'And some nuts,' Harry added.

'Beers yes, but no more nuts. You guys eat them like you're having lunch,' Sam said, uncapping three bottles. 'Besides, they're not good for your collateral.'

'Cholesterol,' Rick corrected.

'Whatever,' and Sam moved away again.

'So,' Rick said after sipping his beer. 'What is the new year going to hold for us?'

'Golf without Sol,' Al said, and they went quiet for a moment.

'I'm going to miss that sonofabitch,' Rick said, and they all smiled.

'True,' Harry said. 'He was a pain in the ass but it will still ache without him.' He raised his glass and they touched their glasses against his to toast Sol's memory.

'What else,' Rick asked, 'for the new year?'

'Well,' Harry started, 'first there are the New Year celebrations. Then there is the Easter egg hunt, then the July Fourth celebration, then Thanksgiving and then it's back into Christmas.'

The other two looked at him with sullen faces. 'And that's another year?' Rick queried. 'Is that all it holds?'

'There's also playing in the Summer Mixed with Louise,' Harry grinned. 'But that won't involve you two.'

'Oh ho,' Al chuckled. 'Does Rosemary know you are playing in that again?'

'I'll mention it.' Harry took a long pull at his beer. 'Sometime.'

'I'll remind you,' Al said with an evil grin.

'Hey!' Rick said suddenly. 'Have you heard the town council wants to take a loop off the main highway and pass it through the centre of town?'

'I heard something about it,' Al admitted.

'What do they want to do that for?' Harry queried; he was never one to keep up with the news. He didn't take a local or national newspaper and he felt the world would circle as usual whether he was aware of it or not. 'Everyone was happy when they built the highway.'

'A loop will improve access and communication is the official line given,' Rick said with some sarcasm in his tone. 'But they're really after more business. They say they did a survey through the Summer on how many cars drive past the town.'

'So why should they stop just because it comes through? There's nothing to stop for,' Al commented.

216

'They have other plans,' Rick said. 'Stop offs with refreshments and a leisure area and motels and things like that.'

'So where is the loop supposed to pass through?' Harry asked.

'Guess.' Rick didn't attempt to hide his sarcasm this time. 'Through the eastern side of town.'

Harry rubbed his hand over his chin. 'You know, something like that could start the Civil War all over again.'

'Just what this bar needs,' Sam interrupted them.

'A civil war?' Harry queried, not understanding his logic.

'No,' Sam said impatiently, 'I'd get more customers.'

The three of them stared at him in silence for a moment before Harry asked, 'And why would they come into here?'

Sam seemed unsettled by the question. 'You come in here,' he said lamely. 'There must be some attraction. Huh?' And he laughed in a stuttering sort of way.

'But if the loop only goes through the eastern side, how will they know your bar exists?' Al queried.

'Perhaps you can have a sign erected on the highway,' Harry suggested. 'It can say something like, "Visit Sam's bar. Built by the original settlers and untouched for decades".'

'And,' Rick said with an innocent smile. 'I also read in the local newspaper that the council will be giving a Star Bar Owner of the Year award. It has to be you, Sam.'

Sam sneered and rummaged around in his brain for a quick riposte, but he kept coming across the same one and decided in the end that it would have to do. 'Friggin nutters,' he mumbled.

'Now that's not a nice thing to say,' Al said with a hurt tone in his voice. 'We'll have to reconsider who we'll vote for.'

'There's no competition,' Sam snapped back. 'And even

if there was, I wouldn't enter it.' He began to move away, muttering to himself.

Rick leaned closer to them and said quietly, 'I could run up an entry form and voting slips on my computer and bring them in here.'

'Now that would be mean,' Al said, his eyes gleaming with mirth.

'We could get some mileage out of it,' Harry said.

'And maybe a few free drinks?' Rick suggested.

'And nuts,' Harry added.

'It would upset Sam when he found out,' Al said.

'I'll do it tonight,' Rick said, and they all chuckled like naughty schoolboys.

16

The town of Wannabee celebrated the arrival of the new year like most other towns with crowds of revellers congregating around the clock tower as the hour neared. They stamped their feet and slapped their arms against the cold; over on one side, a group of youngsters had a CD player pumping out music rather too loudly, and they gyrated to the rhythm as much to keep warm as to enjoy dancing. As the minute hand crept up to the hour, two policemen eased their way into the group and requested politely for the music to be turned off, which the youngsters did without complaint – they too were keeping an eye on the illuminated clocks. As the hand moved over the final minute, people whooped and hollered, and a fusillade of rockets streamed into the air, trailing orange tongues. At the zenith of their journey, they burst across the black night sky like umbrellas of sparkling stars, filling the air with loud cracklings. Children 'ooohed' from their fathers' shoulders and people cheered, linked arms with strangers and began to sing. For a brief time, east and west townspeople joined together without thinking of who lived where and they danced in huge rings round the clock tower, and the square was alive with a rippling tide of bobbing faces. Within a half hour, the square was empty, apart from a few stragglers stealing lingering kisses in doorways. The traffic for the easterners, still feeling the 'bonhomie' of the occasion, queued patiently over the bridges to cross the river. Like Christmas, the hour of the New Year took its time coming and then passed in a wink.

*

It was Rick and Anna's turn to host the new year party at their place. They had taken down the Christmas decorations and replaced them with small American flags draped on cord round the walls and a large banner across the fireplace which heralded the new year.

Al and Phillippa were the first to arrive and she wore the new necklace Al had given her for Christmas. Anna was dazzled by it and the warmth of her welcome and adulation of the necklace put Phillippa in the right mood. Al felt some relief: they had been getting on well for a week but he knew she had a predilection for receding into her hardened shell in company, especially when it was Rick and Harry. While the women went away to the kitchen where Anna was putting the final touches to the food, Rick took Al over to his drinks bar he'd had specially built in one corner, and he stood behind it with his hands on the walnut bar.

'So, what do you want?' he mimicked Sam.

Al looked along the shelves of bottles. 'Have you got some friggin nuts?'

Rick had expected this and stooped below the bar and came up with a bowl of nuts. 'So, don't your wife feed you?'

Al was about to respond when the doorbell chimed, 'That'll be Harry and Rosemary,' Rick said as he went off to the door. 'Come in, come in, gracious folk,' Rick greeted them with a bow and a wave of his hand. He kissed Rosemary's cheek and then held out his hand to Harry, who brushed it aside and gave Rick a similar kiss.

'I didn't want to be left out,' he explained.

220

'Now boys,' Rosemary warned, 'you'll be making me jealous.'

'I didn't use my tongue,' Harry defended himself.

Rosemary waved a hand in mock horror. 'You can be disgusting sometimes, Harry.'

Harry tried to look perplexed. 'I said I didn't...'

Rick was just recovering from the surprise of the kiss. 'The girls are in the kitchen, Rosemary, if you want to join them.'

'Am I classed as a girl too?' she enquired.

'The youngest of them all,' Rick said, giving her another kiss.

'Hey. Who's trying to make me jealous now?' Harry argued.

'Come and have a drink,' Rick said as he led him across the room.

'Say,' Harry stood back and admired the bar, 'when did you have this put in?'

'Just a little thing I prepared earlier,' Rick smiled as he went behind the bar. 'What'll you have?'

Harry saw the bowl of nuts and grabbed a handful. 'This is like home from home.' He looked around the room. 'You'll have to stop cleaning it though. It loses something of the atmosphere.'

'I can imagine Anna letting this place get like Sam's Bar,' Al jested. 'You'd have all the dropouts coming here.'

Rick listened to a set banter between Harry and Al while he poured them three Buds in chilled glasses. He put them down on copper coasters engraved with his name.

Harry was the first to notice them. 'Hey. Look at this. Tell me, do you wash them after use or do you just throw them away?'

'Throw them away? Look, they've got my name on them.' Rick lifted his glass to show them. 'Anna bought them for me when I had the bar built.'

Harry rubbed his hand across his mouth. 'I don't know,' he looked to Al, 'this establishment seems to be a little too high class, for me. He'll complain about me spilling nuts next.'

'I'll drink anywhere,' Al said, raising his glass.

'Me too,' Harry agreed, picking up his. 'Here's to you two guys and a prosperous new year ahead.'

They clinked their glasses together and then drank deeply just as the ladies entered the room.

'Oh. You've had a bar installed,' Rosemary exclaimed.

'It's the best way of knowing where those three are,' Phillippa said, unusually lightheartedly.

'Exactly,' Anna joined in. 'It's as good as a leash round their necks.'

Harry came over and gave Anna a hug and a kiss and then turned to Phillippa; he stood for a moment just looking at her.

'Something wrong?' she asked cautiously.

Harry reached into his pocket and took out a small jeweller's eyepiece and, holding it to one eye, bent forward close to her. 'Very nice,' he muttered. 'Perfection.'

'It's a Menkowitch necklace,' she said, surprised. 'Haven't you seen it before?'

'I'm not looking at the necklace,' Harry said softly.

Phillippa gave out a girlish laugh and covered her cleavage with her hand. 'Al, take this animal away before he starts pawing me.'

Al was taken aback, but pleasantly so, by Phillippa's animation. He went over and put his arm round Harry's shoulder. 'But I thought you liked old grizzly bears.'

'But not the old wrinkled ones,' Rosemary put in with a twinkle in her eyes.

Harry looked deflated, but Phillippa came across to him and wrapped her arms round him. 'But he's still cuddly,' she said. Harry looked over her shoulder to Al and raised his eyebrows. Al just shrugged with a bemused smile on his face.

That start to the evening was just the fuse being lit and, as it progressed through a sumptuous spread washed down with plenty of drinks, it sparkled into life with noisy banter and laughter that they had not enjoyed so much together before. By eleven, Harry suggested a game of charades and to everyone's surprise, Phillippa brought the rafters down trying to act out *Yankee Doodle Dandy*. The Yankee and the Dandy she managed fine, but she mistook what a Doodle was and had the other's falling about with laughter when she tried to act out relieving herself on a toilet.

It was Rick who noticed it was almost midnight and they quickly donned their coats and stepped out onto the front veranda. Rick's house was situated on one of the higher plateaus, with a commanding view over the town and they huddled together waiting for the firework display in the town square. It was shorter than expected but the women 'ooohed' at the soaring rockets and the men 'aaahed' as they died in the night sky, which brought on a fit of giggles before they all hugged each other and simultaneously wished each other 'Happy New Year'.

'Hey, I've forgotten something,' Rick said and hurried back inside. He returned a moment later with a large rocket that he stuck gently into the lawn. 'Let me have your lighter, Harry.' He flicked it, touched the fuse paper and then stood back. It hissed for a moment and then, with a loud 'whoosh', climbed to a good height before lighting the sky with a huge umbrella of silver and gold stars. As these died, it exploded with a thunderous bang which made them all take a step back.

'That should wake up the old fart bag down the road,' Rick laughed aloud.

'Don't be unkind,' Anna scolded him, knowing whom he meant.

'She is,' Rick defended himself. 'She's worse than a flatulent dog.'

'Now that conjures a picture.' Harry tried to make light of it before an argument formed.

'I'm trying not to,' Al joined in with mirth.

'Have you noticed how these three always stick together?' Rosemary asked the other two women.

'Always,' Anna agreed.

Phillippa put her arms round their shoulders and pulled Anna and Rosemary closer to her. 'Like Tweedledum and Tweedledee and Tweedle something else. Were there three of them?' She hiccupped, which made the others laugh.

Anna shivered as the cold penetrated her coat. 'It's time to go in and have a coffee.'

Al and Phillippa drove home in silence for a while. 'Are you okay to drive?' Phillippa asked, not really caring; she knew she couldn't.

'I'm fine,' Al said, taking a corner gently. 'That was some evening. I've never seen you enjoying yourself so much.'

'Are you saying I never do?' Her voice sounded cold and made Al glance over at her.

'No.' He looked back at the road ahead. 'I just meant that tonight you sort of, well, let yourself relax.'

'Meaning I'm usually a party pooper. What is a pooper?' she mused. 'Sounds something awful.'

He ignored her question. 'There were times tonight when I quietly watched you. You were animated and sparkling. And a little drunk,' he chuckled, and put his hand over onto her lap.

She brushed his hand away. 'So you think I have to be a lush to be the belle of the party?' Again her voice had become cold.

Al was confused. What was it with her? One minute she was witty and the centre of attraction and then next, alone with him, her mood swung to the other extreme. He began to wonder if there was something emotionally wrong – he avoided the word 'mental'.

When they arrived home, he held the door open for her and she strode passed him and went straight up the stairs. He closed the door quietly while he watched her ascend and disappear into the bedroom. He took his coat off and went into the kitchen to make a coffee, but while waiting for the kettle to boil, he went off the idea, switched it off and made his way up the stairs. He felt a weariness permeating through his body brought on by Phillippa's mood swing – he really didn't understand what was happening. When he entered their bedroom he couldn't see her and guessed she was in the bathroom. He went over to his bed and peeled off his jacket. Then he sensed rather than heard someone behind him. He turned and stood stock still, not quite believing his eyes. Phillippa was in the centre of the room, standing with her legs slightly apart with her hands on her hips; she was wearing nothing apart from a pair of high-heeled shoes, her necklace and a broad smile. She came slowly towards him.

'Is this how you like me, Al?'

She stepped close to him and began to unravel his tie and unbutton his shirt.

'You like me being the party lush, don't you.'

'I never said you were a lush.'

She ignored his words and suddenly grabbed his shirt, ripping it open to bare his chest.

'Is this how you want me? A bad girl? I can be a bad girl you know.'

Al was aware of her perfume and the nearness of her body as her breasts moved against him, but something inside didn't feel right. This wasn't Phillippa and not how he wanted her. But his silence encouraged her.

She slid her arms over his shoulders and began to run

225

her fingers round the back of his neck, bringing them closer together.

'Phillippa, look...' he began to protest, but she covered his mouth with hers.

When their lips parted, she looked him steadily in the eyes, lowered her eyelids and purred like a cat. His arms had been hanging limp by his side, unable to move, but when she lowered her hands and unbuckled his belt something snapped inside and he placed his hands on her shoulders and began to ease her back.

'Phillippa. Not like this.'

She hesitated and then moved away from him and her face darkened; for a moment he thought she was about to start shouting and ranting at the humiliation of his rejection. But then the smile crept back onto her lips and she eased herself in a feline way over to her bed where she lay down and spread herself apart. She crooked her finger, beckoning him to join her. 'Then take me how you want me.'

Everything around him blurred from his vision and all he saw was her, looking more beautiful than he had ever seen her before, calling to him, wanting him.

Al woke up with a start and sat upright in the bed. He gasped for breath as his chest felt tight and his mind flicked between reality and a dream. The light was still on and when he looked to his side, he was in Phillippa's bed, with her curled next to him. The sheet was dragged down and he could see she was only wearing her necklace. It was no dream – they had made love like never before, or rather she had made love to him. He felt some revulsion. She had dominated him, she had used him until she was satiated, she had been like – he baulked at the word but it remained with him – she had been like a whore.

He got up quietly and went to the bathroom, where he relieved himself and washed his face. He then went to his bed and slid between the sheets. He switched the lights off and lay in the darkness wondering why it had happened like that and hoping it was just too much drink. His fear was that it was something else. He slipped into sleep without finding the answer.

*

A few days later, Harry and Rosemary drove Rob to the airport. His visit was over all too quickly, but with promises he would arrange a date for them to visit. He flew off back to California, leaving behind a warmer feeling with his parents.

Rick's perspective with many things had changed over the festive period and Anna noticed the seriousness go out of his eyes; the moments when he sat in deep thought stopped happening. He met Ricardo and Joshua once a week to shoot pool in a downtown bar and would come home with bright eyes and full of conversation about his game and how Ricardo was doing at his job.

Al's relationship with Phillippa seemed to bump along with some sort of harmony. They never spoke of that night and she never tried a repeat performance. He wasn't sure if he was happy or sad that they had not talked about it. He made a point of booking a reservation in a different restaurant each week and one offered a small dancefloor with a three-piece band playing easy music, where Al had coaxed her to the floor for a slow waltz. The next week she surprised him by suggesting they went back there. He stopped going to the diner and Aritha guessed why. She was sad for herself and happy for him, a strange feeling that she never came to terms with.

*

Spring came to Wannabee earlier than expected. Late in

February, warm fronts moved up from the south and cleared the snow from most places more efficiently than the ploughs. A few patches lingered in hollows to serve as a reminder that Winter hadn't quite passed, but as the days edged into March, shoots and buds began to appear and the grass began to grow. The whiteness of everything transformed through stages of browns and finally into various shades of green. The members of the golf club received letters advising them the course would open in a few days, and the more avid players began going to the practice range to stretch their sinews and remind their dormant muscles how they had coordinated last year to swing a club. Harry met Al and Rick in the locker room and they passed comments about how badly they were likely to play their first game before making their way to the first tee. It was here that the absence of Sol became immediately apparent; they had two golf buggies and one would have to drive alone. They thought about it and then Rick suggested they swap partners each game, which was not wholly satisfactory.

Al took his club and practised his swing. 'Perhaps we should find a fourth partner,' he suggested.

The other two thought about it but it didn't appeal to them. Besides, they couldn't think of anyone. 'We'll see how it goes,' Harry said.

Al stepped up onto the tee area and turned his mind to his game. He swung easy and hit his ball straight up the middle. 'You've been practising,' Rick said as he put his ball on the peg.

'Like riding a bike,' Al quipped, pleased with himself.

Rick took too long thinking about it and thinned his ball; although it went straight, the wet ground took some distance off it. He sighed, picked up his peg and refrained from comment.

'Still five dollars a game?' Harry asked as he stepped up

and took several swings before addressing his club behind the ball.

'Make it ten, you sonofabitch,' Rick said in a familiar tone.

Harry stepped back from his ball with a smile. 'So who's you friggin hustling?' Harry mimicked Sam.

Al leaned against his buggy. 'Are you two clowns playing golf or what?' he asked without rancour, knowing it was their way of breaking the ice.

Harry aimed left, swung harder and cut the ball over to the right side of the fairway. He was pleased to see his ball twenty yards ahead of the others.

'Playing cute,' Rick commented as he got in his buggy.

'Opening up the green,' Harry chuckled as he got in beside Al.

'Amazing what ten dollars can do to a guy,' Al called across to Rick as he started forward.

They all felt good – golf had started again, the Summer was in front of them and they had slipped through the first awkwardness that Sol was missing. He occurred in their thoughts now and then, especially at memorable points on the course like where Sol had managed a spectacular shot into a tree and his ball had stuck in the higher branches; for weeks Sol had cussed up at it every time they passed it. But mostly they avoided actually talking about him. It wasn't until the sixth green that he came up again in their conversation. Harry was holding the flag while Rick lined up his putt when Harry glanced down the fairway and then at his watch. Rick stood away from his ball.

'Am I keeping you from something?' Rick asked.

Harry apologised. 'I'm sorry. I was just thinking.'

Rick took two putts to get down and halved the hole with Al. 'So what were you thinking about?' he asked as he retrieved his ball from the hole.

'That there's no one pushing up behind us,' Harry

explained, 'and we're fifteen minutes ahead of our usual schedule.'

Rick looked at his ball and wiped away a scuff mark. 'We're only a three ball,' he said softly. 'It makes the difference.'

'Let's face it,' Al said, 'Sol wasn't exactly a fast player. He spent more time cursing or looking for his ball.'

Speaking about him seemed to make it easier. 'Do you remember his shot on the tenth, the last time we played?' Rick asked. 'He wound himself up like John Daley and hit it with the speed of Tiger Woods.'

'Except he hooked it straight into the water,' Harry added.

'True,' Al said. 'He never did learn that bit about relaxing over the ball.'

They drove to the next hole, trying to leave the thoughts of Sol behind them. By the time they reached the eighteenth hole, they were all square, four holes won apiece and the others halved. Harry pulled his second shot and visited his favourite bunker to the left of the green. As he looked at his ball, lying clear but coated with wet sand, Rick's face appeared over the cavernous rim.

'Fifty bucks says you can't hole it.'

Harry took a spare ball from his pocket and tossed it up to him. 'Give it to Al. He'll know what to do.'

Rick caught it deftly and put it in his pocket with a grin.

Harry tried to swing down on the ball but caught it thin. It plugged into the sand face, held for a moment and then eased out, trickling back near his feet. He took a new stance and hit again, too quickly this time, and the ball hit just under the rim and rolled back down again.

'Would you like a cigar?' Rick asked.

Harry cursed silently to himself and picked up his ball.

Al putted down from thirty feet to win the hole and the game. 'You sonofabitch,' Rick cursed.

It would be a while before they finally put Sol out of their minds.

After they had showered and changed, the men went to their usual table in the lounge and ordered drinks. They talked about their game and their families and it seemed like there hadn't even been a Winter break. Louise came over and sat down.

'I won't stay long,' she said, apologising for her intrusion. 'Have you heard about Ellor?' she directed the question to Harry.

He shook his head. 'Has she gone to a health farm to dry out?'

Louise flapped her hand at him. 'Nooo,' she dragged the word out in a way to scold his remark. 'She's resigned as Lady Captain.'

'Good for her,' Rick said in a mock, upper-class British voice. 'The right thing to do. Can't have a lush in charge of the young gels.'

'Oh stop it,' Louise flapped her hand at him. 'Don't be awful. The point is,' she addressed again to Harry, 'they've asked me to become Lady Captain.'

'Do you want my approval?' Harry questioned.

'I just thought you might like to know,' she said, not sure if he was making fun.

He tried to hold a straight face but his mouth creased and gave him away. 'That's good news. I hope, anyway.'

'You hope?' she queried.

'Well, Ellor had a habit of hounding us. I trust we shall have a better relationship.'

'You mean, carry on the way you always do, I suppose.'

Harry shrugged and tried to look innocent. 'I suppose.'

'I'll wait and see what you get up to.' She smiled and stood up. As she went to walk away, Harry got up and called after her and she turned. He gave her a brief kiss on the cheek.

231

'I know you'll make a good Captain,' he said softly in her ear. 'I'm pleased for you.'

'Thanks, Harry.'

But then Rick called after her.

'One thing a Captain must learn is that she cannot show favouritism.' Her eyebrows arched in a question. 'Don't we get the opportunity to congratulate you?'

She laughed and went over to them, planting a kiss on their cheeks. 'That's better, young lady,' Al said. 'I hope that is how you intend to carry on.'

'Down boys,' she purred. 'I only give out official kisses.'

Harry sat down and they watched her walk away across the lounge to rejoin some ladies sitting at another table.

'Harry, you never said if you two ever...' Rick started.

'No, we didn't,' Harry said.

*

In late Spring, that period when the air starts to really warm up and the days begin to stretch out, Harry sat in his favourite chair on the back porch. He had put in a day on the garden, running the mower over the grass, trimming the edges and pulling out the obvious weeds, which normally included a few flowers. He slowly supped a glass of JD, smoked a cigar and relaxed – his eyes were beginning to droop with the fatigue of it all. He could smell cooking and smoke from an early barbecue a few houses away and a bird was singing from a tree somewhere; all was right with the world.

His eyes opened quickly and he started forward when Rosemary let the outer door bang shut. She sat down next to him and waited for his eyes to focus so she had his attention.

'I've got something to tell you. I've just been shopping,' she announced.

232

He mulled this over. She sounded excited and her face was bright. 'Were they giving away shoes?'

Her face creased with confused thoughts. 'I don't think so.'

'So what is so exciting about shopping?'

'Oh, I see,' she said, not quite knowing what. 'No, it wasn't the shopping. I was shopping. That's why I went into town. I'd seen a nice two-piece but they didn't have my size. You know, the blue one I told you about.'

Harry didn't remember.

'It's a shame really,' she continued. 'It would have gone so well with the hat and shoes I'd seen in Cromby's.' She paused while she reflected on her disappointment.

Harry waited.

'But I did pick up a nice yellow top. It will go well with my shorts when we go to California. That's not far away now. Don't you think you ought to get some Summer clothes for the trip?'

Harry felt like another drink and a cigar. 'Did something happen in town?'

She thought about it. 'Like what?'

'Like what you were so fired up to tell me,' he sighed. 'We've got lost somewhere between a blue two-piece, a yellow top and going to California. I guess they must be related somehow but I can't work it out.'

'Sometimes, Harry Menkowitch, you confuse me with these conversations.' She tutted with mild annoyance.

'You had something to tell me,' Harry reminded her again.

'I was coming to that. As I was near Dave's shop, I called in to see him. He had just had a phone call and was about to call us. Isn't that a coincidence?' She looked at him, waiting for him to concur but he decided to take a short cut.

'Who was the first phone call from?'

'From Pam. She's just had a test.'

'Is she getting promotion?'

'No. It was a pregnancy test. She's pregnant.'

'She's having a baby?'

Rosemary clucked her tongue and pulled a face. 'What else would she be having?'

Harry reached over and hugged her, as much from finally extracting the news as from the information it contained. 'Well, I'll be. That's great news. Dave said they would be trying for another.'

Rosemary's face clouded a little. 'He told you that?'

Harry tried to shrug it away. 'Just something he said in passing.' Her face showed she wasn't pacified. 'He only said he was thinking about it. He hadn't even mentioned it to Pam.'

'So you were both being secretive.'

'No. It wasn't like that,' Harry began to explain. 'We were talking about him and Rob and how Rob didn't go into the business and what he would do if James didn't want to follow him into the business.' He stopped when he saw the way she was looking at him.

'Well, I hope he discussed it with Pam. It could be a nasty surprise if he didn't.' She got up and went into the house.

Harry shook his head slowly and looked out to the garden. 'I mowed the lawn,' he called out. 'Looks pretty good.' There was no response so he reached under the table for the bottle and poured himself another drink. 'Trimmed the edges and tidied the flower beds too,' he said quietly to himself. He sipped his drink. 'Having another baby,' he murmured contentedly. 'I guess that calls for a cigar,' and he reached down for the packet.

*

Dinsdale's life had been going very well since the new year

dawned and each month it just kept on getting better. The new franchising had been dropped, Ellor Byrne had resigned as Lady Captain and news had just reached him that JDW had decided, obviously with a view to saving face, that he was looking for a buyer for the golf club. To top it all, Felicia had agreed to go with him to Las Vegas for a week, to a golf club general managers' convention. He had attended one a few years before and apart from a few days of speeches, lectures and discussions, the rest of the time would be spent at functions in the evenings and playing golf during the day. As he was not a player, he and Felicia would have plenty of time together to see the town and whatever else came to mind. Since he had invited her, their relationship – which had still been a little cool after the 'cake' episode – suddenly blossomed and they had even stolen a few quiet weekends away in New York.

Dinsdale was also looking forward to something else. During the Christmas party at the Mayor's house, he had found new friends in the right places, said the right things and had been accepted into the Mayor's inner circle – that night he had been invited to a 'little get-together' by the Mayor. The meeting meant a light buffet in the Mayor's official residence, a few drinks, some cigars and a lot of conversation with influential people. Dinsdale felt that whoever controlled the order of things in the universe had suddenly noticed him and smiled. Except for one small thing – he still hadn't found an opportunity to get even with Harry Menkowitch, but the way things were going, he had a feeling it wasn't far away.

Dinsdale said goodbye to his wife with just a wave of his hand and told her not to wait up for him and took a cab into town. The Mayor's official residence was within part of the town council's building fronting the main square. His suite of rooms was set on the top floor of the building and consisted of a secluded room for his private functions and separate living quarters. He only resided there when something happened that demanded he stay overnight at the hub of things, but as Wannabee never had anything serious happen, it was used only for nights like these when it was easier to stay than go home. Dinsdale was surprised by the lavish decor and furnishings, the sumptuous food and drink, and guessed why local taxes were so high. Not that he objected – he had a feeling that if he played his cards right, the opportunity for a payback was coming his way. The attendees were all men who either had top positions on the Mayor's staff or were senior men from local businesses. Dinsdale preened his feathers, after all, he had to be considered a 'top man' to be invited into this company. The evening passed like musical chairs but without the music and with no chairs – everyone circulated round the room, partaking in conversations, and then dropping out and passing onto another one. Dinsdale listened more than spoke and only occasionally was asked for his opinion. The response he gave was based upon what he had just heard and the importance of the person giving it; the technical term for this procedure was 'sucking up'. As the evening wore on, the numbers thinned and Dinsdale had made a number of new contacts, which he guessed would be useful in the future. He was beginning to wonder when to politely make his exit, when the Mayor came over and asked him to step into a side room with one of his closest aides. Dinsdale was flattered and cautious at the same time.

The room turned out to be the Mayor's private office and he waved Dinsdale to a handsome leather-bound chair in front of his desk. He was offered a drink and a cigar but he declined both; he felt they might have been the condemned man's breakfast.

'Listen here, Dinsdale,' the Mayor began as he reclined

rather than sat in a large, executive-style armchair that sighed as it eased its way gently under his weight. 'You've impressed a few people, not to mention myself.'

Dinsdale felt relieved, surprised, flattered and self-satisfied, all rolled into one huge emotion that made his head feel light. 'I do my best, Mr Mayor.'

'Call me John,' the Mayor said with an expansive sweep of his hand. 'Tonight, anyway,' he added with a grin. 'Now the point is,' he hurried on, 'I don't know if you realise it, but next year is the one hundred and fiftieth anniversary of the founding of this town. At least, since it got its name.'

'Yes, I was aware of that,' Dinsdale replied, adding, 'John,' rather awkwardly.

'Well, we've been beavering away at thinking up things we ought to do.' The Mayor stubbed his cigar out in an ornate glass ashtray and leaned back. 'The guys have been working on several projects. The details don't matter at the moment, but one idea needs your help.'

Dinsdale shrugged. 'Ask away.'

'July Fourth, Independence Day,' he said, looking to the ceiling as if for inspiration. 'Now that deserves a special celebration. I thought we ought to hold a special dinner, maybe a dance as well, when we could invite all the folk together.'

'All the folk?' Dinsdale queried.

'Selected folk,' the Mayor corrected. 'And your golf club seems the ideal venue. It has the parking, the space and the facilities. Everything we need, in fact.'

Dinsdale felt a tightening in his stomach. On July Fourth, the club always held its own Independence Day dance and he'd have an impossible job getting that past the board, especially JDW. But then he remembered JDW was trying to sell the club and he, Dinsdale, had been making more independent decisions without referring to JDW. Always one with an eye for an opportunity, Dinsdale said, 'Did you know that Jay Don Winchester wants to sell the club?'

'Why hell no! What's wrong with it? Is it losing money?'

Dinsdale put on his best supercilious smile. 'Quite the opposite. Let's just say he committed a little indiscretion and wants out.' He gave a knowing look that led the Mayor to believe it had to be something to do with sex. 'I can't say I'm sorry,' Dinsdale continued. 'Ten years ago, when the then-Mayor, Democrat Luke Whiting, sold off everything in sight to raise money for that idiotic idea of his to build a hospital and provide a free service for the public, he sold our club to JDW. And he's been milking it ever since.'

Dinsdale sat back and let his words sink in, watching the changing expression on the Mayor's face. Dinsdale knew the current Mayor, John Wesley Cook, was a righter than right Republican who had complained enough about the burden of the Luke Whiting hospital and many other things he had inherited from those 'Democrat Years', as he often referred to them with distaste.

'It has always been my dream,' Dinsdale sighed, 'that some day, the town would claim back its own club.'

The Mayor sucked on a finger for a moment and then looked to one of his aides. 'Make a note Bob – let's get that on the agenda. Maybe we can get a consortium together with some of the local businessmen. Try Guy Holder and Matt Heflin to start with. They'll know of others who might be interested.'

Dinsdale was overawed by the swiftness with which the Mayor made a decision and then swung into action. 'You know,' he said, 'if you could buy back the club, we could combine the new ownership along with the July Fourth celebration.'

'That's true,' the Mayor agreed, warming to the idea. 'I'd guess that most of your members own businesses of one sort or another; there were three of them here tonight.

We'll get moving on it.' The Mayor stood up to indicate the meeting was over and came round with an outstretched hand. 'Many thanks, Dinsdale. I knew it was the right decision to get you into my little band.'

'Any help you want with the purchase ... you know...' Dinsdale winked, '... inside information ... just let me know.'

The Mayor punched his shoulder playfully. 'You're my kind of man, Dinsdale. You hear that, Bob?' he turned to his aide. 'Keep Dinsdale in the picture.'

When Dinsdale left, he got into a cab and sat in the back feeling very satisfied; events had moved fast and in his favour. He felt that with a little positioning he could play a major role in the negotiation to buy the club and cream off a little compensation at the same time. He remembered what JDW had said to him at their last meeting. 'Well, Mr Jay Don Winchester,' he thought, 'not only will you be seeing me and talking with me, but I'll be screwing your balls at the same time.' When the cab had dropped him off at his home, he paused for a moment and looked up at the starlit sky. He smiled up at whoever was smiling down on him.

17

Harry met Al and Rick at Sam's Bar and after settling on their stools with a drink, Rick showed them the entry form and voting slips he had printed. He had written 'Sam's Bar' on the nomination form and they each signed it and completed a voting slip. They waited for Sam to wander to their end of the bar.

'Hey Sam,' Rick said, passing the entry form across the bar. 'There's the nomination form. We're proposing you.'

'So what's this?' Sam read through the form carefully and then looked over at them with a hint of suspicion. 'You know, it's funny I haven't heard about this competition. No one else I've asked knows about it either.'

'But it's on official paper,' said Al, pointing to the heading on the entry form.

'And we're going send it in,' Harry added.

'And here are the first voting forms. We're submitting one each.' Al showed him the slips of paper.

Sam looked at the forms and coloured with slight embarrassment. 'I don't know, fellers. I said I wasn't interested.'

'But we've voted for you,' Rick said, trying to sound hurt.

'But it's only three votes,' Sam said. 'I don't stand a chance against the big boys. There are some posh bars around town offering food and family areas and...'

'But they haven't got what you've got...' Harry said, and announced in a grand fashion '... originality.'

'Here's some more voting slips.' Rick handed them over. 'You get all your customers to sign one. You'll be surprised how quickly they'll mount up.'

'Get that old boy down at the other end to sign one,' Al suggested, looking down the bar at the only other customer.

Sam looked at them carefully but their faces shone with expectation and encouragement.

Sam took a slip. 'I don't know...' But he went to the other end and talked to an old man in a knitted hat and stained raincoat whose beard drooped below the level of the bar.

'Will it cost me?' the old man queried.

'No,' Sam replied. He hesitated for a minute and then said, 'In fact, there's a free drink in it for you if you sign.'

The old man snatched the pen from Sam's hand. 'I'll sign two for an extra drink.'

'No. You can only sign one,' Sam said, taking back the signed form and his pen. 'It's in the rules somewhere.' He brought back the form to their end of the bar. 'I never knew that was his name,' Sam said.

Harry glanced at it. From the crab-like handwriting, he managed to decipher 'Abraham Lincoln'. 'Now that's a name that should carry some recommendation,' he observed.

Al and Rick craned forward to see the name. 'I think it must be an omen,' Rick said. 'I'll call in a week from now and collect the forms and send them in for you.'

'That's real good of you,' Sam said. 'Hey, would you like a drink on the house?'

After their drink, Harry left and called round to his son's place. Pam met him at the door and Harry gave her a special hug.

'Rosemary told me the great news,' he said as she showed him inside. 'We're both really pleased for you.'

'Early days yet,' she smiled. 'So much for me starting my career over again.' But her eyes were bright and her voice reflected her true feelings.

James raced in from another room. 'Hey, Grandpops, have you come to see my new brother?'

Harry bent down and studied the youngster's face. 'No. Where is he?'

'In there,' his grandson pointed to his mother's belly. 'He's not ready yet. Dad says he'll be here in the new year.'

Harry stood upright and gave Pam a sideways look. 'Well, I guess he's got to get used to things. How do you know it will be a brother? What about a sister?'

James thought about it. 'Nah. A girl wouldn't be so much fun. They can't pitch a ball.'

Harry kept a grin from his face. 'I bet she could with you teaching her.'

'Do you think so?' His eyes began to lighten.

'I bet you.'

'How much?'

Harry thought about it, ignoring the look he knew Pam was giving him. 'Five dollars by the time she's five.'

The boy thought about it, and before he could raise the bet, his mother ushered him back to watch television. 'I'll get you a coffee, Harry. Dave's in the kitchen.'

Dave had not long been home from work and was sitting at the kitchen table eating his way through a pizza. 'Hi Harry,' he said. 'So what brings you round here, as if I didn't know.'

'Just passing.' Harry sat down opposite his son. 'Just wanted to add my congratulations.'

'And teach our son to bet,' Pam said without animosity as she passed Harry a cup of coffee and sat down with them both.

'I heard him,' Dave said, finishing the pizza and dabbing his mouth with a napkin. 'Not a bad way, actually. We've been thinking how to prepare him if it's a girl. He didn't seem so keen on that possibility.'

'I guess not,' Pam agreed. 'Trust his grandpa to come up with the easy solution.' She reached across and touched Harry's hand. 'I should have given you a call.'

Harry shrugged. 'A lesson in life. If you can't get to a man through his stomach then try his wallet.'

'Pam learned that one pretty quickly,' Dave said seriously. 'She fills me up with pizza and then empties my wallet.'

Pam flipped a playful hand at him. 'So who isn't allowed to go with me to the shops because he fills the basket with lots of things we don't need?'

'I've heard that one before somewhere,' Harry mused. 'It must be in the Menkowitch genes.'

'It's not long before you and Mom are off to the west,' Dave said, taking the offered coffee from Pam. 'Give Rob our regards.'

'I will,' Harry said. 'Another week and we'll be flying off into the sunset. I'm looking forward to it. Well, almost.'

'What's wrong?' Dave queried.

'Nothing,' Harry began to chuckle, 'but from now until we leave, your mother's head will be full of what has to be done. She's started making lists already.'

Dave began to laugh. 'Do you remember those vacations we took when Rob and I were young boys?' He gestured over to Pam. 'She would make these long lists and then check them off with ticks. He and I used to move things around just to confuse her.'

'And she always said it was me,' Harry laughed with him. 'We had more arguments getting ready for a vacation than in the whole of the rest of the year.'

Pam was not amused and took Rosemary's side. 'Left to man, nothing would get done. I can imagine the hard time she had with the three of you. She needed a daughter to sort you out.'

Harry thought on this as he sipped his coffee. 'Now that would have been something,' he said softly.

*

When Harry and Rosemary finally went to Los Angeles to see Rob, they took – in Harry's opinion – too many cases. He packed one for himself and Rosemary packed two for herself. Then she packed a second for Harry with the clothes she thought he ought to take. A week or so before, she had made long lists of what had to be done before they went, what they should take when they went and what they had to do to get there. Harry did the best thing he could to help – he didn't get involved and stayed out of her way. He knew she was excited and the only way she burned off the expectation was by making endless lists and then rewriting them in a new order. Dave had offered to take them to the airport and, as he and his father put the cases in the trunk of his car, Rosemary poised on the doorstep, reading off the final things to check.

'Water off, alarm set.' She looked at her son. 'You know the combination when you check on the place?'

'Yes mother.'

'And Rob's phone number if you want us?'

'I have it.'

'Tickets?'

'You have them,' Harry said as he joined them.

'I'll just check again,' and she went into her bag, which was bulging with cosmetics, pills and face wipes; somewhere down the bottom, Harry was sure there was probably a bathtub and a set of towels.

'That leaves only one thing,' Harry said, and nodded to Dave.

As she asked 'What?', they each put a hand under her

244

arms and half carried and half walked her to the car. 'You'll complain if I've forgotten something,' she said as they eased her into the rear seat.

Los Angeles was warm and the sun shone every day, but Harry noticed the air didn't feel as thin and clean. It was the number of cars pumping out exhaust fumes, Rob explained as they settled into Rob's house – or mansion, as Harry kept referring to it. They liked the way it was furnished – the floors were beige stone tiles with occasional rugs scattered around and there was plenty of room between the furniture. It gave the impression of great space, which reflected the panoramic view of the Pacific from the west-facing windows. Each day, Rob took them somewhere new. First stop was the homes of the famous, and Rob cruised round Beverley Hills, stopping outside some big place and saying that belonged to so-and-so who was presently living with so-and-so. He took them around Los Angeles and up to San Francisco and arranged a flight across to Phoenix; they hired a car to visit the Grand Canyon and then went down to Las Vegas for a few nights, where they took in a show and a little gambling and then the round trip back to Phoenix for the flight back. Rob seemed to be trying to make up for all his absent years, and by the end of the first week, Harry and Rosemary were exhausted. They were happy when he said they would be spending a quiet weekend at his house.

On their arrival, Rob had introduced them to Miriam, whose hair was so black it shimmered with a tinge of blue in the sunlight; her skin was natural and the colour of coffee. By the way she spoke with short, crisp syllables, Harry thought she might be Mexican or of Spanish extraction; only her deep blues eyes defied this. One evening, when Rob and Rosemary had gone for a walk along the beach, Harry sat alone with Miriam on a balcony overlooking the sea and asked, 'Where do you come from?'

'Los Angeles,' she smiled pleasantly, guessing he thought otherwise.

'And your parents?'

'Here too. They have a drugstore not too far from here.' She saw his look and gave up the game with a short laugh. 'My mother comes from São Paulo in Brazil. That is why I have this tan.'

'And a lovely one it is,' Harry said admiringly. 'Have you known Rob long?' he changed the subject.

'Almost two years. We have been living together for about half of that,' she said, pre-empting the next question.

The balcony faced west and Harry watched as the sun, a huge orange globe, settled on the horizon; it painted a rippling orange streak of flame across the sea towards them. 'I've not seen Rob so happy for many years,' Harry said in a quiet voice, feeling the moment when day was about to change to evening. 'I guess you've played a good part in that.'

'We are happy together,' she replied simply.

'Are you thinking of getting married?' Harry asked.

'Does it bother you that we are living together?'

'Not at all. It doesn't seem so important these days.' He sighed as the sun slipped out of sight, but the sky remained bright. 'It's what you feel for each other that counts.'

Miriam felt grateful for his understanding. 'It may happen,' she said, and then added, 'one day.'

Rosemary and Rob strolled along the sand. They had both removed their shoes and walked close enough to the water's edge so that creamy wavelets, hissing quietly, washed over their feet.

'It's so lovely here,' Rosemary said, admiring the view. The sea and the sun and just about everything to her was perfect. She sighed and said, 'You're a lucky lad and you've made a good choice.'

'We like it,' Rob said. 'Even though it sits on a fault line. But we tend not to think of that.'

'I'm sorry,' Rosemary laughed. 'I meant Miriam. She's a lovely girl.'

'Oh right. Yes,' he untangled himself from the confusion. 'She has a wonderful nature. There's not a bad thought or word in her.'

'That's nice,' Rosemary said as she watched a young girl throw a ball into the sea and her excitable dog charge in to retrieve it. 'Do you see her as someone special?'

'You mean, do I think we will get married?'

'Well I presume that is the next step.' Rosemary wondered if she had touched on a sensitive point. 'Look at that dog.' She stepped away from the subject as the dog bounded out of the sea and shook its wetness all over the young girl and they heard her crying out with delight.

They stopped walking to watch. 'We may,' was all he offered.

'I didn't mean to pry,' Rosemary said, but he put his arm round her shoulder to show it did not matter.

'Did you and dad live together? Before you were married?' he asked.

Rosemary laughed. 'No. But those times were different. But we did ... well, you know.'

'Did what?' Rob asked innocently.

Rosemary was about to explain, with some difficulty, but then she caught the look in his eye. She slapped him lightly on the chest. 'Some things in life have always been the same,' she smiled.

When they were in bed that night, Harry and Rosemary lay back in the darkness and the warmth and both felt content with things. Harry was for going to sleep but Rosemary talked on a bit about their trips and Rob's home and finally got round to Miriam. 'I asked Rob if he was thinking of getting married,' she said.

'That's funny,' Harry murmured, 'I asked Miriam the same question.'

'Oh dear,' Rosemary uttered.

'What's the matter?'

'They'll think we disapprove of them living like this.'

Harry turned over, his sign that he wanted to sleep. 'Knowing Rob, it won't bother him and he'll do exactly what he wants to in his own time.'

In the next room, Rob and Miriam lay quietly in each other's arms. Her hair hung close to his face and he could smell an essence of cedar. 'My mother asked if we were thinking of getting married,' he said into the darkness.

She stirred and turned into him, pressing her body against his. 'Your father asked me the same thing.'

Rob smiled into the darkness. 'I guessed it would come up.'

She lifted her head and tried to see his expression in the darkness. 'Do you think they disapprove of us living together?'

'Nope,' was his short reply.

'So why did they both ask?'

'Because that is what parents do.'

She just said 'Oh,' and snuggled her head against him. 'Perhaps we ought to talk about it.'

He yawned and tightened his arm round her. 'Yep. In the morning.'

She smiled in the darkness. She would remind him.

One day during the next week, Rob took them to his studios. As he drove into the car park, Harry looked up at the large sign fixed on the roof: 'MBGPS Special FX'. He felt an inner pride that his son had succeeded beyond his expectation.

'What's that stand for?' Harry queried.

'The FX is short for effects and the other letters are the five partners' surnames: Menkowitch, Braden, Groenink, Peterson and Sanders. No special order – we're equal partners.'

He turned towards a space with his name on a small sign. 'To the right are the offices and design labs,' Rob pointed out as he parked the car. 'We call them labs because that's where we initially create things. That big building to the left is an old airplane hangar built in the 1930s.'

They got out of the car and Harry asked, 'Why do you need somewhere so big? Don't you do everything on computer?'

'The animation and graphics, yes,' Rob explained as he guided them towards the lab area. 'But we sometimes need sets and scenery to shoot at and then add the computer images in afterwards. We do adverts and smaller stuff as well as the bigger movies.' They arrived at a solid iron door and Rob punched a code into a pad; the door swung open. 'We need security here,' and he stepped back to let them in. 'There are a lot of people who would like to get their hands on our software.'

They took an elevator to the fifth floor and Rob led them into a room that was all white – the ceiling, floor and walls. It was cluttered with so much equipment that winked and blinked coloured lights that to Harry and Rosemary it was like walking into a future age. What struck Harry most was the air – it felt cool and dry.

Rob noticed his father sniff at the air. 'It has to be conditioned and filtered. Dust and moisture are our biggest enemies.'

They saw several people sitting at monitors with various displays and Rob led them there. 'This is our initial design area. It's our think-tank. When we get an assignment, it comes here first for them to play around with it.' A young dark girl with spectacles looked over her shoulder and smiled. 'This is Annie,' Rob said. 'Annie, this is my mom and dad.'

Annie stood up and held out her hand. 'It's nice to meet

you both. I see where Rob gets his good looks from.' They both noticed her hand was cool from the temperature, but her welcoming smile was warm.

'From me or his mother?' Harry chirped in.

'From me, of course,' Rosemary said quickly.

'From you both,' Annie said diplomatically.

'And this is Tom, the head of the unit.' Rob passed to a thin, sinewy character with a goaty beard and a large Adam's apple. 'This is my mom and dad.'

Tom stood up and similarly held out his hand. 'It's good to know he's got parents. We doubted it sometimes.' He smiled broadly to show he was joking.

'Tom thinks I drive them too hard,' Rob added.

'Is there a lot of pressure?' Harry asked.

Tom answered. 'Yes, but it comes from the competition out here. There are a lot of companies chasing too few contracts.' Then he smiled again. 'But we're the best.'

'I'll take you into the hangar next. Thanks Tom.' He led them back to the elevator. 'There's not a lot to see in this building, just people working with computers, but the hangar's different.'

As they rode down in the elevator, Harry asked, 'I suppose your office is at the top of the building.'

'I don't have one,' Rob said casually. 'No need for a desk. I'm a hands-on person.'

Harry saw Rosemary's eyebrows rise in a query. 'It means he works,' he explained.

'We run things pretty easy here,' Rob said as they left the elevator and followed a long corridor. 'Everyone knows that unless we keep on top you can disappear overnight in this game.'

'Have you had any problems with someone stealing your software?' Harry asked.

'Piracy, you mean? Just once.' Rob paused at a large door. 'We had a kid working here a year ago. He was

250

something of a genius but he got greedy. We found out he had stolen some sensitive software and was going to sell it to one of our rivals.'

'My.' Rosemary was startled. 'Did you stop him?'

Rob began to chuckle. 'Hans did. Hans Groenink, one of my partners. He's Swedish and stands about six-foot thirteen. You'll meet him in a minute. We knew the kid hadn't time to sell it on but he wouldn't tell us where he'd stashed it. Whatever we did, he knew he had a valuable piece of merchandise. That was until Hans got involved.'

'What did he do?' Harry was interested.

Rob smiled at the memory. 'I was for going to the police, but Hans sat himself in front of this kid and stared at him for a long while. 'You know,' he said to him at last, 'if we go to the police, you may get five years or so. Maybe nothing. Without the software we'd have a job proving you took it. So I'll tell you what I'm going to do. I'm going to lock you in one of our secure rooms with no food or water and each morning I'll visit you and ask you where it is. If you don't tell me, one morning I'll find you dead.' The kid told us straight away. We retrieved the software and kicked him out.'

'Did Hans mean it?' Rosemary asked, fascinated by the story.

'I asked him that but he didn't reply. I suspect he did.' Rob punched the keypad and the door slid back to reveal a huge hangar area filled with various props, sets, cameras and lighting. To one side, there was a shoot in progress and Rob led them towards it. 'I have to ask you not touch anything. There are some robotics about which could run amok if activated.'

When they neared the set, he halted. 'We're making an advertisement; let's see if you can guess what it's for.' Rob waved to a blond giant who they assumed was Hans. 'You

251

can talk if you want. We make it silent and then do the voiceover and music afterwards.'

Harry and Rosemary stood fascinated by the scene. A beautiful girl in a flimsy nightdress sat on a bed brushing her hair, and then a cat – a white, long-haired Persian – appeared from one side, jumped onto the bed and went over to the girl. She laid down the brush and the cat went up on its hind legs. It reached up with its front paws on her shoulders and sniffed at her hair while she ruffled her hands through its fur. The cat made a soft mew and then suddenly looked round and chased something invisible from the bed.

Hans stepped forward and clapped his hands. 'Great. We'll run through the film and check its okay, but it looks good. Take a break everybody.'

'Well?' Rob asked, turning to them. 'Did you guess what we were advertising?'

'Cat food,' Harry jumped in. Rob looked to his mother.

'Hair shampoo,' Rosemary said.

'You got it.' Rob laughed at his father's dismay.

'How did you guess?' Harry queried.

Rosemary tried to suppress a superior look. 'She was in her nightclothes so she had probably just got up and washed her hair. She was brushing it. And then the cat came on and sniffed her hair. Quite obvious really. By the way, how did you train the cat to do that?'

'We didn't,' Rob replied. 'We hire them from a firm that trains animals to act in these type of things.'

'And why did it suddenly run off?' Harry queried.

'Chasing a mouse,' Rob answered. 'Wasn't it obvious? Didn't you see the little mouse climb up on the bed?'

Harry looked over to the bed where the girl had stood up and had donned a bathrobe. 'You put the mouse in afterwards,' he said. 'A computer-generated mouse.' He looked to his son with satisfaction. 'Am I right?'

'In one. The idea of the advert is that the perfume of the shampoo is appealing to cats and then a mouse comes on, also attracted by the perfume, and the cat chases it away.'

'Won't that make people think that the smell will attract cats and mice?' Harry asked.

'Apparently not,' Rob replied. 'We're only doing what the shampoo manufacturers came up with themselves. They believe that women will be enamoured by the cat.'

'Well, he was furry and cuddly,' Rosemary admitted.

'You see what I mean?' Rob addressed to his father. 'Oh, here's Hans. Hi big feller. This is my mom and dad.'

The tall Swede shook Harry's hand vigorously and then bowed towards Rosemary before giving her a kiss on the forehead. 'Rob said he'd bring you in to see us working.' His voice was heavily accented and his mixture of words made Rosemary smile. 'Do you want to see the finished product? Come. I'll show you.'

He led them to a small monitor and, flicking a switch, stood back to let them see. The advert ran through, but this time with a voiceover and soft music and flashes of the bottle of shampoo. Rosemary was so impressed at the end when the cat chased the mouse that she clapped.

'I'm glad you liked it,' the big Swede beamed. 'That was unusual. It took only a few takes to get it right.'

'I'm impressed how quickly you pull it all together,' Harry admired.

'We have some pretty powerful computers,' Hans explained. 'Once we have all the parts, the computer pulls them together in the right order and automatically adds in the sound and the graphics. Rob wrote that software.'

Harry and Rosemary looked at their son with a new admiration. 'Well, there was me and a lot of other people,' Rob said modestly.

'Don't listen to him,' Hans protested. 'He's a top guy.'

'Have you got time to have lunch with us?' Rob asked.

'Nah. You folks go off and enjoy your holiday. We've got a lot of shorts to catch up on.'

When they had said their goodbyes, Rob showed them some of the equipment round the hangar and then took them off to a cafe on the beach to have hot doughnuts and coffee.

Harry filled his mouth with a doughnut before speaking. 'That's some set-up you got there.' Rosemary reached across with a paper napkin and wiped jam from his mouth.

'It earns a buck or two,' Rob admitted. 'But as I said earlier, there's a lot of competition and you have to keep ahead of the game.'

'But you're the best,' Rosemary said with a mother's pride.

'At the moment, yes. But we're constantly looking for newer and better things.' Rob gazed out over the mirror-like sea. 'Do you fancy a swim this afternoon?'

'I was just thinking how inviting it looked,' Harry said through another full mouth.

'You'll sink with all those doughnuts inside you.' Rosemary gave a little dig as Harry's hand hovered over the doughnut box.

The final week passed quickly and all too soon they were standing in the departure lounge saying their farewells. Rosemary put her arm round Rob. 'Take care of yourself,' she advised as mothers do. 'Try not to work too hard.'

'Of course not,' Rob said in a pat reply.

'And you, young lady,' Harry gave Miriam a hug. 'Make sure he doesn't neglect you.'

'Of course not,' she made the same reply.

They heard their flight number called and Harry and Rosemary sighed in unison. Harry held out his hand to Rob. 'Thanks for a wonderful vacation. I'm really proud of you, Son.'

'Thanks Dad.'

'And as for you, young lady,' Harry turned to Miriam, 'I think Rob is an extraordinarily lucky man to have found someone as lovely as you. And I mean lovely in every sense.'

Miriam was slightly taken aback and delivered a kiss that made Harry step back. 'Thanks Dad,' she said with a huge smile and bright eyes.

Harry was touched by the word dad. Rob coughed, 'We'll ... er ... invite you over again soon.' He paused and then added, 'When we get married.'

Rosemary's hand went to her mouth and Harry's mouth fell open.

Rob laughed at their reaction. He put his arm round Miriam's waist. 'I need to make an honest woman of her.'

Miriam dug him in the ribs the way Rosemary often did with Harry – there's something special about women's reaction to humour.

When they returned home, Rosemary busied herself with unpacking, getting the piles of washing started and generally inspecting the house as if it had somehow altered itself in their absence. Harry also made himself busy, or so it seemed, but he just fiddled around and achieved little.

18

On the Monday after their usual game, Harry sat with Al and Rick in the club lounge and told them about their trip to Los Angeles and about Rob and the lovely Miriam.

'So, they could be getting married soon?' Al asked.

Harry shrugged. 'Maybe. It looks like it, I suppose. They seem too happy to complicate things with marriage.'

Rick chuckled at that and Al understood – 'why spoil it?' he thought. Things had taken a down turn with Phillippa. Perhaps she had tired of their rekindled relationship, maybe she had found someone else. Whatever it was, she had returned to her old ways and he wasn't enjoying it. As a result, he had started going to the diner again.

'I went to Sam's Bar yesterday,' Rick informed them with a gleeful look in his eyes, 'and collected the voting forms. He was quite excited about it.'

'How many did he get signed?' Al asked.

'Nearly forty. Not many, but he gave a free drink to everyone who signed a form,' Rick said.

'Uh-oh,' Al sighed and when they looked at him he added, 'perhaps this is getting out of hand. Especially as he's been buying all his customers a drink. He'll ban us for sure when he finds out.'

'Nah,' Rick drawled. 'Besides, I have the award here. I printed it from my computer last night.' He reached into a large brown envelope and took out a sheet of thick, quality paper coloured a faint yellow that gave it a parchment effect. He showed it to them.

'The Golden Star Bar Award,' Harry read out the words across the top, printed in a grand Cloister Black font. 'Presented to the best bar in Wannabee'. Below that was a dotted line, along which Rick had written in a fine style, 'Sam's Bar'. He read down the page that explained why Sam was the winner of the award. 'Pretty flattering,' he observed.

'But how are we going to present it to him?' Al asked.

Harry chuckled. 'I suppose I could ask Felicia to don her sequinned costume to present it to him.'

'He'd know we've been having him on,' Rick said.

'Isn't that the idea?' Al queried.

'I thought we should play it along without hurting his feelings,' Rick said. 'I thought of getting it framed under glass and sending it to him through the mail with a letter. That way he'd think it came from the Mayor's office.'

'And he'd hang it up in the bar,' Harry said in admiration of Rick's idea.

Al began to laugh. 'He'd sure make a big thing of it.'

'And there was I thinking you were an upright member of the community,' Harry said through a smile.

'Me?' Rick replied. 'Who's been spreading that rumour?'

They waited for a few weeks before visiting Sam's Bar, allowing time for the mail to arrive. One evening they strolled in casually and sat at the bar on stools.

'Three glasses of your finest ale, landlord,' Harry said with a deep dramatic voice.

'You mean three Budweisers,' Sam said. 'As usual.'

'I guess,' Harry said.

When Sam had served the beers he hovered in front of them, cleaning the bar with exaggerated sweeps of a cloth.

'Steady on, Sam,' Rick advised. 'You'll rub the bar away.'

257

'Just keeping up appearances,' Sam said, with a smug look. 'I have to now.'

'Are you expecting the Mayor to visit?' Al asked.

Sam thumbed over his shoulder. 'You haven't noticed?' They looked past him and saw the framed award certificate on the wall behind him.

'Hey, Sammy,' Rick shouted, 'you won.'

Sam shrugged with some embarrassment. 'It arrived a few days ago. What do you think of it? Looks pretty good, huh?'

'Now that's something,' Harry commented. 'Looks impressive.'

'I like the frame,' Al joined in. 'Looks expensive.'

'I guess I've got you guys to thank,' Sam said. 'Have the next beer on me.'

'Well, that's very nice of you,' Harry said, 'but that's not the reason we did it, was it guys?'

'No' they both said in unison.

*

As the days rolled through Summer with endless heat and clear skies, the time came again for the Mixed Competition. As defending champions, Harry and Louise were the last group to tee off. A few days before, Louise had led him to the noticeboard and pointed to the list.

'Do you see who we are playing with?' she said, tapping the board with her finger.

'Ah, the same delightful pair we played with last year,' Harry smiled. 'That looks like Dinsdale's work.'

'Does it bother you?' she queried.

'Why should it? It will be a quiet round,' and in answer to her look he said, 'I doubt if they will be talking to us.' Louise wasn't convinced and Harry put his arm round her shoulders. 'All you have to do is wear those tight shorts and leave the rest to me.'

On the day of the competition, Harry and Louise drove their cart down to the first tee where Babs and Jim were waiting impatiently; they avoided looking at them until they were too close to ignore.

'A lovely day for golf,' Harry enthused. 'It hardly seems a year ago since we played together.' He noticed Babs was looking past him and eyeing Louise's clothing. He looked back at Louise and then back to her. 'She has a whole wardrobe of that stuff,' he said, and winked to Jim. They made no response.

Harry went over to his golf cart to select a club and leaned close to Louise and spoke out the side of his mouth. 'I said tight shorts, but you haven't got a bra on.'

'Does it notice?' she smiled innocently.

'It does with the sun on you.'

'Just doing my bit,' she added. 'I thought it might add another distraction.'

'It does,' Harry said, taking out his driver. 'To me as well.'

Louise giggled. 'Then keep looking at Babs. She'll dampen your ardour.'

When Harry mounted onto the tee, Jim was swinging away, loosening his muscles. He waited until Harry was close to him. 'Is she still going out with you?' he queried.

'I prefer long-term relationships,' Harry replied with a straight face.

'I thought your wife was supposed to be your long-term relationship,' Jim said, keeping his voice low.

'Oh she is,' Harry said, 'but I like a little variety in my life.'

Jim moved away not sure if he believed him. He settled on the ball and drove long and straight and turned with a smug look. 'Nice to get the first one away,' he said in a satisfied way.

'Better than last year,' Harry conceded, noting the

smugness disappear from Jim's face. He then hit straight, but was about thirty yards short of Jim's ball. 'I don't try to keep up with a big hitter like you,' he admitted with a smile. 'You'll have to show me how you do it sometime.'

Harry joined Louise in the cart and drove up level with his ball. Louise selected a fairway wood and eased the ball just short of the front of the green. Jim stood near Harry and looked over his clubs while Babs went off to make her shot.

'You have a lot of wooden clubs,' he commented. 'I use irons on the fairways. They're more accurate.'

'It's my age,' Harry explained. 'I can't hit like you.' He looked up the fairway to Jim's ball. 'I suppose you'd take a five-iron from here if it were your shot.'

Jim walked away. 'An eight at most,' he almost scoffed.

Louise came over. 'What was that about?'

Harry let a smile slip across his lips. 'Nothing. I'll just let him keep bragging.'

Babs hit a high ball onto the green about twenty feet from the pin. Harry drove up to his ball, selected a wedge and walked over to his ball. There was a slight slope up onto the green and he judged a chip and run would be better. He walked back to the golf cart and changed to an eight-iron. As he slowly ambled back, he noticed the other two were watching him with disapproval at the time he was taking. He ignored them, measuring the distance and chipping it stone dead on the hole. With two putts, Jim and Babs parred the hole as well.

'Nice chip, Harry,' Louise complimented him as they drove to the next tee. Harry just smiled.

Off the next tee it was the ladies' turn to drive, and Babs hit a reasonable ball that faded slightly to the right and held on the fairway; Louise sailed her ball about thirty yards past to the left edge of the fairway. Jim studied the lie of his ball and judged the distance to the green – it

260

was not a particularly long hole but the green was tucked to the right with some overhanging trees obscuring the right edge.

'You've opened up the green nicely,' Harry said to Louise. He had meant to keep his voice low, but Jim heard the comment and looked back with some disdain before steadying himself over his ball. He aimed left to slide it round, but when he hit, the ball kept too straight, hit the left side of the green and rolled over a bank and down the other side.

Harry took a medium iron and punched it straight at the pin; the ball flew low but straight, pitched short and ran on towards the flagstick, stopping about ten feet short.

'Not pretty, but effective,' he grinned to the dour faces of Jim and Babs.

The game continued with little said and Jim was careful not to look too much at Louise, except when he was sure Babs was looking the other way. Their scores remained about the same, on handicap, and Harry found it pleasant enough; his game was steady but Louise seemed a little uptight. As they approached the tenth tee he asked her what was wrong.

She shrugged. 'Babs is getting to me.'

'What has she said?' he asked.

'Nothing,' came her short reply.

Harry thought about it and then said, as they neared the ladies' tee, 'Ignore whatever I say and aim to the right side, hitting it as hard as you can.'

Louise gave him a strange look but he just nodded. She mounted the tee, placed her ball on the tee peg and then stood back to survey the fairway ahead.

'Aim over the water,' Harry said casually. 'It's the shortest route and you can carry over the pond easily.'

Louise looked at him and took up her stance. She hit the ball hard as Harry had told her and although it set out right and seemed to be heading into the trees, the extra effort she had put in pulled the ball back; it landed in the middle of the fairway and skipped over to the left side, quite a distance past the small pond. She smiled as she came down the steps and stood next to him. Babs showed some confusion at the shot and Jim mounted the steps and stood close to her, saying something they could not hear. Babs seemed to argue with him and he muttered something before leaving. When Babs hit, her swing was noticeably quicker, and she pulled the ball low and left. It stopped just short of the pond but in some thick grass. Harry guided the golf cart up the side of a bank and onto the cart track.

'So are you going to explain?' Louise asked, sitting next to him.

'I've noticed something about your game,' he said, pausing while they bumped over a step in the path that rattled their clubs in the bags. 'When you swing easy, you hit straight, but when you try to hit it hard it always curves to the left.'

'So why didn't you let me swing as I do normally and hit it up the middle?' she queried.

'Because Babs would have done the same.'

She said, 'Oh,' as she realised what he had done. 'I thought you'd been too quiet.'

He stopped the cart short of the pond and watched Jim peering down at his ball in the long grass. 'So what did Babs say to you?'

Louise seemed reluctant but in the end sighed and said, 'She's made a few remarks about you. But then she said she thought you were too old.'

'Too old for golf?' Harry asked, surprised.

'No. Too old for me.' She looked at him. 'Are you upset?'

Harry laughed softly. 'Nope. I guess I am too old for you. So what did you say to her?'

262

She chuckled. 'I said you had it in the two areas that matter. Between your ears and between your legs.'

Harry almost choked.

The tenth was the turning point for Jim and Babs; they began to argue with each other and Harry and Louise just looked on and said nothing. Jim just managed to get the ball out of the rough grass and Babs scuffed her shot low and too short. After that, any errant shot was the other's fault and, as any golfer knows, when partners fall apart, so does their game.

Although Harry and Louise returned a good score, they only managed third place, but Harry was happy enough; Jim and Babs were again unplaced. Dinsdale assisted the club captain with the prize-giving and it was the first time since the JDW affair that Harry found himself within talking distance of him; for some reason, Dinsdale had been avoiding him. As new captain, one of Dinsdale's cronies gave them their prizes. Harry leaned past him. 'How's it going then, Dinsdale?' he asked and winked. Dinsdale's face coloured slightly and his narrow eyes became slits. He said nothing.

As they walked away, Louise tugged at Harry's arm. 'He's still not forgiven you over Felicia.'

'Nope.' Harry smiled easily back at her.

19

The Summer passed all too quickly and as Harry had said in Sam's Bar one evening with some truth, if they cancelled the public holidays and the festive days, there would be nothing to look forward to, to measure the time against and the years would pass more slowly.

'Nothing to look forward to is right,' Al had said. 'That's the remark of a retired man. It's a choice between expectation and a slow death, and I prefer the expectation.'

'It's the early build-up that annoys me,' Rick partly agreed with Harry. 'The shops fill up with Christmas stuff in September.'

But the festive days remain on the calendar and the year hops forward from one to the next with hardly a pause to gather breath between them. Autumn painted the trees, the cold fronts moved down from the north, the furry mammals collected food to store and fathers were rummaging around attics and cellars looking for last year's decorations and untangling the knotted wires of Christmas tree lights.

The snow came later than usual to Wannabee. It had threatened a couple of times, so the gritting trucks had been loaded and the snow ploughs fitted, but the clouds had passed over, deaf to the pleas of the children below and there remained a cold, dry, crispness in the air. The weathermen at the local radio station had given up predicting an imminent fall and contented themselves with air temperatures and chill factors.

One evening, Al travelled across town to see an old friend of his who was ailing from a prolonged bout of influenza. He was saddened that his friend looked so frail and his usually full face had shrunk to hollows and shadows. On his way back, a shower of sleety rain began to fall and he turned on the heater to stop the windows misting. As he hit a sleazier area on the eastern side of the river, he stopped at a red light and he drummed his fingers lightly on the wheel, looking idly about. It was then that he thought he saw Phillippa standing on the corner across the road, close to and in conversation with a man in a dark raincoat and hat. Something passed between them and then she walked briskly away. The lights turned green and the cars behind started hooting their horns. Al cursed and drove a short way forward until he could make a turn. When he finally made it back to the lights, the area was deserted, and though he drove some way back down the road, he didn't see her again. He pulled into the kerb and sat thinking – he was sure it was her, but what would she be doing in this part of town? He had no answers, and the longer he thought about it, the less certain he was that it was Phillippa. After all, it was very dark and the sleet had partly obscured his vision. Al drove home feeling a heavy rock of gloom on his shoulders.

Phillippa was not home when he got there and, although he hated himself for it, he went up to the bedroom and searched through her drawers and wardrobes. He found nothing, although he wasn't actually sure what he'd expected to find. On the drive back, his mind had woven odd things together especially her ever-changing temperament; high one moment and low the next, and by the time he arrived, he had convinced himself that her mood swings could be down to taking drugs. On finding nothing, he began to curse himself for his stupidity, but the thought kept nagging at the back of his mind. As he descended the stairs, Phillippa entered. He paused halfway down; she was wearing a coat similar to the one he had seen the woman wearing.

'Where have you been?' he asked, moving down.

Phillippa barely gave him a glance and took off her coat. 'It's a filthy night,' she said, going passed him into the kitchen.

He followed her and stood leaning against the door frame. 'How are you feeling?'

'Me? I feel fine apart from getting a soaking.' She gave him a wide smile. 'Do you want some coffee?'

'Thanks.' He moved into the room. 'You seem in a good mood.'

'Why not?' she asked as she scooped coffee into the percolator. 'Has something happened? You went to see your friend tonight. How is he?'

Al was surprised she remembered where he had been. 'Not good. He's been sick for quite a while and it seems to be taking its toll.'

'I'm sorry.' She sounded genuine as she retrieved two mugs from a cupboard.

Al seated himself at the breakfast bar. 'I thought I saw you when I was driving back.'

'Oh? Where was that?' she said lightly.

'I was stopped at some lights. At the corner with Studermens, the department store. I think it's the junction of Lincoln and Souix Falls Drive.'

She thought for a moment and her brow wrinkled. 'That's on the eastern side. No. I haven't been near there.'

Al looked across to the bag that she had put to one side near the toaster – he so wanted to go over and look inside it.

A couple of days before Christmas, Harry picked up Al and Rick and drove them to Sam's Bar for a festive drink. They sat on their usual barstools and sipped their Buds.

It was quiet in the bar and it was not long before Sam edged towards them, wiping the bar with a cloth.

'Say, Sam,' Rick said as he appeared in front of them. 'Don't you ever think of decorating your bar? You have your award to live up to now.' Rick nodded to the frame on the wall.

Sam looked round the room. 'Nah. The paintwork's good for another five years.' He looked pointedly at Harry. 'It's you guys smoking cigars that make it look dirty.'

'I meant Christmas decorations,' Rick corrected him

'Jeeesus,' Sam drawled, 'what do I want them for?'

'Christmas?' Rick suggested.

'Goodwill to all men?' Al put in.

'Peace and joy,' Harry added.

'You sound like the friggin three wise men,' Sam scoffed.

'You might attract more custom,' Harry suggested.

'None of my customers would even notice them,' Sam argued.

Rick looked round at the near-empty bar room. 'That's true.'

'But we'd notice,' Al said.

'You come here anyway,' Sam muttered defensively. 'What's the point? You put them up and a few days later you take them down.'

'I think it's the bit in-between that matters,' Rick commented dryly.

Sam muttered again and moved away; he felt he wasn't winning again.

'What are you doing for Christmas?' Harry asked as a general question.

'At home,' Rick said. 'Ricardo is going away to Florida but Anna's brother and his family are coming to stay. It should be a full house. And you?'

'We're going to Dave and Pam's,' Harry replied. 'I'm hoping Rob will make it, but he phoned last week and said

267

he was on a tight schedule for a film company so he may have to stay in LA. It'll be a pity.'

Al sipped his beer and said nothing. Harry and Rick exchanged glances. Al knew this moment would come and had wondered, without success, how he would handle it. His relationship with Phillippa had not been easy through the Summer and instead of confronting her about his suspicions that she was on drugs, he had simply spent more time at the diner; this had only tended to add to the confusion of his emotions. But then everything had changed for him during the last week when, after their usual game of golf, he had gone to the diner for lunch.

*

Aritha seemed preoccupied and didn't spend much time with him as he ate his usual plate of scrambled eggs and bacon and drank his coffee. When the place had virtually emptied, she came and leaned close over the counter.

'George has got himself a new job.' She referred to her husband by name, which was unusual.

'That's good,' Al said, wiping his mouth with a paper napkin.

'In Philadelphia,' she said.

From the tone of her voice, Al guessed she wasn't over the moon about it. 'A big city,' was his only comment.

'He starts in the new year.'

Al continued patting his lips with the napkin while he searched for something to say. 'So you'll be leaving here.'

'Maybe.'

'Maybe?' he queried, screwing up the napkin and dropping it onto his plate.

She took the plate away, dropped the napkin into a bin and put the plate and cutlery into the dishwasher and came back. 'Want more coffee?'

Al shook his head. 'So why only maybe?'

She touched her hands together and interlocked her fingers as she rested her elbows on the counter and leaned closer to him. 'Maybe I don't want to go.'

Al knew the reason but didn't want to admit to it. 'It may be an opportunity for a fresh start for you both.'

'Al?' her voice almost cracked with the sound of a plea. 'You know people don't change. Not at our age.'

'That's true,' he said quietly. 'I guess I'm too set in my ways to change much.'

Aritha watched his face as he looked down into his empty coffee cup. She felt she knew the answer but had to say it anyway. 'I'd stay if you wanted me to.'

He looked at her and she saw a deep sadness in his grey eyes. 'I can't ask you that,' he said quietly.

It had been said – all the hopes, doubts and fears that she had harboured, and that had deprived her of sleep, had come together to be dashed in five short words. She knew there was no point in saying more and turned away to hide the moisture forming in her eyes.

Al called after her, but she disappeared into the back room. He waited for a moment and then got up, put some money on the counter and left.

That evening, after several hours sitting in his study, he went into the lounge where Phillippa was reading. He sat in a chair opposite; she didn't look up but he could tell her concentration on the book was false and that she was waiting for him to speak.

'I was thinking about Christmas,' he said at last.

'What about it?' she asked without looking up.

'Oh, going away down to the Caribbean or somewhere warm.' He waited for a reaction but got none. 'Somewhere warm,' he repeated.

She laid her book down. 'It's a bit late now. They'll be

269

booked out. Besides,' she lifted the book again, 'I'm going to stay with my sister Betty.'

'That sounds singular,' he commented.

The book was lowered again and he noticed her expression was cool. 'You don't like her particularly.'

'Is that why you are going to see her? Because you know I wouldn't want to?' His voice was half caught between surprise and anger.

She was about to say 'Would you want to come?' but she didn't want to give him the option. 'It's a while since I saw her. It's a family time.'

She said it in a way that excluded him and he got up and returned to his study. He sat in his chair and drew his fingers slowly over his lips while he thought about it; he hadn't guessed things had gotten quite so bad. He thought of ringing Aritha – he had her home number – but he knew that was not an alternative. As much as he now wanted her, he felt he had no right transferring his misery to another family. Instead, he looked through his personal phone book and, finding the name he wanted, lifted the receiver and dialled a number. It rang several times before a thin, almost whining voice answered.

'Betty? It's Al.' There was a pause and he added, 'Phillippa's husband.'

'Oh right,' the voice said without enthusiasm.

'We were just talking about Christmas and how quiet it usually is with just the two of us. Phillippa asked me to give you a call. See if you wanted to visit us. Stay for a week or so.'

'She asked you to do that?' the whining voice questioned.

'Yes.' He tried to put humour into his voice. 'She said if I asked you then you'd believe we wanted you to come.'

'That's true,' she said and he thought he could detect a little laugh in her voice. 'Can't come though. We're going to Vancouver to stay with friends.'

270

'That's a pity,' he lied. 'Not to worry, it was just an idea. Have a good trip,' and before she could reply, he put the phone down.

He sat for a while longer with his finger tracing round his lips again. Then he reached for the phone and dialled another number – it was his attorney who was a close friend and wouldn't mind him ringing him at home at that hour. He made an appointment to see him in the morning.

*

Al came out of his thoughts and rapped his glass on the bar. 'How about some service here?' Sam reluctantly left watching the television and sauntered back up the bar. 'Three Jack Daniels,' Al ordered.

'Just a beer for me,' Harry cut in. 'I'm driving.'

'And a beer will do for me,' Rick added.

'Two beers and one Jack Daniels. A large one,' Al ordered.

Sam served the two beers. 'So, are we celebrating already?' he queried as he poured a generous measure of the whiskey into a glass. 'Do you want ice with it?'

'No ice.' Al shook his head, took the glass and held it up. 'To a new year and a new life.'

Harry and Rick held their glasses up but exchanged glances again.

'So what's the new life?' Sam asked.

'You've just missed a touchdown,' Harry interrupted quickly and nodded towards the television.

Sam cursed and turned away. 'Friggin' hell. They've been playing three quarters without a score and the moment my back is turned they go and do it.'

'That's the problem with customers,' Harry said to the retreating figure.

Al emptied his glass with one swallow and rapped it on

271

the counter again. 'Another JD.' Sam didn't move away from the screen. 'Hey Sam! Some service over here.'

'Yeah. Yeah,' Sam said, coming back with the bottle. He put it on the counter. 'Serve yourself,' and he went back to the other end.

'Now that's trusting,' Al said and almost filled the glass.

Harry watched him drink half the glass. 'Did I tell you I met Dinsdale?'

Al took another swallow. 'You mean he failed to avoid you?' Rick asked.

Harry chuckled. 'He tried to but he was standing at the urinal at the time so he had no place to go. I stood next to him.'

Al refilled his glass. 'So what did you do?'

'Just peed,' Harry said with humour. 'He tried to ignore me but in the end he said, "The course will be closing soon. The snow's coming."'

'And what did you say to that?' Rick persisted, hoping that Al would stop drinking.

'Nothing straight away,' Harry smiled. 'He was in so much of a hurry to get away that he caught his fly-zip in his shirt. As he struggled to pull it back down I just said, "Looks like you need the Winter break" and I left him to it.'

'That was not a gennelmanly thing to do,' Al said. His words were slurring and running together with a small hiccup at the end of them.

'I think it is time to go,' Rick suggested. 'I promised Anna I wouldn't be late.' He dropped some money onto the bar.

'Me too,' Harry agreed and he touched Al's shoulder. 'Come on, Al. It's time to go before you swallow the bottle as well.'

Al swayed off his stool and they both held an arm and guided him to the door. 'Have a good Christmas,' Rick called out but Sam didn't turn away from the game.

'I'll be with you in a minute,' he said absently. A little while later, during a time-out, Sam looked round and found he was alone. He wandered up and collected up the dollars they had left on the bar and put them in the till without counting them. After clearing away the bottles he stood and surveyed the empty bar. 'Merry friggin Christmas,' he said to himself.

As the men stepped outside, they halted and stared at the whiteness everywhere. 'It's snowed,' Al said, swaying and they tightened their grip on his arms.

'And still is,' Harry said, leaning his head against the cold wind and guiding Al across the sidewalk to his car. They finally managed to get him into the front seat and close the door.

'Funny how it creeps up on you when you're not looking,' Rick said, looking down the smooth, unfurrowed road.

'Funny peculiar or funny ha ha?' Harry asked grimly. He wasn't looking forward to the drive.

'Just funny,' Rick said, and got in the back. The pleasure of the evening had gone somewhat.

Harry dropped Rick off first and then drove carefully to Al's. The tyres slid a little but not so much to be dangerous. He drove up the drive, stopped outside Al's front door and switched off the engine. 'I'll see you to your door,' he said and unbuckled his seat belt.

Al had been sitting with his head down, looking like he was asleep. He straightened up with a sigh. 'Do you know the bitch is going away for Christmas.' It was a statement spoken with a bitter amazement.

'I guessed something was wrong,' Harry said quietly.

Al almost sobbed. 'She said she was going to see her sister but she isn't. I checked.' He looked at his house – it was dark, and looked bleak and stark in the whiteness of the snow.

'You can spend Christmas with us,' Harry said quickly. 'Dave and Pam will be glad to see you.'

Al shook his head. 'Thanks but no. I won't be good company.'

Harry was about to reply when Al opened his door and half stepped out. 'Don't bother to get out. No point in both of us getting cold.' He stepped all the way out and held onto the car roof as he leaned in through the doorway. 'I've fixed her, though,' and he closed the door, leaving Harry wondering what he had done. Harry waited until Al had lurched his way up the few steps to his porch and got to his door. He turned and waved with a smile. Harry buckled his seat belt, started the motor and pulled away.

Al watched until he saw the red tail-lights disappear and then felt in his pockets. He went through them all and then again before cursing – he had forgotten his keys. He pointed his finger and somehow made it connect with the bell at the second attempt; he pushed it hard and long and heard it ringing inside the house. He waited but no lights came on. He pressed again, longer this time. A voice from an upper window shouted into the night.

'Who is it?'

'Who?' Al questioned to himself, wondering where the voice was coming from before realising Phillippa had opened the bedroom window. He stepped back across the porch and almost fell down the few steps, grabbing the handrail to steady himself. He looked at his hand encrusted with snow and tried to work out where it had come from.

Phillippa recognised him. 'What's the matter?'

Al looked up from his hand and saw her silhouetted in the window frame. 'What's the matter? I want to come in.'

'Where are your keys?'

He shrugged. 'I don't know. Ask me another,' and he began to chuckle.

'Are you drunk?' she asked, with accusation in her voice.

'I can answer that one.' Al continued laughing and the effort made him sway, so he grabbed hold of the handrail again.

'Then sleep in the car in the garage,' she shouted, and closed the window.

Al stared at the closed window. 'But I haven't got my keys,' he shouted up. He waited, but the light went out in the bedroom. The snow was falling heavier and stung softly on his face; it began to matt his eyelids, so he stopped looking up. He thought of ringing the bell again but then he remembered a spare key hidden in a shed at the rear of the house. He began to chuckle. 'Locked out of my own home, am I? I'll show you, madam,' he shouted up at the window.

He lurched sideways by leaning his weight to one side and then stepping out before falling over; in this way, like a drunken crab, he made his way to the end of the house. The wind was suddenly stronger as he turned the corner and he squinted his eyes against the slanting snow. It was pitch black and he edged forward slowly, trying to remember how the path followed the house. 'Stupid,' he chided himself. 'Ought to know my own house.' Although the track down the side was wide, he staggered with progressive steps over to one side and a bush swept ice across his face. Then his foot hit something and he pitched forward. His hands were deep in his pockets and as he tried vainly to free them his head struck something – bright lights illuminated his mind before a second blow stunned him as he hit the ground. He lay for a moment feeling pain and confusion; he struggled to work out what had happened, but the pain in his head was blocking any coherent thought. At last he managed to free his hands and he touched his head and gasped. It hurt, and his hand came away with something warm and sticky. Out of the pain his mind focused on one thing – he had to get the key.

275

He moved his hands under him, feeling the snow press through his fingers, and tried to lever himself up. But as he brought one knee up to raise his body, his feet slipped from under him and he fell again, grazing his head. He cried out as more pain stabbed through his brain but the wind tossed his cry into nothingness. He lay for a long while until the tormenting agony became numb with the cold and muted to a dull ache that throbbed around behind his eyes. He forgot the key and thought of Aritha; he saw her smiling face and somehow it took away the pain. But then he remembered she was going away and as she turned, he called after her, 'I do want you. Please stay.' She came back to him and held him gently; he could feel her warmth and her softness and he lost himself in her arms, gently slipping into an all-consuming sleep.

*

When Phillippa woke the next morning, she lay back and gazed at the ceiling until she remembered Al coming home drunk. She looked across but the bed next to her was empty and had not been slept in. She felt no alarm, in the state he was in, he was probably asleep in his car or had found his keys and would be in a spare bedroom or on the sofa downstairs. She was in no hurry to see him. She showered and dressed in warm clothes, as she intended to do some shopping, and finally went down the stairs to set the coffee pot going and put some bread in the toaster. It was only after she had done this that she thought of Al again. She checked the downstairs rooms but there was no sign of him. She heard the toast pop in the kitchen but left it to go back upstairs and check the spare bedrooms. After she had done that and not found him, she stood on the landing and paused – if he was in the garage, she realised he would be freezing by now so she went down,

276

feeling a tinge of guilt and slipped on a coat. She searched the car and all round inside the garage but there was no sign of him. The snow had fallen heavily through the night and covered his tracks so this offered no clue to his whereabouts. As she stood outside she clasped her arms round her body and shivered as the cold penetrated her clothing. She would ring Harry – he had probably taken Al to his place. The more she thought about it, the more she convinced herself there was nothing to worry about.

Once inside, she went into the kitchen and tossed the cold toast into a bin and put more slices in the toaster. She switched on the radio and the weatherman on the local station was announcing, with some relief, that the snow had come at last and then reeled off the roads that were impassable until the ploughs got to them. 'If you don't have to go then avoid the snow,' his cheery voice sang out. The toast popped up and Phillippa spread low-fat margarine over it and sat munching through the slices, washing them down with black coffee. The radio was playing *Winter Wonderland* and she hummed along while she thumbed through a magazine. When a news bulletin came on, she got up and switched it off and went into the lounge and picked up the telephone. She pressed some buttons and waited. Harry's voice came on the line.

'It's Phillippa,' she said without a greeting. 'Have you got Al with you?'

There was the briefest of pauses. 'No. I dropped him off at your place last night. Haven't you seen him?'

She was about to say 'Yes, last night', but she stopped herself and said, 'No. There's no sign of him. Would he be with Rick?'

'Unlikely. I dropped Rick at his home first. Then I took Al home. He was...' Harry stopped and remembered that Al had not opened the door.

'He was what?' Phillippa asked.

277

'He was at the door,' Harry said. 'I'll give Rick a call. Have you checked the garage?'

Phillippa became cautious again. 'Why should I do that?'

Harry wasn't about to tell her that Al had too much to drink. 'No reason. Just somewhere to look. Maybe you ought to ring the police.'

'That sounds rather drastic,' she uttered, feeling a tremor of cold pass through her.

'Just a precaution,' Harry advised, and rang off.

She rang the police and a squad car arrived within minutes. 'We were in the vicinity,' the patrolman explained as he stamped his feet against the cold. Phillippa noticed his boots were coated with snow and she was reluctant to ask him in to tread it over her carpets.

'It's my husband – he didn't come home last night.' She noted a certain look creep over the patrolman's face. 'Well, he did come home apparently. But he's not here this morning. His bed has not been slept in. There's no sign of him.'

The patrolman wanted to be asked in, and he clapped his mitten gloves together to indicate it was cold. 'You say he did come home?'

The cold air was moving into the house, so Phillippa relented. 'You best come in. But wipe your boots.'

She stood back and he made a great deal of wiping his feet on the bristled mat, closing the door behind him. 'Perhaps you could explain what you know.'

Phillippa stood in his way to stop him walking further into the house and kept him on the mat. 'He went out drinking with a couple of friends last night. I've rung one of them and he says he dropped Al, that's my husband, at the front door.'

'Did he see him enter?'

'No. He just said he was at the front door.'

'And this morning?'

278

'His bed has not been slept in.'

The patrolman twitched his nose. 'And you weren't worried about that?'

'Why do you ask?' She was made a little nervous by the question.

'I can smell coffee and toast,' he shrugged. 'You made yourself breakfast before calling us?'

Phillippa felt awkward and didn't know what to do with her hands so she raised them in front of her and pressed them together as if she were about to say a prayer. 'I thought he was with one of his friends.'

The patrolman said, 'Okay,' in a way that suggested he wasn't quite sure if he believed her. 'So you got up, made yourself breakfast and then what?'

'It just struck me as strange that he wasn't in. I checked around the house. You know, in case he had slept in a spare bedroom.'

'Does he do that?'

Phillippa felt she wanted to scream at the calm figure who was asking awkward questions, but she managed to keep her voice steady. 'Well, no. It just seemed the thing to do.'

The patrolman just said, 'I see. Then you rang his friend. Who's he?'

'Harry Menkowitch. He said he had dropped Al at the door.'

'And what time was this?'

'I didn't ask him,' she said with agitation creeping into her voice.

The patrolman made a decision. 'Okay. I'll tell you what I'll do. With your permission, I'll get my partner to check outside and I'll go round inside the house.'

'I've already checked, but if you want to then go ahead,' she said, a little tartly.

The patrolman opened the door and called to the car

outside. His partner stepped out and came over. He spoke low and she didn't catch his words. The other patrolman set off to the left as the other returned into the house. 'Do you mind?' he asked as she still barred his way. She didn't reply, but stepped aside. He wandered into the lounge and took a quick look around. 'Have you checked the garage?' he asked as he moved into the kitchen doorway.

'Yes,' she said, feeling that her home was being invaded.

'What's that room over there?' he asked, looking back in the lounge.

'That's his study. *His* room.'

The policeman glanced at her, surprised by her expression, and went over and opened the door.

'I can see why you call it, "His room",' he said with a grin as he surveyed the untidiness. At that moment the doorbell chimed and Phillippa went to the front door. It was the other patrolman, and he looked white and cold.

'Can I speak to my partner, ma'am?' but the other patrolman was already edging passed her.

'What is it?' she asked as their heads came together and they exchanged whispers.

'We'll just check something. Won't be a minute,' and they were gone.

Phillippa retrieved her coat and shoes and slipped them on, following the patrolmen round to the side of the house. As soon as she turned the corner she stopped abruptly and put her hand to her mouth. They were bending over an object which she could see all too clearly was a snow covered body. They heard her gasp and one of the patrolmen rose and came to her side.

'I'm sorry, ma'am. It looks like somebody's fallen and cut their head.' He hesitated, watching for signs that she may faint, but she seemed to have control of herself. 'Would you mind having a look? Just to check.'

She felt him take her arm and she stepped forward

slowly, but she knew it was Al. She stopped over him and when she saw his face, she buried her face in her hands.

The patrolman waited for her to sob, but it didn't come. 'Is it your husband?'

She uncovered her face and nodded.

'Let's go back into the house.' He motioned her forward by briefly touching her arm. As Phillippa moved round the corner, he turned back to his partner. 'Call the station, tell them what has happened and get them to send an ambulance.'

The other nodded but didn't move his eyes away from the inert figure on the ground. 'He's frozen. He must have been there some time. Just look at his face – it looks like he's smiling at something.'

The first patrolman tilted his head to an angle to see Al's face. 'It's probably the cold. It's pulled the skin tight.' He turned and then followed after Phillippa. He was careful to wipe his feet and found her sitting on the sofa, staring vacantly ahead. He was about to speak when the telephone rang. He looked at her but she showed no reaction. 'Shall I get that, ma'am?' She looked up at him briefly and then looked away again. He went over and lifted the phone and listened. 'Is that Mr Menkowitch?' He heard the reply and said, 'This is Patrolman Edwards. Yes. Perhaps you can come over. Yes. Thank you.' He put the phone down and turned to see that she hadn't moved. He hesitated and then went into the kitchen and poured a coffee from the pot and took it back to her. 'Here, ma'am. Drink this. It may help.'

She took the cup and sipped absently. From the moment she had seen Al's body lying frozen in the snow her mind had flipped from thought to thought with no cohesion. She thought about last night when she had seen him staggering below and she had closed the window; she imagined a picture of him groping in the darkness and somehow falling; she saw him laying in the snow and

281

wondered if he had felt anything; she filled her mind with images and there was no room for guilt or remorse. Then she thought of the vacation she had planned – she would have to ring and cancel it.

'Ma'am?' The patrolman's voice seeped into her mind and she looked up. 'There's an ambulance on the way. I'm afraid your husband is...' but his voice trailed off. She was nodding acceptance with a strange sort of smile on her face; he thought of the death smile on her husband's face, and they were somehow similar.

'I know,' she said quietly.

'Mr Menkowitch is on his way as well. Is he a close friend?'

'He's my husband's friend. They were close.'

'Is he the Harry Menkowitch who owns the high-class jewellery store?'

She nodded – it seemed everyone knew Harry.

The patrolman felt uncomfortable and was pleased when his partner came into the room. Instinctively he looked down and noted he hadn't wiped his boots on the mat.

The ambulance arrived. They examined Al's body and then bagged him up and took him off. Harry arrived just after that and the patrolman met him outside and spoke with him alone, asking questions about the night before. 'So you didn't actually see him enter the house?'

'No,' Harry said. 'He waved to me from the door and I thought he was okay.'

The patrolman looked around and spoke as if to himself. 'We wondered why he would be round the side of the house. We searched his pockets but found no keys. Perhaps he was locked out.'

'Perhaps he had forgotten them,' Harry suggested.

'What would you do if you found you were locked out?' the patrolman asked, again in a way that he seemed to be talking to himself.

Harry knew the answer but didn't offer it. 'Perhaps I ought to go and speak with Phillippa. She can't be feeling too good right now.'

The patrolman stepped aside and let Harry pass him into the house.

Harry tried to speak with her but her answers were monosyllabic and she kept turning her head away as if she were disinterested or afraid of talking. He sighed and stood up.

'Is there anything I can do?' he asked, looking down at her, hoping she would show some sort of response. But she got up and made her way to the kitchen, speaking in a casual way over her shoulder.

'I can handle it.'

He was unsettled by her coolness and felt like shouting at her to get some reaction but instead decided to leave. He was feeling numb and the fact that Al was dead hadn't quite sunk in; thankfully, that little mechanism we carry around that shuts down part of the nervous system and keeps the hurt of reality away had temporarily kicked in. As he stepped outside, the two patrolmen came from round the side of the house. 'We were looking for the keys,' patrolman Edwards explained.

'No luck?' Harry asked.

'No,' the patrolman answered. 'But if he didn't have his keys, why would he go round there?'

Harry shrugged. 'To find some shelter maybe. He has a wooden shack where he keeps his tools. It's round the back.'

'I think I'll go and talk with his wife again,' the patrolman said, but he was obviously reluctant to do so.

Phillippa found the further questions annoying and was pleased when the patrolmen finally departed. When she was alone, she made a phone call and said, without explanation, that she would not be going away. The male voice on the line asked why but she just put the phone down. After an hour of nothingness filled with wandering round the house and absently touching things for no reason, she rang the same number again and said she would, after all, make the trip.

The police informed Phillippa that an autopsy would have to be carried out but, as it was so close to Christmas, nothing would be done until the new year. Christmas Day dawned but the thought of Al laying in the morgue took the edge off everyone's fun. Harry, in particular, found moments when he went to a quiet place in Dave's house and sat staring out of the window at the bleakness outside. He couldn't accept that Al was gone, especially in that fashion, and the patrolman's words kept returning to his thoughts. He thought about the years he had known Al and couldn't remember the precise number – they went that far back, but they had been through quite a few things together and had built a sort of affinity between them where words were not always necessary. He tried to enthuse when his grandson wanted to show him a present or play a game with him but Rosemary had carefully eased her way between them and he smiled to her gratefully. The only other bit of joy was Pam's swelling belly; Harry had touched it affectionately and thought ruefully, 'one gone and one coming; such was life.'

The autopsy report said that Al had a high level of alcohol in his blood and the wounds were consistent with falling and hitting his head on a stump of a tree. This tied in with the patrolman's report of finding traces of blood and skin. But it didn't explain why Al couldn't get into his house if his wife was in bed. The autopsy was filed.

*

The day of the funeral was bright and clear; the snow still

lay thick, but the air was clean and not too cold and had an invigorating edge about it. Harry stood with Rosemary and noted the large number of people that had turned up. They stood around in family groups or with friends and waited outside the church, none wishing to be the first to go in. The hearse arrived and they drew back and made a pathway to the door. Phillippa was dressed in black – designer style – and Harry noted she walked into the church with her head held high and looking straight ahead, offering no acknowledgements. After the coffin was carried in, they filed quietly behind it.

'It's hard to tell if she's mourning or just going through the motions,' Rick whispered into Harry's ear as he sat next to him.

Harry turned his head slightly to the side. 'She's probably thinking about the coroner's findings,' he whispered back. 'A lot of people are wondering what actually happened that night.' He thought back to the fateful day when he had sat talking with her and had difficulty finding anything consoling to say. He was sure he grieved Al's death more than she did. When he asked if Al had rung the doorbell, which he was sure he had, she snapped at him and said the police had already been through that. He had got up and mumbled that if there was anything he could do, she only had to ring, but she had not replied or even seen him to the door.

The service was almost embarrassingly short – one hymn and one prayer – so when Harry stepped into the pulpit to give a eulogy for Al, he made sure it was long enough to make Phillippa uncomfortable. He kept the tone light, retelling tales of humourous escapades they had together and he noted even Dinsdale smiled when he told one that involved him. Harry finished on a more sombre note: 'I haven't said a lot about Al's character. But then you all know him and therefore mere words cannot pay enough tribute, except to say we shall all miss him, but shall cherish and be thankful for the warm memories he has given us.'

He stepped down and resumed his seat; Rick leaned his head close. 'Nice speech. Especially as you didn't refer to Phillippa,' he said quietly. 'And I bet she noticed,' he added.

Harry hated the actual burial, it was so final. It seemed everyone else was of the same mind and they stood back in a loose circle. Phillippa stood alone, stark and black against the whiteness around her. When the prayers had been said, she remained alone and aloof from the people who walked passed the graveside, offering a silent prayer and leaving without speaking to her. She kept her head up and stared into the distance as they filed passed her; if she noticed them she did not show it. Harry and Rick waited until last and then stepped to the other side of the grave so that they were facing her. Harry just stared at her and waited until her eyes flickered across to his face. She could not hold his gaze and she suddenly turned and walked away.

'There goes a guilty woman,' Rick commented, watching her stepping carefully up the path to her hired limousine.

'Maybe,' Harry said dryly. 'Whatever she's thinking, she's keeping it hidden.'

'Down to two,' a voice said behind them.

'Thanks, Sam,' Harry said as they turned towards the voice. 'It's nice to know someone's keeping count.'

'Uh? I didn't mean it like that.' Sam looked embarrassed. 'I meant it in an affectionate way.'

Harry patted his arm. 'I know you did. It's good to see you could come. Al will appreciate it.' They both noticed Harry expressed his sentiment in the present tense.

'So who's looking after the bar?' Rick asked.

Sam looked at him sideways to see if he was mimicking him. 'Who do you friggin think? I've closed it.'

'That's a tribute in itself,' Rick couldn't resist another dig. 'And you have a suit on. Did you buy it special?'

'Alright, alright.' Sam shook his head. 'So I don't get out much in this thing but I'm glad 'cos it doesn't feel right.'

Harry could see that Rick had the bit between his teeth and was preparing for another quip, so he interceded quickly. 'We'll probably be down later. We'll have a drink for Al.'

'Okay,' Sam said and began to turn away. 'I'll have to go back now. I've got a guy coming round to estimate a paint job.'

Harry and Rick exchanged glances.

'Wow!' Rick exclaimed. 'Sam's sensitive after all.'

Harry took one last look at the grave, but his mind created a picture of Al lying in the coffin so he turned quickly away. 'Come on,' he urged. 'Let's join the ladies and take them home.' But it was then he noticed a woman standing back among a couple of trees; she seemed to be waiting for them to go. Harry made an excuse to Rick and walked over to her. 'You must be Aritha.'

She nodded. 'And you must be Harry.'

'Yes,' he smiled, trying to ease her obvious nervousness. 'He'll be glad you came.' He held out his hand towards the grave, inviting her to join him there, but she shook her head.

'I don't want to see the coffin,' her words faltered.

'I understand,' he said gently. 'I found it difficult.'

She was holding a small posy of flowers and she held them up to him. 'Would you drop them on his coffin?'

Harry took them and noticed there was a small note attached; he was touched by the gesture. 'Are you sure you don't want to deliver them yourself?'

She hesitated and took back the flowers. 'I guess I ought to.'

He walked with her back to the graveside and she peered

tentatively down into the dark chasm as if it were bottomless. He saw her eyes moisten and then she stooped and dropped the flowers carefully so they lay about where his head would be. When she stood up he took her arm and led her a short distance away.

'He spoke of you often,' he said. 'You brought some happiness into his life.'

Her mouth began to open but her words caught in her throat and she turned away. She had only gone a few paces when she stopped and looked back; she summoned up the effort and spoke with a laboured voice.

'I asked him to leave her. Do you think he told her?'

Harry thought for a moment. 'No. In all the years he had the chance, I don't think he ever said anything to hurt her. That's the sort of guy he was.'

She studied him for a moment and then nodded before turning again and walking away.

*

Phillippa sat rigid – she couldn't believe what she had just heard. Al's attorney avoided her glare and ran his eyes over the passage he had just read out to her. It was brief and explicit, just how Al had told him shortly before Christmas: 'To my wife I leave the house and all its possessions. The house is her Ice Palace; I hope she feels the cold. To Harry Menkowitch, I leave my watch; he made it and I gratefully return it. Thanks for everything, Harry. To the Wannabee Golf and Country Club, I leave all my money and investments.'

He looked up and coughed. 'Of course, you can contest the will. It is rather unusual. But you will have to get your own lawyer to do that.'

Her expression slowly changed from shock to a bitterness that twisted her mouth. 'When did he change his Will?'

He studied her face – it didn't have the sadness a widow's usually has and he guessed the words in the Will explained why. 'You really ought to get yourself a lawyer,' he advised again. 'As executor of the Will, I'm afraid I cannot act for you.'

She stood up abruptly and stared down at the paper he held in his hand. 'You will be hearing from him.' Her words were spat from tight lips and she turned and left the room without saying more.

He put the paper down and looked across his desk at Harry and Dinsdale. 'Well gentlemen?'

'The part about her feeling the cold is rather ironic,' Harry said thoughtfully.

The attorney made a noise in his throat. 'And the golf club will benefit handsomely. His investments are quite considerable, Mr Dryden.'

'I doubt if we'll see any of it,' Dinsdale said acrimoniously. 'She'll take it through the courts. It's not the sort of publicity we want.'

Harry smiled to himself; Al had felled two thorny trees with one swing of the axe.

*

The snow lingered a while and Harry was glad when it finally disappeared during a warm spell; it served as too much of a reminder. Several things happened as the new year progressed towards Spring. The first was the opening game of golf between Harry and Rick when the course opened after the thaw. They had felt they had lost an arm when Sol had left them, but losing Al felt like both legs had been cut from under them. They stood on the first tee, swung their clubs to stretch their muscles and then looked at each other a little helplessly.

'Do you want to drive off?' Rick asked at last.

Harry shook his head. 'You go.'

'We don't have to play,' Rick offered without moving. 'I think we feel the same.'

'Yes, we do have to. I'll go if you prefer,' Harry said, and went over and put his ball on a peg. He looked up the fairway. 'It'll get easier I guess.' He aimed left, hit hard and the ball flew high but kept straight; they heard the fatal clatter as the ball pinballed down through the branches of a tall beech.

Rick said nothing and teed his ball low to the ground. He hit a low skimmer that curved viciously to the right and disappeared into some bushes. He sighed and picked up his tee peg.

'Well, partner,' Harry said with a lilt of humour in his voice. 'One's left and one's right. I'll see you on the green.'

'Last one there's a pooper,' Rick smiled.

They went over to the golf cart and stopped and looked at each other and began to laugh; it was the first time they had shared just one cart between them. 'You take it,' Harry offered.

'No,' Rick bowed from the waist and swung his arm around his body. 'You take it, young sir.'

'Get in the friggin cart and we'll drive up the middle of the fairway.' Harry nudged him into the buggy.

As Harry steered up the middle, they felt some relief and Rick looked over his shoulder back to the clubhouse. 'I wonder if Dinsdale's watching us? He'll slap our wrists for not keeping to the cart track.'

'I don't think so,' Harry smiled.

*

The second event was the birth of Harry's second grandchild. He and Rosemary were awoken in the early hours of one morning by the telephone ringing. Harry reached over, switched on the light and picked up the receiver, but he knew who it was. 'Dave?'

'Yes, Harry. She's started.'

Harry whooped and Rosemary slapped his back. 'Calm down,' she said, 'it's not me having the baby.'

'We'll be there in ten minutes,' Harry said, and put down the phone as he swung his legs out of bed. He went straight to the bathroom to relieve himself and hummed as he sprayed in a circle round the bowl. When he returned to the bedroom, Rosemary was just sliding from the bed covers. 'Come on, come on,' he began to urge. 'We're going to have another baby.'

'We're not,' she corrected him. 'And stop nagging. What's the matter with you?'

Harry got his leg caught as he tried to pull up his pants and he began hopping round the bed to prevent falling over.

'More haste less speed,' Rosemary chided him.

He finally gave up and fell on the bed, where he found it easier to untangle his leg and pull up his pants. He lay there and looked at his wife from an upside-down angle. 'You know the trouble with you, Rosemary? You've no longer got the young kid in you.'

'That's because I have to look after you. You've got enough of a kid in you for both of us. There. I'm dressed.' She stood with her hands on her hips like a school ma'am. 'Do you want me to help you put your clothes on?'

'No,' he laughed, 'we haven't got time for that.'

By the time they got to his son's place, Dave had the bag packed and was ready by the door. Pam was half sitting, half lying on the sofa, wincing with each breath. Rosemary began to fuss, so Harry put the bag in the car while Dave got the engine started.

Dave got out, leaving the engine running to warm. 'James is asleep. Pam has written a long list about what to do when he wakes.'

'I guessed she would,' Harry laughed, 'they always do. Can you manage alone with her? I'm sure Rosemary would like to help.'

'That's okay.' Dave put his hand affectionately on his father's shoulder as they entered the house. 'I think we've got a few hours yet.'

Pam was standing as they entered and the two men guided her out to the car. As they progressed she reeled off some instructions which Harry was sure were on the list.

'Don't worry about a thing,' Rosemary said as they eased Pam into the car. 'You just go and concentrate on bringing your little one into the world.'

Dave helped her secure the seat belt and then they were gone. Harry and Rosemary stood in the drive until the rear lights had turned a corner, and then they realised how cold it was and they went inside.

'What shall we do?' Rosemary asked. 'Do you want a cup of coffee?'

Harry looked at his watch. 'It's not four yet,' he said and stretched himself onto the sofa. He held out his arm. 'Come here. We can have a cuddle and grab a little sleep for a while.'

Rosemary nestled into his arm. 'No snoring,' she said.

'No snoring,' he repeated dreamily as he closed his eyes. 'That goes for you too.'

*

They stood around the bed and Pam's eyes were bright as she held the small bundle in her arms; a little face with eyes shut was just visible through the folds.

'I'd forgotten how small they are,' Harry muttered. 'Hey, Tiger,' he said to his grandson who was standing on one leg and twisting some bedclothes with his hands. 'What do you think of your little sister?'

292

'Are we still on for the five bucks?' he asked.

'Of course we are.'

'Then she's not so bad,' he admitted. 'She's awfully wrinkled though.'

'That's because she's been wrapped up for a long while.' Harry tussled his hair and the boy pulled his head away.

'Here,' Dave said, taking a teddy bear from a bag. 'I bet she would like her first gift from her bigger brother.'

James took it and moved up the bed next to his mother. 'The bear's bigger than she is,' he said, holding it next to the babe.

Pam reached across and took the bear and nestled it in her other arm. 'I'll make sure it's the first thing she sees when she wakes.'

James seemed pleased with this and beamed back to his grandparents.

'Have you settled on a name?' Rosemary asked.

'Louise,' Pam said. 'Louise Rose.'

'That's nice,' Rosemary said, her lips a little tight. 'Don't you think Louise is a nice name?' she asked Harry.

'A beautiful name for a beautiful girl,' Harry said, avoiding looking at his wife.

When they got back to their place, Harry put on a pot of coffee and hummed while the water hissed and dribbled its way through the filter. Rosemary came into the kitchen and slowly smoothed her hand up and down his back.

'Do you think they called her second name Rose after me?' she asked.

'Of course they did,' he said. 'But Rosemary doesn't quite balance with Louise so they obviously shortened it.'

'And when did Dave tell you that?' she asked.

'He didn't.' Harry was honest. 'But I'm sure that is why.'

'You always call me Rosemary,' she said absently. 'You never shorten it to Rose or to Mary.'

293

'Because I like Rosemary.' He put his arm round her. 'What's troubling you?'

'I'm just tired, I guess.' She smoothed his back with her hand a last time and moved away. 'I think I'll go up for a little sleep. Are you coming?'

'I'll have a coffee first,' he said as the percolator coughed the last drop of water. He poured himself a cup and took it to a rear window where he sat and looked out at the garden. Things were beginning to grow; new life was breathing everywhere and, in a sad way, he thought about Al. It's a pity he didn't have children, he mused, it may have made a difference.

The court case over the Will did not happen. Dinsdale knew Phillippa had a strong case and didn't want the bad press, so the club had conceded before it got that far. She sold the house and moved out of town; some said they had seen her driving off with a young man in a car, others said it was by plane. Harry didn't put much store in any of the stories – he was just glad that Phillippa had gone.

The last event of note was a phone call that Rosemary took. Harry was reclining on the sofa, half listening to her conversation and half trying to read an article in *Time* magazine.

'Hello. Oh, it's lovely to hear from you. How are things?' She listened for a short while and then said, her voice rising with some excitement, 'But that's wonderful. Of course we do. Wait a minute, I'll get my diary.' As she delved into her bag, she said over her shoulder, 'It's Rob.' Before Harry could speak, she found her diary and the phone was back to her ear. 'When? Oh, that's fine. Of course we will.' She listened for a bit more before saying, 'And how is Miriam? I bet she is. Be sure to give her our love and tell her how happy we are. Yes. All right then. Bye. Take care.'

Harry waited for her to replace the phone. She sat for

a moment, staring into space. 'Well, are you going to tell me what that was all about?' But he had a good idea anyway.

'Rob and Miriam have set a date for their wedding and want us to go.'

'Now that's something,' Harry said. 'Do you think that's because of what we said?'

'Of course not,' Rosemary said quickly. 'They love each other.' She said this in a way to convey that there could be no other reason.

'When is it? Do we start packing now?'

Rosemary tutted. 'You want everything to happen immediately. They want us to invite Dave and Pam but I'm not sure she will want to travel with the little one. I'll have a talk with her.'

Harry noted how she was already taking control, something she liked to do and would relish the coming time when she could organise everything.

'So when is it to happen?' he asked again.

Rosemary was right, as usual – Pam thought the journey would be too much but Dave was eager to go with them. 'I never thought this would happen,' Dave had laughed. 'I'm not going to miss it for anything.'

They flew together and on their arrival, Dave was given a tour of the house – or mansion, as Harry still referred to it – and he was bowled over by the beautiful Miriam. As he was shown around the house he confided to her some of Rob's bad points, but in a voice loud enough for Rob to hear. 'Don't listen to him,' Rob had called from behind them.

'I'm only telling her the truth, little brother,' Dave had called back. 'She has a right to know these things.' But what he actually confided about was their escapades when they were very young and he had her laughing aloud. 'Did he really do that?' she exclaimed several times.

Rob came over. 'The only reason we did some of those

things is because my big brother suggested them. And he could run away faster and that's why it was always me that got caught.'

They held the ceremony at their house with a large marquee in the garden. Chairs had been laid out on the lawn with a centre passageway leading to a small stage under a canopy that had been erected at the front for the ceremony. Harry and Rosemary had met Miriam's parents the day before and hit it off from the start. Miriam's parents were both very short and Harry was surprised that Miriam had grown so tall – well, about five ten. He moderated it when Rosemary argued that she wasn't that tall and it was her high heels that made her look taller – women stick together.

The five-piece band to one side of the stage struck up as Miriam appeared on her father's arm and even Rob gave out a gasp – she was just so beautiful. While the service progressed, Harry looked round; he guessed there had to be nearly two hundred people there.

'This must be costing a small fortune,' he whispered in Rosemary's ear.

She tutted. 'You'll be inspecting everyone's jewellery next.'

'There are some expensive pieces being worn,' he chuckled, and received a dig in the ribs.

The sky was clear and the air hot and everyone was happy that the service was kept short. 'A shorter service than our mayors are used to giving,' Harry quipped as everyone clapped when the new bride and groom kissed. Fortunately Rosemary didn't hear his comment over the noise so he was spared another dig.

To one side, a large spread was set out, and when all the congratulations had been made, everyone turned to the tables and began eating and drinking. The band struck up while they ate and the first to be satisfied with enough eating moved to the front and began dancing to the music – many of the tunes had a Brazilian flavour.

Rob and Miriam finally made their way over to Harry and Rosemary, at which point, Rob stood, panting a little from the kisses and back-slapping. 'Well, Harry, did I get that right?'

'About the first thing in your life,' Harry laughed. Rob came forward and gave him a bear hug.

When his mouth was near his father's ear, he said, 'You couldn't lend me a few bucks to pay for all this, could you Harry?'

Harry eased himself out of the hug and grinned. 'Just a few?'

While Rob gave his mother a similar hug, Miriam kissed Harry on the cheek. 'You look radiant,' Harry said. 'This is just a little something from us, but I fear your beauty will eclipse it.' He took out a box from his pocket and gave it to her.

Her eyes widened as she lifted the lid. 'Oh, my goodness, it must be a Menkowitch. Rob is always on about your jewellery.'

'My design and Dave's skill,' Harry said proudly, putting his hand on Dave's shoulder.

Rob looked over her shoulder. 'Hey. If we sell that we can pay for all this.'

Miriam turned on him with mock horror. 'Sell it? I shall be buried in this one day.'

A little while later, when Harry and Rosemary were sampling some of the food, Dave came over to his father's side. 'Have you seen some of the stones the women are wearing? Perhaps we ought to open a shop in this area.'

Rosemary turned quickly to face them. 'Like father, like son.'

20

'Here comes trouble,' Rick said, and at that moment Dinsdale bustled across the lounge.

'Did you get my message?' he addressed to Harry without saying a welcome.

'Yes,' Harry said shortly.

Dinsdale hesitated; he stopped from asking the obvious. 'Perhaps you could come round to my office now. It is rather urgent.'

'When we've finished our drinks,' Harry said, and Dinsdale hovered for a moment before walking off.

'So, what is this?' Rick asked, his face not attempting to hide his humour. 'Your old buddy needs your help again?'

'I haven't a clue.' Harry puffed on his cigar. 'And what's more, I don't really care.'

'But you'll go and see him,' Rick ventured, 'just to find out.'

'I guess so.'

'Perhaps he needs an assistant,' Rick added. 'Or a secretary.'

Harry finished his drink and stubbed out his cigar. 'There's only one way to find out.'

Harry went to Dinsdale's office through Felicia's room but she wasn't there; probably out to lunch, he guessed. Dinsdale looked up as he entered. 'Sit down, Harry. I have something of importance to discuss with you.'

Harry sat and waited.

Dinsdale straightened some pens in a pot on his desk. 'I suppose you know the franchising is not going to happen.' Harry just nodded. 'It's not just to do with what happened at Christmas, you know. Well, I suppose it is,' he contradicted himself. 'But it has moved on from there.'

He looked at Harry to make sure he had his attention and he assumed a sombre face. 'What I have to say is of the utmost secrecy. It must be kept in the strictest confidence. I must have your word on that.'

Harry spoke for the first time. 'Perhaps you should stop there, Dinsdale. If this is another plot of yours, then forget it.'

Dinsdale seemed surprised. 'A plot? What do you mean?'

'You know, like the cake.'

Dinsdale laid his hands flat on his desk and nodded as his face assumed a smug smile. 'This is no plot about a cake, Harry. This is bigger. Much bigger.'

'A huge cake.'

Dinsdale ignored the intended sarcasm. 'This is not about a plot but I must have your word this will go no further?'

Harry rubbed a finger along the line of his chin. 'Tell me what it is about first.'

Dinsdale felt frustrated, and his hatred for the other man began to grow. He almost choked on his next words. 'I trust you as a man of integrity. I will tell you but must ask that if you are still not interested, that you will tell no one.'

Harry nodded in agreement. Dinsdale told him about his meeting with the Mayor and the proposal to buy back the club from JDW. 'That has now been concluded,' Dinsdale informed him. 'I managed to arrange a very favourable price.'

Harry noticed the emphasis on the 'I' and guessed he had also creamed off a suitable amount for his efforts. 'So who owns us now?' he queried.

'A consortium.' Dinsdale clasped his hands together as if he were about to applaud himself. 'It frees us from the likes of JDW and a group of men will be easier to deal with than an egotistical...'

'Who are these men?' Harry persisted.

Dinsdale collected himself; he didn't like being interrupted. 'At the moment, it doesn't matter who. A press release will be issued in due course. The Mayor is one of them, although at the moment it is politically necessary not to include him. You understand why?'

Harry did. The town's mayors over the years had perfected the 'spin' technique and the latest one was a master at it. 'And you think you will be able to control them?'

Dinsdale smiled with the look of a contented cat. 'One mind, one thought spells clarity. Many minds and many thoughts spells confusion. I can deal with that.'

'Is that one of your sayings?' Harry asked. He couldn't imagine anyone else thinking up something quite so absurd.

Dinsdale's smiled broadened. 'Yes, actually it is. Don't worry, Harry, I will keep a firm hand on the tiller. You'll see.'

'So how do I fit into all this?'

'Ah yes.' Dinsdale remembered the reason for their meeting. 'This year is the one hundred and fiftieth year since this town was established. The Mayor will be organising special events to celebrate what he will be calling "Founders' Day". I expect you've read about it in the local paper.' Harry nodded even though he hadn't. 'The Mayor has asked if we can have the "big celebration",' and he waved two fingers on each hand like bunny ears to give it quotes, 'at our club on Independence Day.'

'But we have a July Fourth dinner and dance anyway,' Harry remarked.

'Ah. But this year, he wants to incorporate the Founders'

Day celebration with Independence Day and,' he emphasised the conjunction, 'the launch of the new ownership of the club. How does that sound to you? Like three aces?'

From the bottom of the pack, Harry thought. 'So who will be invited to this mass celebration?' Harry queried.

'Just everyone who's anyone,' Dinsdale enthused.

'Does that include the members?'

There were times when Dinsdale could hide his feelings and times when he could not. This time, he tried to keep them under control, but the grinding of his teeth showed his growing frustration with the figure opposite. If it wasn't for his 'payback time' plans, he would have shouted Harry out of the office; he was just not taking it seriously.

'Of course it will include the members,' he said, controlling his voice with difficulty. 'Look Harry, this will be a great moment for our club. It will be a new beginning for us all. And it will bring a lot of kudos. And you can play a big part in it.'

Harry lit a cigar. He knew Dinsdale would normally not tolerate it in his office and this was his test to see how much he needed him. He saw Dinsdale's eyes narrow and follow the spiral of smoke up to the ceiling but he said nothing. 'So what do you want me to do?'

'The fireworks display,' Dinsdale said, trying to ignore the pungent odour of the cigar.

'Fireworks display?'

'I've spoken with the Mayor and he's happy with it. I convinced him you're the best man for the job.'

'Perhaps you would like to convince me,' Harry said demurely, puffing another cloud of smoke.

Dinsdale tried to breathe as little as possible. 'You're an expert jewellery designer. You have the eye for the artistic. We want a display that will take the breath away.'

301

Like this cigar, Harry thought. 'I don't know anything about fireworks,' Harry said.

'You will,' Dinsdale insisted. 'I have arranged it with a local firm. I will take care of all the ordering and purchasing. You don't have to worry about a thing. Just talk to them about the different types, colours, that sort of thing and come up with some spectacular display. They'll do the setting up and the actual firing. You'll be paid for it, of course.'

At any other time and with somebody else making the request, Harry would have seen it as a challenge, but with Dinsdale involved, there had to be an ulterior motive. It could be he was going to cream off some more, but then why involve him? It would need thinking about.

'I'll do it,' Harry said, making a snap decision. The desire of finding out what Dinsdale was up to was irresistible.

'Good man,' Dinsdale almost gushed. 'Here is the business card with the address and number of the firm. The owner's a friend of mine. He'll be expecting your call.'

'I'm grateful for the opportunity,' Harry lied convincingly.

'And the Mayor will know all about it,' Dinsdale said, standing to show the meeting was over. 'You can be sure of that.'

When Harry had left, Dinsdale punched the air in the same way he had when he left JDW's office. 'That guy up there is still smiling', Dinsdale grinned, and he hummed away happily as he opened the window to let out the smell of smoke.

21

A few days later, Harry drove out to the far eastern end of town set near the foothills to a factory bearing the sign 'Pyrotechnic Technics'; below it was added in smaller lettering: 'Demolition and Displays – Our Speciality'. Harry smiled at the contradiction. It was set alone, for obvious reasons, and was situated in three bland buildings, enclosed by high fences and with a security guard at the gate. One housed the serious stuff – explosives for the demolition part of the speciality – and another the fireworks; at a safe distance were the offices housing the staff. He was shown into a sparsely furnished office that needed a lick of paint and someone to sort out all the papers strewn untidily on just about every flat surface.

'Good to meet you,' Thomas Elway said without rising from his chair or offering a hand. The only other chair in the room was piled high with paper so Harry just stood in front of the desk. 'Dinsdale has filled me in.'

Harry suppressed a flippant response. 'I need someone to tell me what all these fireworks of yours can do,' Harry said.

'I can do better than that,' Elway said, and pressed a button on his telephone. 'We'll put on a little display for you. Let you see first hand what they can do.'

Harry was driven in an open Jeep about half a mile from the site where the ground was barren and open. He was driven by a small mouse of a man called Calvin, who had protruding, yellow teeth that affected his speech. The back of the Jeep was piled high with boxes that leapt around as it bumped its way over the rough terrain.

'We have to get remote,' the teeth shouted above the noise of the four-wheel drive and the wind blowing around their exposed heads. Harry held onto the sides, wondering if it would be the boxes or him who would be pitched out first. He was thankful when they finally stopped and Calvin leapt out and began unloading boxes. 'I'll fire them manually here,' he explained, 'but for a display it's all done electronically.'

Harry stood by the Jeep watching the little man perspire as he heaved out the heavy load. He took out a cigar and Calvin stopped and shook his head. 'Not an advisable thing to do.' He motioned to the boxes. Harry looked at his cigar, shrugged and tucked it back in his shirt pocket.

'I have a special launcher here.' The perspiring figure showed him a length of tube that he fixed in the ground some distance away before coming back. 'That's for the aerial stuff.' He looked around the back of the Jeep and then cursed. 'Damn. They haven't put in the slow-burning fuse.' He looked back to the distant buildings and Harry could tell he was measuring the time it would take to drive back there.

'Will this do?' Harry asked, holding out his cigar.

The little man thought about it. 'I guess,' he said reluctantly. He laid out the boxes in a row and opened them up. 'Right! I'll start with the starbursts. These go to varying heights depending on their size and explode with a shower of stars. Some have exploding stars and others have screamers. They're different colours. Are you with me?'

'Right next to you,' Harry said. 'Shall I light my cigar?'

'In a minute. Here, I'd better have it.' Harry handed it over and offered him a light. As soon as Calvin was puffing

304

away, Harry lit another cigar for himself. 'Not bad,' Calvin mused. 'Expensive?'

'That's alright; I'll charge it to my expenses.'

Calvin laughed and then stopped – he wasn't sure if Harry was making a joke. 'Right, I'll fire off the first one.' He applied the cigar to the fuse and dropped the rocket into the tube like a mortar. They both stood back. Harry expected a slow lift-off with the usual orange tail as the rocket steadily climbed, but he was shaken by a sudden thunderous explosion as the rocket was hurled high into the air, too quick to see. It then exploded into a large umbrella of stars, which crackled as they spread out across the sky. Even in the bright sunlight, the display was pretty spectacular.

Calvin roared with laughter at Harry's reaction and slapped his thighs. 'It always gets you like that the first time. You weren't expecting that.' He chuckled for a minute. 'They're not like the domestic ones you buy in the shops. These babies really lift off,' and he waved his hands like rockets zooming to the sky.

'No,' Harry agreed. 'I don't suppose my neighbours would appreciate me firing off things like that. How many have you got?'

Calvin stroked his chin. 'Oh, there are about a hundred different types.'

'I'll go and sit in the Jeep,' Harry said, retreating. 'I'll be able to see alright from there.'

'Right you are,' Calvin said, and selected the next one. He shouted back, 'This one is a screamer.' Harry just nodded and puffed on his cigar.

It was over an hour later when the final rocket exploded into the air. Harry had watched the array of rockets and various candles shooting coloured blobs into the air, all with their own noises and colours that cascaded in different shapes. Calvin came back to the Jeep; his shirt was patched with dark shapes of sweat.

305

'Well, that's about it,' he announced, and got in the driver's seat. 'What did you think of them?'

'Very spectacular,' Harry said. 'But how am I supposed to remember them all?'

'No problem there,' Calvin smiled. 'We have a video and booklet you can look at in your own time. They're all referenced. You just have to write down the order of firing. I'll show you when we get back.'

Before he could start the engine, Harry asked, 'Do you work for Elway?'

Calvin spat into the dirt. 'Yep. Do you know him?'

'No,' Harry said.

'He's one mean sonofabitch.'

Harry made no comment, so Calvin started the engine and set off at a fast pace.

Harry refrained from asking what the purpose was of the demonstration if he could have watched it all on video, but Calvin had been eager and he didn't want to hurt his feelings. Besides, he was more concerned with hanging on and not being thrown out of the Jeep.

That evening, Harry ran through the video and made notes from the reference book. Then he played it through again and made more notes. Rosemary had watched some of it and then got bored and went off to do some chores. She came back a while later with some coffee.

'It's getting late,' she reminded him.

Harry barely heard her and murmured a thank you for the coffee. He was replaying a sequence of rockets and then got up and went over to a CD rack.

'What are you looking for?' she enquired.

Harry didn't answer immediately and took out several CDs, reading their covers and slotting them back. He turned suddenly. 'Do you remember that display we saw at Disney?'

'Of course, it was quite something.'

'They did it to music. They synchronised the display with music.'

She saw his eyes were glazed and deep in thought. 'Isn't that rather ambitious, Harry? Will Dinsdale be expecting something like that?'

'No,' Harry smiled. 'Nothing like that. That's the point.'

She didn't know what he meant but she was sure he knew what he was doing.

Harry worked long into the early hours. Rosemary gave up on him and went to bed around midnight, requesting only that he keep the music low. Harry said yes, but didn't really hear her – he was seeing a new beauty in the showering displays and began timing them and noting colours and noise. He finally found several pieces of music he wanted, and as the night wore on, the colours and sound began to form pictures that coalesced in his mind. He gave up only when his eyes hurt with tiredness, but he went upstairs feeling a whole lot better, quietly humming the music as he prepared for bed. He knew he still had a lot of work to do to perfect it, but he had time. He also had to have a word with Rick about something.

A few nights later, Harry met Rick at Sam's Bar and told him what Dinsdale had requested. He briefly went over what he was doing and Rick sucked on his lips.

'Sounds ambitious,' Rick commented when he had finished.

'That's what Rosemary said but it is possible. All the firing is controlled electronically. It's just getting the timing right with the sequence of the music.' He sipped his beer in thought. 'At least it sounds good in theory.'

Rick supped his Bud. 'You don't sound that convinced.'

Harry grabbed a handful of nuts and flipped one expertly into his mouth. 'It's not the display that worries me. I'm sure Dinsdale's up to something.'

307

'He's probably making sure he makes enough out of it,' Rick suggested.

Harry shook his head slowly. 'He'll do that anyway. No. There's a reason why he's asked me to do it.'

'He's hardly likely to try and sabotage it. Not at his own club – and the Mayor wouldn't be too pleased either,' Rick surmised.

'That could be it,' Harry looked brighter. 'He's convinced the Mayor that I should do it. It's my head, not his, that will be in the noose. Don't you have a relative working there?' he asked suddenly. 'A brother or someone?'

Rick nodded. 'Yes. A nephew. My sister Rose's boy. He's a good type. He's been working there since he left college.'

'Is there any chance of inviting him down one evening for a few beers and a chat?' Harry asked.

Rick nodded again. 'He'll do that. What have you in mind?'

'A little inside information,' Harry grinned. He finished his beer and stood up. 'Let me know when he can meet us.'

They met a few days later at Sam's Bar. Rick's nephew, Stuart, was a big man – tall with wide shoulders and a waistline tending to advance with his years – but despite this, he spoke with a soft manner. He was wearing a lumberjack-style shirt and faded jeans and had a beard that bushed around his face. He held a good position in the demolition side of the firm and they talked for a while about the work he did. Harry found him candid and easy to talk with and gauged his moment when to broach the subject about the fireworks. They sat at a table over by the wall, away from the bar so Sam couldn't listen in and interrupt.

'Do you know a guy called Thomas Elway?' Harry asked, noting Stuart's eyes suddenly looking up at him. There was something about his face that showed he was uncomfortable with the name.

'He works in the other division,' Stuart said brusquely. 'He's in charge of the firework production. Why do you ask?'

Harry hesitated and Rick spoke up. 'I think it best if you explain everything,' he advised. 'Stuart and Elway don't exactly get along.'

Harry was heartened by this and briefly explained what Dinsdale had asked him to do and his visit to the site.

'And you think maybe this Dinsdale and Elway are up to something?' Stuart queried.

'Apart from making money out of it, yes, I think so,' Harry said, indicating to Sam for more beer. 'Perhaps I'm too suspicious, but I know Dinsdale and I know he wants to get even with me.'

Sam brought three bottles over and snapped the caps off, leaving them to fill their own glasses. 'So is this guy replacing Sol or Al?' he asked.

Rick beat Harry to a response. 'Now why would we want to do a thing like that?' he said with an edge to his voice.

Sam shrugged. 'I just wondered.'

Harry didn't answer his question. 'We just wanted a few beers and a little peace.'

'So I was just being friendly,' Sam complained. 'I'm here to please and serve. Anything else I can do for you?'

'Nuts,' Harry said.

'There's no need to be rude,' Sam said, trying to make a joke, and he wandered away chuckling to himself. The others returned to their conversation.

'Is there any way you can find out anything?' Rick asked. 'I know it's not your area but perhaps you can ask a few questions.'

Stuart sipped his beer from the bottle, not bothering with the glass, and burped quietly. 'Excuse me,' he offered. 'I'll see what I can find. I'll have to be careful though. Elway can be one mean bastard.'

'I don't want you getting into any trouble,' Harry said.

Stuart finished his beer, burped quietly again and got up. 'No problem. I've got to go home to my little lady. I'll call you when I have something,' he said to Rick, and then reached over and shook Harry's hand. 'I'll be glad to help you, Mister Menkowitch. I've got one of your watches for my twenty-first.' He pulled back his cuff and showed it. 'It keeps perfect time.'

'An expensive one,' Harry smiled.

'They all are,' Rick cut in; he had been the one to buy it for his nephew.

'Seems a nice young man,' Harry said when Stuart had left.

'He is,' Rick agreed. 'If there's something to find then he'll get it for you.'

It was a few weeks later that Rick called Harry and arranged to meet him in Sam's Bar again. Harry had just finalised the firing sequence and music for the display and was about to take it to Elway; the timing of Rick's call was perfect.

They sat at the table away from the bar again and Sam assumed they must be up to no good. He stood over their table with his hands on his hips. 'So what's so secretive?'

'Family business,' Rick explained. 'A bit sensitive.'

Sam hovered. 'So anything I can help with?' They both looked at each other and then up at Sam. He caught their expressions and mumbled to himself as he returned to the bar. 'Friggin keep it to yourselves then.'

Rick shook his head. 'The next time we come in here we'll have to sit at the bar or Sam will be getting a complex.'

'And he won't give us any nuts while we sit here,' Harry added. 'Did Stuart find out anything?'

'They know you are planning to fire the display in sequence with music,' Rick said.

Harry thought about it for a moment. 'Yeah, I know

that. I had to ring Elway a few weeks ago and ask him if the electronic firing could be sequenced like that. So what?'

'They plan to fire them in a different order and not include everything you wanted,' Rick explained. 'Stuart wouldn't tell me how he found out.'

Harry sighed. 'So the display won't be coordinated.' He imagined what a flop it would turn out to be. 'And the Mayor will have my hide. With Dinsdale telling everyone that Harry Menkowitch designed it all, it won't do Dave's business a whole lot of good either.'

'They're being pretty cute,' Rick added. 'The display will go ahead but everyone will be left feeling it wasn't quite right. Elway will say that is how you instructed them to be fired, so no blame falls on him.'

'And Dinsdale will plead ignorance and both of them will probably cream off a nice little profit,' Harry completed the scenario.

'Would but won't,' Rick said with a hint of a smile.

'What do you mean?'

'It's Independence Day.'

'I know that.'

Rick began to laugh quietly. 'So everyone wants to be with their families. Stuart has volunteered to control the firing.'

Harry's face began to crease into a rubbery smile. 'And he'll use my sequence.'

'Exactly. And make sure all the fireworks you ordered will be included.' Rick fished in his pocket and took out a piece of folded paper. 'And you might want to give the Mayor this.'

Harry unfolded the paper and read it. 'It's an invoice for the fireworks?' He looked to Rick questioningly.

'It's the real one.' Rick's face beamed. 'Did I forget to mention that Stuart's wife works in the accounts section? The one that Elway sent to Dinsdale to give to the Mayor is for half as much again.'

'Well, I'll be...' Harry leaned back in his chair. 'It's at times like this I could kiss you.'

'I'd rather you didn't.'

'Are you shy?'

'Sam's watching. He may get jealous.'

Harry stood up. 'Thanks pal.' He patted Rick's arm. 'Let's go to the bar and I'll buy you a large Jack Daniels. It'll make Sam happy and I want some nuts.'

*

Independence Day dawned to blue skies streaked with inconsequential cloud – the only thing threatening was a high midday temperature. The town celebrations began with a brief prayer service at the old wooden bridge and then cascaded into a noisy procession through the centre and around the square, with trucks decked out in red, white and blue, depicting scenes from the War of Independence. At intervals, the line of trucks was interspersed with bands, mainly from the schools, either marching or on top of flat-loaders. They played various music, from brass band to pop, and the streets echoed with a cacophony of sounds. People lined the roads and cheered each display as it passed, waving American flags on plastic sticks. Children sat on their father's shoulders and licked ice cream and stuck their fingers with candyfloss. It all went well until a horse on the back of a truck – which was depicting Paul Revere's ride to warn the troops – suddenly decided it had had enough of the swaying vehicle and, with his rider clinging on to his hat, leapt from the truck and headed off down the main street. This created a stir of laughter and many comments about the authenticity of his headlong flight. At lunchtime, many families gathered in the South Park area for a picnic and were entertained with music alternating between military brass and modern electronic beat numbers. In one corner, a group of families set up a game of baseball, but there were so many taking part that it was impossible to score a home run past the hundred-or-so outfielders; nobody seemed to mind.

In the evening, the Wannabee Golf and Country Club became the focus and the folk dined casually from a sumptuous hot and cold buffet spread out on an avenue of tables. They mingled and ate and drank and talked loudly and the air was full of laughter and friendliness. A band was situated in one corner, playing unobtrusive music that provided an ambience of soft sound while people talked. Harry and Rosemary stood with Rick and Anna, who seemed animated and full of excitement. Harry was retelling one of his old golf stories when Dinsdale appeared at his side.

'I'd like you to meet the Mayor,' Dinsdale interrupted.

Harry was about to make a quick remark but he caught Rosemary shaking her head slowly from side to side. He sighed. 'All right, Dinsdale. Excuse me, everyone, his Highness calls.'

Dinsdale had already turned away. As Harry followed him through the throng, he said, rather tartly, over his shoulder, 'You address him as the Mayor.' Harry just smiled.

The Mayor was standing among a large group of men, mostly his aides, and Dinsdale stopped just short of them and turned to Harry. 'No games tonight,' he said rather harshly. 'Now, is everything in position and ready?'

'Absolutely.' Harry almost saluted but stopped himself; the fun would come later. 'I've positioned it all on the south bank of the practice ground, behind the line of pines so that they appear over the treetops. It'll add something extra.'

Dinsdale's eyes slowly lost their suspicion. 'Good. I'll introduce you.' He went forward and waited until the

313

Mayor was aware of him. 'This is Harry Menkowitch. The man responsible for the firework display this evening.'

The Mayor's eyes transferred to Harry and his mouth formed a practised smile. 'Hi, Harry. Good to have you on board.'

'Thank you, The Mayor,' Harry said casually. The Mayor's eyes looked unsure. 'Dinsdale told me to call you that,' Harry grinned.

The Mayor's face took on a boyish humour. 'Better than some call me,' he laughed easily. 'So you're the jewellery designer my wife is always going on about. You've cost me a small fortune over the years.' He punched Harry playfully on the arm.

'Well I've been retired a few years,' Harry explained. 'My son runs the business now so you can blame him for the prices.'

The Mayor held up his arm and pulled back his sleeve to reveal a gold watch studded with diamonds around the rim. 'Blame?' The Mayor shook his head. 'My wife gave me this. It's priceless.'

'And tax deductable?' Harry kept a straight face.

A brief shadow crossed the Mayor's face, but then his lips formed a grin and he punched Harry's arm again. 'I can relate to you, Harry.'

'Not if you keep punching my arm,' Harry thought, but said aloud, 'I can remember making that watch.' He looked up to the ceiling. 'It was for your fiftieth birthday.'

The Mayor was impressed. 'And what is the colour of my wife's eyes?' he jested.

'Blue,' Harry guessed. 'And she was wearing a green dress.'

'Really?' The Mayor was surprised.

'I don't know,' Harry said, 'but I guessed you didn't know either.'

The Mayor laughed openly and turned to Dinsdale.

'You've certainly picked the right man, Dinsdale.'

'Oh yes,' Dinsdale said cooly. 'I think I have. It's nearing nine-thirty, Mister Mayor. I think it is time everyone should assemble on the practice area.'

'Oh right, have you the microphone?' Dinsdale handed it to him and, after calling for attention, the Mayor invited everyone to go outside for the display. He made particular mention that Harry was the guy responsible, which got a loud response of clapping and a few hoots.

Dinsdale had arranged for a small stage to be erected for the Mayor and his closest aides and family and made sure he was standing next to him. He insisted Harry stood next to him; he wanted to see his expression as the display unfolded.

'It's almost ten o'clock,' Dinsdale advised the Mayor. 'The fireworks are situated over there,' and he pointed towards the southern line of trees.

'A good night for a display, Harry,' the Mayor said.

Harry looked up at the sky – the sun had set but the sky had paled to a satin blue and the stars were massing in their evening splendour. 'Looks like Nature is putting on her own display,' he said quietly.

The Mayor looked up briefly. 'That's the designer in you,' the Mayor admired. 'I'm sure your display will surpass it.'

At that moment, from speakers situated in a circle around the area, a fanfare of trumpets rent the air. Everyone stood with silent expectation when suddenly, from the line of trees to the north, a fusillade of explosions shook the air and seconds later, the sky was filled with cascades of exploding stars. The Mayor was confused by the direction of the display and quickly looked at Dinsdale. He was about to say something but the music had started with an excerpt from 'The Entry of the Queen of Sheba' from Aida, and with each crescendo of the music, wave upon

315

wave of rockets set the sky aflame. Everyone around the Mayor had been looking to the south and their heads turned north, firstly with surprise and then accusingly at Dinsdale.

Dinsdale leaned towards Harry. 'I thought you said they were situated behind the trees at the southern end.'

Harry shrugged and shouted back. 'I was never good with directions.'

The music slipped easily into the cantus, 'Song of Tears', and giant Roman candles hidden among the trees began to shoot coloured orbs into the sky, accompanied by more rockets. Even Harry was taken aback by his creation; until then he had only had his imagination to conjure the images, but now he was seeing it as he thought God must have viewed the creation of the Universe. He ignored Dinsdale's obvious confusion and growing agitation as the display moved from one piece of music to another, and the visual display, as if guided by the erudite sound, rose and spread and crackled or burst thunderously over the heads of the watching crowd. The final piece was Tchaikovsky's '1812 Overture' and as the display built up to the final crescendo of cannons and bells, the sky and the people's vision were filled with colour and sound. When the last notes sounded, there were a few seconds of hushed silence before one solitary rocket soared into the sky and with a massive explosion which made the people step back, it shot out tentacles of eye-searing whiteness to light every corner of darkness. When this had died, and the crowd was sure it was over and had adjusted their eyes to the night, they erupted in applause, and cheering and whooping filled the air. Harry felt someone pumping his hand; it was the Mayor, who had brushed Dinsdale aside to get to him.

'That was one hell of a display, Harry. Well! My God! Jees! Oh shit, was that something!' The Mayor seemed to

316

be searching for every blasphemy and he ended it by giving Harry a bear hug, which he marginally preferred to having his arm punched.

'Thank you, sir,' Harry said, his voice muffled against the Mayor's coat.

Back in the clubhouse, Rosemary approached Harry and hugged him, whispering her congratulations in his ear. But then he was engulfed by people wishing to add their thanks and congratulations, and he felt his hand would soon detach itself from his arm. The only person who avoided him, for some reason, was Dinsdale. The Mayor sought Harry out again and Harry flinched once more at the arm punch.

'Oh, I have something for you.' Harry reached into his pocket and passed over the invoice.

The Mayor looked over it briefly and then at Harry. 'And what's this?'

'It's the invoice for the display. I was asked to give it to you...' Harry broke off as the Mayor turned to one of his aides.

'Look at that,' the Mayor said. He turned back to Harry. 'Is it genuine?' Harry nodded, but before he could speak, the Mayor had turned away again. 'That's a lot less than the one Dinsdale submitted. Look into it, Don,' he said to his aide. 'And where is Dinsdale?'

Harry went outside, partly to have a quiet cigar and also to seek out Stuart. He found him stowing away his gear in the back of his truck. Harry offered him a cigar and held a match to light it.

'That was some display.' Harry breathed smoke.

'That certainly was, Harry. Even from where I was, it looked pretty, well ... startling.'

'I don't know how to thank you enough.' Probably for one of the first times in his life, Harry had to search for the right words. 'Perhaps these will go a small way.' He handed over two small boxes and after cleaning his hands, Stuart opened them. 'It's my best way of thanking you.' The first box contained a set of studded cufflinks and the second a brooch. In the dim light, Stuart couldn't see what stones they were, but he saw they sparkled. 'The brooch is for your wife,' Harry said. 'Don't get them mixed up. It won't suit you.'

Stuart looked up briefly and coughed a short laugh and then looked down again at the gifts. 'There was no need,' he said quietly, but then his head snapped up quickly. 'But that's not to say I don't appreciate them. Thank you.' He sounded embarrassed.

Harry patted his shoulder. 'Anything else I can do, just let me know.'

'Well, there is one thing,' Stuart said, tentatively.

'Just ask.'

'I've been thinking I might want to take up golf. Rick said you could teach me.'

Harry smiled in the darkness. 'I don't know if I'm qualified. I'm not that good.'

'Rick said that, but he also said you were devious.'

Harry saw Stuart's teeth gleaming white in the dark as he grinned. 'He's right about that,' Harry agreed.

When they finally got home, Rosemary made them a cup of coffee, but when she went into the lounge, Harry was sat in an armchair with his eyes closed. She hesitated and was about to turn when he spoke.

'I'm just resting my eyes.'

She turned back and put the coffee on a side table next to him. 'I'm not surprised. Mine are pretty dazzled too.'

He looked at her. 'You liked it then.'

She knelt at his feet and put her hands on his knees. 'Of course I did. You know, I sometimes wonder what else you could have turned your talents to. Architecture or film sets or something.'

318

Harry sighed in a tired fashion and sipped his coffee. 'I've found the two things that fill my life and I'm happy with them.'

'What's the other one?'

'You, of course.' He stroked her hair affectionately. 'I guess I could have gone on to other things, but when I look back over the years, I wouldn't want to change a thing.'

'What was that business with Dinsdale and the Mayor?' she asked.

Harry laughed softly. 'You don't miss a thing, do you?'

'I try not to.'

22

Dinsdale sat in his office in a dark mood. It was a time when everything around him seemed opposed and whoever it was up there who had appeared to be smiling down on him had really been laughing and waiting for his fall. In the days following the Independence Day celebrations, he had made himself scarce and ventured little from his office. Felicia had taken the brunt of his malevolent mood and had sought out Harry and asked him to sit at a quiet table.

'What's the problem?' he asked, a little cagey, having a good idea what it was about.

'It's Dinsdale,' she said, looking round to make sure no one could overhear them. 'He's been in a real bad mood lately. Do you know what is going on?'

Harry rubbed his chin. 'Not exactly.'

'Then you know something,' she picked up quickly.

Harry considered telling her to have a word with Dinsdale, but that would have been throwing her to the lions – or the bear in Dinsdale's case. But he knew he had to tell her something near the truth.

'I think there was an administrative problem with the firework display,' he said cautiously.

'You mean Dinsdale made some money out of it.' She surprised him. She saw Harry's expression. 'He's done it before, you know.'

Harry shrugged. 'You'd know more about his dealings than I would.'

She sat back and looked very prim with her hands in her lap. 'I just don't understand him sometimes. He has such a good position but he is just plain...' She sought the word.

'Greedy.' Harry supplied it.

'What am I to do?' she pleaded, looking like a little lost girl.

'I would suggest nothing,' Harry advised. 'He's in enough trouble with the Mayor and I don't think he'd appreciate it if he knew that you knew.'

She thought about this for a moment. 'I guess you are right.'

Harry had said nothing to anybody except Rick. He told him about the Mayor's reaction to the invoice and despite seeing the funny side and wanting to relate the story, Rick promised not to say anything. When Dinsdale had to venture out of his office, he took a detour if he saw Harry. He half expected Harry to visit him and gloat, but then he remembered Harry had said nothing about his indiscretion with Felicia or the JDW affair; he accepted – but didn't understand – that Harry was one of those peculiar people who liked to bring you down but didn't kick you when you were on the floor. In some ways, this annoyed him even more and only served to fuel the fire of hatred that seared his insides. One thing was for sure – he was out of the Mayor's circle and should have been thankful not to be prosecuted for fraud but he was not of a mind to thank anything or anyone. When the Mayor had rung, he had pleaded ignorance and said the invoice had been passed to him and that he had simply passed it on – he was only the messenger. As weak as his plea was, he had got away with it, though the relationship he had been nurturing with the Mayor had ended abruptly. But that wasn't the end of his problems – Elway had been after him as well to find out what had happened to the money and the display. Elway had questioned Rick's nephew, Stuart, but he just said he followed the instruction list he had been given. Elway couldn't make a great deal of it without exposing the truth, so in the end he let it pass. One thing that did confound him was where did the real invoice come from? He couldn't follow this through for the same reason – he decided to keep a low profile for the time being, but was determined that one day he would eventually get even with Dinsdale. While Elway had his suspicions about Dinsdale, he in turn had his suspicions about Harry, who was the one who had given the invoice to the Mayor. Where did he get it from and how did he know about his devious plans? How did he arrange to have the display and the music in the right sequence? But as he was avoiding Harry, there was no way he could ask him. He came to the same conclusion as Elway and decided to let it pass in the hope that, with time, it would be forgotten.

Dinsdale straightened the pencils in the jar on his desk and then sat back and stared vacantly across his office. He wanted, as had been his fashion since childhood, to mentally obscure any mistake or anything distasteful from his mind until he had convinced himself that it had never happened. That way he could lie truthfully to his father. But this time it was different – Harry would always be there to remind him just by his presence. As he saw it, he had one of two choices: get Harry out of the club or leave himself. The first choice would be the most difficult – he had already tried twice and failed – but the second was unacceptable; he was too cosy in this set-up. Somehow he convinced himself the opportunity would arise to even the score and, until then, he would have to bite on the leather and wait. As he was consoling himself with the fact that he had at least got away with it, the intercom buzzed and Felicia informed him the Mayor had rung and wanted to see him at his office.

322

*

Harry was mildly surprised when he received an invitation to the Mayor's office. As far as he was concerned, the 'firework incident' was closed. Rosemary insisted he wear his best suit and a conservative tie and made Harry promise to behave himself. Harry was shown into the Mayor's office and saw that he was alone; this was unexpected as he had only ever seen him flanked by his aides who were sort of extensions to his arms and provided the right words when he faltered. The Mayor rose from his chair and came round his desk.

'Harry. It's good of you to come.'

Harry expected a punch on the arm, but the Mayor guided him to a chair in front of his desk. 'Have a drink. A cigar?' he asked, opening a large walnut case on his desk.

'I'll pass on the drink.' He almost said, 'it's too early', but he rightly guessed the Mayor would be having one. He eyed the long, contraband Havanas in the box. 'But one of these will do nicely.'

The Mayor took one out, clipped the end and held a match steady while Harry puffed it into life. While the Mayor poured himself a large malt whiskey, he spoke over his shoulder.

'You know, Harry, I still can't get over that display you put on.' He went back to his desk, eased himself into his chair and put his feet up on the desk.

'That's nice of you to say so.' Harry sucked on the cigar, again surprised by the Mayor's relaxed attitude, with his feet up.

The Mayor saw his look and smiled. 'There are too many times I have to be formal. I like to relax in private.' He sipped his drink. 'I've asked you here for two reasons.' He sipped again and sucked on his lips, savouring the taste of the single malt. 'They're connected.'

Harry blew smoke to the ceiling and waited for the Mayor to tell him what it was about. The two men waited for the other to speak, but Harry was prepared to wait it out and leaned forward to tap his ash into a glass ashtray.

'I thought I ought to tell you about Dinsdale ... before it gets out,' the Mayor started. He put down his drink, slid his feet off his desk and leaned forward. 'We've had to dispense with his services.'

It was a morning for surprises. 'I'm sorry to hear that,' Harry said quietly.

'You are? I thought you would be pleased.' The Mayor's face showed surprise.

'I know he had his shortcomings,' Harry said, ignoring the Mayor's cough of astonishment, 'but he was good at running the club.'

'Did you know he was trying to stitch you?' the Mayor asked.

'I knew that the moment he asked me to do the display.'

The Mayor's face passed through surprise and amazement, but then creased into a chuckle. 'I like you, Harry. You like to meet things head on.'

At that moment, Harry was glad there was desk between them, for he was sure the Mayor wanted to punch his arm. 'I didn't know you had the authority to fire him?' he said.

'When the consortium was set up to buy the club, I put in a small stake.' The Mayor's face showed a little unease. 'It's not generally known, you understand.' Harry nodded; he knew why. 'But I do hold some sway, especially with a matter like this. That guy was crook. Do you know how much he would have creamed off with that fake invoice? He denied it all, but I have eyes and ears in the right places.'

Harry didn't know how much Dinsdale would have made out of it but he could guess it was a lot. Perhaps Dinsdale had become too greedy, he conceded. 'So who have you in mind to replace him?'

'That's the second reason I asked you here,' the Mayor said, but offered no more.

Harry puffed on his cigar but it had gone out. He fiddled with it in his fingers; he knew what was coming and was reluctant to hear it. They played their game of silent fencing again and once more it was the Mayor who showed he had less patience.

'We would like you to take over the club,' the Mayor said finally, referring to the grey people who were behind the decision. 'It was unanimous – you're the right man for it.' He paused and then added, 'You're honest as well. A man we can trust.'

'But I'm retired,' Harry said quickly.

'So?' The Mayor raised his arms. 'Then you have the time.'

Harry felt uncomfortable – he didn't want the job, yet he felt the Mayor would be disappointed, perhaps even angry, if he refused without a good reason. He decided to lie honestly.

'I am honoured by your consideration but unfortunately I have to turn it down.' He paused while he watched for the Mayor's reaction. His face was blank, so Harry continued. 'It's my health, I'm afraid. The old ticker couldn't take the stress.'

The Mayor's face looked concerned but Harry detected a doubting glint in his eyes. 'Should you be smoking cigars?' he queried.

'One a day. That's all I'm allowed.' Harry tried to sound convincing. 'The Doc doesn't condone it but says if it relaxes me then one won't do much harm.'

'I'm sorry to hear that,' the Mayor said. 'You would have made a good general manager. The salary would be good, too.' The concern left his face. 'Never mind, it was worth asking you. But I did tell them I thought you may turn it down.'

'Have you anyone else in mind?' Harry asked, surprised how quickly the Mayor's face had brightened.

The Mayor remembered his drink and drained the glass. 'We always have a contingency plan,' he smiled easily. 'I have a nephew who's well qualified but between jobs at the moment. I'll see how he feels about it.'

Harry repressed a smile. 'I'm glad to hear that. The club needs a good man at the helm.'

The Mayor stood up and held out his hand. 'Thanks for coming in, Harry. I would appreciate you not talking to anyone about this meeting.'

'Not a word,' Harry assured him.

The meeting was over and the Mayor had followed the consortium's wishes, Harry had declined and his nephew was ready to step in – he marvelled how he made everything slip into place. But that's why I'm Mayor, he reminded himself.

Harry only told the inquisitive Rosemary that the Mayor had called him in to tell him about Dinsdale; he knew that the Mayor's offer to him would not become public knowledge. Rosemary was disappointed.

'Didn't he offer you anything for all the hard work you put in?' she queried. 'I thought you were to be paid something.'

Harry hadn't thought of that. He felt that the Mayor had somehow manipulated him and he was disappointed with himself for being outfoxed.

*

Dinsdale cleared his office quickly. He put a large cardboard box on his desk and went through every drawer and cupboard, taking what was his and also what wasn't – he felt the club owed him something, even if it was only an electronic calculator-cum-diary and an array of office gadgets. And, of course, he emptied the drinks cabinet.

When he had been to see the Mayor, it had been unpleasant, with the Mayor ignoring his pleas of ignorance and using an assortment of blasphemies that would have shocked a whorehouse. When the Mayor had exhausted his vocabulary of profanities, he sat down and quietly told Dinsdale that he was to be relieved of his post; he didn't say who would replace him. Dinsdale had reeled from the verbal assault and had stood silently, with every part of his body quivering with rage. But even in this moment of darkest despair, Dinsdale's mind, trained from years of devious deals and subversive plots, tried to salvage something for his future.

'I have served the club for almost twenty years,' he said, keeping his voice level with difficulty. 'In which time I have run it with precision and honesty.' Only the first part was true, he admitted to himself, but the Mayor wouldn't know that. 'I have worked, no, slaved,' he corrected to add emphasis, 'to make it what it is today: a profitable club in which you now have a sizeable stake.' He felt imparting this knowledge may somehow impress the Mayor.

But the Mayor was not impressed. He was more concerned that Dinsdale was angling for a pay-off by threatening to make a case from the fact that he had an inside interest with the club. He took out a small knife from a drawer and began slowly sharpening a pencil with precise strokes of the blade. He looked up suddenly. 'Are you trying to threaten me in some way?'

Dinsdale watched the blade slowly slide up the pencil; he was sure the action was deliberate. 'No,' he answered cautiously. 'I shall leave the town and you'll hear no more from me. For that I would hope to have some sort of pay-off.'

The Mayor shook his head slowly. 'No cash.'

Dinsdale realised there was no bargaining to be had and tried to salvage something, no matter how trivial. 'I shall need a reference.'

The Mayor laid down the pencil and knife and leaned back in his chair. 'Oh, I'll give you a reference. I'll write it personally.'

Dinsdale did not like the tone of the Mayor's voice. It conveyed a different meaning. 'Will it be a good one?'

The Mayor sucked on his bottom lip and gazed steadily at Dinsdale. 'I have a lot of influence and many contacts. My advice to you is to go quietly.'

Dinsdale wondered if the Mayor was implying that he would take out a contract on him, but quickly dismissed it as fantasy. He wouldn't go that far, would he?

Dinsdale had just about finished packing when Felicia came in and looked surprised. 'What are you doing?' she asked, noticing the loaded box on the desk.

'Leaving,' he said, shortly.

'Leaving? But why?'

Dinsdale shrugged. 'The new owners and I do not see things the same way. They want to change how the club is run. I don't agree so I thought it better if I leave.'

'But you can't.'

'I can and I am,' he said, noticing her eyes had not left the box. He flipped the lid closed before she saw what he was taking with him. 'There comes a time, my dear,' he continued with his hands resting on the box, 'when one has to make a choice between standing up for what you believe to be right or living a life as an obsequious toad.'

Felicia looked confused. 'But what will you do? And what about us? You weren't going to leave without telling me, were you?'

He noticed how her questions were initially about him and then focused on herself. 'Of course not,' he lied. 'I didn't want any fuss so I thought I'd pack away my things first.'

'So?' she questioned.

He guessed she was referring to them. 'We shall need to talk when I've got myself sorted out.'

She didn't seem satisfied with that. 'Are you thinking of leaving town?' she asked with a hint of accusation.

'Probably,' he said quietly. 'There's not much for me here.'

'What about your wife?'

Dinsdale smouldered; he'd had a rough time with the Mayor and he didn't want more from her. 'I said I would contact you. I'm sure you can appreciate that this has come as a shock to me and I need a little time to think about what I shall do.'

Felicia relented. 'Of course, Dinsdale. Shall I help you with the box?'

Dinsdale shook his head and tried to lift the box, but he immediately dropped it back on the desk and winced; the bottles of drink made it too heavy. Perhaps he should get a second box, but he didn't want Felicia helping him.

'I'll get one of the staff to carry it to your car,' she offered.

'No,' he said a little too sharply. He wanted to make his exit without anyone knowing before he had left. 'Perhaps you can take one end,' he said reluctantly.

Between them they managed, with shuffled movements, to carry the box to his car. Bemused members watched their crab-like movements down the corridor and though one held a door open, and one offered to take Felicia's end, no one offered to help him. Dinsdale closed the trunk and slid quickly into his car.

Felicia opened her mouth to speak, but he started the engine and drove off without a word. 'Don't forget to call me,' she said quietly to herself. She returned to her office and sat with head bowed in confusion and dejection. He hadn't even said who would be replacing him.

*

The Mayor's nephew, Michael, took up his post of general manager the day after Dinsdale had left. He guessed from her expression and body language that Felicia was not pleased with the arrangement, but with honeyed words he had learned from his uncle, and inviting her out to dinner that night – 'to get to know each other' – he persuaded her that he was not such a bad guy. Such was the fickle nature of people – Dinsdale had left without a kiss or farewell, but this young man was not only pleasant and handsome, but he had invited her out to dinner. Felicia returned to her office thinking that things weren't so bad after all.

Michael sought out Harry when he came in from a game of golf and invited him into his office. He offered Harry a cigar that he noted was also Cuban.

'My...' Michael just stopped himself from saying 'Uncle'. He corrected himself easily. 'The board have told me a lot about you. The Independence Day display and all that. They think a lot of you, Harry.'

Harry watched him as he spoke. His hair was cropped short and his even, white teeth gleamed with a practised smile; his face was clean cut and handsome and he looked athletic in his dark blazer with a club tie and epitomised the image of a young graduate. Harry decided that he disliked him intensely.

'I'd like us to get to know each other,' Michael said. 'I shall need your experience and advice.'

Only while you get your feet under the table, Harry thought.

'I need to look over the whole club,' Michael continued.

'Procedures, administration, the catering, the fixtures. Everything,' he concluded with a sweep of his hand. 'A new broom and all that.'

It was the 'and all that' that bothered Harry. 'Do you play golf?' he enquired.

'Sure do.' The smile was still fixed. 'I play off two. Do you fancy a game?'

Harry shook his head. 'I wouldn't offer much of a game. Besides, I expect you'll be too busy sweeping for a while. The new broom and all that.'

Harry noticed a small twitch in Michael's eyes but the smile remained the same. 'Yeah, you're right. Perhaps some time later.'

Harry stood up. 'You are a young lad with new ideas. On the other hand, I'm an old fart set in his ways. Perhaps you ought to take a look around on your own. I'm sure you'll find something to change.'

Michael remained seated. 'You're a crafty old bastard,' he thought, but he said, 'Okay Harry. I'll do as you say. But you may get a call from me.' He laughed as he pointed a finger at Harry with his thumb cocked like a gun.

'You want to be careful with that,' Harry nodded towards his finger. 'It may go off.'

'Yeah right.' Michael laughed too vigorously. As Harry left, he thought, 'and it may just be aimed at you.'

*

A week later, while Harry and Rick were playing a round of golf, Rick met with an accident that, at the time, he passed off lightly. They were playing down one fairway which ran parallel with the next hole coming the other way, when a shout of 'Fore to the right' was heard from ahead and to the right of them. Rick was addressing his ball, preparing to make his shot, and he looked up at the shout just as a golf ball caught him full on the forehead. He went down without a sound and Harry, some distance away on the other side of the fairway, raced over. Rick was just stirring and trying to sit up and putting his hand to his head when Harry arrived.

'Don't move,' Harry advised and eased Rick's hand away so he could look at his head. 'That's some bump you're growing, and its split the skin,' he said, using his handkerchief to stem the sudden flow of blood that was running down his nose and over his mouth. 'How do you feel?'

Rick shook his head to clear it, but decided it was not a sensible thing to do. 'I'm okay. Just a little stunned.'

The two golfers coming the other way had dropped their clubs and raced over to where Rick was laying. The one who had made the errant shot came panting up. 'I'm sorry,' he gasped. 'Hey, I didn't know it was you, Rick.'

'Would that have made a difference?' Rick asked, moving into a sitting position and holding the handkerchief to his head.

'No. But shit. Hey buddy, how bad is it?' He peered closely with concern.

Rick eased away the helping hands and stood up – the bump on his head was becoming more pronounced with every second, and the blood continued to flow. 'Don't worry about it. Where there's no sense there's no feeling,' he tried to jest, but winced when he touched the bump. 'Does it notice much?'

'It gives you more character,' Harry smiled. 'You look something like a unicorn. We'll go back to the clubhouse. I think you ought to get that looked at.'

'It's nothing,' Rick insisted. 'We'll play on.'

The other three exchanged glances.

'No,' Harry said deliberately. 'We'll go back. It's still bleeding and there's no point in taking chances. You need some treatment.'

'You sonofabitch,' Rick said without malice in his voice. 'I'm three holes up on you.'

'I'll concede the game,' Harry said gently with a smile. 'Now let's go back.'

Rick didn't argue further because his head was beginning to throb. Harry helped him into the buggy and then drove in the straightest line he could manage towards the clubhouse. As he cut across fairways, some golfers waved their clubs angrily at them but Harry just raised his hand and smiled back without explanation.

For a while after, Rick had some really bad headaches but said nothing. The swelling finally began to go down and the ugly blue bruise wore off with time, but the cut left a jagged scar. Anna had argued with him to the point of nagging, but he shrugged off the incident and refused to go to the doctor for a check-up. A few months later, there was little trace and the headaches had disappeared – Rick convinced himself he had been right and the accident was all but forgotten.

*

Felicia found her new boss quite charming. Their evening out had been at a quiet, low-lit restaurant, and he explained how he wanted to use her more as an assistant than a secretary. 'I'd like us to work as a team,' he had said, and she liked the term. A short while after, he had invited her out again, this time for dinner at a large, plush hotel, and after more wine than she was used to, he encouraged her to stay the night with him. While she lay in his arms after a session of lovemaking that left her breathless and exhausted – she hadn't known such positions existed – he had told her about Dinsdale and why he had been sacked. Michael drifted into sleep, but Felicia lay awake in the crook of his arm and felt burned from Dinsdale's deceit and lies. Finally, she cried out, 'Damn him!' into the darkness and Michael stirred by her side.

'What time is it?' he murmured dreamily.

'It's that time again,' she chuckled and moved her body over his.

*

A few days later, Dinsdale called Felicia on the telephone.

'I'm off to Phoenix at the weekend,' he enthused.

'That's nice,' she said with a flat voice.

He paused for a moment; he didn't like her tone or choice of words. 'I've got an interview. There's a club just south of the city. It's for the position of general manager.' He waited for a response but there was none. 'I was wondering if you would like to go there with me?' He waited but she still said nothing. 'We could spend a week down there. Vegas isn't very far away.'

At last she spoke. 'I couldn't spare the time. There's so much to do here.'

He took the telephone away from his mouth and looked at it with surprise before returning it to his ear. 'I thought you would be pleased.'

'Tell me, have you told your wife about this interview?'

Dinsdale's eyes slitted as he raised his eyebrows. 'My wife? What's she got to do with this?'

'Well, surely,' Felicia questioned, 'she ought to know if you are thinking of moving.'

Dinsdale felt his blood rising. 'I don't understand you, Felicia. I thought you wanted to go with me?'

'That was before Michael,' she said.

'Michael? Who the hell is Michael?' The phone was beginning to feel slippery in his sweating hand.

'My new boss. Of course, you don't know about him, do you?' Her voice beginning to purr. 'He's young, handsome and enthusiastic, and he's thought up a lot of new positions for me.'

'Like what?' Dinsdale asked suspiciously.

'Oh, you couldn't imagine. But then you didn't have much imagination, did you? You were just "wham-bam-thank-you-ma'am".'

Dinsdale ground his teeth and she thought it was interference on the line.

'Sounds like the line is breaking up,' she laughed. 'Have a good trip, Dinsdale. I hope you get what you deserve.'

He was about to reply when the line went dead. He slammed down the phone and then became aware that his wife was standing close to him.

'A problem, dear?' she enquired.

'No,' he said bitterly. 'No problem.'

'You've been a little stressed lately,' she said in a quiet way. 'Perhaps the trip down to Phoenix will do you good. I'll go and pack your case so you can leave today.'

'You were listening?' he asked with heavy accusation in his voice.

'Not deliberately, but I suspect half the neighbourhood could hear you.' She smiled sweetly. 'You have a tendency to shout when you are upset.'

Dinsdale said nothing; there was nothing to say. His wife turned to leave, but then paused and said, 'I'll pack your lighter suit. It'll be warmer down there.' She looked briefly at his forlorn figure with a mixed expression of pity and contempt. 'It's a shame about Felicia. She has been good for you over the years.'

He looked up at her and she smiled softly before leaving to pack his case.

23

In early September, it was Rick's sixty-fifth birthday and Anna secretly prepared a surprise party. Except it wasn't such a secret because Rick knew his birthday was near and he noticed her quiet conversations with Rosemary and her occasional hushed voice on the phone. He smiled and said nothing – there was nothing as bad as a secret found out, and he knew Anna was enjoying every minute of organising something.

She woke him early on his birthday and led him out onto the back veranda overlooking the rear garden. She served him breakfast of eggs – sunny side up – bacon grilled crispy, toast and coffee.

'Well,' he said as he liberally sprinkled pepper and salt. 'This must be some special sort of day.'

'No,' she said in an innocent sort of way. 'The sun is shining, the sky's blue and the birds are singing, so I thought I'd give you a treat.'

'And a treat it is,' he smiled, and leaned over and kissed her cheek. 'Specially with you.' He munched into the food and, as men often do, waited until his mouth was full before saying more. 'You know, there's something else about today, but for the life of me I can't recall.'

'Are you playing golf with Harry?'

'Nope. For some reason he said he couldn't make it today.'

'Then perhaps you are going to take me for a surprise picnic in the park.'

He filled his mouth again and looked up at the sky while he chewed and thought about it. 'No. I hadn't thought of that. But if you would like to, we can.'

'Oh dear, we can't. I've just remembered something.'

He sipped his coffee. 'And what is that?'

She went into the house and returned a moment later with three wrapped parcels, putting them on the table. 'It's your birthday.'

'It is?' he asked with mock surprise. 'Are you sure?'

'Of course I am. It's the fifth today.'

'Wasn't I born on the sixth?'

'No,' she laughed. 'Stop teasing and open your presents.'

'I think you're more excited than me,' he observed as he took the first and largest parcel. 'Do you want to open it?'

She slapped his wrist playfully. 'You're supposed to be sixty-five today, so act your age.'

He stopped opening the parcel and looked at her. 'I'm no different than I was yesterday.'

'Of course you are. Today you're sixty-five.'

He slipped his hands over his face and down his body. 'Nope. It all feels the same. Perhaps you are different.' He moved his hand over to her breast and held it for a moment before sliding it slowly down her body. She pushed his hand away with laughter.

'I guess I was wrong. You're the same Rick I've always known.'

'Are you sure?' He held onto her hand. 'Would you like to check me out?'

She pulled her hand away. 'Open your presents first.'

'First?' he queried. 'Do you mean that afterwards...?'

'Just open your presents.'

He shrugged and resumed tearing off the paper.

*

Around noon, Anna said she had forgotten to get some rice for the paella she was preparing for their lunch and sent Rick off in the car to get some. He guessed the reason was to get him out of the way but he went without comment. While he was gone, several cars that had been waiting for Anna's signal drove up their drive and excited voices called to each other. They became a hive of activity, quickly carrying tables and benches to the rear garden on which they laid cloths, plates, cutlery and glasses; the womenfolk arranged small vases of flowers along the centre of the tables. Chilled wine and beer were taken from the cooler and put into big tin tubs filled with ice, and several of the men got the barbecue going and prepared several types of meats for grilling. In the kitchen, Anna and Rosemary began to unwrap the bowls of salads Anna had secretly prepared and stored in the fridge, and Anna's sister began to cut chunks from French-styled sticks of bread and put them on wooden platters.

When Rick returned with the token bag of rice, he saw the parked cars around his drive and smiled to himself. He went round the side of the house and surprised his guests in the garden. 'Hey folks,' he called out. 'What's the occasion? Someone's birthday?'

They all turned and one of the women squealed with her hands to her cheeks, and they moved towards him like a swarm of ants onto something sweet, shaking his hand and slapping his back. Some of the ladies gave him delicate kisses on the cheek, while others slobbered wet ones on his lips, leaving smears of red around his mouth. By the time they stepped back, Harry thought Rick looked worse than when he had been hit by the golf ball.

'Well,' he said, gasping for breath, 'I guess it must be my birthday.' Then he whooped and threw the bag of rice into the air, splitting and showering them like hail. They all began to laugh and he raised his hands, calling for quiet. 'I would just like to say a few words.' They calmed and looked silently at him with expectation. 'Who's for a drink? Me!' he hollered, and dashed through them and made straight for the iced beers.

Harry and Rick's nephew, Stuart, took charge of the barbecue and soon everyone was sat around the tables eating and drinking – the garden was filled with noise and laughter. At an appropriate moment, when most of the food had been consumed, Rick stood up with a can of beer in his hand and called for quiet.

'Folks,' he started, but then paused. 'No. I mean friends. I'm not one to make a speech but I guess that I owe you one. And I'd like to take the opportunity to say a few words without fear of my wife contradicting me.'

'Make the most of it,' Anna said, seated by him.

'Or interrupting me,' he added, and patted her shoulder. 'I don't feel sixty-five and I certainly don't look it.'

'Do you want a mirror?' Harry called out, and Rosemary dug him in the ribs.

Rick waved to him and laughed. 'Thanks Harry. I guess I asked for that. Seriously, though. No,' he corrected himself again, 'it's not a time for being serious. It gives me a warm feeling to have my family and friends around me, not just because it's my birthday. But the important thing is I received a lot of gifts.' He held up his hands as balled paper napkins came flying his way. 'I'm trying to say the right things but old habits die hard. This time I'm serious. Thanks to you all for coming and preparing this party. And a special thanks to Harry and Stuart for burning the meat – it tasted fine. I know a lot of effort has gone into it and Anna has been beavering away to get it all arranged. It was the best open secret I know.'

'You knew?' Anna squealed with mock indignation.

'I had a vague idea from the phone bill,' Rick chuckled.

339

He put his arm round her and pulled her to her feet. 'Sixty-five years is a long time, but it hasn't been long enough with Anna and Ricardo.' He waved to his son who smiled back. 'I'm proud of them and I'm proud to have you all as my friends. Thank you.'

As he gave Anna a kiss, some of the women said, 'Aaah' and then the men began to hoot and clap their hands.

'Thank you,' Anna said quietly but her face became alarmed as Rick's face began to contort. He seemed to be trying to cough and gasp for breath, and his body started to reel over. She held onto him, but his weight took them both down and she found she was falling over him.

'Rick?' she cried out.

Everyone stood up and moved quickly round; Harry eased Anna away and touched Rick's face. 'Get a doctor,' Harry barked. 'Get an ambulance. Get anything.'

Someone ran off to the house and Ricardo came to his side. He lifted his father's head and gasped as he saw that the life seemed to have drained away.

'Harry?' Ricardo looked into Harry's face with astonishment.

'Take your mother inside,' Harry said quietly but firmly.

Anna struggled against the insistent hands. Ricardo tried to soothe her with words, but they were washed away with his tears – he knew his father was dead.

The paramedics soon arrived and confirmed their fears – Rick was dead. He'd probably died before he hit the ground. The men hung around not knowing what to think or do and the women sat around Anna with little to say; the shock was too much for all of them. Ricardo sat with her, his tears still flowing freely.

One of the paramedics stood with Harry. 'It's hard to say what it was from what you've said. We'll get him off to the hospital. They'll have to examine him. It could be a heart attack. You say he was sixty-five today? Could be all the excitement brought it on. Has he had any sort of accident lately?'

Harry cursed quietly to himself. 'He was hit by a golf ball about two months ago.'

'That's interesting,' said the paramedic, but Harry didn't think so. 'Where did it hit him?'

'On the head,' and Harry pointed to his own forehead. 'He refused to get it looked at.'

'Could be a clue,' the paramedic said absently. 'Look, we'll have to take him away.' He paused, finding the next words difficult. 'Will his wife want...?' he broke off.

Harry nodded. 'She will. I'll go and get her.'

*

Anna and Ricardo went in the ambulance with Rick's body; it seemed somehow futile, but she could not bear to leave Rick to be alone, not at this time. She sat by his side as the truck swayed through the traffic, holding his still hand tightly. Tears flowed gently down her cheeks, and when her body shook with a sob, Ricardo eased his hand round her shoulders.

Back at the house, everyone wandered around aimlessly. They kept uttering words of disbelief to each other until finally, for want of something to do, they began to tidy up the plates, glasses and cans.

Rosemary sought out Harry and slipped her arms round his waist. 'You're blaming yourself.' But he didn't acknowledge her words. 'You mustn't, Harry. Are you listening?'

Harry shrugged. 'What can I say? It happened so suddenly.'

'We don't know the cause. Don't go thinking you're responsible.' She moved a hand to his back and massaged him gently.

341

Dave came over – he could guess what was going through his father's mind. 'Hey dad! Come in the house. Young James is a bit upset by this all and needs his grandpops.'

Harry looked at his son and then smiled. 'Then I had better go and cheer him up.'

As he moved away, Rosemary took Dave's hand. 'Good thinking,' she said in thanks.

*

The autopsy report revealed that Rick had suffered a huge brain haemorrhage, probably as a result of being hit by the ball. The word 'if' is a short but barbed word, which tends to stick in people's skin and it remained at the forefront of many minds, most of all in Harry's and Anna's. They felt sad and distraught, but most of all, in some way guilty that they had not insisted he have a check-up when he was hit by the golf ball. Rosemary tried her best to comfort Harry but he was inconsolable.

The funeral came too soon and the fact it was at a crematorium somehow affected Harry more. Rosemary clutched his arm as the coffin slid out of sight behind the curtains. It was too final – at least with a burial you had somewhere to visit where you could imagine the person was present and even gain solace from talking to the figure you still believed to be whole and untouched, simply asleep.

Ricardo had made a speech about his father and, without referring directly to his sexual persuasion, recounted how he and his father had had their differences but that he had always been forgiving and understanding. 'The gift my father has left Mom and me,' he concluded, 'is a memory of a caring and loving man. We shall cherish that forever.'

Anna had managed to sit dry-eyed through the service, but as her son finished, she bowed her head and all the

342

feelings she had controlled until then suddenly gushed out through her eyes – she wept with sobs that shook her body.

*

Harry changed. Not many would have noticed, but Rosemary could see his eyes had dimmed somewhat and his smile was often forced. He was as attentive to her as usual and he took her out more; she even let him go to the shops with her – he needed to be occupied. She wanted to encourage him to go to the golf club, but reasoned it would hold memories that he hadn't got round to yet, so she just made sure she was always there when he wanted her.

*

The Winter came and brought heavy snow that kept them at home a lot. The course was closed and somehow it made Harry more comfortable; during this time every year, he had only met his friends occasionally for a game of poker or down at Sam's Bar so he didn't have so much to miss. He went to Dave's more often, mainly to see the grandchildren, and he always returned home with stories for Rosemary of how they were growing up and what James had done at school and how Louise was talking more. While Rosemary knew most of this, she listened intently and laughed with him when he related some antic young James had got up to.

One evening, just after Harry had left, Dave sat at the kitchen table going through some invoices. Pam brought him a fresh coffee and sat next to him.

'I'm worried about Harry,' she said when Dave had put down the papers and sipped his coffee.

'He's slowly getting over it,' he said between sips.

'I don't think he is. I've been watching him with Louise and James. There are moments when he reaches out and just touches them.' She saw Dave was looking at her in a peculiar way and she tried to explain. 'Tonight, they were playing on the floor and he reached across and touched their shoulders. He kept touching them until they shrugged him off to play with something.'

'He always does that,' Dave said. 'He's a touching man. Haven't you noticed when he speaks to you how he'll often take your hand or slip an arm over your shoulder? That's Harry.'

'No. It's different now.' She sucked on her lip with exasperation at not being able to find the right words. 'He's touching things as if he knows he won't be seeing them much longer.'

Dave just said, 'Oh.' He hadn't noticed, but now that Pam had brought it to his attention, he realised he had been seeing something of a change in his father. 'He's lost three good friends in a short time. I guess it's brought it home that he's next. I can understand that.'

'So what can we do?' Pam asked earnestly.

Dave thought and then shrugged. 'I don't know if he would appreciate it if we said or did anything. He's the sort who needs to work it out himself.'

'We can't just leave it,' Pam almost pleaded. 'At least have a chat with your mother.'

Dave didn't look convinced, but he nodded and said he would.

Like his father, Dave took his own time in doing something, but eventually, when Harry was out, he sat with his mother and spoke about his and Pam's concerns.

'I know,' Rosemary said after listening to him patiently. 'He doesn't say a lot about it – he keeps things like that inside, but I've noticed. You know,' she took her son's hand and cupped it in hers, 'the only thing he's said which really

344

showed his feelings was when we were in the garden. It was late Autumn and we were doing the last tidying before the snows came. There were leaves and things all over the lawn so we swept them up and put them in plastic bags, and then he suddenly stopped and looked up at the trees.' She paused as if lost in the memory. 'He said, "Every year the trees lose their leaves and look stark and bare as if there is no life in them. I think we are like leaves. At some time we crinkle up and just die." He put his arm round me in that special way he has of making you feel part of him. I said, "But the next Spring, the tree comes to life and it all starts over again." He laughed at that.'

'So you think he will be alright?'

'Of course.' She patted his hand reassuringly. 'He'll work it out in his own time. And I've arranged for us to visit Rob in LA after Christmas. The warmth and the change will do him good.'

'I guess so. By the way, how is Anna making out?' he asked.

'So, so. She has good days and bad days.' She sighed at the sadness of it all. 'Ricardo sees her a lot and your father and I took her to the town centre the other day. We treated her to lunch and had a browse round the shops.'

'Harry went round the shops?' he asked surprised.

Rosemary looked sharply at him – she didn't mind him calling Harry by his name directly to him but preferred him to use 'father' with her. She had never quite got used to it. 'He was very good. He treated her like a child going round the shops at Christmas. He wanted to buy her things. I think it did the pair of them some good.'

*

When Spring came and breathed life back into many things, Harry must have caught a lungful for he began to find some enthusiasm for doing things and getting out, and his eyes began to reflect the smile on his lips. One morning, after finishing off a large plate of pancakes, he stood up and went out to the rear garden; Rosemary saw him from out of the window, standing in front of a robinia tree. He didn't move for quite a while, so she went out to him.

She stood next to him and followed his gaze to the tree and then looked back to him. 'What's the matter?'

He pointed to the thin branches. 'You see that? Buds. The leaves are forming. It's what you said.'

'The cycle is starting over again,' she said softly.

'That's right,' he breathed the words, and then announced, 'I'm going to the club this morning.'

Rosemary was pleased but taken slightly aback. 'To play?'

'I'll take my clubs,' he said, and he looked from the tree and smiled at her. 'I thought I would just go down for a drink and see if there's anyone I know looking for a game. If there's not, I'll have a swing on the practice ground. There's no point in me brooding around. Life won't change itself.'

She linked her arm in his – she had known this moment would come and was glad it had arrived.

*

Harry went into the locker room but it was quiet – he guessed most people were out on the course, so he went up to the lounge to get a drink. As he went up the stairs, a familiar pair of legs came into view.

'Harry!' Louise enthused and she put her arms round his shoulders as he came level. 'I haven't seen you for months. You're looking good. How's my favourite partner?'

He returned the kiss she gave him. 'So, so. I'm glad the Winter's out the way.'

346

'I'm sorry about Rick.' She nestled her head against his cheek and spoke softly in his ear. 'I am truly sorry.'

He eased away from her and attempted to muster a smile. 'And you are looking as beautiful as ever. How are things with you?'

'Come into the lounge,' she urged. 'Let's have a drink and a chat.' She linked her arm in his and guided him through the door. 'I have – wait for it – met someone who is nice and kind and handsome. He's everything I've dreamed about.'

Harry stopped and broke away from her arm. 'Couldn't you have broken that to me a little more gently? Does that mean it's over between us?'

She laughed and took his arm again, pulling him closer. 'You'll always be my Harry,' and she pecked him on the cheek.

'That's alright then. I thought I was another discarded leaf.'

'A leaf?' she queried.

'It's just something between Rosemary and me. What do you want to drink?' He signalled down the bar to the barman. 'Your usual?'

'An orange juice, please.'

Harry ordered their drinks and they went over to a table by the window. 'So tell me about this Prince Valiant you've found,' he said as they sat down.

'Well,' she drawled out, 'his name is Greg and he's about my age. He's six-feet-two, weighs about one-ninety, wears mostly casual, except when he takes me out to dinner, has light-brown hair and the most gorgeous dark brown eyes.'

'From that I guess I could recognise him in the street,' Harry laughed. 'Is there anything bad about him?'

Her voice dropped a tone. 'Only that he's divorced and his ex is a complete bitch. Thankfully there are no children to complicate things.'

'There's always a brighter side,' he said lightly as the drinks were served. 'Here's looking at you kid,' he said through his teeth as he raised his glass. 'Is this guy local?'

'Sort of,' but she didn't expand on it. 'You must meet him. You'll get on. He doesn't play golf so it doesn't dominate our conversations.'

'I don't know.' Harry swirled the ice round his glass, looking serious. 'Rivals for your hand and all that.'

She noted the humorous glint in his eyes. 'He hasn't mentioned anything more permanent yet. Nor have you for that matter. I think you just see me as a plaything.'

'Talking about play,' he leaned forward. 'Are you planning to play today?'

'I came down to do some paperwork.' She saw his eyebrows rise. 'Of course, you wouldn't know. After my year as Captain they asked me to become the Ladies' Secretary. I handle all the admin and competition schedules for the Ladies' section.'

'That's nice,' he said. 'By the way, whatever happened to Ellor Byrne?'

Louise laughed throatily. 'She stuck around for a while but when she had to resign as Captain – thanks to you – she found that people began to say what they really thought of her. She's still a member, but doesn't come here often. I see her around occasionally.'

'She was too puffed up with her own pomposity. It's nice to know she got what she deserved,' Harry said without regret. 'Can you fit in a few holes with me today?'

'I can fit in a complete round if you want. To heck with the paperwork,' Louise said, remembering that Harry was on his own now. 'Matchplay with five dollars to the winner?'

'To the winner,' he emphasised, recalling the time she won with a half. 'No shots?'

She looked at him with something of a smirk. 'How many do you want?'

'Now that's fighting talk, young lady.' He finished his drink. 'I'll go and get changed and meet you in the buggy park out front.'

Not having played since last Summer, Harry took a while to get his game going, and by the ninth he was four down. As they stood by the tenth tee, Louise asked, 'Are you sure you don't want any shots?'

He looked sideways at her. 'Do you want to up the bet to ten dollars?'

She looked sideways at him. 'Are you trying to sucker me, Harry Menkowitch?'

'Of course I am. I've noticed you've struggled over the last couple of holes,' he said with a straight face.

'We halved them. You haven't won a hole yet,' she quipped back.

'That's about to change now,' he said, and mounted the tee. After an elaborate practice swing, he drove his ball right into the rough grass by some trees.

'I like your tactics,' she laughed. 'Are you trying to make me feel over-confident?' She went forward to her tee and drove her ball straight and long down the fairway.

Despite losing that hole and going five down, Harry managed to pull his game together, and by the eighteenth he was only one down. He got out of the buggy by the tee and looked up the fairway.

'I'll have to make an allowance for the left-to-right wind,' he said to himself, but loud enough for her to hear.

'There's no wind, Harry,' she said.

He wet his finger and held it up, murmuring something she didn't catch. He drove to the left and the ball angled back to the centre of the fairway. 'Yep, there's a wind all right,' he said, putting his club back into the bag.

'You faded that ball deliberately.' She poked him in the ribs as he got in the cart.

'I guess I might have,' he grinned as he drove to her tee.

349

Louise stood on the tee and tried to detect some wind. She looked at him suspiciously, wet her finger and held it up.

'Not sure?' he enquired.

'There's no wind,' she said firmly, and struck her ball straight up the middle. When it landed, it hit a small grass mound and kicked right and nestled in the light rough. 'That was a bad bounce, not the wind,' she said quickly before he could say something.

'Of course,' he said.

His ball was furthest from the green and he took a five-iron, swung too easy and pulled it left, just short of the cavernous bunker. He cursed quietly to himself. Louise found her ball was sitting pretty and eased the ball on the green, about twenty feet from the flag. She smiled at him smugly when she got in the cart.

'It's not over yet.' He forced a grin.

He parked the cart near the bunker and got out to survey his ball. It was lying clean, but he had to get it up over the bunker and then stop it quickly as the flag was not far past it. Louise sat in the buggy while he walked round the bunker and up the slope onto the green. For a moment he disappeared from view, and she was just getting out of the buggy when he reappeared.

'What are you doing?' she asked.

'Just getting the distance right,' he said, and took a wedge from his bag. 'Watch how a master plays a difficult shot.'

'I'm watching,' she said, standing to one side. 'Don't top it and put it in the bunker,' she added as he stood over his ball.

He stepped back. 'I love it when you talk dirty,' he grinned. He addressed his ball again and hit it hard and low; it just skimmed the rim of the bunker and disappeared from view.

'Now that could be in the rough on the other side,' she chuckled. 'Nice one, Harry. I'll have to remember how to do that shot.'

'It had a lot of spin on it,' Harry said in a casual way. 'It'll be on the green.'

'Yeah, right,' she said as she walked up the slope with her putter. As she came onto the green, she stopped and waited for him to join her. 'There's my ball. No sign of yours though.'

He looked mystified and sauntered over to the hole. 'Hey. Well look at this,' he said, peering down at the hole.

Louise leaned forward and he detected a little gasp escaping from her lips. 'How did...?' she stopped and reached down and took the ball out of the hole and turned it over in her hand. She noted his initials on the ball and looked up at him with amazement. She was about to say something when she noticed the wide smile on his lips – his hand was raised, holding a five-dollar note. 'Why, Harry Menkowitch you are the most despicable, devious, crafty, conniving old man I ever played with.' She stopped and began to laugh, throwing her arms round his neck and kissing him. 'And I love you.'

'Steady on,' he reeled back from her hug. 'Prince Valiant may be watching.'

'I wish he was,' she said with joy in her voice. 'He'd love you too.'

'Is he gay as well?' Harry asked. 'That boy is just about everything.'

She slapped him playfully. 'Next Wednesday,' and, in answer to his questioning look, added, 'we'll have another game. Put it in your diary.'

'Are you sure you want to play with a despicable, devious, crafty, conniving old man?'

She took the five dollars from his hand. 'There's no one

else I would rather play with. And now you can buy me a lunch,' she laughed as she walked away to get her ball.

*

When Harry got home, Rosemary was in the kitchen preparing something for their dinner that evening. 'Did you have a game?' she asked and then answered her own question. 'I guessed you might from the time you've been gone.'

Harry kissed her cheek and then went over and poured himself a coffee. 'Yes. I managed to find someone.' He put his mug on the table and sat down. 'I was a bit rusty at first but I enjoyed it.'

'That's good. Have you arranged another game?' Rosemary asked as she slit some beans.

'Next Wednesday,' he said between sips of coffee.

'Who was it with? Someone I know?'

Harry just said 'Yes' and then moved quickly on. 'I've had lunch so I won't want much tonight.'

Rosemary huffed with a little annoyance. 'I can serve this tomorrow. We'll just have something light tonight, if you wish.'

'Sounds fine,' he agreed.

Rosemary put down the knife, wiped her hands on a cloth and came over and sat at the table opposite to him. 'So who is this new playing partner?'

'You know, it's the darnedest of things. There I was with no one to play with and I was thinking I would just have a drink and come home, when who do you think I met?'

'Louise,' Rosemary said in a flat sort of way.

'How did you know that?' he queried.

'Just intuition.'

Harry shrugged. 'I guess she felt sorry for me having lost the last of my playing partners.'

352

'Probably.'

'She's met a young man,' he continued, undaunted by her expression. 'She sounded pretty keen on him.'

'That's nice.'

He put his mug down. 'Does it bother you if I play with her?'

'Of course not. Don't be silly.'

'That's good because we've made a date for every Wednesday.'

Rosemary played with her hands. 'You know, I've been thinking.'

He waited for her to add something and noted an uncharacteristic nervousness around her mouth. 'Well?'

'I've been thinking,' she repeated. 'What with so little for me to do during the day and you getting out playing golf again; I thought I needed something to fill my time. I've never played but I've always admired the game.' She paused, but he said nothing. 'I thought I might have some lessons.'

'Lessons at what?' he asked cautiously.

'Golf,' she said quietly.

'You want to play golf?'

'Only with you. It would be nice being together.' She looked a little forlornly at him. 'Would you like that?'

Harry toyed with his mug between his fingers. 'You don't have to. Not just for me. Is it because of Louise?'

'Don't be silly,' she laughed, but it came out more like a cough. 'Why should I worry about a young stripling like her? My, you're old enough to be her grandfather.'

'And young enough to be her father.' Harry began to grin and she felt unsettled. 'All right, if that's what you really want. I'll have a word with the Pro at the club. We'll see how you get on with it. But in the meantime, do you mind if I play with Louise?'

'Of course not,' she brightened a little. 'Are you sure you wouldn't mind playing golf with me?'

Harry slid his hand across the table and took her hand in his. He held it loosely and sighed in a tired way. 'I married you for better or for worse and I guess the worst thing to happen is to have to play golf with you.' He watched her face closely and saw just a hint of an uncertainty in her eyes before chuckling and squeezing her hand.

*

Rosemary had several lessons and she surprised Harry with how quickly she grasped the fundamentals of the game. After her first round of golf with him, she joined the Wednesday game with Louise, and when she had progressed to a reasonable standard, Louise introduced her to the Ladies' Section; she began to play more regularly. Harry felt he was the spare arm of the trio for their Wednesday game and so excused himself by saying that he had found someone else to play with. It was an elderly chap who had no sense of humour, and Harry soon lost interest. Besides, he found he was beginning to struggle round eighteen holes. At Rosemary's insistence, he went for a check-up and ended by having a triple heart-bypass operation. After that he gave up cigars, limited himself to one JD a day and generally took things easy. He found a new interest in his garden and would often greet Rosemary with an array of freshly cut flowers when she came home from a game at the club. She returned one day with her first trophy she had won in a Ladies' competition.

*

Dinsdale didn't get the job at the golf club near Phoenix but stayed down there and ended up as manager of a large toy shop – his wife had filed for divorce and won a handsome settlement, which left him near broke. He still dressed smartly in a suit and an impeccable white shirt that one of the shop assistants – with whom he had moved in – devotedly pressed for him.

*

Louise married her Prince Valiant and Harry was the best man at their wedding. As she expected, he embarrassed her with his speech, but he never referred to the episode with the cameras – some things are best left untold. Within a year she gave birth to a boy, whom they named Harry.

*

Harry passed on a few years later – one morning he just forgot to wake up. Rosemary, Anna and Louise stood together at the funeral, holding hands for comfort, each thinking similar thoughts.

*

Rosemary moved into a smaller house and continued playing golf with varying success. She filled her days, but in the evenings her thoughts always drifted back to Harry – he'd left a big space. She formed a closer friendship with Anna and eventually she moved in with her; the evenings became more comfortable.

*

Felicia's romance with Michael slowly petered out when he'd learnt all he needed from her. She left the job and met and married a butcher who had a shop in the centre of town. She kept the sequinned costume in a box in the attic along with the photograph of her rising from the cake – her one moment of stardom.

*

Harry's son Dave kept the jewellers' shop expensive and successful and was disappointed, but proud, when James went to university to study Law. His daughter, Louise Rose, showed her father's talents from a young age, and after college, she joined him in the shop. On her twenty-first birthday, he took her outside the shop to show her the new sign: 'Menkowitch and Daughter'. He was sad only that Harry was not still around to see it all.

*

Harry's other son Rob and the lovely Miriam were blessed with five children. His skills with computer graphics for films earned him a good reputation and a sizeable fortune – he retired early and moved to San Francisco. Rosemary visited them once a year and, while rejoicing to be with her son, regretted that Harry had never seen Rob's children.

*

While most things change with the seasons, Sam's Bar didn't, except it was never the same without the three 'friggin nutters' frequenting his bar. He never did find out about the joke they played on him and the framed certificate still proudly rests behind the bar.

*

After an insider-dealing scandal involving the Republican Mayor, John Wesley Cook, a Democrat became Mayor of

Wannabee, and the loop road was forgotten – the town remained insular and changed little. The townsfolk were comfortable with that.

*****